PRAISE FOR
A REAL ANIMAL

"Emeline Atwood's Lucy is a marvelous, maddening, monstrous creation, and *A Real Animal* is an irresistible whirlpool of a novel."
—Joy Williams, author of *The Pelican Child*

"Emeline Atwood's *A Real Animal* is a strange and astonishing and entirely original book, full of darkness shot through with light, wild and tender. Atwood writes brilliantly about our interior, personal wildernesses, the snarling, wounded animal at the heart of any person. Lucy is an unforgettable narrator: compelling, terrifying, lovable, surprising, human. She, and this book, are extraordinary."
—Elizabeth McCracken, author of *The Hero of This Book*

"The gorgeous writing in *A Real Animal* makes its protagonist's risky behavior all the more harrowing—Lucy's intelligence does not necessarily protect her. I feared for the young woman with the extravagant sense of what intimacy looks like, creating near-constant suspense in this powerful debut."
—Amy Hempel, author of *Sing to It*

"In a moment when we often find ourselves numb and distracted, Emeline Atwood has given us an enlivening and powerful novel about what it means to dwell and be changed. It gets under your skin. Atwood is an ambitious writer, as at home in the colloquial as she is in the lyrical. A tremendous accomplishment."
—Stephanie Wambugu, author of *Lonely Crowds*

"*A Real Animal* is an absolute marvel—at once dark and luminous, raw and poignant, feral in its originality and brilliant in its delivery. Emeline Atwood is a breathtaking writer, and her first novel is a lithe, muscular, and beautifully dangerous tour de force."
—Bret Anthony Johnston, author of
Encounters with Unexpected Animals

A REAL ANIMAL

A REAL ANIMAL

a novel

EMELINE ATWOOD

CATAPULT  NEW YORK

A REAL ANIMAL

Another version of the chapter "Orphanage" first appeared in the Spring 2023 issue of *The Kenyon Review*.

First Catapult edition: 2026

ISBN: 978-1-64622-296-4

Library of Congress Control Number: 2026931574

Jacket design by Patrick Sullivan
Jacket painting of bull © Daniel Cacouault / Bridgeman Images
Book design by Olenka Burgess

Catapult
New York, NY
books.catapult.co

Printed in the United States of America

10 9 8 7 6 5 4 3 2 1

For Livvie

PART I

EMERGENCY SERVICES

As the leopard, I had no memory of ever having been anything other. The leopard was me completely, how it seemed I'd been forever, and the confusion I felt when I woke up wasn't because I was a leopard but because, in my half-asleep state, the breeze that had been brushing my short hairs back, pushing the ends of my whiskers every now and then against my cheek, wasn't actually wind off the savannah but musty recycled air emanating from a strange and sterile thing—which I later understood was just the small rotating desk fan that Frances, my best friend at the time and college roommate, liked to keep on. I'd been sleeping on my side, cheek pressed to my shoulder, one arm extending out long beneath me, drooping over the side of what should've been the branch of my baobab tree. Immediately, I knew I was out of place. I remember the power and heat of my body in that moment, how my shoulders and hindquarters quickly cramped up, my throat vibrating involuntarily, how I felt aware and in control of every single nerve as each began lighting up inside my long, alert body.

Frances and I considered ourselves to be extremely tidy girls, which was why we chose to live together all four years of college. We took pride in our dorm room and liked showing it off to our parents whenever they visited, to prove we were grown-ups who knew how to take care of a space. Everything we owned was either white or light blue, which Frances said was the color palette best for brightening. Frances also taught me how to moisturize before bed and how to write down three expressions of gratitude in the morning. She kept all the fans on so that the room wouldn't ever get stuffy because we both hated stuffy rooms. Every night, she turned on this little diffuser that her mom had given her, which puffed out euca-lyptus oil, to help cleanse the space. This diffuser was some-thing that leopard me observed for quite a while, befuddled and a little distressed. An automatic timer shut it off every morning at six. That's how I was able to tell the crisis manager later what time it was when all of this happened, because as the leopard, I remember watching the diffuser, trying to sort out what it was, all while being very aware of another body breathing nearby. The diffuser was making its sputtering, then shushing sounds. With its ovular bottom and narrow spigot, it appeared to be a plump, skinny-headed dove, but the mist emanating from its head was like nothing I'd seen, and I was uncertain whether it was alive or not, when sud-denly it went quiet.

In the quiet, I didn't move a muscle, only sniffing and blink-ing, taking it all in. All the smells the fans were circulating— the coconut oil coating Frances's hair, the Starbucks iced coffee melting on the desk, the sweaty peep-toe booties by the door—only called attention to the fact that the space containing me had no escape. There was something sick going on. Something reeked of sex and death. I had to get outside and into a tree.

People probably think the reason my friendship with Frances ended was because of the leopard incident. We never spoke to each other again. But it didn't end just because she no longer wanted to be associated with me. It also ended because of the way I saw that dorm room and took in Frances's body in the bunk below me, through the leopard's eyes and the leopard's mind, after I leapt down from the top bunk, landing on all fours lightly, then curved my shoulders toward the human mass that was Frances, her chest rising, falling, a little whistle sneaking in and out of her nose; I remember placing two paws on the bottom bunk, then bringing my nose close to those dark bangs that cut across her forehead, which she insisted on straightening every morning, which she sometimes retrimmed with my desk scissors. I still can't unsee the way I saw her then, the silliness and fragility of her body, the redundancy of her existence, her breath exposing a weak, unconscious heart. Clearly, I was precious and she was not.

Weeks later, it made me ill to picture the way Frances had wiped smudges off our Walmart furniture with Clorox, how she had once glued a piece of plastic back onto the chipped corner of our faux-wood desk. She had paid attention to all the wrong things. The case study interviews she'd agonized over all senior fall, the special stockings she bought that were reinforced against runs, the internships she'd taken meticulous care to secure to get the right job after college and every next right job after that. She was going to be a consultant in New York. I had accepted an offer at a casting agency called AUTHENTIC in Indianapolis (associate recruiter, forty-six thousand dollars a year). But after being the leopard, I felt stupid for ever wanting any of the same things Frances had. The leopard was so much more powerful than she was, and as I sniffed the coconut oil on her scalp, as I took in the state of her life and considered thwacking the back of her skull with my paw to check just how alive she was, I ended up deeming her body so unthreatening it wasn't worth further inspection, and for years after this, Frances remained cast in my mind as a fool for not knowing how she appeared to creatures other than herself.

I slinked out, my paws light on the carpet, totally silent, following my nose and the glow of light to the great outdoors. I took little steps down the hall, stopping at every tiny sound, looking around, then taking more little steps. One step down the stairs. Another step. Another. My paws on the stairs a tap, tap, tap. Something infuriatingly itchy started rubbing against me and I whipped my mouth back to my hip. Finally, I clamped onto it—the pink boxer shorts emblazoned with the university logo that I'd slept in since freshman year—and ripped the fabric with my teeth, then shook my body to get the material off me. Another itch sent my teeth back around and I pulled and pulled and pulled until the T-shirt split.

Finally, I was outside, strutting on all fours across the cold quiet quad. The tree rose up before me, and I dug my claws into it, my toes pressing into the bark, and climbed as high as I could until all the scary things—the far-off bodies, the rushing cars—were far below. I settled on a sturdy, horizontal branch where nothing could reach me. Up there, my body sprawled out belly to bark, all four limbs dangling over the sides of the branch, sun heating up a spot above my tailbone, I felt safe. I pressed my cheek to the tree and slept.

—

The sirens arrived later in the morning. The commotion had started building while I was still asleep, as students on the way to their 9:00 a.m. classes began noticing me up there. It was the biggest oak on campus, the old famous one, planted right in the middle of the quad. At first, I awoke incensed by the noise, but when I peeled my cheek off the branch, and felt the weight of all their eyes and registered that the attention of the assembly below was pointed up at me, I got scared and scooted back along the branch to conceal myself in the foliage.

But the lights and sirens wouldn't leave me be. They created a kaleidoscope of creatures in the tree. I didn't doubt my ability to stay both hidden and far away from them until one of the firetrucks extended its ladder up. I hissed and bared my teeth at the man trying to beckon me. He backed off. I did the same to the set of men that arrived in the bright-yellow bucket of the utility truck. I needed them to know I could rip their heads off if I wanted to.

Eventually, they had the idea to bring my mother onto campus—a three-and-a-half-hour drive for her—and put her in the cage of the cherry picker. It was her very pale face appearing in the leaves that snapped me out of my leopard state. I remember turning back into myself then, and suddenly feeling extremely unbalanced and very high up. The shock of seeing my mother while a leopard, and then the gut-rupturing second it took to become Lucy again, was so powerful that the thought crossed my mind (my human mind, Lucy's mind) that it might be a good time to just roll off the branch and end my life. But I didn't roll off the branch; I let them approach me instead (which was how I learned with certainty that I was actually someone who preferred to live).

The men managed to get the cage containing my mother close to me, just a couple of feet away, and then it was easy to slide inside under the rail. The relief of being out of the tree, coupled with the terror of being so close to my mother after occupying such a state, made me cry in a way that felt like I was shedding several versions of my whole life.

As soon as I was near her body in that cage, my mother didn't let me go. Both of her arms wrapped around me with alarming ferocity. She was much shorter than I was, but I wouldn't have been able to wriggle free even if I'd tried my hardest. On the ground, a man tried to put a yellow towel around me, since I was naked, but my mother took it from him and draped it over my shoulders herself, patting me as if to dry me off. The supervisor of our dorm, a female PhD student whose name I've since forgotten, passed my mother a plastic CVS bag that contained the pink boxer shorts and gray T-shirt that some student had collected on the stairs. There was heated talk between my mother, the dean, and the EMTs about how to transport me to the hospital to get evaluated. The EMTs wanted to take me in an ambulance, and the dean agreed, but my mother clearly won, because I ended up in her Subaru, a silent drive aside from the blinker and the tinkling of her long earrings whenever she changed lanes.

At home, my mother made me corn soup. Then we didn't speak to each other for two weeks. That said, she didn't let me leave her sight. We simply existed in the house together, neither of us leaving the premises. She inspected every aspect of what I did, even if I was just alphabetizing the books on the shelves in the den or splitting open an Oreo. The first night, she entered my bedroom every hour to check on me.

The second night, she blew up an air mattress on the floor and that's where she slept for the entire two weeks of not speaking. My dad came in and out, to and from work. When he was home, we chatted with him a little, just not to each other. I couldn't figure out what my dad knew or didn't know about the leopard. For his entire life, he never mentioned the incident around me.

Silence, historically, meant my mother was extremely angry with me, but this time there was a feeling of relief in it. At twenty-one, soon to be twenty-two, I was home again, spending every day in my PJs, flipping through the old picture books my dad used to read to us before bed. It felt like college hadn't really happened, like even high school hadn't happened. The more familiar, realer world was this one I was back in with my mother; I was her child again. Once more, my mother was cooking for me. She was doing my laundry. There wasn't ever a question as to whether she was close by. I lay on my belly on the cold kitchen floor, or I lay on my belly on the rug in the den, reading those wide-format *Calvin and Hobbes* paperbacks word for word, studying every speech bubble like I used to do in elementary school. As if no time had passed. In the mornings, my mother and I sat on the front stoop together, not speaking but drinking tea and eating chocolate digestive biscuits, observing the squirrels and the rabbits. In the afternoons, the window seat by the front door was my favorite place to be because of how the sun came in and warmed the cushion; the seat looked out across the street onto a big grassy field that in the summer was teeming with swallowtails and deer. Before dinner, my mother and I would go to the side porch to eat crackers and cheese, and wait for my dad to come home, me sitting on the swing and my mother in her green comfy chair, her legs tucked up under her. My mother was an avid moisturizer, her legs always smelling of SPF and slick as a seal, yet somehow they managed to stay tucked without slipping.

My mother was a small thin woman who took good care of herself. Her muscular arms and calves had always made her stand out among the other mothers. Her dark hair used to be as long as my sister's but now she kept it short and cropped around her ears, so it was easier to maintain—about her physical appearance, there was never a thing out of place. The scarves and shawls she wore in the spring and fall she'd wrap around herself tightly, tucking in the ends. Her clothes were always perfectly sized and color coordinated, but this was less about style and more about balance. She wore belts and tucked in her shirts. The freest part of her were her earrings, which were always long and dangly: a pair of silver wind chimes, tiered pearls, or silver feathers with turquoise stones that her friend Jordie had once brought her back from Santa Fe.

That year, my older sister, Patty, was in Chicago, doing two semesters of improv training, away from the East Coast for the first time ever. I broke up some of the silence by calling her from the bathroom, turning on the fan and shower so my mother, stationed somewhere outside the door, couldn't hear. I could tell my sister found the whole situation unnerving. She sounded most protective of our mother. She kept checking, "But you feel good now, right? Is Mom okay?" I didn't want to talk about how I was feeling now. I wanted to talk about how it had felt to be the leopard. But Patty wasn't curious about that. In fact, she seemed completely unwilling to discuss it.

I longed to talk to someone about this new recognition of

what my body could do. The leopard was, without a doubt, the most magical thing that had ever happened to me—I'd never felt so connected to another being, so inside of something else—and I wanted to describe it to someone, to discuss it with them in depth, to watch another person become as infatuated with it all as I was. Even just watching the squirrels and the rabbits with my mother, the way they quivered in the grass and then darted in and out of the rhododendrons, how their twitchy little bodies were panoramically aware of what was going on around them, I knew that no one could connect with them in the way I now could. As the leopard, my needs had never felt so simple to identify. Each need that registered in me had been easily addressed: I felt tired on that branch, so I slept; I felt scared, so I backed into the leaves. There'd been silence around every instinct. Now, as I moved around the house, trying to name what had happened, the noise in my head seemed not only pitifully unproductive, but also entirely what made me Lucy and not a leopard. And as a result, I felt grief over having to be myself again.

Still, I wasn't convinced that I hadn't actually been the leopard. The fact that I had scaled seventy feet of tree seemed evidence enough. I wondered if maybe what my mother and I weren't talking about was the fact that she had seen me as the leopard, then watched me transform back into Lucy, which must've been shocking, and now she had to reckon with this new knowledge that she had a daughter who was also a leopard. I talked myself out of that theory though when I accepted that for the school to call my mother, people obviously had to have identified me, Lucy, as the girl in the tree. Still, I was desperate to know what I had looked like to them—how much of a leopard had I appeared to be? I couldn't figure out how to open the conversation with my mother: Mom, did I actually look like a leopard or was I just behaving like one? It was very difficult during those silent weeks to get any sense of perspective.

As a kid, I never understood what I'd done to cause my mother to stop speaking to me, even after she'd inevitably ambush me with answers, pulling me aside privately, away from my sister and dad—trapping me in the hallway, or in the driveway—to finally break the silence and accuse me in a quiet, frightening tone of all the terrible feelings I'd made her feel, often referencing things I'd done after the silence started—like getting home too late from school and missing dinner, or not helping her carry in the groceries—but never clearly identifying what had provoked her to go silent in the first place. Sometimes she'd say it was my attitude, my general lack of gratitude, how I rolled my eyes at my dad, how I could be so "vicious" to my sister. When I've asked my sister about this since, she says she has no idea what I'm talking about. She can't remember our mother ever giving me the silent treatment, and she can't remember me ever being that mean. I can't remember a time when our mother ever got mad at my sister, and Patty at least agrees with that.

As I got older, I started wondering if there was a different way I could behave during her silent treatments to prevent, or at least assuage, the shock of the eventual ambush, which was always the worst part. My mother moved with a lot of precision and could be viperously quick, making sudden eye contact, grabbing my hand to cross the street, latching onto my wrist to keep me from wandering off—everything felt under her control, preplanned, highly targeted. The longer the silent treatment, the more shocking the moment it broke, and the anticipation of that moment always sickened me to the point where I'd have done anything to avoid it. So, I got home late; I missed dinner; I stayed as far away from her as possible. Which only added ammo to the ambush. Once, in high school, I forced myself to do the opposite, to see if it helped, but she later accused me of only acting helpful and kind as a way of making her feel guilty and cruel. She was always ready to prove I was one misstep away from turning evil, that if I wasn't careful, I'd become like her brother. Strangely, all the other adults in my life adored me. I always raised my hand, never spoke out of turn, followed directions. I grew up constantly confused as to who was right about me—my teachers, my friends' parents, my soccer coaches, or my mother? Thankfully, I now understand, without needing anyone else's assurance, that I'm not a bad person, even when I reevaluate certain decisions I've made. I understand now that no single decision makes a person any less good or any less bad.

The leopard episode closed out college for me. At that time in the semester, classes were finished for seniors. I had completed all my credits—final papers turned in, exams done, thesis grade received. So, I never stepped back onto campus. My diploma was mailed to me. My college friend group had been made up of five girls and seven guys. All twelve of us had met freshman year and stayed close, and now they had enjoyed a clean finish to a formative period together.

I never heard from most of those friends again, but a few days after graduation, on my birthday, Cole came over to the house, and his arrival is what ended the two weeks of silence between my mother and me. He came in the middle of the day; my dad was at work. I'd been organizing the books in my bedroom when my mother's steps ascended the stairs.

"Cole's here," she said from the doorway. Her face was all bone. "Don't invite people over without telling me."

"I didn't invite him over," I clarified.

She shook her head, perceptible only because of her earrings. "I'd like to know in advance if someone's coming," she said.

"Me too," I agreed. I truly hadn't known. Part of me had worried that Cole might show up, even though he lived forty-five minutes away, but it was very unlike him to impose without checking first to make sure it was okay. He was a careful guy; he liked to wait for clear cues. He had been texting me no more than once a day to let me know that he was thinking of me. I hadn't opened a single message, but I saw the previews with one or two or three red heart emojis and, all lowercase, "thinking of you," "love you," "lemme know how you're doing when you can." Every text had made me queasy. I really did love Cole a lot, but unfortunately, I couldn't stand to be myself around him anymore.

My mother went back downstairs.

"She's upstairs!" she sang out. Cabinets opened and closed. "Want a seltzer? Diet Coke?"

Soon he appeared in the doorway, in black running shorts and the white Henley I got him from Gap for Christmas sophomore year.

Immediately his face fell into something like embarrassment. "Is it bad I'm here?"

I hadn't gotten up from my stomach on the floor, which I knew could come off as rude, but I was worried if I moved even an inch, I'd vomit. Cole shrank against the wall, holding his elbows. His pale hairless legs looked so skinny. He shaved them for swimming.

"My stomach hurts," I explained. "Bad cramps, or I'd get up."

"You're good. Stay there," he said. He stepped around my mother's air mattress and sat on the end of the bed. "Sorry."

He still had his sneakers on. We were quiet. He was probably waiting for me to speak, since conversations were normally led by me, but when I kept quiet, he eventually said, in a weird high voice, "We missed you at graduation."

Finally, I pushed myself up and sat next to him on the bed, so he could show me pictures. We hadn't touched each other yet, but when I got on the bed, he shifted a little as if to come closer to me, but I flinched and he stopped. He handed me the phone, six inches between us.

A few of the photos included Frances and the other girls, but most were just of the guys, Cole's closest friends. Unbeknownst to Cole, that year I'd slept with every single one of them. They were all in their black robes, in front of the library. Cole was the shortest. He had freckly skin like mine and red hair shaved so close to his scalp that from far away he looked bald. In one picture, Miles was on Cole's shoulders, their robes off but caps still on. In another, all seven boys stood seriously in front of the library. Next to Cole was Danny, with whom Cole shared a room for three years, twin beds side by side. After each time we had sex, Danny made me pinky promise that we'd "never ever tell." None of the guys knew about one another. Each thought he was special and illicit. But they were all the same. I'd had sex with other guys that year too, not pictured. In his cap and gown, Cole looked a little like Caillou.

"That's fun," I said, handing back the phone.

"It was weird not having you there."

How long was he going to stay? The smell of his coconut deodorant was unbearable.

In a crackly voice, he repeated that he missed me. "I'm

not sure what to do." He always sounded exasperated, like he was holding his breath, whenever he shared his feelings. "I'm worried I haven't been a good boyfriend with everything." He was out of air.

"How's Frances?"

"She thought it was best to give you some space. But I was—" He inhaled sharply. "I started thinking that was the wrong call."

"It's okay." We were quiet for a little while. His breath leveled out.

I moved back to the carpet, because of the cramps. He got off the bed too and sat on the floor, cross-legged, against the dresser. He started untying his shoes.

I asked, "Did you see me when I was in the tree?"

He removed one shoe, then the other. "Yeah," he said. "It was pretty scary."

After a few moments, he asked, "How did you get up there?" He was blinking a lot.

I told him I had climbed, confused by the question.

He pulled his knees into his chest. "That's wild."

"What did I look like when I was up there?"

He didn't get it, so I clarified, "Did I look like Lucy?"

"I wasn't sure what was going on," he finally said, not looking at me. "You were really high up." He picked something out of the carpet. Dog hair, maybe. "I don't know. What were you trying to do?"

"Are you scared of me now?"

"No," he responded quickly, looking up at me for a second, then back at the carpet. "It was scary. The situation. Not you." A pause. "Sorry. I know I'm not saying the right things."

He looked up at me again, his face so devastating in its abject helplessness that I had to lower my gaze. Then he moved his right hand toward me on the carpet, as if to crawl my way, but again I shuddered, involuntarily, and he stopped immediately, yanking his hand back to hold his socked foot instead. He dropped his head. I hadn't been touched by anyone since getting out of the tree, since my mother wrapping that towel around me, so my skin was screaming for him to just come over. But Cole wasn't like that. He didn't like to initiate. That first week of freshman year, for example, I had to be the one to kiss him.

We didn't say anything for a little while and the longer we were quiet, the more Cole seemed to shrink. He wasn't a big talker, but he loved listening to me. I would come back from class, for instance, and talk his ear off about everything I had learned. I usually got sick of hearing myself speak before he did. It was something about him that I already missed.

I stayed on my stomach gazing at him as he continued picking at the carpet, as if looking for little treasures.

"Is this Sadie's, you think?" he asked at last about the dog hair. He was twirling it so slowly between his thumb and index finger as if it were a fragile, precious artifact.

"Probably not," I said.

"Princess is really sick. My mom might have to put her down."

"I don't think I can do this," I decided to let him know.

"It's okay," he said to the carpet. "I'm here for you." He sounded very young and far away. Then three times in a row he said that everything was going to be okay.

"I think I need some time to be on my own," I explained.

He picked up his head, finally looking at me in the eyes, and started nodding a lot. He hugged his knees into his chest. "That's completely okay," he said. "Whatever you need. What can I do to help?"

Cole always wanted to help. He was a good person. He was like my mother in that he'd never left the Northeast. Yet, despite knowing very little about what the world was like, he still wanted to save everyone in it. His life goal was to start a company that would support him, his mother, and his twin sister but that would also help people. He spent college trying to figure out what that company should be, always picking people's brains, searching for ideas.

I said, "I think we should break up. It makes the most sense, especially with me moving to Indianapolis."

This knocked the wind right out of him. His whole face was dazed and blank, his mouth tiny.

I apologized. "It'll be too hard for me to focus on myself if we're still trying to make things work with you here. It won't feel like I'm getting a fresh start."

"We can still make sure it feels like that," he said, his voice evaporating.

He said, "If that's what you need, we can make sure it feels like a fresh start."

There was a lot of silence. Then he said, forcefully, "Everything's going to be okay, Lucy. You're going to feel better. Things are going to feel normal again." He was sounding more confident, finding his reasonable, practical voice that he used in class or when he was around my dad. "You're going to start feeling more like yourself. I know that." He took a deep breath, and his chest protruded and stayed protruded. "I know I haven't been supporting you in the right way," he said, his chest collapsing back to normal. "I think— I think I haven't wanted to make you think about things that you don't want to think about. But I've been reflecting a lot, and I think this year I've been trying to act like everything's normal, but because of that, I haven't been doing enough. I haven't been checking in, or giving you what you need." It seemed like he was done, but after a couple seconds he added fiercely, "And it's not on you to tell me what you need. It's on me. It's on me to get better at giving you what you need without you having to ask."

"I just have a lot to work through on my own," I said. "I need to be on my own."

At this, he dropped his forehead into his hands. He held his head in both hands for what felt like fifteen minutes. I remained on my belly, in a sort of cobra pose, my neck sinking into my aching shoulders. Downstairs, I heard dishes clinking, drawers rolling open and then closing, the low calm tones of *Fresh Air*. She was making dinner. His body was so still, not a single quiver, completely breathless, face hidden.

Senior year was the only year that I cheated on Cole, and he never found out, despite the fact that, for over ten months, Cole and I didn't have sex. First of all, once you start sleeping with other people, it's very difficult to start having sex with your actual boyfriend again. Second, Cole and I had already stopped having sex after I'd been raped during my internship in Australia that past summer, an event that Cole and my mother and my dad and my sister all knew about. And Cole, after this, had stayed with me, despite the fact that I didn't want him to touch me anymore, totally ignorant of the fact that I was letting all these other guys touch me, which only made the reality of my cheating all the more difficult for me to stomach. But I was pretty sure my indiscretions weren't ever going to get back to Cole because of how trusting and generally content he was in the world. Before that, our relationship had been quite happy.

We had started dating the first month of freshman year and had proceeded to date all through college. Every night from seven to ten, Cole studied in the library and every morning from seven to nine he went to the gym. He had very severe allergies to sesame seeds, sulfites, and tree nuts that had significantly limited his life, and most nights he meal prepped, still sitting with us in the cafeteria but eating food he had prepared in the proctor's kitchen of our dorm. He had very good manners and was very good at following rules. Cole was raised Catholic and kept a desk drawer full of index cards where he wrote down any mistakes he'd made that day, just to keep track. This was less about punishing himself for moral failings and more about learning from the rare night he drank too much, the time he skipped class, the time he didn't call his mother on her birthday out of spite because he was mad at her over something she'd said to his sister. He'd been doing this since he was a little kid. For all I know, I'm the only one he ever showed that desk drawer to. Our other friends teased Cole for never drinking enough and never staying out that late, but I was proud to be his girlfriend. He was so good at taking care of himself.

The summer internship had taken place in a suburb of the Gold Coast called Elanora. It consisted of landscaping a private residence, as part of their "beautification" project, and living in a tent on the property with the other interns, as well as backpackers who were there to fulfill the farmwork requirement of their working holiday visa. I had picked this internship from the college career office because I liked the idea of being surrounded by koalas in a tent out in a rainforest so far away. No one I knew had traveled much, and certainly no one I knew had ever traveled the world alone. I would be the first. I had never even left the country before. My mother had never left the Northeast. Her father had died in a plane crash when she was little and because of this she didn't fly. But I had this idea about having friends all over the world. Everyone else I knew from school was working in an office that summer, so I felt brave for doing something different. All through high school and early college, I spent summers working at a charter school program in Mission Hill, where my dad volunteered two nights a week as an after-school math tutor. The Australia internship felt amazingly original.

Elanora wasn't as pretty as I wanted it to be, or as it'd been pictured in the program brochure. The coastline should have been gorgeous—nearly thirty miles of white sand beach running from Coolangatta to Surfers Paradise—but the high-rises of Mermaid Waters ruined it. All along the beach were charmless cheap hotels, holiday resorts, billboards, and tall red cranes. The internship was located at the top of Buckingham Way, where you got a three-hundred-sixty-degree view of the ocean to the east, the skyline north, the man-made canals south, and suburbs. Outside my tent, I was able to watch cockatoos, these magnificent bright-white birds with orange crowns, and hear the sweet low pitches of red king parrots, and count the parakeets, which shot through the air, tiny and neon green.

On my fifth day, I went on a long aimless run toward the beach, through the winding streets, to try and find the prettier parts of the area. About a quarter mile down Guineas Creek Road, a large black bird swooped very close to the side of my face, clicking at my ear. I was surprised at how close it was flying by me, but I kept on running, assuming it was just trying to snatch at my headphones.

The next day, however, when I took the same route down Killara Street to the beach, I paused at the turn from Ware Drive onto Galleon Way, remembering the peculiar, clicking bird from the day before. Glancing down the road, I spotted a slim silhouette atop one of the lampposts about a hundred meters away. The instant I noticed it, the silhouette swiveled around and made a beeline for me, rocketing through the air, as massive as a crow, black-and-white wings cocked, talons outstretched, eyes bright and orange. Never in my life had I felt so targeted.

I lunged at a nearby tree, a young thing planted in the middle of the sidewalk, and snapped off a low branch. I started beating the air with it. The bird was at me in less than a second. It was screaming and I was screaming. Then there was a thump and a sharp pain around the top of my head. The bird had made contact above my eyes with its claws or beak. I staggered back, tasting blood, vision cloudy. Meanwhile the bird was still trying to claw out my eyes.

I sprinted across the street. I could make out only the flashes of it pursuing me, could feel the heat and agitation of its black-and-white body behind me. In front of a pasture across the street, there was a small farmhouse with a red pickup in the driveway. I dropped down onto the ground and army-crawled under the truck. Keeping my body flat to the gravel, I pressed my forehead into the pebbles, covering the back of my neck with my hands. All was still. I could smell the engine of the truck, the rust and gasoline. There was a quiet ticking.

Careful not to make a sound, I slowly turned my head so that my cheek pressed into the pebbles and I could look out under the right side of the truck, which faced the street. And then, in the middle of looking, a set of claws dropped down in front of my face onto the gravel.

The bird was about a meter away. I could see the white tail feathers, the swoop of black stomach, the belly feathers twitching. The rubbery feet started padding toward the front of the truck. Then they disappeared. Then they were back in front of me. The tap of them on the ground was a tiny noise.

I kept anticipating the moment when the head would drop down and those big orange eyes would make contact with mine. After a few circles though, the feet didn't come back. But I wasn't an idiot—I knew the bird was waiting for me.

I considered the possibility that someone might get inside the truck while I was still under it and run me over. For a couple of hours, I stayed hidden beneath it, my body throbbing so much it felt like I was floating. I stayed awake but closed my eyes until it felt like I was in a small boat on an undulating sea. Then it felt like I was being carried face down on a raft atop the backs of men. Then it was nighttime, and I was being lifted like a koala by my dad, moved from the car seat to the house, surrounded by cicadas. Finally, I opened my eyes, my neck stiff, the top of my head tingling, cold and open to the air.

I crawled out from under the truck, toward the front right tire, then pressed my back up against it, peering into the trees, the sky. No bird. When I finally determined it was safe, I ran across the street, as fast as I could, back up Ware, back up Killara, and back to the property.

My closest friends in the program were a group of Czech backpackers, consisting of a couple and three single guys.

They were all older than me, in their late twenties. I was flattered that they enjoyed including me in their card games after dinner. Thanks to my dad, I was rather talented at cards.

When I made it back that evening after the encounter with the bird, my Czech friends explained to me about magpies and their swooping season. I couldn't believe there weren't more signs advertising this danger to foreigners. The Czech guys also told me that the birds had magnificent memories, so my face would be imprinted in that magpie's brain for its entire life. The bird would probably live another fourteen to seventeen years, so I couldn't go down that road ever again.

I spent the rest of my time in Elanora petrified of the magpies. I flinched every time something came too close to my face, even if it was just a moth. I noticed that the neighborhood kids wore these helmets with long needle-like spikes sticking out when they biked to school. It seemed to me that the Gold Coast was infested with these beasts, their talons clasping all the electrical cables. These birds were always hopping around the sidewalks looking for bugs. There were black things constantly bulleting through the sky, which I couldn't escape being under. But the magpies did sing really pretty songs in the morning—multiple-noted, whistling tunes. Out of all the birds, the magpies had the prettiest song.

My daily work for the internship involved shoveling gravel into bags, then wheelbarrowing those bags down the dusty hill to where the Czech boys were laying sandstone walls into the property's cliffside. The shoveling caused a terrific pain between my shoulder blades and dried out my knuckles. It was boring, monotonous work that took up six hours of the day. I tried to find interesting things to say about it when

I used the early hours to call Cole, Frances, my mother, or my sister. I told them about how, at night, I heard wild animals shuffling around my tent—wallabies especially, their feet bouncing through the leaves, and the sound of koalas coughing. I also told them about the card games I played with the Czech boys after dinner.

The man who ran the property was named Norbert. He was a large German man who was always barefoot, in cargo pants and a Hawaiian shirt. He got drunk a lot and when he walked around at night to photograph the koalas he sometimes peed in the leaves outside my tent. He was passionate about wildlife photography and liked showing me pictures on his computer of the mother koalas and their pouched babies. In his past life, with his first wife, he was an anesthesiologist. Then he moved from Munich to Australia and started over as a wildlife photographer who hosted backpackers. Norbert's new wife was a Malay woman named Wendy who cooked extravagant dinners for all of us once a week. During the day, she worked in Byron Bay. To get to work on time, she had to leave at four in the morning, so Norbert had an austere no-noise-after-nine rule. He also had a lot of rules about when and how to clock in for work, which could be done only in fifteen-minute increments, and each fifteen-minute increment corresponded exactly to the amount you owed him for renting the tent. I suspected this system was mostly about satisfying the backpackers' strict farmwork requirements. Norbert also had rules about how to properly clean his mugs. He hated coffee stains.

The night he raped me, he'd come out to where we were all sitting around a fire by the Czech boys' tent. He sat next to me and offered me a cup of sweet Spanish liquor. That whole summer, I hadn't had much of anything to drink because my mother had told me it was a terrible idea for girls traveling alone to get drunk. But I felt rude not drinking what Norbert offered me and it was close to the end of the internship. I woke up, hours later, naked and vomiting. Even though I was vomiting, he continued moving in and out of me. Then I passed out again. The next time I woke up I knew I needed to leave right away. The blue-white window next to us told me it was morning and also that we were downstairs in the garage, where all the tools were kept. I felt so devastated by what was happening, my own vomit plastered to the side of my face, that I thought about throwing myself off the cliff outside. But every time I tried to leave the mattress, Norbert—who was half asleep—yanked me back down, and I actually felt grateful to him because he was keeping me from going off the cliff. Finally, when Norbert was totally asleep, I managed to extract myself from under him. Instead of heading to the cliff though, I went out to my tent and started gathering all my things: my book, my lime-green travel toothbrush, my running shoes, dusty from the gravel. I stuffed most everything into my big navy backpack, then all my leftover things into my two smaller ones. I took my laundry off the line, fished a sock out from under the pillow, zipped up my tent, then slung all three of my backpacks over me.

At that hour, it was hard to tell the difference between the possums screaming and the cockatoos. I didn't stop walking until I got all the way to the top of the hill, where I then did a magnificently slow and accidental tumble onto the grass, my body still foggy and unbalanced from whatever had been in the Spanish liquor. A car passed by, and I waved my hands at it. It was the third car I waved at that stopped.

The guy driving deposited me somewhere near the airport in Coolangatta, by an inlet and a place called Goodwin Park.

There was a picnic table, a red swing set, and a wooden fence, its posts topped with sculptures of herons, each cocked in a different position, made from twists of copper-colored wire. Little yellow-headed birds pecked around puddles of mud where the tide was low and full of small sputtering waves.

I started walking down the sidewalk but made it only a few yards before sitting down on the ground again, on top of my backpack. My vagina was sore and pulsing. Everything smelled musty and I worried the smell was coming from my body. But when I laid back on top of my backpack, I found the answer in the fig tree above me, where hundreds of big, furry bats were dangling from the branches. I realized a lot of the screaming in the air was theirs.

A woman named Penelope was the one who found me under that tree. Her face appeared over me as I was looking up at the bats. It was just past five in the morning. She was clutching a cup of tea, the tail of her pale-yellow bathrobe dragging on the wet asphalt.

"I saw you through my screen there," she explained nervously. She had a rosy face and short, blondish curls, and her voice was high and spotty. "Do you like milk and sugar?"

I peered up at her through my hands, which were sticky with strings of snot and tears, some fingers stuck in my mouth, some stuck to my cheeks.

"I knew you looked like a milk and sugar lady," she said when I took the small blue cup. "If you're comfortable, you can come with me inside. I live just there." She gestured across the street again. "I can fix you some brekkie."

Penelope's place was one story, one bedroom, one bathroom, big enough for two beach chairs. A sign on the wall said NO SMOKING, but there was an ashtray underneath it. Penelope kept looking in her refrigerator, asking me if I liked certain things—Meat? Feta? Eggs? How many? Potatoes? What about beans? I told her feta was my favorite and she set down a plate full of breakfast.

For several hours, I sat with Penelope at her table as she eventually got the story of the night before out of me. My clothes had started feeling itchy and tight but she wouldn't let me take a shower yet. Above Penelope's couch, there was a poster of two giraffes, a baby giraffe looking out at you, and a big giraffe leaning over it, kissing the top of its head so hard the baby's forehead was wrinkly, all smooshed from the pressure of the big giraffe's lips. Penelope told me she wanted me to call my mother because she had a daughter herself and if something like this ever happened to her, she'd need to know. Over the course of those hours at her house, Penelope—in an effort to make me feel better, I think—told me what felt like her entire life. I learned that her daughter, Felicity, now lived in Brisbane with her own daughter. I learned that Felicity grew up with a heart condition, but it hadn't stopped her from becoming a skydiving instructor.

Eventually, Penelope managed to get me to call my mother.

"Oh no. Okay. You're okay, baby," my mother said as I explained through the phone what had happened. Then she asked to speak to Penelope, so I handed over the phone. By the time we were both done talking with my mother, it'd been decided that I was to go to the hospital. We were able to walk there from Penelope's house.

In the emergency room, Penelope told me this hospital was the same one where she'd given birth to Felicity thirty-four years ago. Inside, I met a social worker, who managed my whole situation as the doctors did all the things they needed to do to keep me from getting pregnant or diseased. They took samples that they said they'd keep in a kit for six months in case I decided to do something about what had happened. The whole time I was in the hospital room, Penelope kept coming in and out, whenever permitted. She was talking to my mother on her phone in the waiting room, then checking in with me on different parts of the plan that my mother was laying out. Penelope was starting to annoy me. She wouldn't stop talking about her own life. In between procedures, she kept trying to tell me and the doctor about how her daughter had died thirteen times in this hospital as a newborn, and nobody believed her until she pinned "the quack" to the wall and forced him to face her blue-black baby himself. That's how they found out about the heart condition. "Mothers always know best. Wouldn't you say, Doc?" She kept craning over my doctor's shoulder to look at his computer. I started wanting her to go away.

She told me that my mother was planning to come to Australia to get me. This idea horrified me, and I insisted that I could manage getting on a flight home by myself. When the doctors were finished with me, and Penelope and I made our way on foot back to her house, I got on the phone again with my mother and assured her I was fine to get home on my own. My mother emailed over a flight ticket, then told me she thought it'd be a good idea to call Cole and let him know what was going on. The thought of calling Cole had been preoccupying me the most. Cole hadn't liked my story about Norbert peeing outside my tent or the way I'd described his bare feet.

Before Penelope let me disappear through the automatic doors at the terminal, she had me promise that I'd text her to let her know when I was at my gate, text her again when I got into Boston, and keep her posted on how I was doing.

"Will you do that for me, sweets?" she said, rubbing circles into my upper back, as we walked together to the door, her hazards on behind us. She tucked behind my ear the hair that'd fallen from my bun, then patted my cheek. I told her I would. When I was at my gate, minutes before boarding, I finally called Cole. I also called my sister.

Both my mother and sister came to Logan to pick me up. On the phone, I had instructed my sister to instruct my mother to never mention a single word of the rape to me ever again. I didn't want to talk about it with either of them anymore.

Heading down to baggage claim, I saw them before they saw me. My mother appeared small and tense, wildly looking around like where, where, where. I'd gotten her all worked up. My sister spotted me as I neared the end of the escalator. My mother rushed over, presenting me with two pints of blueberries, a roll of chocolate biscuits, and a thermos of her sweet chai tea. She kept reaching up to touch my face, her whole hand on my forehead, then both her hands on both my cheeks, then back to my forehead. When she stopped touching my face, she wrapped her arm around my waist and led me out to the car, where my sister was putting my things in the trunk.

Because my mother followed my sister's instructions, my dad ended up being the only person who ever said anything explicit to me about Australia. When my mother disappeared upstairs that evening to switch the laundry, my dad sat next to me on the couch as I was finishing a second mug of tea. He put a hand on my knee, looked me in the eyes through his round glasses, and said, "Lucy, I'm so sorry about what happened to you."

"Thanks," I told him. "It's okay." Then I stood and left the den, unable to bear it.

That night, as soon as he got off work, Cole came over to our house, driving an hour and a half in traffic to get to me. I was in bed, under all my covers, my back to the door, when my mother let him in. I heard his feet on the carpet. Without saying a word, he got into bed behind me, pulled me toward him, and just held me like that for a very long time. I was in a big black sweatshirt and sweatpants, the hoodie tied tight under my chin so my face was in a scrunched circle, barely visible.

I really did love Cole. But after Australia, I just could not get myself to have sex with him again. At first, it was because I thought he didn't want to have sex with me anymore, after knowing what had been inside me. So, I made sure to not even present the option of sex to him in order to spare myself the rejection. This fear, however, obscured from me the fact that I was the one who had no desire for him anymore. I was so wrapped up in trying to mitigate what I suspected to be his evaporated attraction to me that I wasn't paying attention to what my own sexual impulses even were. I realized this the night in September when, in Cole's senior year dorm, Cole finally, gently, tried kissing me. All action by Cole was always intensely premeditated—so, by some calculation, he must've determined that it had been long enough since we'd had sex to warrant his trying something different. But a few things happened when he did this. First, I understood that Cole hadn't been touching me for the last month not because he was repulsed by me, but because he was trying to be sensitive. Second, I realized that his suspicion of me had been correct—I wasn't ready to start having sex with him again. Third, as

soon as I realized that the little spiders on my breasts were actually his fingers, I shuddered and became a limp noodle, all
of my muscles dissolving. At once, he stopped and rolled onto
his back. I felt him breathing very softly next to me, staring
at the ceiling, the space between us prickly. I knew then that
he'd never try again. He was going to wait for me. He was a
patient, disciplined person; he'd wait forever if he had to.

Halfway through that fall, however, I noticed I was able to
have sex with other people, just not Cole. This discovery took
place at a party Cole hadn't attended due to an imminent eco-
nomics exam. At the party, a sophomore I didn't know started
talking to me, and I felt overwhelmed with desire for him.
The feeling was so welcome, I just let it happen, though the
guilt the next day was excruciating. I couldn't spend a second
thinking about what I had done because of how bad the guilt
was. Instead, I turned my body off to keep it from splitting me
in half. Still, I felt panicked. I knew I had to tell the sophomore not to tell anyone about what had happened. But when I
met up with him to explain, he didn't seem to care at all that
I had a boyfriend and said he was down to keep sleeping with
me; he wouldn't tell anyone. His apathy was startling, but I
was grateful for it. It matched the numbness I was trying to
summon in myself, the only thing keeping me in one piece.

Cole and I were still sleeping in the same bed our regular
number of nights a week, and snuggling up to watch movies, but it was platonic and ticklish—his touches so light they
didn't feel like anything, his hands like dandelions. He didn't
touch me beyond hand-holding and hugs and soft back rubs.

I felt extremely tortured keeping all my affairs a secret. The
first mouth ulcer popped up in March, and then they didn't

stop. I'd get one after another, sometimes two or three at a time, and the worst part was, as soon as one started healing, another would open up somewhere else—on the inside of my lower lip, above my top teeth, on the roof of my mouth, blooming in the mushy part under my tongue. That spring, at any given moment, my mouth was usually housing two or three ulcers at various stages of their life. Luckily, no one could see them. Likewise, no one knew what I was suffering through. The ulcers were violent. They arrived in a sequence, they weren't healing, and I feared it was going to be like this forever. Every time I spoke, ate, kissed someone, drank—even if I was only drinking water—I was in pain. I remember detesting Frances because she kept asking me questions, wanting to chat, without understanding that moving my mouth to utter even a word was feeding a bestial headache, a reservoir of tears building up behind my eyes, yet I didn't want to reveal to anyone what was happening to me.

In April, I checked myself into the university's urgent care clinic, where the doctor took samples of my throbbing mouth, had me pee in a cup, and asked me to swab my own vagina. Then he inquired about all my sexual partners and ran a bunch of tests. So badly, I wanted to get examined by this doctor and then fixed—this doctor who seemed to think, like I did, that I had some awful lasting sexual disease (even though it ended up being just ulcers). I thought, This must be what it's like to deal with something permanent. A sense that everyone save Cole was about to discover all my lies descended upon me. I knew that I had to change, but I also had a terrible feeling that this was exactly who I was, who I always would be. Sitting on that paper sheet that was ripping in half beneath me, I told myself not to worry: You're only twenty-one years old. None of this counts yet.

—

The day I broke up with Cole, I remember so clearly the way he released his face from his hands, pressed a palm into the carpet to stand, picked up his shoes, and in his white ankle socks walked out. I got up too then and followed him out of the bedroom. He padded down the stairs, holding his sneakers. From the other room, my mother asked if he wanted to stay for dinner. When he didn't respond, she approached the back door, appearing at the bottom of the stairs. His bright-red face made her face turn bright red. She had also loved Cole very much.

She hugged him, her hands gripping the back of his head, then his shoulders. She kissed his forehead, then pressed his face into her chest. When she released him, he bounced on his feet to tug on his shoes one at a time. He waved limply back at her without fully turning around, but she caught his hand like a butterfly. It was a brief squeeze—he clearly didn't want to linger any longer—and as he pulled away, he said something like, "Okay, bye," in a very high voice. Then the screen door smacked shut. I was standing halfway down the stairs at this point, my hand on the railing, looking at all of this as if it didn't belong to my life at all, so I was shocked when my mother turned immediately upon Cole leaving to make fierce eye contact with me. To prepare for the ambush, I sank onto the steps and squeezed my head into my knees, wrapping my hands around my neck. But instead of pouncing, she said, "Oh, sweetie," and approached me gently. Then she said, "Let's go on a walk. Okay? Come."

My mother's favorite walk went up Rockdale Road, down Allendale, up Heritage Hill Lane, down Shaw, through the town cemetery, around Bridle Pond, and back up Rockdale to home. She liked to go on a walk every day, for at least forty-five minutes, at around 9:30 or 10:00 a.m. Sometimes on weekday mornings, her friend Jordie would join her. On the weekends she'd walk with Patty or me.

When my mother walked, she liked to carry two small red three-pound dumbbells. She also always wore a baseball cap, even on cloudy days (she and Patty both burned easily). My mother was a fast walker but because my legs were longer, I had an easier time keeping up with her than Patty or Dad. She and my sister were both five foot two and always seemed a lot smaller than me because they were short as well as skinny. I worked hard to stay as thin as them since my height already made me look so much bigger, especially when the three of us went out walking together. My mother told me my broad shoulders reminded me of her brother's.

There had been a storm the night before, which had sent a rare twister through our town, something that hadn't happened in the area for over a century. It hadn't disturbed our neighborhood, but it had uprooted a lot of old trees and made the town verdant and wet.

So many greens had gotten drawn out, branches still tipping down around us in a quiet cackle, telephone poles collapsed, black wires strewn. Several trees had been lifted up and tossed. I couldn't believe that the giants hadn't been able to hold their own against the tornado, but when I pointed this out, my mother said, "Well, you can see their trunks are rotted through."

And then, she said, "Can we talk about what happened at school?"

There was surprisingly little rage in her voice, but it was shaky with anxiety or restraint. She told me that she didn't understand what I had been doing in that tree, how I had gotten up there, or what animal I was pretending to be. I seemed alright to her now, she added, like myself. But she needed reassurance that I wouldn't pull a stunt like that ever again, at least in her lifetime.

She ended by saying, "You understand how this whole thing seems like a giant cry for help. You clearly wanted attention."

"I didn't do it for attention," I said. I felt hurt having to say this to her. I also wasn't sure it was true. We were approaching the front gate of the cemetery, and I was still trying to detect exactly how mad she was at me.

"Well, it was humiliating."

"I'm sorry."

"Don't say that," she said sharply and I flinched. "That's not what I'm looking for." There was a good amount of silence again, the only sounds around us being the rush of cars on Shaw, the distant screams of little kids, and all the water from the storm draining away endlessly, the rushing gutters. My sneakers squishing, getting soaked through.

Then my mother took a very loud breath, and said, "I'm just trying my best. I tried my best last summer. But I'm just a person. I'm your mom, but I'm also just a person." We were in the cemetery now. She stopped at the bottom of the short hill that led up to the pond, put her hands on her hips, and took three deep shaky breaths, staring at the sky. Then she dropped her head like it was the heaviest thing in the world and said, "Your dad keeps having these dreams about you getting ripped apart by sharks. He's been waking up in cold sweats."

I didn't like hearing this. My dad had always been my ally. My mother could sometimes get angry with him the way she got angry with me.

"Can I know why you and Cole broke up?" she asked. We had started walking again.

"I think I need to be on my own for a while," I explained. "I want to be single."

"Was he aware that you'd been feeling this way?"

"I think a little bit."

"He's been so caring with you," she said. "He's such a good person." My mother and dad were college sweethearts.

"It's going to be too hard with me in Indianapolis and him here," I went on. "I'm ready for a fresh start."

She let out a huge, dramatic sigh. "I want to talk to you about that also," she said. She told me she didn't want me moving to Indianapolis. She wanted me to stay in Boston.

"But I start in a few weeks," I said.

She launched into a long explanation then: She explained that she'd rather I find a job closer to home, and that she had talked to some of her friends and there were a lot of good options for employment here that would keep me close by, which would give me some more time to live at home and feel better. She didn't want me moving somewhere far away so soon after everything. She said it was completely unreasonable for me to move.

"Silly," she said. "Needless."

But moving to Indianapolis felt more essential to me than ever. It was because of Indianapolis that I had any chance of surviving all of this. Everything from the past year was only going to be okay precisely because Indianapolis was a place for me to go, get better, then come back from. I already had big plans about who I was going to become there. I was going to become ten pounds lighter, make a ton of money and even better friends. In Indianapolis, I would build healthy routines and become a good person again. I was already looking forward to the person I was going to be when I moved back home in a year or two—worldlier, more beautiful, ready to be back among my friends and parents, who would've gained enough distance at that point from the versions of me that no longer mattered.

So I let my mother know that I would be going to Indianapolis no matter what. "I'm going to Indianapolis," I said.

This prompted silence again, a very threatening one this time that nearly rivaled in size the silence of the last two weeks. We kept walking between the graves. We reached the pond, where kids and parents were skipping stones. We stopped to watch them. They weren't actually skipping stones. They were just throwing rocks. The pond was higher than I'd ever seen it, and the air was full of dramatic kerplunks, the mud running down to the shore stuffed with paw prints and goose tracks. A boy slightly older than the others sat reading on the big rock where I used to spend a few minutes sitting on my way home from school as a kid, to watch the ducks. Sometimes I just needed to be somewhere quiet and outside.

"Well," said my mother finally, making me jump. A sharp inhale through her nose. "I'm sorry you two broke up. I love Cole. That must be very hard."

Under a nearby bench, a round pale speckled rock caught my eye. I took a couple of steps over to it and picked it up. It was big and smooth. I held its superb body in my palm, excited to chuck it into the pond alongside the other rock throwers. A satisfying sound of submersion and heaviness would enter the air, this time mine.

"I'd really like us to move on from this whole thing," said

my mother. "Can we do that please? I need reassurance from you that nothing like that will ever happen again."

For a fleeting moment, with that rock in my hand, I felt harangued by anger that my mother had decided it was up to her to choose how to move on from the leopard incident, especially since I was feeling like I never wanted to move on. I wanted to hold it inside me forever. Already, a very sad part of me suspected that I would never become the leopard again, the same part of me that wanted to be the leopard forever. That same part also suspected that the more time that passed, the more I'd be able to convince myself that it had all been pretend, even though what my body remembered of the leopard felt just as impossible to make up as it did to inhabit again.

Behind the fence on Eliot Street rushed an unending sequence of cars, each one shepherding their fuzzy headlights through the damp, misty air, one after the next after the next. A toddler in a blue cap and overalls kept running toward the ducks, then running back toward his dad, clapping his hands together. At one point, the dad lifted the toddler onto his shoulders and they stood together in front of the water, pointing. One brave goose kicked out into the middle of the pond, splitting it down the center, trailing sun behind it in the water.

"Well? Can we do that? Can we move on from this?" she asked again, a note of decisiveness in her voice, as if she was being generous, doing us both a favor.

I said yes.

"Good," she said. "I think we should hug."

So, I dropped my rock, and we hugged. It was too short to really feel like anything. At the end of our walk, upon reaching our front door, my mother told me that starting now, she'd like us to hug once a day. This had been suggested to her as a good thing for us to do. She said she'd like us to try and do our hug first thing in the morning, before having our tea, so we wouldn't forget.

And, as it turned out, my mother and I were both able to move on. Nothing like the leopard would ever happen to me again. But ever since then, I've had this vibrant understanding of other species, this special intimacy with wild animals that I know wild animals also feel around me. I know something now about fear that's not quite human, about predation that's different from what others might think they know, about why cats like lying out in the sun so much. I also know that I can be dark, that I can keep secrets, and that I can scale trees.

INDIANAPOLIS

In Indianapolis, I started dating a man named Ellis who liked watching me have sex with other men. That whole year, I didn't know anything about the city except the inside of my apartment, the inside of his, the route I drove to work, my cubicle at the casting agency, and the 10th Street Café, where I first met Ellis because for weeks he was my waiter. My sister had advised that the best way to feel at home in a new city was to make yourself a regular somewhere local, so that's what I'd done with the 10th Street Café. I took my book there every day after work, sat in the booth with west-facing windows, ordered hot black coffee and a side of tamarind-glazed Brussels sprouts.

We'd been seeing each other for about three weeks when Ellis first brought up the idea of other men. He was inside me when he said, "You know what'd be hot? Watching you fuck someone else." I didn't say anything at first. He was on top of me, my legs wrapped around his back.

"You want to watch me fuck someone?" I reiterated, after a few moments.

"Yes," he said. He stopped moving then and held himself inside me. This made me suck in my breath. Then he put a hand on the back of my neck, just under my hairline, lifting my head up off the pillow so his mouth was against my cheek. "I want to watch you fuck another guy."

"You'd like that?" I asked.

It was hard to talk with him that deep inside me. I was almost out of breath.

"Well, I can do that," I managed.

The next day, at the 10th Street Café, Ellis slid into my booth at the end of his shift—the same way he'd done the day we first met, when I was still surprised that someone grown-up like him would be interested in talking to me—and asked if I remembered what he'd brought up in bed the night before. I told him I was confused how it would work.

"How are we going to get these men to fuck me?"

"Tinder," he replied.

"We just ask them over Tinder? No one's going to do that."

"Sure, they will."

"No one will just fuck me in front of you like that."

"Oh please," he said. "Look at yourself." Ellis thought I was really pretty. He explained that any guy who's into girls, when given this type of opportunity, would take it, assuming they weren't too brainwashed yet about what they should and shouldn't like.

"Everyone's scared to ask for what they really want," he explained. "People are scared to be who they are."

"Alright, let's try it," I said.

"You're dreamy." He took my hand from across the table and put three of my fingers in his mouth. "I always wanted to find a girl who likes what I like," he said, taking my fingers out.

It was the end of 2018. Lots of people were using Tinder but not me. For our purposes, it proved to be quite useful. Apparently, Tinder was full of normal guys who were unopposed to getting involved with our sort of proposal, and I wondered if people on Tinder were always getting asked by others, or asking others, to do stuff like this. The account was set up on Ellis's phone, so he handled all the messaging, but the profile was me, my photo, and that's who the men thought they were talking to. Their first messages back to us mostly sounded surprised or amused. The majority ended up being amenable to "having sex with me in front of my boyfriend," if not enthusiastic about it. The rules were clearly laid out ahead of time. They weren't allowed to talk. They had to leave as soon as they finished and they had to finish when and where I told them to. Ellis preferred out-of-towners. Sometimes he wrote out more detailed instructions for them that he'd let me read over first—like how long I planned to give them head, if I wanted them to go down on me too, whether they should fuck me standing up, from behind, or with me on top. Ellis thought it was good to entice them with what was going to happen beforehand so they could feel confident coming in. Other times, he liked keeping it loose so we could both be surprised. Whenever they arrived, Ellis would go downstairs to get them while I waited topless and alone in the middle of his small apartment. The first time we ran it through, I was so nervous waiting for Ellis to come back with the stranger that the thump of my heart was making me sick. I knelt in the middle of the floor, upright and alert, wearing a thin red thong with strings that went all the way over my hips, the rest of my body stacked on top of my knees, arms crossed to cover my breasts, which were small and pointy.

They were usually younger guys, between my age and Ellis's. After the first few times, I got less nervous, so the guys tended to be more nervous than I was. To help them relax, I learned to scoot on my knees over the tile, toward where they stood in front of the door, then I'd place one hand on the back of their thigh to be supportive. The slower I moved, the better. It relaxed everyone. It told them they were in good hands. Sometimes, I'd look up to check in with Ellis, who'd be sitting shirtless on the couch watching us, pants still on, just unzipped.

"Yeah, like that," he'd say.

Indianapolis still wasn't where I wanted to be for the long haul. I'd always pictured my sister and me raising kids across the street from each other. It was unclear how long I had to work at AUTHENTIC before it'd be acceptable to leave— no one had taught me how to decide when it was a good time to end something. But Indianapolis was a fine place to be, I decided, at twenty-two and twenty-three—a useful hiatus. I told myself: Just stay in Indianapolis for as long as it takes to improve yourself without everyone watching. One year, maybe two, depending on how long it takes to turn into something extraordinary.

My only friend in Indianapolis besides Ellis was Darnie

Phillips from Cincinnati, the coworker who was closest to my age. Our job at AUTHENTIC: Real People Casting consisted of calling real people and convincing them to audition for commercials. The first commercial I got assigned was for Walgreens, and we needed real people who were suffering from one of three different diseases: diabetes, arthritis, or cancer—specifically terminal cancer. Darnie and I had to get creative about how to find these people and spent a lot of time online looking up walkathons and support groups on Facebook. When you finally reached someone who was willing to talk with you on the phone, you couldn't say that the commercial was for Walgreens. You had to say, "a major pharmaceutical brand," then ask a series of questions to see if they checked all the prerequisites, such as location ("Are you from the Midwest? Chicago? Fantastic."), race and age ("Over sixty? Black? That's great."), and type of cancer ("Terminal? You're sure? Excellent. And has it ever been in remission?").

AUTHENTIC's website was all bubble letters marketing our new opportunities, advertising what we were seeking. Each bubble-letter description was superimposed on stock photos of happy couples embracing each other on beaches at sunset. SEEKING: MEN WITH EARLY-STAGE ALZHEIMER'S. SEEKING: GIRLS WHO DROPPED OUT OF SPORTS DUE TO A LACK OF BODY CONFIDENCE. SEEKING: FOURTEEN-YEAR-OLD FEMALES WHO EXPERIENCE BLADDER LEAKS AND/OR URINARY INCONTINENCE. SEEKING: MEN WHO OWN A MERCEDES-BENZ. SEEKING: PARENTS WHO SUFFER THEMSELVES FROM BED-WETTING, HAVE BIRTHED BED-WETTERS, AND CAN SPEAK OPENLY ABOUT CHILDHOOD BED-WETTING. SEEKING: EXTREMELY SWEATY PEOPLE. Darnie and I became friends at the end of my first week, when she was still assigned "Veterans Who are Considering, or Have Considered, Suicide" and spent a lot of time taking breaks on the ninth floor in the corner by the espresso machine. I didn't have a desk yet, which meant I had to float around the ninth floor all day or camp out in a phone booth.

Darnie Phillips was twenty-four and still a virgin. She'd never even kissed a boy. Despite this, she didn't seem to think that she and I were that different. She lived near Fountain Square and had two cats named Chaos and Midge. I was certain that Darnie's whole problem with men was the smell of kitty litter in her apartment. I even sent her a link for an advanced litter box that promised to make the smell disappear, and while I waited for her to order it, I gently asked if, in the meantime, she might consider moving her litter box from the front hall into the bathroom. The problem was that she didn't think the kitty litter was a problem. She was used to it. Once, I watched her feed Midge a piece of deli meat straight from her sandwich. I was pretty sure this was why Midge's shits were so stinky.

Darnie cared so much about being a good AUTHENTIC employee that she never said anything to her manager about her dad dying of suicide when she was nine, which I found out only after I asked her about the photos on her armoire. I had to excuse myself to her bathroom immediately after she told me because it felt silly to cry over her tragedy in front of her. But before I could speak to her manager secretly on her behalf, she was moved off the suicidal veterans due to underperformance and put on bed-wetting. It was a much better fit. Speaking to bed-wetters turned out to be something Darnie was excellent at, and soon she was surpassing the quota.

—

Unfortunately, with Ellis, I started smoking cigarettes and I couldn't see myself ever stopping. Besides that, I liked his ideas. I liked how dismissive he was of society's rules. He believed that all the *should*'s and *shouldn't*'s were fake. He said that people who liked things just because other people liked them were penguins. But he and I were tigers.

When Ellis and I talked to each other, it felt like neither one of us had ever talked to anyone so much in our whole lives. It was still eating me alive that I'd cheated on Cole. I was so anxious that it indicated I was someone who'd never be able to be happily married, that I was destined to cheat on people for the rest of my life. When I confessed all of this to Ellis, citing my need for infidelity as the worst thing about me, he told me that he used to shoot heroin when he worked as a crane supervisor.

"That's not as bad as cheating," I said. "You're only hurting yourself."

"You don't think heroin is as bad as cheating?" He threw his head back and laughed. Both his feet were up on the scratched maroon booth, and he had his shoulders pressed against the window.

I probably spent too much time talking to Ellis about my college infidelities, but it wasn't something I felt like I could figure out with anyone else; he was the only person I'd told, and I was so relieved that, knowing this about me, he didn't think I was a bad person.

I tried to convince him. "I caused pain. I broke an agreement. I lied."

"That bloke's not in pain. He doesn't even know about it!"

"But it would cause him pain, if he knew." It still felt very important that I preserve myself in Cole's memory as someone to whom bad things had happened, not as someone who'd done bad things. And it was too easy to imagine any of Cole's friends deciding to confess to having slept with me, rationalizing it as the right thing to do, seeing as none of them owed me confidentiality anymore, especially when up against the possibility of their own redemption. But the truth would destroy Cole. He'd lose all hope in humanity. His dad had left his mom when Cole was six for a whole other family he'd had in Maine.

"You care too much about whether people think you're good or bad," said Ellis. "That's their problem."

"I understand that what I did was bad," I explained. I needed reassurance that I was going to be okay. I needed unequivocal redemption. "I might even be a bad person deep down. I'm not trying to defend that."

"You were just doing what you wanted. There's nothing wrong with that," said Ellis, laying his palm face up on the table so I could put mine on his. Ellis had spiderwebs tattooed on the backs of his hands. He interlinked our fingers. "You know you can do whatever you want in your life," he reminded me. "You don't need to be anything. You can just be happy."

"There has to be more than that," I told him. There had to be.

Ellis shook his head. "You can't do anything that counts with your life if what you're thinking you want, what you're saying you want, and what you're actually doing aren't all the same thing." Whenever he was on his shift, he liked to pack his mouth with cinnamon gum. He had a narrow bite, full of long teeth.

"That's good, isn't it?" he said, the gum smacking around. He always had at least three pieces in there at a time. "I came up with that. That's how I define unhappiness."

"I won't be happy unless I'm a good person who's being good to the people around me."

"That doesn't make any sense! When you're happy, you're good enough. What you're saying is an oxymoron. See? I'm smart." Ellis got a kick out of the fact that I went to college and he was still just as smart as me. He liked telling me about how he'd been the cleverest kid in grade school but got bad marks because he spent his exams drawing up extremely creative comics about alien invasions just to mess with his teachers. He wished his mom was alive so he could get her to text him pictures of his old exams so I could see.

"Nothing matters anyway," he said. "You and I aren't going to change the world. We're not special like that."

"I want to be," I reminded him.

"I remember wanting that," he said. "But it's all fake. You'll see. What's the point if you're just doing what everyone else is doing? Then you're just living the same life as them."

Everything clicked for me, very specifically, on a Tuesday afternoon at work, a few pages into reading a short story on my laptop about a clown murderer. For the rest of the day, I couldn't speak to Darnie or anyone else in the office. I suddenly felt disgusted by almost everyone I'd ever known, and it felt essential that I leave the office immediately and get myself over to Ellis's to inform him that I finally got it, I could finally tell him about my dreams, because I was someone who could achieve anything. I felt foolish for pretending before that I wanted to be a good person who made a positive impact on the world.

The short story had been told from the clown's perspective as he went around a suburban town murdering all these normal couples at gas stations, on picnic benches, even in their own kitchens, interrupting, with his ax, the tiny, unremark-able moments that these normal couples had been tricked into thinking were private and romantic. But the clown un-derstood something about the idiocy of everyone that made him capable of murdering the people who didn't get it, and I was finally getting what the writer and maybe all good writ-ers were trying to say. People, when reading the story, might not realize that they were the people the writer was mocking. That was the big joke that the writer was in on, along with me and Ellis and other rare people who also got it. The writer wasn't mocking the clown. He was mocking all his readers who thought they were capable of getting it and weren't. That everyone wasn't a clown murderer suddenly became insane to me. I could be a clown murderer. Darnie couldn't. I felt myself becoming magnificent and huge. I was also terrified. I actually felt sick to my stomach after reading the clown story because something in me had shifted massively and too quickly. I was scared that this meant I really was going to live forever looking down on other people, and I needed reassurance that this free-dom I was experiencing wasn't going to make me incapable of loving them, especially my family and friends who I now felt were at this lethal distance beneath me. Luckily, I had Ellis.

"We can still be happy and connect with those people," he reassured me when I finally arrived at his place after work, my surroundings still as coreless and echoey as they'd been in the office. For instance, I could see the myriad ways his bookshelf could've been positioned in the space, one centimeter to the right, three to the left, at any angle. We lay on top of his bed. "We can just mess around, play our games, and know this about ourselves. We don't need to go around actually mur-dering people. It's still more fun being us."

"I just want to have a big existence," I admitted.

"You're already having it," confirmed Ellis. His cheek was resting on my inner thigh. I was propped up on his pillows, now examining his ceiling fan, one hand numbly atop his skull, his soft black hair. "Most people never get it. They just keep doing the things they were told to do when they were infants. But you're out here fucking men in front of me every night!"

"I think we're the most romantic couple on the planet," I agreed. "We love each other in a way they'll never understand."

"We are in love, aren't we?" He bit my upper thigh, held on, then shook his head madly. Whenever he pretended to be a dog, he tensed up all his muscles to the point of his whole body vibrating even though he wasn't biting that hard. I patted the top of his head with my weak, tingly hand. It felt like a maraca. Above us the ceiling fan turned really slowly, then stopped.

"Power's out," I announced. The power in his apartment went out a lot because of construction down the road.

Whenever Frances and I used to compare breasts in our dorm room, I always felt so bad about mine. But now that seemed adolescent. None of the guys on Tinder turned us down. They all took us up on our offer. Ellis was consistently star-struck by this. After they'd leave, when it was his turn with me, he would approach me ravenously, push down my head, then pull me back by the hair so I could watch him finish. Then, he'd pet my hair and say, "See, you're way hotter than a hooker. They're lucky they get to have you for even a second," and I'd feel so good about myself, so relieved, and so happy to not be trapped in that relationship with Cole, which had been so terrible at the end.

My exact level of attractiveness had always been something I'd worked hard to gauge—even at a young age, I knew it was important to know this about yourself. I was the only one in my family with freckles. They covered my whole face but weren't anywhere else, except for a faded one on the inside of my right wrist. I was used to my freckles but had gathered through my classmates and some of the mothers that they were unusual. Most of the time, I grew up feeling desperate to erase them. One time, our neighbor Mrs. Hall called them "exotic" and I cried to my sister about it, who then reassured me that I was in the top ten percent of beautiful people, which only confused me more. I remember sitting on the monkey bars one night in elementary school, waiting for my mother to finish talking to the other mothers after my sister's flute recital, the cold metal bars pushing into the backs of my thighs, and wishing on a star to become the most beautiful girl in the world, the girl that every boy in my class was secretly in love with, even though I barely spoke back then, was largely unknown, and had just one friend (Isabella, whom I befriended in kindergarten because she had freckles too).

But now, with Ellis, I saw how they all wanted me. The more guys I fucked in front of him, the more confident I felt out in the world: I'd see a guy in the street, and think, If given the chance, you would. It was nice to continue to prove this. Everybody should spend some time having sex with as many people as possible, I thought, just to get a rough idea of how desirable they are. It was a powerful thing to know about your body—because if less desirable, then the attraction of a single person mattered more. But most people were too scared to put themselves out there in the way I was. Luckily, because of doing this with Ellis, I now knew that, as long as my body stayed this way, I was okay. I had already decided to be someone who prioritized my looks. It was worth it to stay small, which meant eating only the bare minimum of what stopped hunger. The scary part, of course, was that every day was a day when my body could change for the worse—there was only so much I could control. So, every day it was important to confirm again that this was still true about my body. And every time another guy on a new night took us up on our offer and came over and got off, it was a relief.

The more guys who came over, the more each individual guy became every guy—over time, none of them felt like strangers—and the more I realized I needn't ever rely upon the desire of just one man, which more importantly meant I needn't ever depend upon my own desire for just one man. With each new guy, all the things I thought I knew about myself dissolved, but in a good way: I could be anything to anyone and anyone could be anything to me. How did nobody else know this? So many people had no clue because everyone was too scared. I'd watch the man above me become thoughtless before finishing, and I'd think—the things you think you know about yourself, the things you think make you unique are nothing, because you couldn't help it either, you couldn't pass up the opportunity to come over here secretly and fuck me without speaking, for free. You're just like him and him and him and him and him. People thought that the point of life was to hone a consistent version of yourself, to become stable, compact, honorable—no contradictions, no gaps. But in fact, it was all about being as free as possible. Free to be anything! There were so many ways of being, and it was about making sure every way remained available to me at any point in my life. And now that I understood it didn't matter what people thought of me, I was no longer trapped in having to be just one version of myself. I could change as much as I liked.

Still, I got nervous as work came to a close and the evening approached. What helped, before heading over to Ellis's, was just sitting by the river for a few moments, no matter the weather, to catch my breath. It seemed important, in a landlocked city that had such easy access to running water, to visit it once a day. I'd sit in the sun on the concrete wall and watch people pass—runners, bikers, dogs, scooters, strollers. People in cities loved to run. Everyone in leggings and bright sneakers and colorful colors. I'd sit there until they all became a blur. Then I'd focus on the birds. Before Indianapolis, I'd never attended to the way different sorts walked differently: the yellowlegs tiptoed around feet first, skeptically, whereas the sandpipers led with their needly beaks; the plump pintails processed in mopey circles through the reeds; hawks floated casually above. I'd sit there in the cold, with the sun on my shoulders, pressing my palms into the rough concrete slab, making my skin pebbly, and watch the birds move around, and try to exhale for as long as possible, something my mother used to tell me to do before big exams, and just feel myself sink.

It wasn't until my parents drove the car out in the middle of March that I realized just how inadequately I knew the city of Indianapolis. I had nothing to show them when they arrived. I hid my cigarettes. Luckily all my mother wanted to do was fill up my apartment with better food. My mother's mother died of cancer when my mother was my age, so my mother was tethered to the idea that eating specific foods would ward off disease. Cancer was the last thing she wanted for herself or any of us, which was a shame since both she and my dad would end up dying of it. Still, I couldn't stand to have her filling my fridge and cabinets with these things that I grew up eating: kale, broccoli, blueberries, organic almond butter, garlic. My parents spent three nights with me, sleeping on the air mattress they brought from home, along with my foldable bookshelf and two soft-pink beanbag chairs, in which they sat for almost the entire weekend as we hung around my apartment, eating the groceries and playing cards.

On their last day, my mother declared that she'd like to get outside for some exercise, so I took them to Starkey Park. On the ride there, my dad sat up front with me and my mother sat in the back.

"I'm thinking of an animal," said my dad, as soon as I stopped at the first red light.

"Lucy," snapped my mother. She got nervous when I drove. She didn't like hard stops.

"I've had this one in my head for a while," continued Dad. "It's a good one."

My mother didn't like us playing games while I was driving. She wanted me to focus on the road.

"Don't distract her, Abe."

"She's fine, honey," said my dad about me to my mother.

"She hasn't driven in a while," said my mother about me.

"Is it a bird or a mammal?" I asked my dad.

"I thought it had to be a yes-or-no question," said my mother.

"It is yes or no," I explained. She didn't understand our game. My dad and I had perfected an algorithm over years of playing twenty questions in the car—only animals—when he picked me up from soccer practice on Wednesdays after school and we always got stuck in unavoidable standstill on I-93. We both liked to study species taxonomy books—my dad worked for the city as an environmental review specialist, mostly in the capacity of arborist. I got so good at twenty questions on those car rides that I was able to guess practically any animal in the world in ten yes-or-no questions or fewer.

I said, "He can either answer yes, it is either a bird or a mammal. Or no, it is neither a bird nor a mammal. He doesn't need to tell me specifically whether it's a bird or whether it's a mammal, just if it's in the category of either bird or mammal."

"No, it's neither a bird nor a mammal," said my dad.

"Is it a sea creature or an insect?"

"Yes."

Clearly, my mother still didn't get it because she then chimed in from the back to ask, "Is it smaller than a bread box?"

"Yes, it's smaller than a bread box," answered Dad.

"Can it be domesticated?" asked my mother.

"Mom!" I said to stop her.

"What?"

"No, it can't be domesticated."

Despite my mother's faux pas, I ended up guessing my dad's animal in eight: a locust.

"Twelve," said my dad, counting his fingers. "Not bad."

"Eight," I corrected. "Not including Mom's."

"Twelve," he said. "You two are on a team. Who wants to go next? Honey?"

In the rearview, my mother had fixed her gaze out the window. She didn't like driving on highways and looked tense. She shook her head. "Clearly, I don't get the game," she said.

By the time I thought of an animal for my dad to guess, we had already arrived at the trailhead. After we parked, I evaluated the map and then told my parents—with impulsive, inexplicable dishonesty—that in Indianapolis, people liked to hike barefoot, and that barefoot was the best way to experience this path.

About twenty minutes into the hike, my mother had clearly become displeased with me. More so, the barefootedness of the hike had exposed her as small and old. She'd started out with gusto but, trying too hard to keep up, quickly got flustered, then embarrassed. I watched as my dad—sunscreen matting on his pale hairy arms, the back of his neck and top of his head bright pink—stopped to help her pick the most effective path around the roots and rocks. She clamped onto his bicep, looking clumsy and feeble. She nearly twisted her ankle on some unevenness I couldn't see, and when she stumbled, her light-blue mesh sweater—which was tied around her waist—slipped off into the mud.

At last, she stopped looking at the ground and stood up to her full five-foot-two height.

"I don't want to do this anymore," she announced.

Then, she looked up at my dad and said, just to him, "Can we go?"

She said this in a low, breathy tone that I had never heard her use before. I realized: this is how they spoke to each other before Patty and I were born. It was a tone just for him, and suddenly I was watching an old, barefoot couple interact, who had nothing to do with me.

My dad and I looked at each other.

"We can go," I said in response, but my mother was no longer speaking to me.

At six the next morning, I drove them to the airport. My mother hadn't said a word to me since the walk. When I dropped them off at Terminal A, she got out of the back seat without acknowledging me and headed toward the automatic doors. My dad, flustered by the traffic stacking behind us, clumsily kissed my forehead as he unbuckled his seat belt, then bolted to the trunk to retrieve their luggage. Rolling both suitcases behind him, he caught up with my mother, passed her a handle, then ushered her through the parting doors, a hand on her shoulder.

Driving back to my apartment, the sun still wasn't up. I got off at the wrong exit by accident and ended up on a different interstate entirely, one that slung me around and around, over ramps, under ramps, in fast circles. I was driving down roads I didn't know in a strange state that felt perpetually half built, and suddenly on the road there appeared chunky orange signs and bright massive floating arrows. Dim purple stegosauruses were rising up out of the dust. Closer, they turned into cranes. Several times I had the sinking feeling that I was driving the wrong way down the road because under all the overpasses and over all the underpasses, I lost track of my rights and lefts—a nest of white-headed pigeons flew out from under a bridge straight into my headlights and spun themselves into stars. I knew I needed to stop and catch my breath, but I couldn't pull out of the circles, and the minute I understood this predicament, I also realized that I was, in fact, very high up, on a part of the interstate built on stilts over the earth, bordered by only a dinky guardrail. Each bit I traversed coiled back underneath me as I drove up and around and up, this piece of the interstate spiraling me higher and higher above the rest of the highway until it seemed like I was the only car in the entire universe.

I suspected it would be several months before I'd hear from my mother. Once again, it was tricky to identify what exactly I'd done to cause her to cut me out.

"She's anxious that I moved so far away from her," I suggested to Ellis on my birthday in May, when I arrived at his apartment after work. Something about my Indianapolis life had clearly upset her, either the hike or something else I'd done that she'd deemed intolerable. "She's hurt that I chose to move so far away from home, so now she's cutting me out of her life because she's worried that I'm trying to cut her out of mine. But I'm allowed to live wherever I want. She hates when I make different decisions. But different's not bad."

Ellis's studio was smaller than mine, a three-hundred-and-fifty-square-foot room, so the full-sized bed, couch, and kitchen all shared the same space. Neither Ellis nor I had been in Indianapolis long, so like mine, Ellis's apartment had very little in it. Out of habit, every time I went over, I opened the fridge, but it was usually empty except for a pizza box and two or three yellow Gatorades. Even though our apartments were basically the same, his was best to hang out in because the previous tenants had left a couch.

"Can I see a picture of her?" he asked me. We were sitting on the couch. My toes were tucked under his thigh.

"We look really similar," I informed him.

"Can I see a picture?"

I showed him the one that my sister took of me, my mother, and my dad at my high school graduation.

"Something about the hike put her in a bad mood. And because she got into a bad mood on the hike, and because the hike was my idea, she thinks I'm the reason she got upset. But I'm not responsible for her moods! She always blames me."

"Your dad's quite short," said Ellis after staring at my screen for several minutes.

"I'm wearing heels in that."

"They love you a lot," he said, and handed me back the phone.

I backed up into where he was resting against the arm of the couch. I pressed my back into his chest, wanting to get him to put his chin on top of my head, which he sometimes did. I liked feeling his chin nuzzle into my skull. Instead, he linked his arms lazily in front of my ribs and bent his knees so he was squeezing me between his legs. I wanted him to squeeze me harder, but he wasn't catching on.

"Whatever. I just won't go home again," I said. I didn't need to go home. In theory, I could avoid her forever. I pushed my body into his chest, to get him to hold me tighter. I always suspected I was capable of familial estrangement, something my mother used to tell us she didn't believe in. She used to say that estrangement shouldn't ever be an option. It was a bold position for her to take, since she had an estranged brother herself. Ellis disconnected his arms.

"Should we try and get a guy over here tonight?" He reached for his phone on the coffee table. I turned over onto my stomach and pushed my nose into his hip bone. I wanted to bury my whole face. "Are you up for it?"

"Hey," he said, when I wasn't saying anything. "We don't need to."

"We can," I said. I lifted myself off the couch, everything about me heavy. I kept the bathroom door open while splashing water on my face. I wanted him to take my entire body into his arms.

The man who came over that night was English, like Ellis, but from Essex, not Hull. From the messages, we learned he was a backpacker moving through the Midwest on a road trip with two other friends, very much like what Ellis had been doing when he himself landed here. The English man was young and nervous—not as young as me but younger than Ellis—and had short legs, cuffed cargo pants, and eyes that were kind and apologetic. His name was Angus.

Mid fucking him, something happened that was different. Angus had started choking me, but he wasn't stopping in time. I hadn't quite caught on to the fact that I was losing my breath until it was already happening, because I'd been thinking about other things. I'd gotten really good at thinking about other things, like work or weekend plans or Darnie's cats, while making it seem like I was still present in the moment with the guy. It took me a second to remember I was even having sex, when Angus started pushing his huge hand down on my throat.

As I was losing my breath, I had a full conversation in my head with my mother, then with someone else.

"Hi, Mom," I said.

"Lucy, hi."

"I probably don't have much time left."

"Sweetie?"

"I don't have much time left," I repeated, my voice splintery. "I'm really sorry."

"Where are you located?" This wasn't my mother now. The phone had been handed to someone else.

"Will you tell my mom I love her," I said. I didn't know to whom I was speaking, but whoever they were, they certainly weren't going to find me in time.

When I woke up, it was just me on the bed. Ellis was standing above me, gazing down, looking scared. The English man had been pushed onto the floor, where he sat dazed, like a little boy. Both men were staring at me, both with their pants still off.

"You alright, baby?" Ellis said. His legs looked skinny enough to snap in half. I wriggled myself up against his headboard and reached for the sheets without finding them. I found my white T-shirt instead and put it on.

"I think there's something in my eye," I said. An eyelash maybe, or loose makeup.

"What the fuck, mate?" Ellis said to the English man.

The English man's mouth was half open, as he looked from me to Ellis. For a second it seemed like the three of us were all friends, hanging out half naked, maybe a little stoned.

"Sorry," he mumbled. It was like he'd been woken up too early and too suddenly. "You alright?" he asked me.

"I'm Lucy," I told him, in case he'd forgotten. I suddenly felt really embarrassed for him. I decided to go to the bathroom.

I wasn't sure what it'd be like when I left the bathroom, but I could hear Ellis and the English man talking through the door. It seemed like they were speaking in normal tones. When I came out, both had their pants pulled up, but both were still shirtless. Angus was on the floor with his shoulders pressed against the wall, his hairy arms resting limply on top of his knees, his pale belly, which drooped over his belt, also covered in dark hair.

"I was there only three or four days," Ellis was saying. "You'll have a good time. It's better this time of year."

Angus looked up at me immediately. He still seemed scared.

"What are you guys talking about?" I asked from in front of the bathroom door.

"He's headed to Boston next week," Ellis said. He was sitting on the bed.

"I'm from there," I told Angus.

"You sure you're okay?" Angus asked. He had shy small brown eyes.

"I'm good," I assured him. "What are you doing in Boston?"

"Just touristy stuff," he said. "What are you doing here?"

"In Indianapolis? I moved here for work," I said. "I got a job here."

The silence felt tense. Slightly panicked, I decided to change the subject.

"Want to know something?" I told them, settling myself on the edge of the bed. It really did seem like we were all friends. "I can guess any animal in the world in ten questions or less."

There was a little pause, then Ellis laughed. "What are you saying?" He was always amused by my talents.

"Think of an animal," I said to Angus. "But it's got to be an animal that anyone would know. A random person on the street should be able to know it."

Angus looked confused, but I knew that he and Ellis had to play with me right now. There wasn't much else that either of them could do at that point.

"Okay," said Ellis. "I've got one." It was easy to get Ellis to play almost anything. We both liked games. Cards, mini golf, racing each other at the crossword, making bets on what color the next car would be that passed us on the street. He was too competitive to pass up the opportunity to play.

"To be clear," I said to him, huddling closer to Ellis on the bed and putting a hand on the back of his calf, "if I asked a regular person on the street about this animal, they'd know what it was and be able to visualize it?"

"Yes."

"And answer simple questions about it?"

"Yes."

"Whisper it to him," I said, pointing at Angus.

"Little miss serious," Ellis said. But Angus pushed himself onto his feet at my command and walked over to Ellis. I covered my ears as Ellis whispered the animal to Angus, then Angus walked back over to the wall, and slid down again onto the floor.

"Okay," I said to both. "I bet I can get it in ten questions or less."

"Go on," said Ellis.

"Is it a bird or a mammal?"

"Piss off, that's two questions," said Ellis.

I explained how it was actually a yes-or-no question.

"Oh, I get it," Ellis said. "You've got this down to some kind of science, don't you?"

"Is it a bird or a mammal?" I asked again.

Ellis glanced at Angus. Then he answered, "No."

"Is it a sea creature or an insect? And by sea creatures, I'm including all fish and also things like octopuses, seahorses, clams, oysters, lobsters—"

"I get it."

"And by insect, I'm including arachnids, worms, flies, that sort of thing. And scorpions."

"Yes, it's a sea creature or an insect."

"Is it a sea creature?"

"Yes."

"Is it a type of fish? As in, it's fishlike in appearance."

I was getting closer. After a couple more questions, I knew it was a fish that one would commonly eat, like a salmon, trout, cod, tuna, haddock, or mackerel. I listed off all the fish that were left.

"Is it one of those?"

"Nope," said Ellis.

"Is it one of the following: sardine or bass?"

"Nope."

"It has to be."

"It isn't."

"It has to be a sardine or a bass." I looked at my fingers.

"It's a sprat."

"What's a sprat?"

"What's a sprat? Come on." Ellis looked at Angus and Angus, still silent, smiled.

"It has to be something a normal person on the street would know," I reminded them.

"It is," said Ellis. "That was sort of impressive though. Alright. What are you lot up for? Should we give it another go?"

"Do you know what a sprat is?" I asked Angus.

"Of course," said Angus. "Common fish in the UK, isn't it?"

"I don't know it."

"Clearly not," Ellis said.

Angus said, "I thought that was pretty good though," and he smiled. He liked me.

Ellis removed my hand from his leg, got up off the bed, and went over to the couch.

"Alright," he said. "You good now, Lucy? Should we give it another go?"

The second time around, at the end, Ellis said, "Finish in her eyes."

After Angus had left, I couldn't stop crying. My eyes stung and I had a necklace of little bruises around my collarbone from where Angus had pushed into me with all ten fingers. Then I said, "One day you'll love me too much to watch this."

Ellis got really angry then. "Fucking hell. You're making me feel like a freak."

But my eyes wouldn't stop crying and I could barely see through them. I went back into the bathroom and stood at the mirror, throwing water in my face, thinking about how my eyes might never go back to normal, and my eyes, which were green with yellow in the middle, were my favorite feature. When I came out, Ellis stood up from the couch, still shirtless, his shoulders up to his ears like a spring.

"This was your idea," he said. "You wanted to do this."

"It wasn't," I said. The air conditioning was stinging my face. I had goosebumps down my arms, and stubble prickling on my legs.

"I'm letting you get fucked by all these guys, aren't I? I'm doing you a favor. I'm letting you do whatever the fuck you want."

"I just want to have sex with you," I said.

"That's what you want?"

"Yes."

He stared at me.

"What?" I said. "Are you bored of me now?"

"You're making me out to be a monster."

"I'm not."

"Yeah, you think I'm a lunatic. You're making me feel ashamed of myself."

"I'm not making you feel anything."

I wasn't going to look away first. I wasn't even going to move my face.

"You think I'm a sicko. You're making me out to be the mad one." His mouth was too small. He looked truly disgusted with me. The skin around his hairline turning red, his bony shoulders still all the way up by his ears. He spat on the tile floor of the apartment.

"Wait, stop," I said, suddenly desperate. "I was kidding." I stood up from the bed and headed over to him and tugged on his smooth wiry arm, but I still couldn't look directly at him because of how ugly my eyes were. They were bright red and puffy. I was likely having some kind of allergic reaction. Then my head snapped to the right. Ellis had struck me across the face.

I was still dizzy when I felt him fasten his hand behind my left ear, threading his fingers through my hair there. But instead of pulling me in for a kiss, he yanked his fist toward his chest which caused me to swivel away from him. Then he banged my forehead into the wall twice. This all happened very quickly in the moment; I can remember the choreography now only after puzzling it through later. I was limp at the end of his fist, attached to him by my hair and released only when he folded me over onto the bed, placed a knee into my back, then yanked upward. It was a big enough chunk that part of my skull felt exposed to the air for the first time. It had never felt so hot and so cold at once. There were little bulbs at the ends of the hairs Ellis was holding in his hand. I could tell because he was holding them close to my face.

"That's my hair," I told him.

So, I left the apartment. I walked up and down the street and smoked three cigarettes. I started walking down New York Street toward Darnie's, then stopped. Darnie didn't know anything. For a while, I watched two centipedes squirm around in a puddle on all their little legs. I had an awful habit back then of seeing my name written in things. Darnie's was all the way on the other side of town. She was probably watching movies on her laptop in bed, the warm bodies of both cats on her belly. I thought, Maybe the extraordinary thing can be Darnie losing her virginity. Once Darnie loses her virginity, I can go home.

As soon as my face stopped stinging, I headed back to the apartment and climbed up to the fifth floor. Ellis was naked on the bed with his guitar. He stopped playing when I came in.

"Okay, I'm sorry," I said.

"You mean it?"

I nodded. "Did you like that?"

"Of course I did," he said.

I went into his bathroom. The bald spot wasn't as big as it felt.

When I came out, I said, "Let's play again."

"Is that what you're on about? You know I know you can do it."

"Think of one."

"You're clever, okay. You're the cleverest girl in the world."

"Is it a zebra?"

"I'm not in the mood, baby. I'm too tired."

A muscle in my chest was still throbbing from the cigarettes.

"Think of one."

Now he looked cornered and tigerish. He spat on the floor again, then looked up at me, his eyes light brown (almost yellowish) and bright under his long dark lashes. "Alright," he said.

"Is it a zebra?" I asked.

"What about your algorithm?"

"Is it a chimpanzee?"

"Lucy, come on."

"Is it a chimpanzee?"

"You tricked me. You said you wanted to do this. Remember?"

"Is it a walrus?"

"It's not a walrus."

I decided to sit on the floor in the middle of the room. The tiles were cold. I crossed my legs. I was a frog princess. He found his tank top in the corner of the room and pulled it on over his head. Then, still standing, he turned to face me, looking down at where I sat on the floor.

"A crocodile?"

"No." Ellis threw up ten fingers. He folded down four.

"Reindeer."

"No." He ticked down another.

I decided to throw something at him. I cast about the room to find anything. I scooted on my butt over to the couch, then reached up to fish a pack of cigarettes out from between the couch cushions.

"Giraffe," I said. The cigarette didn't quite make it and we both watched it land on the ground by his feet.

"What are you doing?"

"Lobster." I tore up the cigarette, spilling its insides onto the floor, then I chucked its butt at him. "Coyote."

"Fucking hell. You're mad."

I stood up. I backed toward the glass door with all his cigarettes, toward the balcony. I wasn't sure if he was going to come this way or not but at least I had the cigarettes.

"You're such a little cunt," he told me. Another cigarette butt hit him squarely in the chest. He put on his shorts.

When he was gone, I got onto the bed, scrunched my knees up into my chest, and squished my forehead into the pillow like I used to do as a little kid, while behind me big cats loomed, pacing around the room, their rumps shuddering. "Wildebeest," I said, and I conjured a wildebeest. "Elephant," and the room got loud with them. Soon I was a tiny baboon on a puff of green leaves surrounded by long grasses swinging all together under the sun. Cheetahs hung in the baobab trees. A couple buzzards keened. The sun was round and full and a lion kept pawing at my cheek with its big furry pad. I was trying to fall asleep, but the lion kept pawing.

"But was it me you were thinking of?" it kept asking. "Was it me?"

When Ellis came back, my eyes were open even though I hadn't yet lifted my face from the pillow. Gently he got into bed on top of me, his warm body pressing down on mine, and he kissed the top of my head, then my cheek. "I'm sorry about that last bloke. I was just trying something different. I don't want it to always be the same."

"I know."

"You're so pretty and perfect," he said. He blew on my bangs to brush them off my face. "If you died, I can't decide what part of you I'd eat first."

"Thanks," I said, and he held his lips against the side of my neck.

He noticed me shudder but instead of getting mad, he softened and went, "Sh, sh, sh," rolling me on top of him now, my stomach on his stomach. He nuzzled his nose into my armpit. "I know that was intense with the cum in your eyes. I was just trying to keep it original for us."

I just didn't want to be injured, I told him. If we could avoid it, I'd prefer to remain uninjured.

"I know that, baby. You're my baby, okay? You've just been right-handed your whole life. It's not just about training your left hand. It's also about undoing the instincts of the right hand. That's all."

"Those instincts are so ingrained in me," I agreed, my throat still scratchy.

"Sometimes you have to get a bit violent to stay original," he explained.

"Right," I said. "Machiavellian."

"What's that?"

"Like, the ends justify the means."

"You mean utilitarian."

"I think Machiavellian is more specific to this situation," I said, my sentence a couple of words too long for the amount of breath I had.

We were quiet for a while. Then, with his nose still in my armpit, he said, "That's why you're going to leave me."

I said, "I'm not going to leave you." I was confused. He was the one who had left me earlier.

"You're more brainwashed than me because you went to too much school. But I'm in love for the first time ever! You know that? I've never felt like this before. I'll be gutted."

"I'm the same," I let him know.

"You are, aren't you? You'll never be able to be this way with anyone else but me. Angus wishes he had a missus like you."

We were quiet for a little longer, just breathing together. The fan thumped. My body felt like it was levitating.

"He messaged you on Tinder by the way."

"Angus?"

"He thinks you're cool. He said that you and me blew his mind."

Then he added, his voice muffled by my armpit, "I'm going to be thinking about you long after you've stopped thinking about me. You're the only girl who's ever let me be myself."

"One day you're going to get bored of me," I confessed. I was worried about it.

"Oh please," he said. "Look at yourself."

I reiterated, "I don't want you to leave me either."

"Yeah, but you went to university. You've got a mum and dad. I'm just going to be that git you were with once that you're going to tell stories about, but I'm always going to love you," he said.

"Stop saying that. We're not going to leave each other," I said. I really needed us not to leave each other. He put my whole ear in his mouth.

"There, there," he said, releasing my ear and tightening his arms around me.

Later that weekend, to celebrate my birthday, Darnie and I went to an art exhibit that Darnie had been dying to see all spring. We both ended up staring at a black-and-white painting called *One Bull and Two Dogs*, neither one of us able to find the dogs.

"They're there," said Darnie, pointing.

"No, they're not," I told her.

"Well, they've got to be somewhere."

Afterward, I dropped Darnie off at her apartment, then drove dead east on New York Street back to his, the sun bright red and setting. I was out of wiper fluid and my windshield was still covered in sap, which, with the sun, made driving a terrifying and vibrant thing to be doing. As I squinted at my windshield, all I could think about were all the people I used to know. There used to be so many of them. Where were they? There was no one out, not a soul on the street. Guess what, I said to myself. You did it. You're the smartest person alive.

THE EXTRAORDINARY THING

FOR MONTHS, THERE HAD BEEN A BABY GROWING IN-
side me and I didn't know it. I found out when it fell out of
me onto the bathroom floor of Darnie's apartment the weekend in mid-September when she was in Austin for a bachelorette party and I was cat-sitting Chaos and Midge. The
bride-to-be was a college friend of Darnie's nobody thought
would ever lose her virginity much less become the first in the
group to get married. Almost all of Darnie's friends were in
their mid-twenties and still virgins, including Darnie. I was
staying at her place because Chaos and Midge needed constant human attention.

All week, I had been feeling ill without any idea of what
was going on inside me. The cats were the ones who witnessed it. They were rubbing their cheeks against my elbows
and thighs while I was on all fours on the tiles, certain that
something important was happening and also pretty certain

it was death. It might just be that time for you, my own voice sang out to me. This is your body giving out. The cats and I sat together in the aftermath. They watched me scoop the maroon up off the floor with both hands and some toilet paper, then drop it in the toilet. For several seconds, I had to look really closely at it just to make sure, but then it was all there— shut eyes, tiny nose, egg head. A tiny violet baby-shaped sac, as if wrapped in cellophane, like if you pressed on it with two fingers, it'd burst. For a bit, we all watched it ink out into the water. I didn't flush. Midge supervised from the sink. Chaos, at some point during the event, had managed to leap up on top of me and sling her long body over my right shoulder. I thought to myself, I don't know how I'm going to talk to anyone about this.

What stunned me was how the half-finished baby in the toilet with its little fingers and feet was such a clear consequence of all the unprotected sex I'd been having with Ellis. Yet, despite years of education and guidance from my mother, my teachers, media, and the government, the possibility of an unplanned pregnancy had never occurred to me. After all, consequences were something Ellis didn't believe in, a magical quality of his that made me feel fearless and capable of achieving any dream. The idea that you couldn't always get everything you wanted didn't exist for him. When I asked how he'd been able to quit heroin, he'd said, "It's all mental, isn't it? When you've got minds like ours, you can do anything. It was easy." "What about cigarettes?" I challenged, to which he'd replied, "I could stop if I wanted to. I just don't want to."

I had started describing all of my dreams to him, even making up ones I didn't know I had. But now I worried that the baby in the toilet indicated that I had become ruined in some permanent way. I worried it might mean I'd never be able to have any real kids later. The need to talk about it with someone overcame me, to receive endless reassurances that such an experience actually meant very little, that in fact nothing was wrong with me, that this event had nothing to do with anything, that it happened to a lot of people, and that I could literally flush it away and be fine.

Darnie's apartment was decorated cozily. Her doting mother had done everything for her; she also visited frequently, sleeping on Darnie's couch and baking gluten-free cheesecakes. Apparently, after Darnie's dad died, Darnie's mom had reassured her that she would never date again. Strangely enough, the effect was that Darnie was now twenty-six and had never even kissed anyone. It was something that she was working on in therapy. She told me she was straight and very attracted to men, which aligned with how she seemed to move through the world. But I guess there was a possibility that she was putting it on.

The apartment was too small to contain the kitty litter for two cats. I resolved that weekend to fix the kitty litter issue, not only for my benefit but for Darnie's. I tried moving the box around to different places in the apartment—the bathroom, under the bed. The cats followed me, clearly confused as to why I was so obsessed with relocating the place where they pooped.

I arrived at Darnie's on Friday after work. By the evening, Chaos and I had become best friends. We'd always been friendly with each other, whenever I was over at Darnie's to watch *Seinfeld* and drink wine and gossip about Darnie's many work crushes. But now Chaos and I felt deeply connected. She had huge batty ears, a small head, and a white face with one black spot on her chin, like a goatee. Although she had a skinny frame, old age had given her a tummy that dragged on the floor. She was still energetic. She amused herself by taking a running start, leaping onto my lower leg, then scaling my clothes with her claws to sling her big belly over my shoulder. I wondered if Chaos climbed Darnie like that, though Darnie was much shorter than me, so it would be a less impressive feat. Once on my shoulder, Chaos could never manage to get down, so I learned to slowly squat to the level of the dresser or bed, where she could then step off delicately, licking herself all over to regain some composure, as if she hadn't needed my help at all.

All weekend, I kept buckling over from stomach cramps. Whenever I got into Darnie's bed, or lay down on the couch, Chaos took the opportunity to gently tap my face over and over. Sometimes, while tapping my face, one claw would accidentally hook onto my cheek or lip and she'd seem just as surprised as I was, patiently leaving it there until I unhooked her myself. Then she'd draw her small head back into her neck turtle-like. Once recomposed, she'd go back to rubbing her head against my bent legs, massaging her cheek on the corner of whatever book I was reading. It must have felt good, scratching the side of her face on sharp corners like that. Sometimes, I held out my fingers at a firm angle for her to rub against.

When Chaos slept on top of my stomach at night, she became an immovable mass. I tried to wriggle out from under her, but she wouldn't get off. If anything, when I wriggled, she just purred more. Because of the cramps, I lacked the energy to really give it my all when attempting to shove her off, so I instead pretended as best I could that she was just a vibrating heating pad.

Midge took longer to warm to me, which at first I confused for shyness, but really, she was just coy, probably because of her natural good looks. She had a beautiful lightning bolt white stripe that cut down the center of her face and a flirtatious, theatrically aloof nature.

I knew the moment Midge warmed to me when, instead of darting away like she usually did when I entered the apartment, she changed her mind mid-sprint, turned around, then shyly, on tippy toes, circled the kitchen, doing a clumsy dance, knocking half intentionally into the couch legs, while purring and blinking her big green eyes up at me. I took this as my cue to sit down on the floor waiting patiently until she made her way over. I'd wait there all day if I had to. About a foot away, she flopped onto her side, and stretched her legs out all the way, hyperextending her toes so she was basically backbending on the floor, showing me her fluffy white tummy.

Sunday evening, Darnie came home to find all three of us still in the bathroom together.

"Lucy? What's that?"

"Don't look," I told her. I had my eyes closed but reached up for the flusher, and finally, I pulled it down.

"Are you alright? What was that?" Her voice was high-pitched over the sound of the spiraling water. Midge had darted from the room.

"I am fine," I confirmed. "Don't worry."

"I'm calling nine-one-one," said Darnie.

"Don't do that," I said and pushed myself up off the sticky tiles. Chaos tried to keep hold of my silky pajama shirt but ended up sliding off me onto the floor. There she began purring and pressing into my legs, her paws stepping around what was left of the mess.

"Why's it so hot in here?" I asked.

"I can open a window," said Darnie. "I think we should call someone. You're sick."

"I'm not sick," I said. From outside came the pitter-patter of Midge. She was doing her sprints up and down the hallway. "But I'll take a Tylenol."

Darnie opened a drawer. There was the rattle of pills. I asked for four extra-strength and she gave them to me. She also gave me sweatpants and a sweatshirt to put on.

Outside the bathroom, I settled on the couch and so did Darnie, facing me with her legs crossed on the cushion. She pulled a beige throw pillow into her chest, hugging it. Neither of us spoke for a bit.

"How was the bachelorette weekend?" I eventually asked. I grabbed a pillow too and hugged it into my own chest. It was gray and scratchy. "Did you do the bar crawl thing?"

"Do you think we should go to the hospital?"

"I feel better now," I told her.

"I think we need the hospital. I don't think I'm going to be very helpful with this."

"You're fine," I said.

Both cats jumped up onto the couch. Midge's purring consumed the apartment.

"Everyone's coming to take care of me," I said, rubbing my hand along the entire length of Chaos's body, all the way to the end of her tail.

"Who's coming?" Darnie snapped.

"Oh, I just meant the cats."

But there had been a note of panic in Darnie's voice. She was maybe worried that I'd invited someone over, like Ellis. Darnie had become suspicious of Ellis. The day after the hair-pulling incident, I'd made her come into the bathroom with me at work to help me figure out how to pull my hair into a ponytail without revealing the bald patch. I was one of those people who could focus only with my hair up. My sister had been the one good at hair growing up and did mine a lot before school, so I never learned. But Darnie was a bobby pin queen. "I got it caught in a door," was what I told her. "How'd you manage that?" she said, a pin between her lips. She was so focused she was almost sweating. "I was half asleep," I said. "A freak thing."

Another time, when Ellis was sticking his nose in my armpit just to be silly, it tickled too much and caused me to accidentally kick him in the scrotum. This made him pin my arms back over my head and bite me under the collarbone. "That's what you get," he said. "I think I'm bleeding," I replied. I had to hurry into the bathroom to pad at myself with tissues. He had not meant to make me bleed; it ruined the joke. Luckily, I stopped the blood easily, but the next day the bruise came, and I couldn't cover it up. When Darnie asked me what happened, this time, I told her honestly, "Oh. This was Max"—which was the name I used for Ellis because for some reason it felt powerful to lie to Darnie about the name of the guy I was seeing. But I could tell that my saying this about the collarbone bruise made her rethink the hair incident.

The problem was I couldn't stop the marks from forming, especially because of the other guys we invited over and everything Ellis was telling them to do—each used different amounts of strength, and my body was getting worn down— so I decided to start owning the injuries by showing Darnie each one. But my nonchalance, which I'd intended to come off as charming or at least edgy, seemed to have started rubbing Darnie the wrong way, creating a distance between us that made me anxious. She wasn't texting me as much on the weekends or giving me updates on her crushes or inviting me over for wine after work, which in the fall she'd done at least three times a week. Darnie was my only friend in Indianapolis.

As soon as I stopped petting Chaos, she started tapping me with her paw. I closed my eyes and draped my neck back over the armrest, as if I were at a salon with my hair in the tub.

"Do you think there's something permanently wrong with me now?" I asked Darnie.

"Were you pregnant? Is that what we were looking at? Is that what happened?" She sounded scared, her voice pitchy. She sounded the way my sister sounded when confronting me about something.

"That seems to have been the case," I said.

"Did you know?" Darnie asked. Then she said, "How'd you not know?"

I didn't bother answering this. Darnie didn't know about anything.

"What do you think it means?" I asked, still with my head hanging back. Chaos was being incessant with her tapping. "Do you think it means I'll never be able to have kids?"

Darnie didn't say anything.

"Do you think this means there's permanent damage?" I wanted to keep asking her this question forever.

"I don't think so," said Darnie.

"You're right. It's probably not such a big deal."

"That's not what I mean."

"I don't know how big a deal it is," I admitted. I really didn't know how to gauge it or relate to it at all. If my body was ruined forever, I'd rather just give up on prioritizing its longevity and do whatever I wanted instead. If my body wasn't ever going to belong to anyone other than me, I shouldn't feel guilty about smoking cigarettes, for example.

I shared this with Darnie.

"What do you mean?" she asked.

"It's like that game everyone used to play on their phones," I clarified, "where you're trying to get that little bird over all the hills, but if you don't get over the first hill fast enough, it's basically impossible to beat your old score, so it's not even worth playing. That game always stressed me out." I always thought that was a bad way to build a game.

"Tiny Wings?"

"Games are better if there's always an opportunity for a comeback," I said.

Then I said, "Chaos, stop it," and pushed Chaos off the couch. Chaos sat there on the floor, shocked, staring up at me.

"What?" I said to Chaos. "You're being annoying." But it came out angrier than I wanted it to and when I glanced up at Darnie, she looked like she'd been the one shoved.

We stopped talking for a bit after that. We just sat on the couch together, both of us biting our nails. I hadn't taken the side of my thumb out of my mouth since getting on the couch. I seemed to be committed to peeling all the skin off.

Chaos tried to jump back up but Darnie pushed on the side of her body and said softly, "Chaos, no."

I got a good chunk of skin from my thumb in my teeth and ripped it.

I said, "By the way, I tried moving your kitty litter around. But I really think you need to get a different litter box. This whole weekend at your place I've felt nauseous."

Darnie was silent for a second. Then she said, "Probably because you were pregnant," but it came out mean, and I felt my own viciousness snake into me. I'd never heard Darnie speak with such a bite in her voice before. We were normally very gentle with each other. After all, we hadn't known each other that long. We were only coworkers.

"You realize that smells get stuck in the fibers of your clothes and stuff, so you'll start carrying this stench around with you. You don't want that, Darnie. I'm telling you. You don't want people thinking that you smell like cat shit."

I knew that I was hurting her feelings, but I couldn't stop.

"I mean I was at your place for just four days and I'm worried that I stink now," I said. I finally relinquished my left thumb and started in on the other one. "I know I don't smell yet, because you don't smell yet. But it's also possible that I'm just too used to you, so I can't even smell it on you anymore. But I can definitely smell it in here. Do you invite people besides me over? Because I wouldn't until you figure this out. I was here four days, and I never got used to this smell. I have no idea how you've gotten used to it. How can you not smell it? It's actually crazy to me. Can you really not?"

"You know you can leave if you want," said Darnie. "You don't have to be here."

"I'm saying this to help you," I told her when I stood up. "Not to criticize." But she was crying.

—

I walked the full three miles down New York Street from Darnie's apartment to Ellis's. I'd been thinking about breaking up with him for a while and I knew, as I walked, that this time I was going to do it. I'd do it as soon as I got there.

The plan was to break up with Ellis, then very quickly head back to Darnie's to make things right. If I walked fast, it would only take me about forty minutes to get back to her. And there was no way I'd get through the breakup without her, especially the immediate aftermath. Ellis and Darnie were the only two people I had in this city, and I was someone who always needed at least two close people. In college, I'd had Cole and Frances. From kindergarten to high school, I'd had Isabella and my sister. If I broke up with Ellis, I would definitely need Darnie.

What I couldn't decide as I walked over was whether to tell him about the baby in the toilet. I couldn't decide if it was something I should ever tell people about, if it could become an interesting part of my history or if it was just disturbing. It was maybe something people hoped for all their lives, a sympathetic event that could legitimize any later bouts of depression. It could be my tragedy, my defining moment. I could use it to explain who I was to people. But maybe it was something that happened to a lot of other girls, and didn't distinguish me that much, and making it into my tragedy would only expose me as out of touch. I felt relieved that I didn't know about the baby until it was already dead; I didn't have to give birth to it or pay to have it aborted. All I knew was that I was someone who eventually would want kids. But what if this was a sign that I wasn't supposed to be a mother? I had never been someone to whom babies were naturally drawn, which had upset me when I was younger. Babies and animals were always approaching my sister. I'd grown up desperate for animals to favor me, but the horses down the road never liked pushing their wet noses into my palm as much as they liked touching Patty. They'd always go right over to wherever she was standing by the fence.

I had texted Ellis that I was coming over, so his door was unlocked. He was inside eating chips and salsa, watching a nature documentary, leaning forward on the couch with his elbows on his knees, his face close to the screen, stuffing Tostitos into his mouth mindlessly.

"Come here, baby," he said when I opened the door. "You'll like this."

He strung two fingers in two of my belt loops when I got closer, pulled me onto his lap, then wrapped his arms around my lower stomach. I squeezed his forearms, so he tightened them. We hadn't seen each other all weekend. I was still in Darnie's sweatshirt.

"How were the cats?" he asked, chewing the chips loudly against the side of my neck.

"Good. We're all best friends now," I said. "Darnie's upset with me though."

"Why? Did you kill one of them?"

"No," I said.

"You cold?" he asked.

I was shivering. "The AC's blowing right on me."

"I can turn it off." He kissed the back of my head, stood up, and went over to the wall. The room hushed up after he punched the button. Halfway back to the couch, he stopped and said, "Here. I know what you like," and vanished around the corner into the kitchen. I heard the kettle click on, then start to whir. He was going to make me a chai. Both of us had grown up with mothers who made chai, though his did it with real spices. Mine just used tea bags.

He came back around the corner with a thermos full of chai for us to share, then arranged the two of us on the couch so that I was between his legs with my back against his chest and his red-and-brown woven blanket draped over our legs. He held the thermos in front of us. The white skinny bottle pressed into the bone between my breasts.

"I don't know why I'm here," I told him as wildebeest flashed across the screen in front of us, all from a bird's-eye view. I had to press my right cheek to his chest to watch.

"On earth?" said Ellis.

"No. Like here with you. In your apartment."

"Why's Darnie upset with you?" he asked.

"We got into a fight over her kitty litter." For ages, I'd been telling Ellis about the kitty litter. "There's no hope for her, I fear. I felt so sick just being around it all weekend."

"Well, I'm glad you're back here with me," said Ellis, spinning open the top of the thermos and sipping it above me, his chin on top of my head. I felt like falling asleep.

"There's this crazy scene I need you to see. Are you watching? It's coming up." He tapped me on the cheek, then pulled down the skin under my left eye with his thumb.

"I sort of feel like having a cigar," I said, opening both eyes.

"A cigar?"

"I'm really in the mood."

"There's that Sky Mart on the corner now," said Ellis. He took the thermos out of my hands. "Is this sweet enough?"

"It's good," I told him.

"Let's just have a fag."

"I want a whole one," I said. Lately, he'd been making us split.

He paused the film before his favorite scene.

Out on the balcony, I asked, "If someone told you that for just thirty dollars you could go to the moon, but it would take a whole six years of your life, would you?"

"It doesn't take six years to get to the moon, does it?"

"Just pretend."

"Why thirty dollars?"

"Pretend," I said. We each smoked our own cigarettes. It was on this balcony that he had taught me how to take the smoke all the way into my lungs instead of just holding it in my mouth. Now, I exhaled it from my nose like a dragon. Below us a young woman was picking up after her dog, a black Pomeranian whom I heard her call Bear. She was the only other person out. She was talking to her dog in long full sentences, unless she had earbuds in that I couldn't see.

"It's crazy that all this was built by people," said Ellis, leaning over the railing. He rapped his knuckles on the steel. His cigarette butt fluttered all the way down to the ground. "This whole structure. That used to be me. And I was absolutely smacked. The whole time."

"I think I'm only just realizing that I'll never be an astronaut," I said.

"You want to be an astronaut?"

"Not really," I said. "But I'm realizing I'll never be one."

"Probably not, baby," said Ellis.

Back inside, I told him that I wanted to go on a trip.

"I've been saying that for ages, haven't I?" he said.

"Well, I'm ready to go now," I said.

"We should get away for at least a month, then," said Ellis. "Maybe longer."

"I only have a week of PTO left. Unless we wait to go next year."

"What are they going to do? Fire you?"

"Let's go away for a week in November. Thanksgiving week."

"We can't go anywhere good for just a week," he said.

I told him, "I want to be surrounded by animals in nature somewhere."

"I told you I've been wanting to go to Maui."

"Can we go in November?"

"Let's go now," he said.

"Can we get married?"

"We can get married tomorrow. I told you I want to get married. You're stealing all my ideas," he said, but he kissed the back of my head again, then nibbled on the top of my ear.

"Yeah, I want to get married," I said.

"Wait—watch this part. This is the part. Watch," Ellis said, and he cupped my chin with his hand to spin my head toward the television.

It was a scene of snakes hunting an iguana on a volcanic island in the Galápagos. The apartment filled with the sound of snake bodies, hundreds of them, raking over the rocks and then the patter of iguana feet darting away as what looked like millions of snakes teamed up to descend upon the little lizard. They tackled it, then wrapped their bodies over it in a massive, slimy, living ball of brown yarn.

"It's such a crazy world," I said, letting out all my breath as soon as the snake hunt was finished. "I feel so stupid being in it."

"Everybody feels that way," said Ellis.

"I wasn't saying I was any different," I said. But surely help would be coming for me soon. Surely there would be a way out of this.

"Your little ribs." He had cupped his hand into my upper belly so his fingers were practically wrapped inside my rib cage. "I could pick you up like this."

"Mine aren't littler than yours. Everybody's bones are basically the same size."

"You think mine and yours are the same?" He cracked up. We compared hands.

"Obviously, my finger bones are longer," he said.

"Our skeletons are remarkably closer in size than you think."

"No. You're so, so little. You're so much littler than me."

"I'm five seven," I said. "You're five nine."

"Don't insult me."

"That's how tall you are."

"It's the way you're saying it." He put his whole hand on my ribs and pushed down.

"I still feel like a cigar," I said again, wriggling out from under him. Ellis rearranged us on the couch again so that he was behind me with his arms in front.

"We're the perfect sizes for cuddling," he said.

Then, at the television, he asked, "Should we go somewhere like that?"

"No," I said. "Not like that." As soon as it concluded, Ellis put on a different nature documentary and peeled open another bag of chips.

"Maybe somewhere like that," I told him when an aerial view of the Serengeti appeared.

"No, somewhere like that," we kept saying to each other as different parts of the earth were presented to us, "or like that or like that or like that or like that or like that or like that."

OPEN WATER

THE NAIL TECHNICIANS WERE ALL VIETNAMESE, except the woman doing my toes, who was Thai. I told her I was interested in traveling to Thailand. She told me she'd been in Maui for eleven years. The television seemed to be repeating a clip of a massive brown python attacking a mouse, although the attack itself never played out. Instead, the camera flipped between a zoomed-in shot of the snake, never its full body, just parts of it—scales, meaty head, a single black eye—and a clip of the mouse, its white-flecked cheeks, quivering whiskers, its weensy twitchy ears. Sometimes a different mouse and different snake would appear, which meant I kept missing the moment of attack. Staying glued to the television was tricky since I couldn't help but look away whenever my pedicurist asked me a question or I had to reply to Ellis, who sat chatting my ear off in the massage chair to my left. I wasn't sure I even wanted to see the snake attack the mouse, but it was frustrating to keep missing it.

The small single-room nail spa was in the Azeka Plaza parking lot, the same lot as the B&B dive shop, a block from our two-week rental. Ellis and I were the only people getting pedicures but an extremely thin, pale girl with a shaved head and a silky orange scarf wrapped around her neck was getting an acrylic manicure in front of us. Long sparkly purple nails. Another girl whom I assumed to be her sister sat on a stool next to her, watching. They seemed like sisters only because of how they were sitting there so seriously with each other, not talking, as if they'd been forced into this room together, as if the bald girl didn't actually want to get acrylic nails and her sister had been made to supervise. When the bald girl tilted her head up to watch the television, I noticed that her cheeks were super smooth, like the inside of a shell. The other girl had a long brown braid down her back, tied off both at the bottom and at the base of her scalp with pink elastics, which made me think she'd braided it herself. The girl with the braid seemed younger than the bald girl, maybe nine or ten years old. The bald girl looked older, but probably just because she was bald.

Ellis turned his head to me, pressing his cheek against the blue cushy chair, which was vibrating madly. We were both still in our swimsuits. A yellow sundress covered mine. Ellis wore orange trunks and a black tank top splattered in rainbow paint. He had his black hair buzzed at the sides and tall on top.

"How was making out with that guy?" he asked, as my pedicurist grated a pumice stone against the bottom of my feet, making me twitch around. "He really went in for it."

"Relax," I told him.

"The *tenacity*," said Ellis. "Tell you what. I enjoyed it, me."

"That's great."

"I actually want to hear how it was. Did you like it?"

"Mister? What color?" said the woman rubbing rose lotion onto Ellis's feet.

"Purple and orange, please," Ellis replied, looking down at her.

"Purple?"

"And orange, please. One purple and then one orange." He pointed at his toes. Then he turned to me again, pressing his cheek against the cushion, and asked, "Do you reckon I alternate, or shall I have one foot all orange and the other all purple?"

"Alternate," I said.

"He is crazy," added Ellis's pedicurist, shaking her head at me but smiling as she patted his feet dry with a towel. JAMIE'S A CUNT was tattooed on the top of Ellis's left foot in a messy scrawl, and on the inside of his ankle a Hamsa hand. "Last time he was here, he was asleep." She grabbed his ankle and moved his leg side to side to shake out his hip.

"You've been here already?" I asked him, bewildered.

"Yeah," said Ellis. "I was so tired I slept through the whole foot massage and that's my favorite part." Then he said to the pedicurist, "You do splendid work by the way."

"When were you here?"

"Came yesterday to decompress, when you were off on your bloody hike."

"I thought you were taking a nap."

"I was."

The two girls in front of us stood up then. The bald girl went to the counter to pay, while the braid girl stood at the door. Both silent, obedient. Then they left, the door dinging.

"You came here just for a foot massage?" I asked.

"Is that not allowed?" said Ellis. Then he added, "Should we do another night dive at Mala Wharf tonight? That was well nice. That was our best dive yet."

I closed my eyes to indicate that now it was my turn to decompress. My pedicurist had started massaging my feet, but Ellis kept chattering away about whether it was worth us trying a new location tonight even though we knew our best chance of spotting sharks would be at Mala. He also kept beeping the buttons on his massage chair settings.

"Oh, I'm sorry," he finally said, over all the beeps. "Am I interfering with you relaxing?"

"This?" the nail technician asked, holding up Ellis's foot so he could look at the hideous shade of orange she'd painted onto his left big toe.

"Perfect," he said. "Can I see the purple too?"

The nail technician painted a few strokes of purple on his other big toe.

"You are sure?" she said, holding up both feet.

"I'd like one toe purple and the *next* toe orange. You get it? Yeah, like that. *Alternating*."

The woman started in with the orange, painting every other toe. Then she twisted open the purple and did the rest of the toes.

"You like it?"

"Love it," Ellis said to her. "You're amazing." Then he looked down at my feet. "Yours look nice too." Mine were a light bright blue. "What's that machine?"

"I'm getting gel."

"What's that?"

"It keeps it from chipping."

"Wait. Why didn't I do that?"

The door to the salon dinged again. A tall, skinny woman with tan, wrinkly skin and crow-like features entered, tugging behind her the bald girl from before. The crow-like woman went right up to the woman behind the counter, pointing a finger from the same hand she was using to clasp the bald girl's wrist, yanking the girl's arm up with her as she pointed.

"Excuse me." She spoke with a sharp, Russian accent. "You charged my daughter too much. I am confused. Do you not do Kamaʻāina here? What is this? No respect. No aloha." And the woman spat on the counter. I had never seen one stranger spit at another stranger like that. It made me think at first that the interaction was fake.

"No, madam," said the woman behind the counter. This woman wore tan wedge sandals, which I'd noticed when Ellis and I first came in. This woman in wedges picked up the large blue appointment book, then clopped around the counter to fan out the pages in front of the Russian woman. She flicked through them until she found the page she needed and pointed at it. "We charge her forty. Normally, for acrylic, it is ninety. See? We charge her less than half."

"We will pay only twenty," declared the Russian woman. "It is ridiculous to charge forty. You see my daughter here? She has cancer. And you charge her forty." And the woman spat again, this time on the book.

"Yes, but madam, we don't work for free—" said the woman in wedges, stepping back from the woman but forgetting to close the book. I could hear in her shaky voice a note of boldness as she tried to stand up for herself. "We are sorry about the cancer, but we don't work for free, and we already charge her less than—"

"Ridiculous," interrupted the Russian mother, then she pulled her daughter's hand toward the woman to show her the nails. The orange scarf loosened from the daughter's neck and fell onto the floor. I nearly thought her head might fall off with it. "See this one? Already breaking. Ridiculous." Her daughter's bald head hung down toward the ground. I decided to stare at my toes instead, feeling embarrassed and sad for the nail technicians who were now implicated in this display right in front of me and Ellis. My pedicurist—who was a tiny, older woman in a pink mask—was staring at the Russian mother while still holding one of my feet in her hands. I felt so stupid for being here with one of my feet in this woman's hands. The whole world was ridiculous, me most of all.

Then, from next to me, Ellis said in his slow, loud drawl, "Seriously? You're ridiculous."

The Russian mother spun around to look at him.

"What is ridiculous?" she said.

"You," said Ellis. His voice was too loud; he was talking in that overly amused tone that could uncoil at any moment into a cackle. "If twenty dollars is so important to you, here," and he shifted onto his left hip in the salon chair to reach back for his wallet with his right hand.

"Ellis, stop," I said, grabbing his arm to keep him from inserting himself, to push his hip back down, though he hadn't moved from his chair. He shook his shoulder to get me off him.

"Who are you?" the woman said to Ellis, tilting her pointy chin up even though she was sneering down at him. "Who are you to get involved?"

"You're involving all of us," said Ellis, waving out at the salon with his hand holding the frayed, slightly wet wallet, to indicate me and the six nail technicians. "Here. Take it," and, still sitting in the salon chair, he extracted a twenty-dollar bill, the Velcro of his wallet unsticking, and held it out at the woman.

"Fuck you," said the woman, striding toward him rapidly on her long, sticklike legs, her thigh muscles seeming to swing off the bone. Then she spat into his face.

Ellis let out a loud "Ha!" then said back, laughing, "Fuck you."

The woman took another step toward his chair, but before anything more could happen between the two of them, a man came barreling through the door.

Upon first glance, this man looked like a real live werewolf, chiseled and lean, shirtless, a tattoo of a skeletal hand on top of his heart. He had a scruffy yet classically handsome face, eyes wild and full of black. The blond hair covering his tan body was close in color to his skin, which was part of what made him look so furry. He wore cargo shorts that dropped below his knees and red rubber Crocs with white mid-calf socks.

He bounded right up to Ellis, who continued to vibrate in the massage chair, his purple-and-orange toenails still propped above the basin to dry.

"Did you just say 'fuck you' to my wife?" the werewolf yelled at him. He was American.

"I did," said Ellis. "If she wants twenty dollars so bad, take it," and this time he waved the bill at the man. Again, I leaned over my armrest to grab Ellis's shoulder, to pull his hand out of the man's face.

"Stop," I tried. This man was scary, and I knew whatever was escalating needed to stop immediately for the sake of the rest of us in the nail salon, who had all gone quiet besides me.

"I could beat the shit out of you. Look at you with your faggy nails. I could beat the shit out of you. I could take that smile off your face. I could knock your teeth out, you ugly stupid fag. I could stop you grinning like that." The man was bent over Ellis's massage chair, his hands gripping the armrests, his jaw clenched so hard it was twitching, his face inches from Ellis's. The man was close enough to me too that I could smell the oils on his skin, bergamot and body odor.

Ellis was no longer smiling. Slowly, leisurely, he tilted his chin up at the man, turned his face to the right, then cupped and uncupped his left hand, beckoning.

"Go on then," he said. His tone was quiet and slightly lazy now, which made the American man's hot, agitated musculature seem all the more absurd. With a single finger, Ellis tapped the side of his cocked jaw. "Hit me. Go on."

"Fuck you," said the American man, then he spun in a circle toward the door. "Let's go," he said to his wife and bald daughter, but the wife was swooping back in on Ellis, still gripping her daughter's wrist.

"Hit him," she screamed at her husband. "Hit him!" She released her daughter now, and the girl stumbled backward all the way to the window, bumping the back of her head against the glass. It was just a small, accidental tap, but my heart seized.

"Hit him," the woman screeched again.

"I can't here," the man explained to his wife, distressed. He clasped his hands behind his head, winging out his elbows, showing us his fluffy armpits, and paced around frantically.

"Come out here," he instructed Ellis. "Come outside."

The man stepped out the front door, holding it open for Ellis, who remained seated.

"I can't come out there," Ellis said, waving dismissively at the man. He gestured down at his feet. "My toenails are still drying."

The man didn't know what to do with this. He said, "Look at you. You're so scared. You're shaking you're so scared."

"That's cause I'm in a massage chair, mate."

"Come outside. I'm going to beat the shit out of you."

"Yeah, alright," said Ellis. "Let me just finish this massage cycle, then I'll come out."

"Stop it," I heard myself say again to Ellis. "Stop antagonizing." I was terrified. I was worried the werewolf might have a gun or a knife.

The next thing I knew the man had come rocketing back into the salon, straight at Ellis, and began railing on him—five, six, seven punches all to the side of Ellis's face. Ellis's head kept whipping toward me, again and again, knocking into the cushioned headrest of the massage chair, getting bloodier and bloodier, his mouth filling with red. Ellis was just taking the man's punches, laughing as he took them. The salon was full of the sound of bone on bone. Then, suddenly, the man decided to stop, bounding back out of the salon, yelling at his whole family—which I now saw included three kids: the bald girl, the girl with the braid, and, also peeking around the door, a plump little boy with bangs, both hands in the big pocket of his gray hoodie.

"Let's go. Quick!" the man shouted at all of them.

In seconds it seemed like the family had vanished, but then the man appeared again in the doorframe, pointing at me and saying, "You. Fuck you for laughing. Cunt." Then he disappeared.

It was a ludicrous thing to say since I could not have been further from laughing. Ellis was the one still shaking with laughter, but the man had definitely pointed at me.

A motorcycle revved. Then, the werewolf was once again visible through the doorframe, this time on his motorbike with the little hoodied boy on his back and, in his lap, the girl with the braid. Apparently still desiring another final word, he yelled at Ellis, "Welcome to Kihei, bitch," and then, at last, he motored away.

Ellis's mouth was full of blood. Laughing like that, he looked like a lunatic.

"I live here," Ellis yelled back at the now vanished man, incredulous that he'd ever be confused for a tourist, even though tourists were exactly what we were.

"What the hell, Ellis," I said, livid and horrified by what had just happened. The nail technicians and I were all looking around at each other with wide eyes.

Ellis appeared truly deranged, blood between each tooth. He had taken all those punches without even moving his feet from where they were propped up.

"Fuck him for calling me a tourist," he said. He put his hand up to his mouth, spat, examined the blood in his palm, then brought his hand back up to his mouth.

"We are tourists," I pleaded.

"I'm sorry. I'm so sorry," said the woman in wedges, who was suddenly at Ellis with a towel in one hand and a phone in the other. She unfolded his fingers to mop the blood out of his palm, then patted his face with the towel. She was doing these things frantically, but with great precision. "I call the police. I call the police now," she said, waving her iPhone at me and Ellis. "Get him another towel and ice," she commanded my pink-masked pedicurist, who was still holding my foot. And with that, all the women in the salon unfroze and started moving around.

My pedicurist brought over some ice wrapped in a blue washcloth. She held it up to Ellis's face. He spat blood into the brown paper towels that another nail technician had stacked on his lap.

"What a dickhead," he was saying. "My face isn't even swollen. He hit like a girl."

"Oh my god," I said. "You're unbelievable." I stood, pink foam still between my toes. "Let's go. We're going."

"Thank you for sticking up for us," said the woman in wedges, taking the ice from the pink-masked pedicurist to hold it against Ellis's face herself. She placed a hand on his forehead as if he were a sick kid. "They pick on us, you know, because we're Oriental," the woman said. Then she turned to me and ordered, "No charge for him."

"No," I said. I'd already taken out all the cash we had. "Of course we're paying."

"No charge for him," the woman said again to me, fiercely.

Then she clopped her wedges over to the counter and picked up the big blue book. "You see," and she held the large book out in front of me, pointing at the cursive. "The acrylic nails are usually ninety. You see?" She pulled out a plastic menu of services from between the pages of the book so that I could look at it. "We charge her only forty. But we don't work for free."

"You shouldn't," I said.

The salon door was still stuck open, and a pretty young woman now came through it.

"I heard commotion," said this young woman. It looked like something was sprouting from the top of her head, but it was just her ponytail of short black hair. She wore a denim skirt, tight white tube top, and on her forehead tiny oval sunglasses with rainbow rims. "Should I call the police? I got the license plate off the bike."

"We have a security camera too," said the woman in wedges.

"No cops," said Ellis from his chair, where he was now bending over his knees to pluck tissues out from between his purple-and-orange toes. "Don't worry. But can I please have that footage?"

"We're going," I said to Ellis. "Come on. We're leaving."

"Can I please have that security tape?" Ellis begged the woman in wedges. I went over to him, tugging at his arm to get him to follow me out. Handing me his ice pack, he said, "How hilarious will that be? It's literally just going to show some maniac beating the shite out of a guy in a massage chair." He let out another loud "Ha!"

We stepped onto the sidewalk in front of the salon. The pretty young woman followed us out. Now Ellis noticed her and took her in hungrily.

I went into the salon one last time to apologize to all the women.

"You give me his phone number," the woman in wedges said to me.

I tapped open my phone and read out Ellis's number and the woman took it down.

"What video is this?" I asked. The woman glanced up at the TV, then back at her phone.

"Ten hours of snake and mouse," she said. "Tell him I will text if we call the police."

Out in the parking lot, I told Ellis that I gave them his number.

"No point," he said. "I'm not pressing charges. Christ, though. I've got to get it together, don't I? That was mental. Should we have a pint?"

He was asking both me and the other woman.

The other woman looked a little frightened, but also impressed with Ellis.

"How's your face feeling?" she asked him. She wore three delicate gold necklaces, one a choker and the other two dropping in between her breasts. She was bustier than me, but her thighs were thinner. People here were quick to make friends with each other, if only for an afternoon.

"It won't even swell," said Ellis. "He hit like a girl." Then to me, he asked, "How many punches you think he got? Did you count? You reckon it was six or seven?"

"You didn't hit back?" the woman butted in.

"Nah. Not worth getting in trouble over something like that."

"I'm worried they're going to come after us," I admitted, as the three of us crossed the parking lot to Dog & Duck Pub, where Ellis and I had already become regulars in just six days. Ellis had his arm around my shoulders. I gave him back his ice pack and it started dripping onto my shoulder as he pressed it into his jaw.

"Oh please," said Ellis. "The guy's a mug. I'm sad his kid has cancer, if that's true. It's fucked up both her parents are such nutters. Poor thing."

"You sure they're not going to come after us?" We were staying just across the street. We'd be easy to find.

"Chill out, Lucy. The sod's gone. He's a tease. Like you." He kissed me on the cheek.

"Don't get your blood on me, Ellis," I said, wiping my cheek.

"You mad?"

"Yes," I said. "That was crazy."

"It was, wasn't it," he said, dropping the ice pack in a trash bin. "Absolute madness. Fancy a drink though? I'll buy us all a round."

Ellis and I had arrived in Maui the day before Thanksgiving and had planned to stay a week, but he was already acting like he didn't want to leave. He had convinced me to book a one-way ticket. He was the type who liked going somewhere, then staying for no reason other than already being there and feeling curious about what staying would be like. Ellis was also convinced that if you stayed somewhere longer than three months, you were no longer a tourist, and he was determined to collect residency in as many places as possible. He liked planning out exciting next steps for himself, with me included.

We'd come to Maui to learn how to dive, a dream of his that in the last six months had also become one of mine. He had introduced this dream to me over the summer by showing me a documentary that he and his mother had watched the month before she died, when he was taking care of her back in Hull. A prolonged case of the flu, complicated by years of emphysema, was what got her. In the first half hour I understood the film wasn't a real documentary. It was a mockumentary. It was about scuba divers who'd excavated an ungodly amount of treasure from under the sea, all of which was now being kept in an exhibit in Venice that surely didn't exist.

"This can't be real," I suggested halfway through, meaning that I truly didn't think it was, but Ellis, believing I was simply blown away, agreed.

"It's crazy, innit?"

"How come I've never heard of this before?"

He'd replied, eyes still fixed on the television, "That's what they do. They keep stuff like this from us."

The glow of childlike thrill on his face—his delight that he was impressing me with something I'd never heard of—made me correct course. I wasn't going to ruin his dream. And ultimately, his conviction was so captivating that I tried to believe it was real too. When the film ended and he said to me seriously, as if disclosing a deeply personal secret, that he aspired to be a treasure-seeking scuba diver, not in some other lifetime but in this one, and venture deeper than anyone had ever dared go, collecting treasure out of the most unexplored depths of the ocean, I decided that I wanted to be that too. It's a little pathetic, looking back, because even though I knew the whole time that the documentary was a hoax, without even needing to Google it (though years later, I did), many of the things we took to be true about the fake film were what led to the Maui trip and formed the basis of Ellis's very real diving ambitions.

The Maui trip was the first time I'd gone somewhere without letting anyone know, besides Ellis. It made me realize in a new way how my body belonged only to me, and I could take it anywhere; I could explore the whole world without saying anything to anyone.

We spent the first three days of our trip completing the open-water course to get certified. I got off to a tough start: during the pool portion, when we were practicing confined water skills, I panicked even though we were only in the shallow end. This occurred within the first twenty minutes, during the partially flooded mask drill. Underwater, you were supposed to peel up the bottom corner of your mask to flood it halfway, then tilt your head back while exhaling out of your nose; the water was supposed to then drain out the bottom. But when I lifted my mask, water got into my nose and eyes, so even though we were just kneeling in the shallow end, barely submerged, I felt like I was drowning. I stood up in my fins, abandoning the rest of the group, who were still on their knees in a semicircle three feet below. Our instructor, Nicky, surfaced with me, pulled down his mask, and spoke sternly. He reminded me that if I panic like that in the ocean, my lungs could rupture. Panicking makes you hold your breath, but if you hold your breath while shooting up to the surface, the air expands inside while your lungs remain compressed. And the greatest proportional pressure change happens ten feet from the surface, so even in just the deep end of the pool, I'd be toast.

"No worries," said Nicky, placing a hand on my shoulder. Mostly I was worried he was going to kick me out of his course. "Heaps of people panic on that drill. That's why we practice."

But later, Ellis pointed out to Nicky, "No one else panicked."

"Some people are more prone to panicking than others," Nicky replied.

"So Lucy's a panicker, is she?" Ellis cackled, then pinched my hip through my wetsuit. He looked triumphant. He thought he was so much better than me.

For the rest of the course, I tried really hard to be the best in the group, to be everything that Nicky asked of me, channeling my old study habits and supreme eye contact from my A-plus high school and college days. As we geared up, Nicky, now charmed by me, picked me to help demo the skills on land for everyone before getting in, such as buddy breathing and the buddy check. Sticking with your buddy was the second most important rule after Always Keep Breathing. I was nervous about the four ocean dives we still had to complete off the boat, which were required to get our certification. Once certified, Ellis and I would theoretically be able to dive on our own, without a guide, though Nicky reminded us—singling out Ellis in particular—that even with the cert, you still had to dive with a buddy and follow PADI protocol.

"I want you and your buddy so close together you're practically touching," Nicky said as the boat pulled up to our first dive site, Molokini Crater. Maui was still visible in the distance, but we were pretty far out, surrounded by at least ten other dive boats all tied up to the same buoy. It was nearly six in the morning. "In fact, hold hands. Especially you couples," Nicky said, referring to me, Ellis, and the honeymooners from LA.

I just wanted to get the course over with. I was certain my ears wouldn't equalize on the way down, and Nicky would have to send me back up the line to the boat on my own, a humiliation. It was also possible I'd panic again and shoot up without intending to, then die of lung overexpansion before even reaching the surface. All morning, I reminded Ellis about holding my hand. I needed him to follow the buddy rule. He was the type to forget it. On the boat, I kept pulling Nicky aside for some extra reassurance. He knew I was nervous and told me that Ellis and I could be the buddy pair to go right behind him in line. This calmed me down because I now trusted Nicky with my life, and Ellis didn't mind the special treatment. He loved the idea of being up in front and first to see everything.

As soon as we descended into the warm ocean, my fear disappeared—the sea rushing up around my body, my body suspended with water on all sides, a hundred plus feet of visibility expanding out forever. Suddenly the only thing in the world I cared about was the feeling of that water all around me. I wasn't even paying attention to the fish. I was flying. The ocean made clear the extent to which I could control my entire body with breath. It was a revelation: Inhale, I went up.

Exhale, I went down. Breath was the only sound inside me, and it was strong and pure, a shush, shush, shush. Instead of feeling connected to the others on the course as we all experienced this new element together, I forgot about everyone except Nicky, whose fluid underwater body kept convincing me, as I obediently followed his bright-yellow fins butterflying around the crater, that I was in love. I felt in love with my body for the first time. I was finally getting reacquainted with myself, but a distilled version, two percent—just breath and nerve, only the essentials. The more time we spent in the sea, the more I wanted to stay down there forever and when, at the end of each dive, we'd ascend, I'd sputter up stunned yet thrilled by a wonderful reminder of who I was. It was the most I'd ever craved death. Not as a way of escape, but as a way of getting the water to be both inside and outside of me. If I ever chose to die, I decided it could only be this way. Even if I reached ninety-five, and my kidneys started shutting down, death coming naturally, I'd still make my kids take me out to the sea, give me a tank and regulator, and let me kick, kick, kick, till I was sixty feet down, a hundred, two hundred, till I was full of a perfect thoughtless blue, just blue light sinking.

Ellis thought he was the best in the group at diving and wasn't subtle about proclaiming himself a natural to everyone on the boat, even though Nicky warned us that most people think they're better at diving in the beginning than they are. That said, Nicky did seem genuinely impressed with Ellis's buoyancy skills. But what Ellis ended up enjoying most about diving were the nudibranchs. This was unexpected seeing as he'd ruthlessly mocked one of the guys on our course for pointing out every shrimp and sea slug as if the small things were sights to behold.

"Can't be asked to have my nose in the rocks like that," Ellis whispered to me that day on the boat, pantomiming the way the man had used his pen-sized flashlight to examine the crevices of the crater. Ellis believed that the goal of each dive was to see as many huge pelagic creatures as possible—manta rays, whale sharks, gray sharks, giant turtles, schools of dolphins— and go as deep as we could with the air we had.

But once we started diving on our own from shore, Ellis got bored of the turtles and became obsessed instead with finding the small stuff. In just three days since finishing the course, we'd managed to go out on twelve more dives just the two of us, renting tanks and gear from the shop for twenty- two dollars a day, making bets on who could find the most nudis and surface with the most air. Ellis had pocketed a nu- dibranch guide from B&B, and was determined to spot the rarest ones, even though most were rare since the reefs were dying.

"It's depressing, innit," said Ellis, his face mean. "People are idiots."

But I didn't care about the nudis or the fish or the color- less corals. I pretended to like them and pursue depth as much as he did, but only as a way of protecting my real reason for diving—the feeling of that water. Finally, I was getting the point more than he was. I now knew what it was like to be a fish and what it was like to be a bird.

This trip was the first time Ellis and I had been out in the world together as a couple, and it was thrilling being seen this way. Someone like Nicky was telling us to hold hands underwater since we, like the honeymooners, were also a couple. There was something unusual about the two of us together and I loved having it witnessed. I loved the way Ellis looked with his tattoos on the beach, next to me, who didn't have any. I loved that he was thirty-nine and I was twenty-three. There was something impressive about that, especially when I thought of Nicky reading our certification documents and understanding that I was a mature woman dating a real man. Most of all, I loved that when we were in public together, people were seeing us laughing and having fun. Ellis could make me laugh more than anyone besides my sister. Out in the world, we were getting even more of a kick out of each other, making up inside jokes, making fun of the other divers and how bad they were at diving, how their LPIs dragged on the sand, their fins clumsily kicking into the reef. I was realizing that he was someone others enjoyed too. People found him cool, funny, and charming.

Ellis and I liked hanging out at the B&B shop after we returned our gear in the afternoons. We were regulars. We ate Rice Krispies Treats with the staff in the back room and in just a few days considered ourselves part of the crew. Leading up to our trip, Ellis thought that smoking cigarettes would prevent him from passing the course and had quit cold turkey (not me, because age was on my side)—but soon realized that all the dive instructors smoked, and he was back at it. Sometimes I could see the former junkie in him, especially when he took a drag after a few days without having one. His face got the same way it did during sex—his eyes would deaden but ecstatically, rolling back into his head, face looking suddenly full of blood, jaw slack. I'd only see a flash of this but in those seconds, it seemed like there was no way to know what might happen next.

—

The third night of our trip was when Ellis suggested that we exchange secrets.

We were in the plunge pool of our Airbnb, sipping seltzers under the stars, like honeymooners, when he said, "Let's say something we haven't told each other yet." The trip had already made us closer, and we were both feeling giddy about it.

"I'll go first," said Ellis. "You can't tell anyone this. I've never told this to anyone. Fuck, I'm sort of nervous."

"Okay," I agreed. I felt nervous too.

"I've sucked cock before," he finally said. "Okay, tell me yours."

Unfortunately, hearing him say this made me feel really sick, but I chose not to have any reaction to his secret except to quickly say, "Interesting, interesting. Okay, let me think of one."

I had a few to choose from. For some reason, maybe because Nicky was an Aussie and it was on my mind, I went with, "When I was in college, I lived in Australia for a summer and this old guy raped me."

"How do you mean?"

"He drugged me and then I woke up in the middle of the night and he was having sex with me. He was in his sixties or seventies, and Norwegian, I think. Or German." Maybe Swiss.

"I didn't know you lived in Australia."

"Just for a summer."

"I keep forgetting you're a little rich girl. You and me are so different."

"It was like an internship. It wasn't expensive."

"Doesn't matter," he said. "Internship! Ha. Fucking minted."

He placed his drink on the side of the pool and fell back against the jet, his elbows resting on the edge. He was staring at the stars, looking irritated. Sometimes it seemed like he really hated me.

"What you said doesn't count as a secret," decided Ellis. "Secrets have to be about right now. They can't be things from the past."

"Yours was about the past," I said. My voice was small, whereas my body felt several sizes bigger than it was. But all fluff. I floated toward the other side of the small pool and pressed my own back up against the jet. The night had gotten chilly for swimming, but the water was moderately heated, the jets the most.

"No, it's not. It's about how I want us to shag a guy together at some point. A guy who'd be down to fuck a guy and a girl. It's about how I *also* want to fuck a guy. Not really, though. It's just something I would do. Okay, I'm gonna stop. You're making me feel weird."

"Oh," I said. I also felt weird.

I pulled my knees to my chest, then floated on my back for a bit. We were quiet, just moving around the pool on our own, sipping our drinks, looking at the stars. A cat screamed somewhere. Then Ellis said, "Did you like getting raped?"

"What do you mean?"

"I had a friend that happened to. In Doncaster. And she said she sorta enjoyed it. Your secret could be that, for example. That you want to get raped. Or, you know what, that you want to fuck an old guy again."

"I'd rather fuck an old guy," I said. I realized that part of what was making me feel weird was that I'd let myself believe that Ellis and I had left the sex stuff behind us, which was part of what was making the trip so pleasant. Our happy diving days had made us seem like a normal couple, and I'd been enjoying it. I'd also gotten tired of all the random guys. A week before the trip, I'd contracted a UTI that made me miss a full day of work because I had to be hooked up to an IV at an urgent care clinic for seven hours.

"I'd watch you fuck an old guy," said Ellis. "That'd be well hot."

"I don't think they're on Tinder."

"I bet we can find some old loner on the beach."

"Maybe," I said.

I must've been quiet too long, because he said, "It bothers you, don't it?"

"What?"

Picking my head up from where it'd been floating back on the water, I was surprised to find him staring at me, not at the sky, and not looking happy. The pool lights made his chin and neck glow green.

"It bothers you."

I didn't know what to say but didn't want to make him repeat himself again. Before I could say anything else though, he said, "Yeah, you're bothered," his voice tight.

Quickly, I said, "It doesn't bother me." But he was right: it felt like I had missed something. A great big hole had opened my stomach. But I couldn't have him thinking I was bothered. I didn't want him to feel ashamed about anything. "I love you," I said.

It was hard to identify what the problem was, except that at no point had I thought that this thing we were doing had anything to do with anybody else's body other than my own and who got to have it. That was supposed to be the reason why he wanted me to fuck all these guys—it was supposed to be about how much all of them, who were nothing to us, wanted my body and how at the end of the night Ellis was the one who won it. I couldn't even consider that it was about anything other than that.

"Forget it," he said. He still sounded venomous.

We floated around in silence.

"I'd watch you fuck an old guy," he said. I realized he was close by me in the pool now, and he was pulling me into him by the hips. "I'd watch you seduce some old wanker at a bar."

He wrapped his arms around my back. I wrapped my arms around his back.

"I'll keep that in mind," I said. He still smelled of sunscreen.

He tightened his arms around me. "You don't care about what I said, right? Just forget I said all that."

"Okay," I told him. I placed my chin on his shoulder. "I love you."

After about an hour at the Dog & Duck Pub, the pretty young woman who'd joined us at the nail spa left to meet up with her real friends at The Triangle. Ellis and I stayed. We were sitting on our favorite beanbags on the beach under an umbrella. Ellis was drinking beer and I was having my gin and tonic and his foot was tapping against mine. A little table was stuck in the sand between us, for our drinks.

"Let's stay," Ellis said again, interrupting something I'd been saying about work. "Fuck Indianapolis. Such a typical existence, innit? Let's stay and do our divemaster."

"But what would we do here for work?" I asked. Money had been on my mind. I was almost out of it.

"Our divemaster," Ellis said to me, like I was an idiot. We had learned that many shops, B&B included, let you exchange shop work for the professional cert. But it didn't pay.

"We can't get paid for that," I let him know.

"Oh please," he said. "You'll be fine."

Ellis had saved up a lot from two decades of working, plus he had money from selling ketamine on the side, whereas I had only $534 in my checking account, which I needed to save for whenever we booked flights home, since my credit card was maxed out and I had nothing else. My paycheck on the first always had to go entirely to rent. I had been using my parents' emergency credit card to pay for bits of this trip, like the boat rides and equipment rentals and food, hoping nobody would notice, but then my dad left me an apologetic voicemail about having had to cancel the card due to suspicious charges but promising to give me and Patty new ones at Christmas.

"I bet Nicky makes hundreds of dollars a day taking people out," Ellis was saying. "You and I could start our own company. We could take people out on nudibranch tours. We're already masters, aren't we? We wouldn't even need a boat. We'd be the best instructors on the island. Way better than these freaks."

"Where are we going to live?"

"The place we've got. We'll extend," he said.

So far, everything Ellis had said we'd do together, we'd done. Because of this, I had to take his ideas seriously. He knew how to follow through. I could see the way a life in Hawaii might take shape for us. It'd be a unique thing to do, and it wasn't like I was tethered to anything back in Indiana: I could easily quit my job at the casting agency and bid adieu to that city of smokestacks for good. It was exciting to think of, especially the quitting part. I was in the middle of thinking about money again when a sudden snap of pain attacked me around my sternum. I realized I missed my mother. It came out of nowhere. Another snap, and I missed my sister. Ellis was still leaning back on the beanbag, looking at the night sky, mindlessly tapping my foot, monologuing through the pros and cons of stretching out the divemaster course versus getting it done quickly, but all I could think about was how my mother and sister had no idea where I was. I was also realizing that I had no clue where they were either. I assumed my dad and mother were still in Boston where I'd left them. My sister could be anywhere. Where were they at this exact moment? It hurt my head to even guess.

"Hey, look," Ellis said suddenly, in a low voice just for me, returning me to where I was: here, on a beach, at a bar, in Maui. Then, singsongy, he added, "Here's your chance."

Ellis had his eyes on something behind me, so I craned my neck around. An older white man was settling himself down on a red beanbag. A server came over to take the man's drink order, and the man—who looked awkward, laying supine on the beanbag like that, his elbow sticking out at a weird angle, not casual—tilted his chin up to tell the waiter what he wanted.

"He's alone, I think," noted Ellis. Then he took a sip of beer and raised his eyes at me.

We both observed the old man at Dog & Duck a little longer. He had a bald head and white beard and a beer belly that hung over his belt. Ellis decided to go up to the bar so that I could approach him on my own. I took my gin and tonic with me and headed off down the sand, feeling a little nervous, then settled myself on the beanbag next to him. The man looked surprised but pleased that someone like me was sitting down.

"Well, hello there," he said. He hitched up his belt, his belly jiggling a little, and sat up as well as he could in the saggy beanbag, the beans crunching under him.

"I thought you might want some company," I said. "I was just sitting by myself over there. I'm Lucy."

"How nice," he said. He was American, maybe Canadian. He wore a silver Rolex and had on a blue Hawaiian shirt and khakis. His brown belt was loaded with gadgets: a sunglasses case, a wallet, a Swiss army knife. He was wearing white sneakers, which looked funny on the sand. "What brings you to Maui, Lucy?"

"Scuba diving," I told him. "What about you?"

His name was Richard. Richard said, "I've taken a trip like this every year since my divorce. I'm a diver too. Where have you gone out?"

"Molokini," I said. "And then just a lot from shore. Makena and Mala."

"How 'bout that visibility at Molokini?"

"Pretty spectacular," I said. "Were you out there today?"

He shifted onto his hip to extract his phone from his pocket. Then he pulled a case off his belt, snapped it open, put a pair of glasses on, and started scrolling on his screen. "I've got something I think you'll like," he narrated, looking down at his phone. "Just a second. Just one second . . ." He finally found the photo—the bellies of two turtles silhouetted against the surface, with light pouring in all around them. "How about that?" said Richard.

"That's beautiful," I told him.

"My grandkids will get a big kick out of this," Richard said, clicking off the screen and setting the phone down on the table between us. "My granddaughter loves turtles."

"Do they dive too?"

He chuckled. "They're all under the age of seven, so not yet."

I sipped my gin and tonic and Richard drank his whiskey and lemon. I was at a loss. I wasn't sure what I was supposed to be talking about with him anymore. We were both looking out at the water. I wondered if Ellis was watching us. Then Richard said, "Well, what else have you been doing here in Maui, Lucy?"

"I went up to Haleakalā yesterday," I replied.

"Did you? I hope you didn't do that after diving," he said.

"What do you mean?"

"The elevation." And then he had to explain, "It can cause the bends."

I had forgotten all about the bends, how apparently my body was packed with little nitrogen bubbles that could explode open my innards in high altitude like a shaken-up soda can. Nicky had drawn a diagram on the whiteboard during the course, but I hadn't been paying attention really. Suddenly I felt foggy in the head. "Oh, yeah, I know," I said. But I had dived yesterday. We'd gone out in the morning. "Oh no," I added.

"You did dive yesterday? Not Molokini though?"

"No, just from shore."

"Oh, that's better. If you weren't deeper than twenty feet, you should be just fine."

"Are you sure?"

Richard nodded. "Oh yes. I'm sure you're fine," he said warmly.

I needed him to tell me that again, but Ellis was suddenly next to us.

"Alright?" He had a new beer in his hand. Richard looked up at him, confused.

"This is my boyfriend," I told Richard. "This is Richard," I told Ellis.

"Oh, hello," said Richard and he and Ellis shook hands.

Ellis sat down with me on my beanbag. Scooting over, I said to him, "I forgot about not hiking after diving. I shouldn't have gone to Haleakalā yesterday."

"What you on about?" Ellis asked me. His accent sounded spiky and harsh compared to Richard's slightly drunk yet warm slur.

"I'm sure you're fine," said Richard. "Didn't mean to worry you." But my heart was flapping around. "Well," said Richard, crunching a hand into his beanbag to help himself stand up. He hitched his pants up again, snapped his glasses back into his case, then hooked the case onto his belt. He moved slowly. "I hope you two have a lovely rest of your vacation. Very nice to meet you, Miss Lucy. Thank you for the company."

"You didn't ask him?" Ellis asked as Richard walked away from us up the sand.

"He's a grandfather," I said.

"Would you fuck him though?"

"I don't think he'd want to. He's got grandkids."

"Would you though? Let's just ask him. He's the same as everyone else."

Ellis hopped up off the beanbag and marched over the sand toward the bar after Richard. I felt mortified. I also wasn't totally convinced I didn't have DCS. My limbs did feel a little numb, like my hands were full of rice. I tried to shake out my hands, but the feeling didn't go away. These bubbles in me could erupt at any second. It was dark over the water except for a semicircle of squid-fishing boats. Their lights looked like an encroaching army.

"Did you find him?" I said when he came back.

"He's gonna meet us at our place in an hour," said Ellis.

"Seriously? What did he say?"

"He was flattered, actually."

"Are you sure?"

"I mean it took him a second to not think I was a total

nutter, but it made sense to him after I explained what we were into and why you approached him and everything."

"And he wants to?"

"He said he'd give it a go." He scowled at me. "You embarrassed? You look embarrassed."

"I'm not."

Our Airbnb was a small one-room bungalow on Uluniu, next door to an auto detailing shop. When Richard got to our place, I was already waiting topless on the bed. Ellis let him in. He was wearing the same shirt and pants he'd been wearing at Dog & Duck and stumbling a bit.

"Well alright then," he said, stepping into our place, taking me in. He looked extremely nervous and a little drunk. He grunted and headed toward me. I felt quite exposed and awkward, which was not normally how I felt—usually the young guys off Tinder didn't seem that real to me and I always knew exactly what to do to calm them down. Since we instructed them ahead of time not to speak when they arrived, it always remained up to me how to get it started. But Richard was a real person, and also an old man. I couldn't even look him in the eyes. Ellis took his seat on the couch, an expression of anticipation and bemusement on his face.

"You can just go over to her," Ellis instructed Richard. Richard still hadn't stepped more than a couple paces into the room. Already everything about this felt different from how Ellis normally liked it, since he preferred to witness in silence a guy's initial entrance into the room, titillated by any awkwardness or hesitancy he sensed in the guy, and excited to see how the guy decided to make his first move. But Ellis now seemed enthralled by his break in the script.

"I must say. This is certainly a surprise," Richard said, looking down at me, where I was kneeling on the bed.

"I bet," I said, finally summoning some confidence into my voice. "I'm happy Ellis caught up with you."

"Certainly was a surprise," said Richard again.

He had his hands on his hips. I started to untuck his shirt, then undo his belt. He moved his hands to the buckle to help me. His hands were veiny and shaking. I looked up at him. "It's okay," I said. "I got it."

"Let her do it," Ellis said from the couch. He still had all his clothes on. Usually he had his pants off at this point, or at least his fly undone.

When I got Richard's pants off, he was small, especially up against his bulging belly, and totally soft. I tried to take it in my mouth, but nothing was happening. He kept bringing his hands to it, sort of pushing my head away to try and help, but then Ellis would say, "Let *her* do it, mate." I could hear some heat building in Ellis's voice; the more times he had to say this, the longer it took Richard to get hard. The whole thing was excruciating, especially with Ellis getting more frustrated. Finally, I just pulled Richard down onto the bed on top of me, mostly to eclipse Ellis's view, to keep him from seeing Richard continue to fumble with his own penis.

"I'm sorry. I can't," Richard said. He was on all fours, and I was under him, his palms pressing into the mattress outside my shoulders, his belly drooping into mine. His scalp was full of sunspots. He looked bashful, yet also a little jolly, as if relieved to just admit to his inadequacy, almost as if he expected me to join him in laughing off this blooper of an event, an actor stopping mid-scene. "I'm sorry," he said, smiling and shaking his head. "I can't do this."

But then Ellis was upon us, his face appearing over me,

behind Richard's head. He grabbed Richard by the shoulder and threw him backward off the bed. I heard the man thud onto the ground. "I told you to let her do it, mate," Ellis said, his voice full of hate. I sat up and crawled to the end of the bed. Ellis stood over Richard. Richard was looking up at both of us, stunned, in the same supine position he'd occupied earlier on the beanbag.

Then Ellis got onto the floor on top of Richard and started punching Richard in the face over and over again. I'd never seen Ellis move with such strength and volition. Whenever he hit me, it was usually just once or twice, not multiple blows, and never as hard as he was hitting Richard. He was taking many swings, extending his right arm all the way back behind him, then letting it go. It flashed through the air so fast it looked like he was whacking Richard with a long instrument, like a baseball bat, but it was just his arm. The force was such that Richard kept sliding backward across the floor until he and Ellis were at the wall opposite me. Ellis had his other hand fastened on Richard's right shoulder, pulling up on the loose skin. After about thirty rabid seconds of this, Ellis stopped.

The room filled with heavy breathing. He stood over Richard's broken body, which was still mostly clothed, except for the tan pants and tighty-whities which had slid halfway down his thighs from the journey across the floor.

"Get up," said Ellis. He kicked Richard and thankfully Richard grunted. Ellis told him to get up again. And again.

Without pulling up his pants, Richard crawled toward the door. There was a gash on his scalp and blood dripping down his cheeks. It was getting all over the floor. I closed my eyes. The screen thwacked shut. From outside came another kick and another grunt. Then the screen whooshed open and thwacked shut again. I opened my eyes. Ellis was pressing his forehead into the window, facing out, back to me, panting like a hyena.

"Is he still out there?" I asked, terrified. "He's going to tell on us. We have to leave."

"Stop," said Ellis, turning around. He walked over to the couch. He spiked up his hair with his sweaty palm, took off his tank top, flung it across the room, and fell back into the cushions, extending his legs out in front of him. He let out a long, extravagant sigh.

"He's going to tell on us."

"Stop looking at me like that."

"I'm not."

"Stop making your eyes like that."

"We have to leave. Please. I don't want to be here anymore. What if he dies?" I was already taking stock of where all my things were in case sirens arrived and we needed to pack up fast. Richard was too fragile to take a beating like that. Someone would find him and call an ambulance, and the ambulance would ask him what had happened, and he'd tell on us and then we'd be dead. Or, he might die from all the punches, making us murderers. "Is he still outside?"

"Relax for just a second, baby. My head's 'bout to fucking explode."

We sat in silence. Ellis's chest moved slowly up and down from his big, lengthy breaths. Then he folded his belly over his legs.

"This one's already chipping," he said. "That fucking woman."

"I don't feel too good," I said. "I feel really sick."

"You don't have DCS, baby. You're fine." He was still looking at his toes.

"I think I'm going to throw up."

"You've got to be quiet, baby. I've got a proper headache."

I was able to stay quiet for only a few moments before saying again, "He's going to tell someone." This whole island was packed with traps now. Werewolves. Richard. There were probably others also after us. How best to eliminate all trace of us before leaving? It looked like a crime scene in here. We'd need bleach for the floors or at least a Swiffer with PowerMop pads.

I decided to get off the bed. I found my yellow sundress on the floor and pulled it over me. Then I slipped on my sandals.

"You going somewhere?" Ellis said, without looking up from his toes.

"I'm just putting on my clothes." I sat back down on the end of the bed, facing him.

"No, it's alright," he said, sitting up and picking up his phone. "I might have a girl over."

I was confused. His mind and my mind were in totally different places. Where was he?

"I'm going to get a *girl* over here," he explained, drawing out the words.

"What do you mean? You want me to fuck a girl?"

"No. I'm going to fuck her."

"You want me to watch you fuck someone?"

"No girl is going to let you watch. Only guys are down with that."

"Wait," I said, still not understanding. "What do you want?"

"I want to have a girl over," Ellis said, this time overenunciating every consonant like I was a child. Then he looked up at me from his phone and we made eye contact. The rice was returning to my hands. "You have a problem with that?" he asked. "I've been letting you fuck all these guys. I think I ought to be able to fuck someone new for a change."

"Fine," I said. "I'll go, then."

"Right," he said. "You can probably come back in a couple hours. She says she won't be here till eleven."

"Who is she?"

"Jen." Jen was the pretty young woman from the salon whom we'd met earlier.

"Alright. I'm going," I said. I grabbed my small backpack—my carry-on—where I kept all my most important things: my laptop, my makeup, my phone, my dive journal, a book, my wallet, my passport. All those things were in there ready to go. I was missing only my toiletry kit.

No Richard outside. No cars. No flashing lights. I could hear the music from The Triangle, but there was no one in sight. I walked down the dirt path through the trees to the safe and anonymous beach. I decided to walk the beach all the way to Maalaea. My body had been erased from the chest down, either from the stress of the situation or DCS. No arms, no legs, no belly. Just wind and salt on my face. What if Richard died? Then I would have to die too. I wouldn't be able to live with it. I considered walking all the way to the airport and booking a flight out. But what if, once home, none of this went away? What if I felt paranoid and twitchy and numb like this my entire life? What if going home didn't fix this? And worse, what if I could never actually get myself home? Then what was the point of any of this?

At Keaka Beach, I stopped to watch a homeless man who was lying under a mango tree near a blue portable toilet in the public lot. He was lit up by the streetlamp, in beige socks, no shoes, no shirt, asleep but tapping his big toes together. A ring of rotten mangoes encircled him like an offering, and a red checkered cap covered his eyes. This bird with a long orange beak and white feathers was there, too, walking in circles around him, pecking at the mangoes, and for a while it looked like the bird was tiptoeing around so as not to wake the man up, and then, my mind made it such that the bird was the man's son, and the man was sleeping in the grass of a living room, and the bird was carefully stepping around his snoozing father, tidying up some things, the patch of discolored feathers atop his head a kippah. I stayed there, unable to stop staring at them, counting the steps of this shy, quiet, Jewish bird, wondering whether the man was even homeless at all. This probably was his home. Sometimes I really wasn't sure whether I'd survive my life. Obviously, there were ways to survive, and people had survived worse. But I also didn't know if I'd be able to.

Ellis was smoking a cigarette on the front step when I came back through the trees.

"There you are," he said as I emerged.

"Hi."

I stepped around him and headed inside. The bed was all messed up. The door smacked shut behind me. Then it opened and smacked shut again.

"You don't love me anymore, do you?"

"Yes, I do," I said. I didn't want to get on the bed that Jen had just been on, but then I thought about how Richard had been on the bed too, and the Dutch guy, so who cared. I walked around the edges of the bed, straightening the comforter. There was a sweaty stain in the middle of the bed, but it could've been mine.

"I embarrass you."

I turned around. He was sitting on the couch again and now he held my gaze easily. I knew I had to be careful. When Ellis was on the brink of getting fed up, his face usually got twitchy and his shoulders scrunched, all tense, but luckily his body didn't look like this. Just tired and relaxed, legs spread, hands behind his head. He was observing me, leaning back. Just making conversation. He wasn't trying to start something.

"You don't embarrass me," I replied.

"What about the TSA guy," he mused. When we were flying to Hawaii, the TSA agent in the airport hadn't let us go up together—he made me and Ellis go up one at a time.

"I wasn't embarrassed." I sat on my hands at the very end of the bed, still a little fidgety.

"How come you never introduced me to your parents?"

"What?" I wished we could talk about one thing at a time. The room started spinning out of nowhere, so I rolled onto my stomach and shut my eyes and tried not to breathe through my nose in case the bed smelled. I didn't really care what happened next. I just wanted to avoid throwing up.

Ellis was still talking. At first his tone was pleasant and light but the longer I kept my face pressed into the bed, the louder he got.

He was saying, "I want to get twenty guys in here and let them all have a turn with you. I want to watch them fuck you till you pass out. I'm gonna get that git to come beat the shite out of you. Or ole Nicky. See? I know what you like. Should I get Nicky over here? You fancy him, don't lie. Want me to get him over here to fuck you till you're dead?"

Then, at last, he got quiet. A few moments passed. Behind me, his bare feet thudded around on the floor. Then the shower turned on.

When he came out of the bathroom, I had successfully pulled myself under the bed. I watched his feet walk around the room, leaving wet footprints. The white towel that was wrapped around his waist touched just above his ankles.

"Lucy?" he called out. Then under his breath: "What the fuck."

His feet padded across the room to the couch, then stopped. He was picking up his pack of cigarettes. His feet walked to the door, and it thwacked open. He exited. It thwacked shut. After a few seconds, it thwacked back open, and he came inside. His purple and orange toes faced me. They got closer. But his feet weren't headed for the bed. He was going back to the bathroom. He thought I was gone. I heard the bathroom door open, close. The sink turned on. Then his feet were back. They moved to the door again. The screen opened. Then shut. This time, I heard him from outside call out, "Lucy? Lucy?" He stayed outside for a couple minutes. He was having a cigarette. I was certain. Still, I didn't move a muscle. When he came back in, his towel dropped to the floor. And then the bed collapsed over me. I tried to breathe tiny breaths. He was flipping through Instagram stories on his phone. He coughed. Little snippets of videos played, one after the next after the next. And then, without any warning, his head dropped down over the side of the bed, his hair touching the floor. His eyes met mine.

"Gotcha," he said.

I was so surprised that I shot out my hand and dug my nails into his face.

He yelled, and yanked his head away, causing me to scratch his cheek in three long marks. The bed collapsed down above me again, creaking.

"You cunt."

His feet thumped down. Then he was on the floor too, dragging himself on his stomach under the bed toward me. I backed away, but his hand had fastened around my wrist, and he was pulling. I sank my teeth into his forearm, and he roared out, but didn't let go. I bit down harder. I could taste his blood, his skin tearing. Still, he didn't let go. Then I was out from under the bed. A kick to my ribs and I slid across the floor, crumpling up into a little ball.

Somehow, I managed to get up on all fours. He was a few paces away, standing in front of the bed, slouched over, holding his bleeding arm, tongue out yet expressionless. I stared back at him. We stayed like that, just taking the other in, panting at each other.

Then he made too quick a move and I leapt at him, sinking my nails into whatever part of his body I could get. But he rapidly threw me back onto the floor, then sat on my stomach, pinning me down, his bloody forearm pressed across my collar. His teeth now clamped down on my breast, and I shrieked. Then they sank into my neck, again and again.

"Ow, ow." I was finally able to speak. "Ow."

"You little freak." He bit me two more times. "You like that? Is that what you want?" This time he held on, shaking his head like a dog.

"Ow," I said again. My shoulders ached. I couldn't get a full breath. "Please."

Finally, he stopped and with a sharp exhale, he let his body fall down on top of mine to rest. We stayed like that, our aching bodies breathing into each other, calming down.

He sounded close to tears when he finally started pleading, "Come back to me, baby, please. Please." His warm lips were against my cheek. He was petting my head. He was shushing me and sniffling and stroking my hair. "It's okay, baby. Just come back to me. Come back to me please." He was tapping my cheek over and over. Then he put his whole mouth around my ear, enveloping it in warmth. He could've bit it off if he wanted but he simply sucked on the lobe—gently. I couldn't feel his teeth at all. His rough tongue poked into my earlobe. It tickled a little bit, but not enough to make me squirm. The hand that had been tapping my cheek was now resting limply next to my face on the floor. I lifted my head up only a little, then dropped my forehead down onto the back of his left hand so that his knuckles pressed in between my eyebrows. He tightened his fingers into a fist so that I could rub my face more easily into his knuckles, massaging back and forth. It felt good. Skull on bone. The pressure was making soft colors balloon behind my eyelids. I wanted to rub my forehead against his fingers forever. I was rubbing out all the nitrogen bubbles. I was making myself solid again.

"There you are," he whispered. "You're my baby. You know that? You're my baby, baby, baby." He nuzzled his head against mine. The sound of his thick black hair rubbing back and forth across my skull was like a soft, distant saw at the back of my brain. He kept nuzzling and nuzzling and nuzzling his head to mine, until we fell asleep.

The next morning, Ellis still wanted to go deeper than our open water certifications permitted. He wanted to reach a hundred feet. He wanted to feel narcosis.

"Nicky says only stupid people go past regulations."

"Please. They set those for the lowest common denominator."

But we were too broke to pay for the advanced cert, or any more boat dives. It was impossible to reach a hundred feet just from shore, unless we drove to Nuʻu Bay on the southern side of the island, which Ellis had read about on the forums. It was listed as an advanced site with occasional rips and the snorkel report marked its visibility that day at a low six. We'd also have to take our time on the way back to off-gas, since the drive went up through Kula. But we packed snacks and decided to make a day out of it. Time was ours.

Nicky was staffing the shop that morning, along with some girl around my age, who had on heavy dark eyeliner, even heavier than mine.

"We're back," announced Ellis, the bell tinkling above us. I was still twitchy. I couldn't keep from casting around in case any of the people who hated us appeared. We had frequented the same four spots for two weeks. We were so, so, so easy to find.

"Back again," repeated Nicky. His eyes lingered on my face and then on Ellis's, but he didn't say anything besides, "Wednesday will set you up." The eyeliner girl was Wednesday.

"Where are you headed?" she asked, pulling two regulators off hooks behind the desk. She was maybe Spanish. I watched Ellis watch her.

"Makena," Ellis lied.

The six tanks rolled into each other on the back seat as our rental car climbed up Pulehu Road, past all the farms, into Kula. We had four 80s and two 63s, just in case we had time for a third dive. Ellis was driving. I had my left heel propped up on the window and was already ripping open a bag of cheddar chips. Luckily, Ellis and I could talk about anything.

"Look at this," he said, flipping down the sun visor, then tracing his fingers over the scratches on his cheek. "You're a little freak, aren't you."

"You were being really awful last night."

"Me?"

"Yeah. You were being an irreverent twat."

Ellis cackled. "Say that again."

"Which?"

"Twat."

"No."

"You say it so funny. You say *twot*. It's *twat*."

We drove past a group of kids playing outside a house near Keokea, and Ellis changed the subject: "Did you see those kids playing on the road?"

"Yeah."

"That's awesome. They're just playing with sticks. They're just drawing stuff in the road." Ellis couldn't get over the kids. It's what he talked about for the rest of the drive. "They don't know anything else, do they? They just need sticks and mud. See? We don't need all this shite we think we need. Kids just need sticks and they're happy. I love that. I wish I was doing that. I was that sort of kid, you know. I could entertain myself for hours just by drawing lines in the dirt. Maps and stuff."

The road to the dive site took a while to find. We had to cut through a flimsy wire fence with Ellis's dive knife to get off Piilani and onto the back road. We'd read about the road on the forum, so we knew what to generally look for. The road was meant for a four-wheel drive, but Ellis managed to maneuver our Civic around the massive divots, scratching up the sides only a little on the brush. Thankfully, the site itself was obvious. There was a place to park, a porta-potty, and steps that cut into the cliff, leading down to a black sand beach. The marks of other divers were also there—O-rings in the dirt, a collapsed Aqua-Lung weight pocket, a two-pound hard lead, which Ellis pocketed just in case we needed it.

Ellis placed the keys on top of the front wheel even though my small backpack of valuable things was inside the car. "It's good enough. No one's here," he explained.

"Where's your stuff?"

"Like what?"

"Like your phone and wallet."

"Left it at the place. Don't know why you brought all this."

I stuffed my backpack under the passenger's seat just in case someone peeked in.

We geared up on top of the cliff, then carefully walked down the steps, fins in hand. I made Ellis do a buddy check before we got in. It took us forever to kick out past the black stones to even reach enough depth to descend. Ellis kept putting his mask to the surface to check.

"Vis is still bad," he said. "Bollocks. We should've brought torches."

I was worried about sharks in conditions like these.

"They won't bother us."

"The tiger sharks might," I said. "It's murky." Nicky had told us that most tiger shark attacks were cases of mistaken identity. When diving at Makena, even I could confuse the boogie boarders above us for turtles.

"We're the tigers out here, baby. Come on."

"I don't know if this is a good idea." The water felt quite strong at the surface.

"Should we just go down and take a bearing out? I'm tired of kicking. We could just swim out at seven meters till we get to the shelf." Ellis looked at the compass on his left wrist. "If we follow three hundred, we should hit the drop-off."

"You can't be guzzling your air, then," I told him.

"Sod off. I've beat you on air every dive so far."

"No, you haven't."

"Yes," he said. "Let's just descend. At half a tank we'll turn back."

We descended to twenty feet. After fifteen minutes of diving along Ellis's bearing, we reached the shelf. We each still had two thousand psi left. The water was getting colder and darker, the colors disappearing from the corals as we kept descending. At seventy feet, Ellis found an octopus in the wall. He hovered next to it. I sank by his side to also examine it. We were getting better at controlling our bodies. The octopus was staying still but changing colors. I felt mindless, noiseless, dark. The calm black water around me was resolving an emptiness in my body that for the last year of my life, and possibly many years before that, had sporadically registered in me as a deep grief. I'd always suspected that such a state could exist again where this emptiness was quenched, and it was so lucky that diving had led me to it.

Finished with watching the octopus, Ellis looked at his wrist, then swiveled to line up his body with the compass bearing again and started kicking. I followed his neon-yellow fins. As we kicked, our depth continued to drop. The water kept getting colder. My computer was telling me I was at eighty-three feet, ninety, ninety-five.

At a hundred feet, I tugged on his fin. He turned around. I signaled to ask how much air he had left. He was at fourteen hundred and I was at fifteen hundred. He turned back around and kept kicking along the shelf. There were three bright-red nudibranchs by a cluster of pink anemones—we pointed to them at the same time. Ellis took his regulator out of his mouth to make the sign we invented to signal manta ray— opening our jaw with an exaggerated, goofy look of shock and awe. We had both gotten good at taking our regulators in and out of our mouths whenever we wanted.

We were getting even deeper now, a hundred and twenty feet, a hundred and twenty-eight. My air dropped rather suddenly from fifteen hundred to eleven hundred psi, because of the compression, so I now had less than half a tank. I tugged at his fin again when I realized this and made a signal for him to ascend a bit, so we could turn around and head back along the shelf. But he shook his head and made a rival sign to go deeper. I made my signal again. He looked up at me, spreading out his arms like Jesus. Again, I made the thumbs-up sign and, finally acquiescing, he started rising slowly toward me. When he was within reach, I grabbed his arm to look at his computer. His max depth said a hundred and fifty-one feet. I checked his air gauge. He had only seven hundred psi left, which was two hundred away from the emergency zone.

It was far past time to ascend. I was worried we might not make it, but I felt more confused than scared. Was this narcosis? I couldn't think straight. It was so dark and murky that the only way I knew up was up was because my suddenly rapid breath was making us rise. But the visibility got worse as we ascended. I held on to Ellis's air gauge like a leash, just to keep him close to me, and every few seconds pulled him in to check his levels. He didn't seem scared. He kept swatting my hand away, his eyerolls made more obvious inside the black frame of his mask. It got so dark and murky that I lost track of the shelf. Then, something started beeping. I tapped my computer to light it up. The screen was showing numbers I didn't understand, and it wouldn't stop beeping. Something was wrong. There was a twenty in the middle of the interface and a three on the side where the safety stop was supposed to appear, but I wasn't at fifteen feet yet. I had no idea what the computer was trying to tell me.

I tried to show Ellis my watch, but suddenly realized he was nowhere. I had accidentally let go of his air gauge. The visibility was so bad, I couldn't tell which way was up and which way was down. An underwater current had started beating into me. It was taking too much breath to kick against, and I feared it was pushing me farther out to sea, away from shore, though I was so disoriented I didn't know which direction the shore was even in.

I realized: I'm alone down here now. I couldn't make out any fish. Just dark, cloudy water. The only thing left to do was monitor my depth, take in the tiniest breaths possible, and ascend in the direction that made the number on my watch tick down. The computer was still beeping, and I had no clue how to interpret its digits, but my air was running out and there wasn't time. At fifteen feet, instead of doing the safety stop we'd been taught, I decided, based on the hundred psi I had left, to just ascend as slowly as possible, even though my near-empty, floaty tank was making it hard to go slow. Because of this, my computer started beeping even more madly. But at last, my hand broke through the surface, and I was up. Quickly, I pulled out my weight pockets, dropping them into the ocean beneath me, just as Nicky had taught us to do in situations like these, and I inflated my vest by kicking up and blowing into the hose.

Finally, fully inflated, I fell back onto my vest, catching my breath, sun on my face. My heart wasn't even beating that fast.

I was grateful and at peace, not scared, and it was glorious, even as the wind started picking up and I clocked just how far I was from shore. I could see the cliffy coastline, and after scanning for a minute or so, I spotted the portable toilet where our car was parked. It was football fields away. It would take forever to kick back. But it was also okay: I had risen, and I had all the air I needed. It was all around me. There was enough of it for everyone on earth. The sun felt so good on my cheeks.

Slowly, I scanned every bit of ocean I could see. I was the only thing on top of the water, all the way to the horizon. There weren't even any buoys. No boats. Just the ruffles of little waves. Incredibly, my breath was long, strong, and deep. I started kicking toward shore, at first calmly, then ecstatically. I felt so grateful to be me. The current at the surface wasn't as bad as it'd been below. I wasn't even worried about the tiger sharks anymore. You can do this, I said to myself as I kicked. Just one way back now. You know how to do this. You're not a panicker. They were all wrong about you. No one knows about you but you. I kept kicking and talking to myself like this. At the same time, I kept scanning the surface for Ellis. I just had to keep kicking. It was the only way. You know yourself better than anyone. Who knows you? You do. You know you. You know you, you know you, you know you. This was the anthem I let run through my head as I kicked, the long vowels turning it into a siren.

And then, I noticed him. I hadn't seen him pop up because the ocean out there was getting rough from the incoming wind. What I first noticed were just his yellow fins sticking up. But then there he was, all of him—far off, bobbing in the water. As I studied the speck, I realized he was not only waving at me but also getting closer. He was alive and kicking too. I started kicking harder. Kick, kick, kick, kick,

kick, kick. I just had to make it to shore first. I had enough of a head start. He was still pretty far out. I couldn't tell if he was yelling at me; the wind made it hard to hear. Now my breath was picking up, my heart thumping hard under my vest, my throat tightening. Thankfully, after fifty-six minutes of kicking according to my computer, I felt my ass bump up against the rocks of the long, shallow beach, and the moment it did, I slipped out of all my gear, shedding my fins, BCD, and tank, and galloped free and barefoot over the black stones, bruising the bottoms of my feet repeatedly, up the cliff toward the car, my anthem changing into "I did it, I did, I did it," which after a few rounds just sounded like "idiot, idiot, idiot." My face was full of salt and snot. I knew I could do it, though. I had made it. Of course, I had. I knew!

At the car, I braced myself before looking back at the ocean. There he was, still far out, those yellow fins sticking up out of the bright sharp waters. But he didn't seem to be kicking anymore. He was just out there, bobbing. I watched for a few more minutes, breathing slowly, and then I got in the car.

I cranked the driver's seat back, letting my body rest for just a moment. Did I have DCS? Who knew. Were my lungs still intact? Yes. Here I was, breathing. I had made it back. I pictured the fabric of my lungs flapping with each inhale, each exhale. I was fine. I had survived! I remembered the weird numbers that had appeared on my dive computer and took out my phone to google what they meant. But no service. Okay, I thought, it might be time to go. But go back slow. Not through the mountains if possible. I'd drive the other way.

The Civic and I took our sweet time driving down Hana Highway, my hands tingly on the wheel. I'd read about this road on the list of touristy things everyone was supposed to do in Maui. People raved about the views. Well, here I was doing it! But I was doing it backward, cruising past the traffic, which was stacked and meandering oh so slowly around the curvy road, at its worst between Hana and Paia. How come no one else knew to hack it like this? Everyone was so afraid of being different. At Hana, I pulled off to get gas and finally got a flash of service. Google told me that my computer had been telling me to do a deco stop, which meant I was supposed to hover at twenty feet for at least ten minutes to off-gas before ascending. But how? I would've run out of air. Upon reflection, I determined that I'd done everything perfectly. I was the natural after all, and I was still alive. I was full to the brim with nitrogen, but alive.

It was exhilarating driving this famous road the other way. I reached Kahului after three and a half hours. In the cell phone lot of the airport, Google told me that even with a dive as deep as the one I'd just done, I had to wait only twenty hours till I could fly. My nitrogen was getting more absorbed by the moment, more integrated into my tissues, maybe even into my bones. Better, faster, stronger. I left the rental car in the cell phone lot. They'd find it, I was sure.

Indianapolis wasn't an option. There was no way I was going back there. The cheapest flight I could get for exactly nineteen hours from now took me to Dallas, with a thirty-minute layover in Honolulu. Delta, $436 one way. This left me with a solid sixty-seven dollars in my checking account. You'll figure it out when you get there, I said to myself. I just had to make it to Friday, December 13, and ka-ching. Tomorrow was Thursday. Did I know anyone in Dallas? I wish I had more friends. I slept on a bench just past security until it was the next day. I tried to inventory all the friends I had who would still count me as one of theirs. Once I got to Dallas, I'd start reconnecting with people. But now there was nothing I needed to do except get on the plane; I was so happy that the decision was already behind me, even though I wasn't yet on the plane. It was thrilling to make decisions so quickly. It was also totally okay to lose touch with people too. Ellis had taught me that.

When Ellis and I were flying to Maui, the TSA agent at the airport in Indianapolis had motioned me up first before directing Ellis to stay back. After looking at my license, the agent had tilted his chin toward Ellis and asked, "That your boyfriend?"

"We're just friends," I'd replied loudly, just to fuck with Ellis, since he hadn't called me his girlfriend yet even though we were in love and it'd been over a year.

After, when we were putting on our shoes, Ellis had said, "See? No one thinks someone like me can get a girl like you." I felt flattered, but he wasn't being cute. He was mad. "That's what everyone's thinking. That's what that git was thinking when he told me to stay back."

"He was just trying to do one at a time."

"The Chinese couple went up together."

"They're probably married."

"We could be married."

I still have moments when I look back and think: Was that really me? Everyone probably thinks this when looking back at parts of their past. It happens to me when I think about him getting socked in the face at the salon, about myself standing up in the shallow end with water in my nose, about the bright-red nudibranchs and brown brain corals that looked like tumors in the murk, about watching the safety video on that plane to Dallas trying to figure out if the flight attendants in the safety video were real flight attendants or actors. I was seated next to a brother and sister who were about my age. They had their tray tables down and were sharing Chicken McNuggets and ketchup. Right at the moment of takeoff, when the plane at last unhitched from the ground, the vents above us started dumping thick gray air into the cabin in a way I'd never seen before, and it seemed clear to me that something terrible was happening and that everyone on the plane was freaking out, looking around at each other, panicking about what was happening, but only due to the brother's soft hand suddenly touching my wrist did I realize that everyone was actually turning around to look at me, because I was the only one panicking, and they were all just trying to figure out who was causing so much commotion. After the brother, sister, and two flight attendants calmed me down, the brother and sister offered me some of their McNuggets. The exact same phenomenon occurred as we were landing. This time, I was certain the plane was going down, that I was going to die before ever making it to Dallas, before ever letting my mother, dad, and sister know where I was. A small team of firefighters ended up having to greet me at the gate and escort me to baggage claim, because on the plane, my heart had begun beating so fast that I thought I was having a heart attack. The flight attendants who observed me and my beating chest had thought so too. At the gate, the medics took my vitals, confirmed I was physically fine, then wheeled me out in a wheelchair to the curb. They asked if I was meeting anyone here in Dallas, and I said yes, my boyfriend was at home, cooking dinner, and that I was feeling well enough to take a cab there.

But between these two incidents, when we were at our cruising altitude in the air, that part was lovely. We were soaring over so many herds of small white clouds, fat pudgy angel babies with chubby arms and legs huddling underneath us, waiting to be picked up and swaddled. One angel-baby cloud scuttled away from the rest and was hanging out by itself over a reservoir. Then we were through the clouds and Texas emerged below us. Above some nameless lake, white boats skittered across with their tadpole-like tails. Actually, they looked more like those long-legged water striders that skate atop the surfaces of ponds. Then the lake turned into a river that split off into smaller rivers. It looked like a dragon with tons of talons and tiny arms.

BAD TIME

WHEN I WALKED IN WITH THE COFFEES, I FOUND MY
sister equipped with a blue Clorox bottle, her arms dressed in
the long yellow gloves that had been hanging above the dish
rack. She lifted herself up from where she'd been scrubbing
the cabinet door and stood for a quick, serious second in front
of the sink. Meerkat-like. I thought she'd stood up to tell me
good morning, but she was evaluating a spot on the wall to her
right. Then, with a spritz, spritz, she got on her tiptoes to wipe
down the microwave. In this kitchen, the microwave was between two cabinets, positioned strangely high above the stove.

"Was there a spill?" I asked.

"Don't set those down there," said Patty. I had placed our
two coffees on the coffee table, but on coasters. "I haven't
done that area yet."

"What spilled?" I asked. Whatever it was had clearly gotten everywhere.

"Caroline had Zach over here again," she explained in a breathy exasperated tone. "He's a nosebleeder. It's just who he is. He walks around with a roll of toilet paper and his nose just drips blood onto everything. Caroline's used to it."

I hadn't been aware that anyone besides me, Patty, and Caroline had been staying here last night, but obviously Zach left tracks.

"And is this the standard post-Zach protocol?" I asked, wondering if Patty disinfected the surfaces after every time this guy Zach came over. And if that was the case, my next two questions were: How many times a week did Zach come over? That maybe was too probing a question into the sex life of Patty's roommate. But I made a note that later, at the party, after we all got a bit tipsy, I could probably ask Caroline about Zach and find out. My second question was: Was Caroline aware of Patty's Lady Macbethery, or was this post-Zach routine something that Patty kept to herself and now me?

But Patty ignored my first question about standard protocol, even though I thought it was sort of humorous, and kept spritzing. She sprayed the books, the bathroom door handle, my boots by the door. In line with my intention to be as agreeable and helpful as possible that visit, I chose to not repeat my question but ask Patty instead, "How can I help?"

Patty was now rescrubbing the kitchen counter. Everything smelled strongly of lemon zest disinfectant.

"Alright, Patty, this is getting freaky now," I finally said, when I was almost done with my coffee and she still hadn't touched hers. "I think we're good."

"We're not good. Look at this," she said passionately, whirling toward where I leaned against the fridge to pull me by the wrist to the couch. There was a dark spot the size of a zit on the mint-green throw pillow. "Nose. Blood." She punched her finger at the stain without touching the fabric. "That pillow's trash now. And we're having people over tonight. He just flings his bloody tissues everywhere. I've found his nose blood on the faucets, inside the fridge, on cereal boxes, on my toothbrush, on the toilet seat, and obviously all over the floors."

I decided to change the subject. "How'd you sleep?"

Then I added, remembering, "What's with that red light? Were you seeing that?" I'd had trouble sleeping because this apartment across the street had a bright red light filling their entire window all night. It was transfixing. Did they own a terrarium? Dragons? Snakes? I hated snakes. Patty slept with a sleeping mask, so it was possible she'd never noticed it.

"It's weird, I know," she replied, understanding.

"It's like Dracula's lair over there."

"They've got it on every night. I looked it up. I think it helps with sleep. Very strange."

"Okay, Patty, time to stop this madness," I advised. She was putting another pad on the Swiffer to go over the floors yet again. "You should focus on getting ready for your show. I'll make sure the place is bloodless by tonight."

"Did you get the beers?" Patty asked. I hadn't yet. I explained that I couldn't carry the beer and the two coffees at the same time, but my plan was to go back to the bodega when she left for her tech rehearsal.

"Remember Logan likes only light beer. That's all he drinks," she said. She had stopped with the Swiffer and sat down next to me on the couch, finally picking up her coffee.

"Any brand in particular?"

"The cheapest. Coors."

"You got it," I said. Logan was her boyfriend. Apparently, they'd been dating for five months, which was a long time for Patty, possibly the longest relationship she'd ever had. I'd found out about him when we had talked on the phone the day before I planned this visit and only two days before I showed up. The fact that Patty had a real live boyfriend was thrilling.

"You see that weird spot on the lampshade?" asked Patty. She was studying a corner of the room to the right of the TV. She bit her lip.

"It's just a shadow," I let her know. "From the plant, I think."

I wanted to hear more about Logan, so I followed her into the bathroom as she started straightening her hair and putting on makeup. She had to get to the venue by twelve thirty for up to four hours of tech. Her show was supposed to start at five. It was opening night.

"It's been hard for us to get into a regular rhythm," she explained, dressing her lashes in several coats of mascara, cranking her chin up toward the mirror while leaning over the small sink, a bit of ink peppering the basin. Why was it that us mascara wearers always applied it with slackened jaws? Growing up, Patty started wearing makeup a couple years before me. She may have even started pre–middle school, spending a full hour in the bathroom every morning, making herself pretty. "He's in VC so he's out of town a lot and I've been working late almost every weekend. But I think you'll like him."

"He lives in DC?"

"Sorry?" She pushed a thumb across her eyelid, then blinked a lot.

Patty was paler and pinker than me, pale to the point of translucence in the winter. She had thin dark hair like our mother, whereas I had reddish-brown hair that Patty had once called chestnut. Patty had also inherited Mom's breasts and constant worrying, whereas I had Mom's cheekbones and her single protruding left rib. The two of them suffered from an anxiety that caused them to follow all the rules, pay attention to pointless details, and stay on top of things. They both kept daily planners, for instance, and had excellent round hand-writing. They weren't the type of people to ever walk our dog off leash. My dad was by no means a risk-taker, but he used to walk Sadie off leash with me. Even though he was balding, his hair had once been closer in color to mine. We also both got runny noses in the winter, and a homeless woman once told us our chins were shaped like the bottom of a bottle.

"How'd you meet him if he's in DC?"

"He works in VC," she clarified. "Venture capital."

"Oh," I said. Patty was still working a bunch of hourly jobs. For years, her schedule had been a Tetris of cramming together these hourly jobs while living in New York. It stressed me out, thinking about how the time in every one of her days trans-lated to dollars she could be earning. But the idea of a rich boyfriend made me worry that he held all the power in their relationship, and I needed Patty to be the one in the relation-ship with the power.

I walked out of the apartment with her. I realized my heart was thumping in a scary way, just under my throat. It was so loud I was becoming aware of the space between each thump. I tried to pay attention as to whether there was something irregular happening in those spaces, but my heart was going too fast for me to focus.

"Are you feeling nervous about tonight?" I asked.

"I'm nervous about filling the seats," she answered. "I just hope people come."

At the corner, she turned left—the venue was thirteen

blocks downtown—and I crossed the street to the bodega. When I was halfway across, she called out to me, over the cars and delivery people on electric bikes whooshing past, to remind me to also pick up Solo cups, a big thing of seltzer, and anything else I thought would make for good snacks, like tortilla chips and peanut M&M's. She was wearing big pink mittens and a pink winter hat with flaps that covered her ears. She looked like a poodle from a distance. I felt so happy to be helpful.

I could see the Hudson at the end of Forty-Ninth. Above the green awning of the corner store, in the sky far off, there appeared a dribble of birds. Dribble of birds, I repeated to myself. That was pretty good. I didn't want to forget how I'd seen them that way. I wondered if anyone else, upon spotting birds in the sky, had ever thought *dribble* before, or whether the phrase was uniquely mine.

Thursday was when I'd arrived in New York, and my flight back was Sunday. I had to work Monday; I was still in the first month of my new job. But I was hoping that this visit, though short, would set in motion a pattern of Patty and me visiting each other in this casual, pop-in-for-a-weekend way. My main goal was to be as easygoing as possible that weekend; keeping this visit simple and joyful was key for establishing this type of routine.

But relearning and then adhering to all of Patty's systems did take a lot out of me. I had forgotten about all of her specific little rituals from growing up, the way she had to eliminate every toothpaste stain from the sink before bed and pluck any visible hairs out of the carpet. She also never liked being hugged or sharing clothes. It wasn't that Patty's New

York apartment was particularly clean; it was just clean in a particular way. For example, that weekend, we were sharing her full-sized bed, and Patty made me shower right before getting into it every night, even if I had showered earlier in the day. I was supposed to rinse off immediately before bed, and I was supposed to wear these pink rubber shower sandals that she had for guests. I was supposed to wear them in the shower, then wear them when walking from the bathroom to the bed. I was to shed them on the doormat that she'd placed by her bed, right before climbing into bed, so that the soles of my feet wouldn't bring any dirt under the covers. I wondered how in the world she adjusted this routine when she invited romantic interests into her space, such as Logan, but I didn't inquire into this yet, to be sensitive. I was also wondering if she wore her retainer when Logan was over, or if she took a night off from that. She also soaked her hands in Vaseline, seemingly every night, and crammed them into mittens as a way of healing her eczematous knuckles. Because she shared the apartment with Caroline, the common spaces were clean but not monstrously clean. The rugs had stains; there were crumbs on the coffee table. The couch didn't seem to have ever been vacuumed and the slightly cracked window blew leaves off the house plants and into the corners of the room. Patty kept the window slightly cracked even in the winter—in case of carbon monoxide, she said. Patty had never minded a cold home. I considered my apartment back in Texas to be overall cleaner than hers, though I certainly wasn't as anal as she was about the hygiene of the bed.

The reason I was visiting her on such short notice was simple: Patty was having a bad time. She admitted this to me on the phone when I called her in mid-January for the first time in over a year. Luckily, my sister was good at sending texts, especially to remind me of our parents' birthdays and occasions like Mother's Day; she'd text to say she was sending a gift and signing it from both of us and was that cool with me? It was always cool. Even though our family group text was active enough, I was still in the middle of a long period of not speaking directly to my mother, of which I wasn't sure Patty was aware. Patty was a suppressor, so she'd never bring up unpleasant realities such as this, plus the now vast physical distance between me and our parents defused the fact that my mother and I hadn't spoken since March. Ten months. Even though my mother and I hadn't talked, I still called my dad to share small problems:

"Your stomach hurts? I think I know what's going on. How many sesame seed bagels have you been eating?" For his entire life, my dad had believed that his diverticulitis had been due to his daily sesame seed bagel.

Whenever he called me, it was usually to check in on the car: "How are the tires? Did you take it for an oil change?" But unfortunately, I had abandoned the car in Indianapolis and had already been notified twice by authorities and threatened with a fifteen-hundred-dollar bill via email, which I hoped might go away if I continued to ignore it. I was never going back to Indianapolis after all. So there. Thankfully, the title was mine, so I figured I had some time before I'd have to come up with some story about the car whenever my dad found out I no longer had it (which he never did). Patty was under the impression I had driven the Subaru from Indianapolis to Austin. But really, I'd bought a blue 2006 Crown Vic off Craigslist for eleven hundred dollars cash in an H-E-B parking lot outside Dallas, using two-thirds of my final AUTHENTIC paycheck. My parents had also sent me a money transfer for the holidays, when I said I wasn't coming home, which held me over till the new job. But I felt a lot of distress over the Subaru and couldn't spend too much time thinking about it in an abandoned lot, getting sold for parts. It made my teeth hurt. It made me hate everyone.

So there I was, mid-January, driving around my new neighborhood in North Austin, feeling like I hated everyone, seeing people on the sidewalks and absolutely despising them, when I realized quite suddenly—no, I don't. I don't hate everyone. I hate everyone except my sister. It came out of nowhere, this realization, and I was immediately caught in the throes of longing to be near her. My ache to be with Patty—insufferable, extraordinary—sunk a boulder into me that wouldn't budge. At first, the thought of calling her felt unbearable because of how much I missed her, but I eventually found the courage to face the distance that had accumulated between us, and she picked up on the third ring. God bless her, it felt like no time had passed.

"I've been going through a breakup," I told her when she asked for my boy update. "So, yeah. It's been a bad time over here."

"I'm having a bad time too," she said, taking on my lightly melancholy tone. She was walking to the Upper West Side to babysit and it sounded windy out. She told me that she worked too many hours but was still broke, that they kept finding roaches in their shower, that last week her roommate's ugly pug stepped on glass and left bloody paw prints all over the floors, and that believe it or not a small theater in Soho had agreed to let her do a preliminary three-week run of her one-woman show, as long as she handled all the marketing, but now she was stressed about filling seats. She barely had time to rehearse or get the word out, because of her other jobs. Hearing how bad her life was crushed me. I'd betrayed her, I realized, falling out of touch like I had. I'd abandoned her, and now she was floundering in life. And up until this phone call, I'd let myself live in ignorance of her. I was stupid for thinking I could get away with that, for thinking that no amount of time that passed could ever destroy sisterly ties. But it was foolish and selfish and ungrateful—I could see that now—the way I'd neglected our relationship.

Patty was good on the phone. I'd always found it difficult to say much when catching up that way. I was better in person. This was the thought I had after we hung up, the end of our conversation vaguely awkward. At the point when the conversation should've ended, a long silence arrived, where neither of us was saying goodbye, and the emptiness felt weird after the ease with which we'd successfully updated each other. My sister was the person I should've felt closest to in the world, yet that final silence between us was agonizing.

At last, I said, "Well, I should really get going." Only after saying this did I realize that maybe she'd been waiting for me to share more. Maybe she had expected me to talk to her on her whole walk up the West Side, and I should've made up stuff about my Texas existence until the conversation came to its natural end, which would've been upon Patty's arrival at babysitting.

But Patty said, "No worries, sounds good. Bye." There was no "I love you" or "I miss you, sis," and I had to sit with this afterward. I had an iced coffee in the cupholder of my car, and I chewed on the ice like cud, considering how badly the conversation had ended, unable to ignore my stomach, which, ever since the single direct message Ellis had sent me on New Year's, kept bubbling up with this horrible gastrointestinal pain at randomly inconvenient times. Oh, I felt so depressed, thinking about my sister. The guilt was killing my gut. I also felt thirsty or something. I needed something to steady these terrible, swishy feelings in me. But what could I do? I had really fucked up our relationship. The number of times I had ignored her texts had made a difference between us. It had caused that ugly silence at the end of the phone call. I was only twenty-three and she was only twenty-five, and I tried to reassure myself by thinking, Don't worry, distance happens at this stage of early adulthood when people move all over, trying to figure out their lives. Your sister gets that. Cut yourself some slack. And then, a miraculous insight rescued me, out of the blue, and the insight was this: You might just be bad at keeping in touch with people *over the phone*. That's all. You're not a bad person. You're just a person who's bad at texting. It's not your skill set and that's okay. But you know what you *are* good at? You're good at showing up when people need you. And on the phone, Patty had said that she was going through a bad time. So here was an easy opportunity for me to be a more present, active, loving sister.

Upon my arrival, my sister thought—perfectly reasonably— that I was coming to surprise her for her show, although I had totally forgotten about this part of our phone call. She was makeup-less and baggy eyed when she opened the door, a few pimples on her chin. Man, I thought, she is going through a bad time.

I felt relieved by the serendipity of my timing. Coming for the show made it seem like I had paid good attention during our phone call to what she'd been saying about filling seats, and now here I was, bringing my body to fill a seat. She also told me that she and her roommate Caroline had planned their housewarming party for that Saturday night as a way of celebrating the first night of the show. This party was also going to be the first time that her new boyfriend, Logan, would meet all her friends. A lot was happening that weekend in the life of Patty.

"Is Logan also coming to the show?"

"No. He doesn't land till six thirty, so there's no way he'll make it. But he is coming to the party."

I was nervous for Patty's show. Patty had always been a theater kid, but I never liked watching her perform. She used to have this stutter that made her unbelievably shy. It only happened when we were in a group of adults we didn't know that well, which at times included relatives. I had trained myself to step in and speak on her behalf whenever it started happening. By the time we were in middle school, Patty had remedied the stutter with speech therapy, thanks to our mother's persistence, but I could never stop bracing myself for it. And my body took on this same bracing still, whenever I saw Patty onstage.

Her show that evening was not good. She was nervous and unpolished and I was certain everyone could tell. The audience was full of fake laughers forcing their laughter out. Unfortunately, the venue was fuller than I was expecting it to be, more than half the seats of the one-hundred-person space occupied. After the show, I realized that about thirty of the people were Patty's friends, and they were all planning to attend the party later. It was crazy that Patty had thirty friends, and not just friends who were invite-able to a party, but friends who were also down to attend her show on a Saturday night.

The show was only an hour even though it was slated for ninety minutes. It was short because of how fast my anxious sister had sped through it. Afterward, I stood among Patty's friends on the sidewalk as we waited for her to emerge from the backstage door. Several people had brought flowers. Several also introduced themselves to me, telling me I must be the sister, that Patty had told them to keep an eye out for me. A few raved about how funny Patty had been, how much they adored the performance.

When Patty emerged, her group of adoring friends engulfed her. I hung back to be polite and give space. There was another guy hanging back with me. I had noticed this man in the audience earlier. He had been sitting next to Caroline (a fake laugher). But the man had not been laughing. He had a stupidly attractive, well-groomed face (his facial hair in perfect rectangles) and was too tall. The whole show, he had taken in my sister with an expression of confusion and mild disgust. He was too attractive a man to be at this type of show.

I introduced myself to him as Patty's sister.

"Oh right. You're staying with them for the weekend. I'm Zach."

"Oh, hi," I said. Of course this was Zach.

"The show was great," he added in a monotone.

"Really?" I said. "I thought it could use some polishing." What was I doing?

"Yeah, you're right," said Zach. "I was just being nice." Then he added, "I find that type of humor contrived. Every bit ended the same way. But good for her putting herself out there."

I could have murdered him. I wanted to push him and his stupid face in front of a speeding cab. The audacity to insult my sister's show to me of all people. Who did he think he was and who did he think I was? I had permission to say it could use some polishing because I was her sister. He obviously didn't have that permission. I didn't want him anywhere near me or my sister for the rest of our lives. Luckily, he got sucked into a conversation with some other people, and we were able to escape him.

Walking back to Patty's apartment amid the group of fake laughers, a group of what now seemed like way more than thirty people (we took up a whole block of the sidewalk, walking in twos and threes), I felt scared about every part of Patty's life. She didn't have any real money. No salary. She was forcing her brand-new boyfriend into shower slippers every night without realizing how excruciating a request that was to make of anyone. She didn't know what she wanted out of life. She was embarrassing herself by putting on these one-woman comedy shows. She had to give up on that dream at least. Would I have to be the one to tell her? I didn't know. But was I supposed to let her go on with these people like Zach critiquing her behind her back? And were these thirty people even real friends? Who was to say. Did everybody pity her? Had everybody come to see her out of pity? I had to rescue her from these throngs of fakers and all these guys like Zach who absolutely sucked. Thank god her new boyfriend, Logan, hadn't come to see the show tonight. That would've been a humiliation. He would've ended it with her right then and there, immediately upon her exiting the backstage door, in front of everyone. I would have to get my sister to abandon her theater dreams as soon as possible, or at least convince her that inviting Logan to her next show was a god-awful idea. I really didn't want Patty to end up alone. Gosh, my

heart was loud. The jacket zipper under my chin was thud-
ding against my collarbone, and with my hood up, the thud
at first sounded like my heart, then it started sounding like it
was coming from many distances away, to the point where I
kept confusing it for the sound of a basketball on pavement.
But there were no kids playing nearby. No, no, I kept telling
myself. That thud is just the zipper becoming echoic because
of my hood. Sound got funny in the winter. It fucked with
your sense of proximity. It hushed everything. Even in Hell's
Kitchen.

My first task: make sure that Zach the nosebleeder, that
miserable fuck, didn't step foot in Patty's apartment ever
again. Luckily, he wasn't in our group that was walking together from the theater. Better yet, when we all got inside
and shed our coats and staring pouring ourselves drinks in
the red Solo cups I had picked up from the store, the white
refrigerator suctioning and unsuctioning, the crew spreading
out, everyone loud and happy, I didn't see Zach or Caroline
anywhere. I wished there was some version of this life, either
now or later, where I could replace Caroline as the one living
with my sister.

I spent the beginning of the party with an ear out for anyone else who dared say anything bad about the show. But
everyone seemed to be keeping up the act. I overheard one
conversation between Patty and the Asian girl with the massive engagement ring on her finger who had been sitting two
seats down from me. The Asian girl was passionately unpacking parts of Patty's show to Patty, gesturing animatedly with
her heavy finger as she gave my sister feedback on where to
tighten and where to slow down, but none of the things she

was saying sounded mean. And my sister was nodding, smiling, asking questions, taking notes on her phone.

Eventually, I found myself in the kitchen chatting with Patty and three of Patty's closest friends—Sydney, Irene, and Anne. Girls whom Patty had met at college that now all lived in New York. Sydney and Anne had joined my family one year for Thanksgiving.

Patty was being funny to all of us about Zach's nosebleeding from that morning. When she told stories and made self-deprecating jokes like this, in the context of close friends, Patty could be really funny. I joined in on the fun by re-enacting my version of the morning to them, exaggerating the crazy way Patty had spritzed everything. All of us were laughing. At one point, Patty got down on her knees to pretend to sniff the floor for nose blood.

"I mean I get it," I said, all of us cracking up. "I like to keep my place super clean too."

Standing up again, Patty scoffed. "Oh please," she said.

"What?"

"You're not clean. Your stuff is all over my place."

"No, it's not."

"You leave a ton of trash around."

"I do?" I asked. Patty laughed and her friends did too. Everyone was being jovial with each other, but I felt tears build up behind my eyes out of nowhere.

"That coffee mug is yours, for example," said Patty. "And that iced coffee from this morning." I had forgotten to throw out my iced coffee from earlier. It was still on the coaster. She continued to point out all the traces of me that I had left around her apartment. "Your shoes that you've flung over there. Your books there and there and there. You're really making yourself at home here."

"I'm your sister," I explained, hating that my voice came out choked.

"I'm just saying that you really spread out," said Patty, unaware that she was upsetting me or simply not caring. "You'll see when you start packing. It's going to take forever to gather up all your things."

"But don't worry—she's not keeping tabs," said Sydney, joking.

Some guy pulled Patty aside then, wanting to offer suggestions on her show.

"That guy's a big deal," said Sydney softly to the three of us as we watched Patty and the guy head to the other corner of the room. "He's in the industry."

"Why is he here?" I asked. "How does she know him?"

"I think he's sort of interested in her. Romantically. But because of that, she's been keeping a distance. I don't know. I like him more than this Logan guy."

"What do you think of Logan?" I needed the scoop.

"We're not into it," Sydney said to me, glancing at Irene. Sydney was a gym nut. I remembered her once bragging to me about spending two hours every day at the gym. Lifting. But it looked like in the last couple years, she'd let herself go. "Patricia *says* he's her boyfriend but we're not sure they're exclusive. We've said this to her face too, so I don't feel bad repeating it here."

"They only see each other once every couple of weeks," said Anne. "She says they've been seeing each other for five months, but it's not like five months of seeing each other all the time. It's five months of occasionally seeing each other."

Anne was a flautist. I remembered my sister telling me about Anne's college recitals. Patty used to play the flute too.

"We're pretty sure he's still seeing other people," added Sydney. "My coworker matched with him only a few weeks ago. Not great." I clearly looked horrified because Sydney said to me, "We told Patricia this. Apparently, they had an exclusive conversation last month. But he better show up tonight. He has a lot of work to do to win us over."

Unfortunately, this was the point in the evening when I started to get a little drunk. I had also noticed, during the conversation, that Zach had arrived. I had watched him follow Caroline through the door, both holding packs of seltzers. But I didn't want to move away from my group of Sydney, Anne, and Irene. My slight drunkenness was softening my killer instincts. I decided to supervise him from over here. I liked being a part of this group of girls anyway, my sister's inner circle, and they seemed pleased to have me among them.

What they were saying about Logan was not a shock. In fact, it was less of a shock than the idea of Patty having an actual boyfriend. It had been Patty's pattern since college to call men her boyfriends who weren't really boyfriends. Basically, Patty called every boy she'd ever kissed a "boyfriend," even though they didn't consider her their girlfriend. I didn't think Patty even knew what it was like to have a boyfriend who did real boyfriend things, such as taking you out to dinner, introducing you to his friends, going on trips, spending the holidays together. I'd had two real boyfriends, not including all the guys I kissed in high school: sweet Cole in college and Ellis after that. Patty claimed she'd had four, but these were just guys that she'd kissed maybe twice in undergrad, then obsessed over. I realized that I was the delusional one for thinking that her pattern could've changed with this Logan guy. Not that much time had passed in life after all, even if it seemed to me like a lot of time had passed since I'd seen Patty.

"Well, if they are exclusive, then he's a cheater for being on the apps still," said Irene.

"Once a cheater always a cheater," added Anne. "I don't know how she trusts him."

"Well, cheating's not *that* bad," I chimed in.

They laughed, thinking I was kidding.

"Seriously," I said. "I think we can cut him some slack for that."

"What do you mean?" said Sydney.

"I mean that we all have the desire to cheat at some point. We can't all be bad."

"I don't have that desire," said Sydney. "What are you saying?"

"I mean that we all have the desire to have sex with people other than our partner," I explained. "Some people act on that desire. Others don't."

"Well, that's because acting on that desire can be really hurtful," piped up sweet, simple Irene. She had a pixie cut and bangs and was at least five inches shorter than me.

"I don't have that desire," Sydney said again.

"I think acting on any desire can be a good thing. It can be liberating," I said to Irene. "Some people have the courage to follow their desires, and others don't. We're all just animals." And they were penguins, these girls. Huddling together in this kitchen. Especially Sydney.

"But cheating is a betrayal," argued Irene. "It's a really painful thing to do to the person you're with."

Sydney nodded vigorously. "I've been cheated on before,"

she revealed, as if this was a shocking thing to reveal. I ignored her and responded to Ms. Irene.

"I don't think it's that hurtful," I challenged, gazing down at her. Then I offered, "When I was living in Indianapolis, I dated a guy who liked watching me have sex with other guys in front of him."

The three of them stared at me. It was exactly the reaction I was hoping for. Stun these fake laughers out of their fakeness. These girls had experienced so little in their lives. And they were clearly desperate to hear about me.

"It's best to accept that both you and your boyfriend have these desires and then just allow yourselves to indulge them," I explained to the penguins. "It's better to do that than condemn the desire."

"But I don't think everybody has that desire," said Sydney. She was all worked up. She probably had a lot of pent-up energy from not going to the gym. "It's a hundred percent okay if *you* do, and I validate you for acting on yours. That's wonderful. And it sounds like you and your partner had a mutual understanding. But I don't think it's fair to say that we're all the same."

"Trust me. All men have the desire to cheat," I said. I knew more about men than any of them. I suddenly felt very grateful to my past self for gathering so much information about men.

"If your partner cheats, it's close-minded to punish or judge them," I continued. "It's an oppressive thing to do to someone. I think that expecting your partner not to cheat is a form of oppression. You're constantly making them deny their desires and give things up for you." It felt good to challenge these girls, to push their thinking. "I wouldn't care if my partner sleeps with someone else. I'd be hurt if they didn't want to be with me anymore. But sleeping with someone else doesn't mean that that someone doesn't love me. Fidelity is an unfair test we put our partners through that's entirely beside the point of what we truly need from them. It's a test of how much discipline one can exercise in order to prove one's commitment. But it's apples and oranges. Resisting desire doesn't translate into promoting more desire for your partner. It just doesn't. Cheating shouldn't ever be the sole grounds for leaving someone."

"Well, I disagree," said Sydney, pushing her Solo cup into her lips. She looked unattractive with her arms crossed like that and a look of self-righteousness, which made her face rich with wrinkles.

Regardless, I continued, "I just feel like we all have these desires that we're too scared to have. But having desire is a good thing. It makes you alive. And we should all be trying to liberate our spirits as much as possible. I guess I'm just a free spirit type of person," I concluded. Granted, my concluding statement came out flatter than I had anticipated but luckily, at that same moment, the Asian girl with the engagement ring came over with a handle of tequila and a platter of limes and salt and asked if we wanted to take pulls, so this distracted from the anticlimactic end to what had been a rather invigorating monologue from me.

The reason I decided to strike up the same conversation again, this time with Zach, was to make sure he knew that I contained violence. After two pulls of tequila, I made my way over to where he was sitting on the floor, looking at his phone, his back against the couch. I plopped down next to him.

I started the conversation by asking him how long he and Caroline had been together.

"Caroline's my cousin," he said, indignant or disgusted—it was hard to tell. "I just crash on her floor when I get too drunk after work. I commute in from Greenwich."

"Greenwich?"

"My parents are there. I'd rather save money than live downtown."

"Are you dating anyone?"

"How very forward of you." This made him put down his phone and shift his shoulders to face me. He was grinning.

"Please," I said. "I'm not interested in you. I actually hate you."

"Sure, you do," he said. "Sure." But he was doing a bad job keeping up his grin because he wasn't one hundred percent sure I was kidding. "And yeah, I'm dating someone. Are you?"

"Is she pretty?"

"She's gorgeous. Want to see?"

I didn't really. Instead, I asked, "How many days a week do you go to the gym?"

"Six. Sometimes seven," he replied without missing a beat, but he raised his eyebrows.

"Do you list hiking as one of your favorite activities on your dating profile?"

"I'm dating someone."

"Do you have any tattoos?"

"Yeah." He smirked.

"How old are you?"

"Twenty-three."

"Do you read fiction or nonfiction?"

"Nonfiction."

"Was the last book you read a presidential biography?"

"Why are you asking all this? What are you trying to find out?"

"I'm trying to find out if you're the type of guy who likes to choke girls in bed." I felt hilarious, saying this. I almost cracked myself up. I was thrilled that I had thought of something so clever and shocking to say. I was enjoying my ability to keep people on their toes at this party.

Zach laughed. He was amused. "Yeah, I do like to choke a girl on occasion, if that's what you're asking. I mean, if she's into it."

"Do you like to watch other men have sex with girls also?"

"You mean like porn?"

"I mean, would you watch your girlfriend get fucked by another guy?"

He laughed. "What? What are you saying?" He cast around, still laughing, as if looking for someone else to join in on the joke. But there was only me.

"I used to date a guy who liked watching me have sex with other men in front of him."

"Oh, like cucking? Yeah, I've known people who are into that. Are you poly or are you just into the cucking thing as a fetish?"

Weirdly, I felt suddenly speechless. But after just one speechless second, I said, my voice strangely breathy, "What do you mean? What's *poly*?"

"What's *poly*?" He looked confused. "Have you been living under a rock? I mean, do you identify as a polyamorous person?" He said this slowly, as if I were an idiot. "Like, you don't like being with just one person at a time. I sort of identify that way, I guess."

"No," I said. "I like being with one person." I hated how breathy my voice had gotten.

"So is the cucking thing just a fetish, then?" The word *fetish* felt embarrassing to me. Hearing him keep saying it was embarrassing. "It's quite a trend these days."

"What do you mean?"

"Being into the whole cuck thing. A lot of people must be into it. It's all over porn."

"Is it?" My voice sounded very far away. I had lost the thread of the conversation and wasn't sure how to get back in control of where I had originally wanted it to go.

When I was probably twelve or thirteen, I was with my dad at the hardware store, picking up Christmas lights, and another dad was there with his daughter, in the same aisle. The other daughter and I noticed each other since we were about the same age, both of us trying to assess the other without making eye contact. She was playing with a yo-yo, catching it in her hand every time it bounced up. She had a long, horsey face. Not an attractive girl. Not the type to be popular. I had on my favorite baseball cap and still had braces so, to be honest, I wasn't looking too hot either. But I remember feeling bad for this girl and her horsey face. And then at one point, the yo-yo hit a weird bounce and it leapt up and knocked her in the chin. She looked taken aback, scrunching her chin into her long neck, blinking a lot, then glanced over at me to see if I had witnessed this. She caught me looking, and quickly looked away, turning her back to both me and her distracted dad, and headed off by herself down the aisle. My insides were absolutely screaming for her. I felt so bad that I had caught her in this tiny moment of humiliation. I felt so bad I wanted to sob. That's what it felt like in that moment at the party with stupid Zach. Like my heart had leapt up out of its normal rhythms and knocked me in the chin.

—

"Do you not watch porn? Here, I'll show you." Zach pulled out his phone. He played me a video. After this, I pointed at other videos on the home page and made him play me little clips. I was entranced and horrified. I had watched porn only once in the locker room with the other soccer girls in the ninth grade, as part of a hazing thing. But that was it. Porn was never something I'd been drawn to or even thought about. Growing up, I turned myself on by rereading scenes from YA fiction I liked, or remembering sex scenes from movies and TV shows, or just making up stories in my journal about boys I knew from school.

"I've done that," I told Zach toward the end of another video.

"Really? That many?"

"Yeah, about." There was nothing original or transcendent about any of it.

"At the same time?"

My stomach felt horrible again. Swishy, turbulent. I had to go to the bathroom. I had somehow spun into feeling tremendously sad for myself all at once. And I felt stupid about the previous version of this conversation that I'd had with Sydney, Irene, and Anne. With all my heart, I hoped that everyone would forget everything I'd said. How could I undo it? There was so much heat and liquid building up behind my face.

"What are you guys doing?" asked Patty, appearing above me and Zach, looking down at where we were sitting next to each other in front of the couch.

"Watching porn," said Zach. "Care to join us, Patty-cakes?"

"Nope, I do not care," Patty replied. Then she said to me, holding out her hand and twiddling her fingers, "Want to come help me concoct my lemonade punch?" She was trying to give me an out. But I felt like lead on the floor.

"In a sec," I said. Then I turned to Zach. "By the way, no girl is actually into getting choked. It's just something we pretend to like because we think it makes us seem hot."

My stomach still hurt so badly. I didn't want to move a muscle out of fear that I might completely lose control of my bowels. "You're stupid if you think any girl likes getting choked in bed," I said.

"I sort of like it," said Irene. I hadn't realized that she had sat down on the couch above us. Her legs were tucked up under her. She was wearing frilly pink socks. I wondered if she'd seen us watching the porn.

"No, you don't," I told her.

"I've been choked before," she said. Maybe she was trying to flirt with Zach. I wanted to let her know that he was two years younger than she was. He looked older but he was my age. Also, he had a girlfriend.

"You're wild," Zach said to me, shaking his head. Then he stood up from the floor. "I'm getting another beer."

"I think it's a little different in the queer community," Irene said to me.

Sydney approached us. "What were you all doing?" she asked, sitting next to Irene.

"They were watching porn," tattletaled Irene.

"What about porn? I like porn," said Anne. She was standing over us, her lips pressed to the rim of a beer, speaking into it. "Well. Some porn," she clarified.

"Really? I hate it," I'd decided.

"I think porn can be empowering," said Irene. "It promotes

sexual openness. It can create space for people to explore sexual curiosities in a way that's safe and private." Irene had a quick, high, quiet voice. Like a nymph.

"I agree, but I think it's also made nonconsensual violence in the bedroom more acceptable," said Sydney, "which can be confusing for people."

"You should've seen what Zach was just showing Lucy."

"Don't shame them," Sydney said to Irene.

"Oh, I'm not. I just don't think *that* porn is the porn that Anne and I are talking about."

"All I'm saying is people are confusing passion for violence these days," said Sydney. "We *think* some of the things we do is expected and dare I say *normal*, like waxing our vaginas, but we're just being sold a bill of goods."

"Yes," I agreed. Then to further support Sydney's point, I added, "Nobody actually likes getting choked. That guy Zach thinks that real girls actually like being choked in bed."

"Well, some people are definitely into that."

"Yeah, but that's really, really rare," I said. I wanted to go back to the part where Sydney and I were agreeing with each other.

"I think that's pretty close-minded," said Sydney. "I'm all for experimentation and kink, if people discuss it and consent to it. If the experimentation gets aggressive, I would hope that the people exploring it have already worked to establish trust and boundaries."

"But that's not how choking happens," I said. Now I was getting worked up. "People are getting choked left and right in the bedroom now. Same with anal. Guys just go in for it without asking." I spotted my sister closing in on us, so I directed some of what I was saying toward her, as a word of caution. "I just think that we should all be extra careful about who we sleep with," I said. "I think if you're having sex with someone for the first time, you should tell them preemptively that choking is a behavior you don't like and that you don't want to do anal either, so that you don't get surprised in the middle. I think we should make sure to set the expectation as: sex should be gentle and regular at first. Don't you think?"

The room had become a lot emptier. I realized it was just me, Anne, Sydney, Irene, and my sister. Across the room, Zach exited the bathroom in his boxers, a roll of toilet paper in hand.

"I'm gonna be sleeping on this couch, ladies, if that's alright," said Zach. "Caroline's got a guy in there."

Sydney, Anne, and Irene all agreed that it was time to leave anyway. They helped collect some Solo cups and tossed them in the trash bag that Patty held open by the door.

After everyone left, an uncomfortable silence moved in between me and Patty. Patty showered first and when I joined her at the sink to brush our teeth, all around her eyes was red, but maybe that was just from taking her makeup off. She spit into the sink silently, then padded out to the hall in her slippers.

She was already in bed, sleeping mask on, mittens on, when I came into the room. She peeled her sleeping mask off just one eye to observe me getting into bed.

"Did you wear the shower shoes?" she asked in a husky voice.

"Yes," I lied. She grunted, then rolled over. Fuck, I had forgotten about the shower shoes but I didn't think Patty could see from the bed so she would hopefully not know I was lying.

"Light seems extra bright tonight," I said about the red

window across the street. I was worried she was upset at me for watching porn with Zach during the party, or for the conversation I'd had with her friends about cheating, choking, and porn. I was worried I had revealed too much to everybody about who I was and what I'd done. I wasn't drunk anymore so I was starting to feel ashamed for how loud and talkative I'd been.

"Patty?" I knew I was keeping her awake when she wanted to sleep. The sound of my voice in the room reminded me of when we were little, sharing a room together, and how I sometimes woke her up in the middle of the night because of this recurring bad dream I used to get about her turning into a witch and melting.

"What?" she said, pushing her sleeping mask up onto her forehead and rolling over onto her back to stare at the ceiling.

"Is it okay that I came here this weekend?"

"Yes?" She wasn't sure why I was asking.

"Are you sure it's okay that I came and surprised you?"

"Yes, yes," said Patty. Now she sounded aggravated. She wanted to go to sleep.

"I'm sorry you had to host me on such a busy weekend, but I'm glad I could be here for your show," I said.

"It's all good," said Patty. "Go to sleep."

But about an hour later, I woke up to her crying. Maybe it was only a few minutes later. Time was hard to tell in the dark.

"Patty? Patty? Are you okay?" I asked. I reached over her to flick on the lamp. She was crying a lot. Long, horrible heaves that sounded like a heavy door opening and closing. I patted her back. What had I done, what had I done?

"It's okay," I whispered. Her crying wasn't slowing down, her shoulders shaking.

"I'm here, I'm here," I told her. "It's going to be okay."

"Logan didn't show up," she finally admitted, "after I told everyone he was coming."

Oh, I felt so relieved! This was what had been upsetting her. Nothing about me or anything I'd said. It was usually never me in the end. I should've known: this was the same way she'd cry growing up, all of her sadness coming out at once. It'd usually happen after something I said, even though both me and Patty knew her tears weren't ever my fault, despite our mother's suspicions; I just happened to be the unfortunate trigger a lot of the time. Mostly, Patty was happy. Then I'd tell her she was taking too long in the bathroom and boom—she'd start sobbing.

I realized that Sydney, Anne, Irene, and I had all silently acknowledged earlier in the evening that there was no way this Logan guy was going to come to the party. He wasn't a real boyfriend, just a man that Patty had made bigger in her head. I had understood this hours ago. I had also accepted the fact that he would likely end things with Patty over text very soon. It was like I had seen all of it happen before it had happened to her, and I had forgotten that Patty was still inhabiting her delusional world where she believed he was going to come. She'd even had me buy beer for him.

"Has he texted you?" I asked.

"He said he was too tired. He texted that at eleven thirty."

"Well, at least he's not ghosting," I said.

"That would be insane. We're dating," she reminded me.

I didn't say anything. Patty popped in her retainer and turned her back to me again, pulling a pillow into her chest.

"Well, if you're dating, he should've come tonight. Being tired isn't an excuse," I said.

She flicked off the lamp. The red light across the street got bright again.

"Do you wear your retainer when you're with him?" I asked. Looking into the red light without blinking, then staring at the wall, created saucers in the air. It turned our bedroom into outer space.

"No," she said. "I'm going to sleep."

"Good," I confirmed. Right answer.

"Can I see the text he sent you?" I asked. I wanted to keep the conversation going. I needed to somehow convince her that he wasn't a real boyfriend, then convince her to abandon her performing dreams and get a real job.

"In the morning," she said.

I knew I needed to let her sleep, but I said, "I forgot Irene was queer."

"Yeah," said Patty. "They're dating Lenny."

"Is Lenny queer?"

"I don't know," she said. "I assume." Keep talking to me, please, I thought. Ask me a question, ask me anything. I wanted us to stay up together, talking about everything, until I had to leave for the airport. We still had so many hours left.

"Was I okay earlier at the party?" I asked. "Did I say anything weird?"

"You were fine," said Patty, her back still to me. "You came off a little strong at one point, I guess. But no one cares. Let's sleep."

"Sometimes I just feel so confused," I said. I'd take back everything I'd said if I could. "I hope I didn't ruin anything."

But she didn't say anything else. She was asleep.

Around three in the morning, I left the bed to go have sex with Zach. I made sure to wear the shower shoes on my way back in. I accidentally woke her up getting back under the covers. The bed was too small to be subtle. She peered out of her sleeping mask.

"You okay?" she asked.

"Yes, yes," I reassured her. "Go back to sleep."

In Texas, I liked driving. I-35 that first year had no traffic—just a flat, fast road. By the summer, I could make it to San Antonio in fifty minutes, and Waco in under an hour and a half. On 290, on a cloudless night, if I hit Giddings by sunset, all the light got sucked into this one spot by the cell phone tower, then drained down, and the wooden utility poles that stacked back over the hills became silhouetted until they looked like a line of antlered elk marching off. Then, in the dimness, the streetlights would turn on and cast down, each beam starting to come into its own, craning over my car, greeting my windshield one after the other after the other, like my own happiness coming down to meet me, then passing me on. And driving like that, I'd remember how I was someone who wanted to live a very long time. I wanted to get very old; I needed to know what that felt like. It seemed magnificent that anyone could make it that long, and no one who wasn't ninety knew what it felt like to amount to something so enormous. Sometimes my curiosity about what it'd feel like to be her made me want to become her so bad—the old woman version of me. Driving up and down I-35, sometimes I wanted to be her more than anything. I wanted to be extraordinarily old, and barely recognizable, and in possession of immense sets of knowledge, the knowledge you get only from decades of learning the same things over and over. I wanted to know everything in the world by heart. I needed to make it that far, to feel the age when living longer isn't the point anymore, when life is no longer about the ecstasies of the everyday but about retelling the memories, when you don't need to care anymore about where you're headed or where else you need to go or whether you're headed the right way, when the only direction to look is down and back, all the work at last behind you. Obviously, there were steps that had to be taken if my body was going to get me there. Because there were also moments when I saw that old woman who was me at ninety looking back down the highway of her life, saying, Please don't be me, please don't be me.

PART II

NEON-GREEN GUY

WE HAD TO STOP BACK AT LIAM'S FIRST TO PICK UP HIS swimsuit. I waited in the truck while he ran in. I had asked him to help me out with an errand that morning, so we were already running behind, at risk of arriving after the crowds, but I'd needed his truck to drop off my kitchen table to a woman on Pleasanton who'd bought it off Craigslist and was paying cash. What bothered Liam was the principle of it. He thought the buyer should pick up the table, or that I should have at least charged for the delivery. But I just had to be rid of it.

Liam was inside for what felt like a long time. I checked my face in the mirror, reapplied blush and some eyeliner, then examined the stubble on my shins. At last, the truck door clicked open, and Liam slid back in behind the wheel. He buckled up.

"Sorry, that took a little while," he said. He had both hands on the wheel but hadn't started the truck. "There's been some drama with the neighbor. The window's shattered and there's blood everywhere."

"The window next door?"

"Yep, that unit," he confirmed. "It's pretty crazy."

We looked at each other, then both unbuckled. We knew we needed to find out more about the drama. That's also when I started putting some other things together, like the two police cars parked on the other side of the street that I'd noticed in the rearview, and the two police officers standing on the sidewalk talking to a young woman in purple spaghetti straps, whose back was to me, but whose short brown hair and slight figure I recognized. I knew that woman. I'd seen her come in and out of Liam's building loads of times.

Liam's apartment was one of the only old brick buildings in the area. It reminded me of New England. He lived on West Fourteenth, next to a veterinary clinic, in the quiet dead zone six blocks south of West Campus. It was a teensy studio, three hundred and fifty square feet, but U-shaped, so you couldn't see the kitchen from the bed or the bed from the kitchen. He was on the first floor, next to the three outdoor laundry machines, which often knocked against the wall in the evenings. In August, I had moved in temporarily for the nine weeks in between my leases, working from home at his desk. We had been dating for several months at that point; I was ready for us to move in together permanently, but he said he wasn't yet. I had two new jobs, both virtual. The first was working as a remote online notary, contracted by a software platform called Proof that automated the public notice process for local newspapers and government offices. The second was ghostwriting newsletters and thought leadership for a twenty-six-year-old CEO who was trying to build houses in the sky.

I spent a lot of time getting to know what his place looked like during the day. It turned out Liam almost never saw his apartment in sunlight since he got to his shop by 8:30 a.m. and left after 6:00 p.m. and weekends he spent out and about. Liam owned and operated a custom furniture and millwork shop off Cesar Chavez, and he'd built all the furniture inside his apartment: a white pine credenza, a coffee table that fit exactly as it should in the L-shaped nook of the sectional, the shelves about his desk, the desk. He said that what made a place beautiful wasn't the stuff you put in it, but the built-ins. He made his place look like it had built-ins by the way his white pine pieces melded in with the apartment: he had added a plank with a live edge to the windowsill above the sink; he had built a sliding contraption in the pantry so that the trash can could be rolled in, out of the way; his bed had night-stands built into its sides that looked attached to the wall. By studying all of Liam's things, I realized for the first time how I was looking into the insides of real trees. It'd never occurred to me before that the length of the line in the wood indicated the height of the tree, that the longer the line the taller the tree. By peeling open a chopstick, Liam had explained how you had to line up the long grain to make furniture maintain its shape, since wood expanded and contracted over time. Cities like Austin were packed with quick builds that time hadn't yet tested—luxury buildings like Marq Uptown that had the same framing and interior finishing as modular homes—and as soon as he said this, I knew I agreed with him: I could feel the insecurity of the buildings in this city, all of them trembling on the cusp of replacement or collapse. But Liam's pieces were built to last.

"So many people don't know about stuff like this," I told him a lot, to make sure he understood how special he was for knowing what the world was made of and how it got put together.

Liam and I got out of the truck and walked down the little alley to his door. Right away I noticed the splotches of blood on the path. Above us, a woman and her tiny dog were making their way down the exterior staircase that ended right in front of Liam's door. On the bottom railing, both his bike and the one he built me were locked up.

The woman was on the larger side, wearing a tight purple T-shirt. She had short brown hair cropped around her ears and a little white dog, so fluffy you couldn't see the dog's face.

"This is pretty wild," Liam said to her. We were both leaning against the wall to make room for the woman and dog to pass, so they wouldn't have to step on the glass.

She stopped on the last step. "I know!" She'd been looking shy before, perhaps unsure of whether to talk to us, but now she seemed overjoyed that Liam had initiated a conversation. She tugged the dog closer to her to keep it from stepping off the stairs onto the broken window, saying in a baby voice, "No, Rosa, heel."

"What happened?" Liam asked.

"You didn't hear it?"

"We weren't here."

The dog's skinny blue leash was wrapped around the woman's legs, and she kept saying, "Rosa, Rosa, Rosa," until she twirled in a circle and the dog unwrapped itself. Then she tightened the leash, awkwardly stepped down and around the glass on tippy-toes, then stood facing us on the blood-splattered path.

A guy opened the door to our left, coming out with a laundry basket full of whites. The woman was still dancing around with her dog. That day, I happened to look silly and young in my bright-green overalls, white sneakers, and pink bikini top. Out of everybody present, Liam was by far the most adult, a real grown-up trying to get a handle on the situation. Although he was one of the most attractive men I'd ever seen, Liam had a faded look about him, from all the sawdust, that made him appear older than he really was. He could also look a little run-down because of his acne scars and stubble-slash-beard and the black gunk under his fingernails. At night, whenever we watched movies, Liam used a razor blade to remove hundreds of splinters from his palms, slicing into his skin without even looking.

"Do we know who did this?" the laundry guy asked, glancing around.

"It was that guy," said the dog woman. "That guy was down here shouting, and then he punched a hole in the window."

"Oh shit," said the laundry man.

"What guy?" asked Liam.

"The neon-green guy," I answered. I realized that I knew exactly who the dog woman was talking about. I'd seen him around the complex during the day. He was sometimes out back by the dumpsters, sometimes coming out of a car in the parking lot, once carrying boxes. I thought he lived here, or was in the process of moving in, although the one morning that I saw him standing between the two dumpsters, I'd reconsidered.

I turned to Liam. "You know that guy. He's always wearing neon-green socks and neon-green running shorts."

Liam looked at me, then back at the dog woman. "Who?"

That's when Liam's next-door neighbor showed up, accompanied by a police officer. I had seen this guy multiple times. He was taller than Liam, with shaggy brown hair down to his shoulders, and always looked stoned, loping around with his eyes half closed, dangling his keys as he walked from the back lot, where he liked to park his red Chevy, to the door. His keys had a very distinct dangle. He was probably twenty-three, twenty-four.

"It's all here," he said to the police officer. The dog woman was standing in their way, but Shaggy Hair craned around her and said to me, Liam, and the laundry guy, all of us pressed against the wall in a line, "Sorry about all this, you guys."

Then, Shaggy Hair flopped his lanky arms around, gesturing nonspecifically, and saying to the officer, "So yeah, it's like—this is the blood, and that's the window."

The police officer had a camera. He beckoned the dog woman to move away with a "Can you please . . . ?" and she fumbled with her leash, then sort of hopped-skipped-tippy-toed around the glass to get in line with the rest of us against the wall, taking her place next to the laundry man after bumping her belly up against his bin. He lifted it over her head so she could duck under it with her dog.

The officer took photos of the path, then shook Shaggy Hair's hand and left.

"What happened, man?" Liam asked Shaggy Hair.

"Yeah, sorry about this, man," said Shaggy and he pushed up his bangs. "It was that guy. He just came over this morning and was shouting and punched a hole in the window. I tried to get him to go away, but he wouldn't stop. I came out here to try and grab him, and that's when this happened to my sleeve."

Shaggy turned his left shoulder to us, and we all noticed that a sleeve from Shaggy's red T-shirt was missing.

"Oh shit," said Liam. I think we'd all assumed that the missing sleeve was just part of Shaggy's overall vibe.

"I bet this is going to cost a shit ton to fix," said Shaggy, stepping directly onto the glass to check out the hole in his window. He was wearing black boots with large silver buckles. "I'm about to get smacked."

"Surely you won't have to pay for it," I said. "They'll pay for it, right? The apartment."

"Nah," said Shaggy. "They won't care about me and my drama."

"Why are there eggs?" asked Liam. I hadn't noticed until that moment, but there were, in fact, several brown organic eggs on the ground, plus their empty carton, most of them uncracked.

"The dude had groceries," said Shaggy, and he bent down to pick up one of the eggs. "He had a bag of pretty nice groceries." For some reason, Shaggy handed the egg to me.

I took the egg, examined it, then nodded at Shaggy and said, "Yeah, pretty nice."

Nobody was asking what I thought was the obvious question, so I added, "Why was he trying to get inside your place?"

"I guess he went grocery shopping before," Shaggy said to me, still staring at the egg.

"Is the guy unhoused? Who is this guy?" asked Liam.

"He's always around," the dog lady piped up. She was still trapped against the wall behind the laundry guy and his laundry bin. "He followed me once when I was walking Rosa."

"He followed me once too," I said. I wasn't sure if this was true, but I felt compelled to say it in solidarity with the dog lady and as a way of increasing the tension, and as a way of doing something to Liam, though I wasn't quite sure what. That guy hadn't ever really followed me. What I was thinking of was the time he was standing between those two dumpsters and I was walking to my car, and we made eye contact from our opposite sides of the street.

"What?" Liam said to me.

"He followed me once to Starbucks," I said.

"Yes!" said the dog lady, and she craned around the laundry bin to make big eye contact with me and eagerly nod her head. She even reached both her hands out to me in the air and for a moment, I thought—if the laundry bin wasn't there—we might have clasped hands.

"Why was he trying to get into your place?" I asked Shaggy again.

"Well, Anna was there," Shaggy said matter-of-factly as if we all understood what this meant, and he sat down on the bottom step of the exterior staircase. We were all quiet. We were all probably wondering what to do with this new piece of critical information since I assumed none of us had any clue who Anna was.

"I've got a shop vac inside my place," Liam said. I couldn't believe he was moving us on from the most important thread in the conversation so far. "I can get this cleaned up."

"Oh, man, that'd be great," said Shaggy earnestly, looking at Liam like he was an absolute godsend.

Shaggy stood up and he and Liam shook hands. Shaggy's name also turned out to be Liam. My Liam disappeared into our apartment. That's when the dog woman took her cue to leave, less reluctantly than I would've expected seeing as we were all finally getting somewhere with this mention of Anna, looking back to tell Shaggy Liam, "Sorry you had such a terrible morning." The laundry guy also headed upstairs, saying something similarly empathetic to Shaggy. I watched the dog woman chat animatedly with her long-haired white pup—a Maltese? A terrier?—as they hurried down the stone path, out the iron-framed alleyway door, and across the street. My chest split open down the middle, watching her.

It was just me and Shaggy Liam standing outside now, waiting for my Liam to come back out. I wanted to ask Shaggy Liam more questions about who Anna was and what Anna had to do with anything. I was already coming up with a pretty solid idea of what was going on, even without Shaggy Liam's intel. Important pieces were coming together.

But before Shaggy and I could really dig in, a girl came around the corner, the girl in spaghetti straps I'd seen on the street talking to the officers, the girl I now suspected to be Anna.

She sat down on the step that Shaggy Liam had just vacated, right next to our bikes. She clutched a bright-green vape in her hands and started sucking on it. She wasn't wearing a bra. She looked shell-shocked, expressionless.

But I smiled at her. After a second, she smiled back.

"Hi," I offered. I wanted to ask her if her nails were fake. They were long with bright-pink tips. But I didn't want to make her feel self-conscious about anything or give the impression I was studying her too closely.

My Liam came back out of the apartment then, with his orange shop vac on a long extension cord. It roared and he started sucking up the glass.

Shaggy Liam said to him, "Do you know who I can call about this?"

"Yeah, I've got the number. One sec." My Liam finished up, then rolled up the slinky black tube and started scrolling through his phone. I was so proud of my Liam for everything I already adored about him—how capable he was at taking care of things, how handy. My Liam, for example, clipped all his keys onto his belt with a carabiner.

Anna was still sitting on the steps looking like a phantom.

"It's going to be brutally hot in there if you don't get this fixed," my Liam said after Shaggy Liam typed the maintenance team's number into his own phone. "I can bring by a piece of plywood tonight as a temporary solution if you want."

"Really?" said Shaggy Liam. "That'd be great, man."

"Yeah, no worries. Sorry you're having a bad day."

They shook hands again.

After Liam put away the shop vac, we got back into his truck and buckled up. We were heading out west to a popular swimming hole in the Hill Country. It was the middle of the day now, and we'd be lucky if there was any place to park, but Liam knew a lot of secret spots, so if this one was too busy, we could drive out to another he had in mind. Central Texas was in a drought it would never get out of. It didn't matter how much rain came; apparently, it'd never be enough. So, for everyone here, the hot months were always about finding water.

"What did that mean," I said on the drive, "when he was like, 'Well, Anna was there'?"

"What was that?"

"Remember? I was like, 'Why did the neon guy try to get into your place?' and he was like, 'Anna was there.'"

"Pretty weird."

There was so much to unpack!

"That was funny how you and the other woman were both like, 'Yeah, I know that guy. He's followed me before,' and I'm just standing there like an idiot," Liam added.

"It's so weird you don't know who we're talking about!"

I described the neon-green guy again for Liam just to

prove how much I knew. But Liam shook his head. He had no idea who I was talking about.

"I think there's a love triangle going on," I said. I'd been working up to announcing this theory for a while. "Remember the Corolla that was keyed? I think that's connected."

A few weeks back, Liam had pointed out a car in his lot that'd been scratched up with the word *cunt* over and over. I hadn't even noticed it until he said to me one morning, "Check that out." It also had a threat—"if I see you here again I'll kill you cunt!"—scraped in.

"It's not a coincidence." I was confident.

Liam shook his head. "I don't think those things are related."

"Of course, they are," I announced. "They're two extremely violent things happening at your apartment separated by mere weeks."

We were on US-290, going fast, passing the shopping centers that all looked the same. Liam was no longer interested in the story of Anna and Shaggy Liam, probably because there was only so much we could figure out on our own without more facts, so I changed the subject.

"I keep seeing the marionette sculpture from that exhibit in the small telephone poles," I said. We'd just been to an exhibit at a gallery in Alpine. One piece had been a Native American man made of beer cans and string who danced whenever the stereo turned on. "And the big telephone poles look like Eiffel Towers."

Liam didn't say anything.

I tried again: "I hate how freeways in Texas have all these stoplights."

"They're not freeways. They're highways."

"What's the difference?"

"Oh, baby, yes," said Liam, slapping the top of the steering wheel. "Let's talk about *interstates*." I had nailed it. It was with great joy that Liam engaged in topics like this. As a kid, he used to study maps.

Liam explained how all the interstate numbers ending in zero run east-west and the ones ending in five run north-south. This was true across the entire country. And the numbers that end in neither are not interstates, but state highways, although state highways could end in anything. Freeways, apparently, were what people living on the coast call interstates.

In the middle of this, I interrupted to point out, "I've been to that exact gas station before," as we approached the Chevron. "Is this the same road we took to Crystal City?"

"No. We're north."

"Well, I'm pretty sure I've been to that exact gas station." Closer, however, I realized it was permanently closed. It didn't even have any pumps.

"Well, I've been to that exact galleria," I said at the next exit, pointing.

"I don't think so," said Liam. "I feel like we're in a sitcom right now where two people are just talking past each other."

"I feel like we're talking about the same thing," I said. He was being funny, but I was hurt. "You're talking about interstates and I'm talking about how everything looks the same."

We were quiet for a little while, just listening to the music—DIY pop-punk. I watched buzzards land on the shoulder, then take back off, and I waited for the landscape to open. Sometimes, a bend in the road would suddenly expose canyons and cliffs in a way you'd never expect. Liam was fine with the rocks and lines of the Hill Country, all its dry riverbeds and tiny suffering trees. The mesquite and Ashe juniper. He loved getting intimidated by big sky. There were never enough colors for me, but I liked when the height came out of nowhere.

"What's that?"

"Oil horse. Actually, it might be called a pump jack."

"It looks like an ostrich."

"It might be called a gas bronco. Can you look it up? Type *oil horse* into Wikipedia."

"Oh wow. There are a lot of synonyms. Pumpjack. Also called a donkey pumper, a nodding donkey, a pumping unit, a horsehead pump, a rocking horse, a beam pump, a dinosaur, a sucker rod pump, a grasshopper pump, a Big Texan, a thirsty bird, or a jack pump."

"What was that one? A Big Texas thirsty bird?"

He was so delighted, I didn't want to tell him about the comma.

Next, we talked about the difference between a tree and a bush. Liam thought it might have to do with whether it has one trunk or many trunks.

"Actually, with mesquite," I said, still on Wikipedia, "environmental factors change the way it grows. 'Mesquite adapts to the pruning effects of weather and grows in a new way, hence changing its identity from bush to tree.'"

Liam considered this. "That's powerful stuff," he said.

"When you go back to do the plywood tonight, you've got to get some answers," I said finally. I couldn't help myself.

"I'll find out what I can."

"We need to know the whole story."

Liam laughed. "We might not get the whole story."

"Well, I need to know," I told him. "I can't not know."

He turned off the highway. At the end of the dirt road, windmills were fading in a long line on top of red hills, the sun making everything hazy.

"That's so cool," noted Liam, looking at the same wind-mills I was looking at.

At last, we arrived at the swimming hole. Liam was happy that it wasn't as busy as it could've been. We spread our pink towels out on the sunny rocks and lay back. I loved a big sunny rock and told him. He was proud that he'd brought me to a place that I loved.

"What are those bugs?" I asked, pointing up. "Those bugs are so big I can see them from here." There were three massive bugs buzzing around the cypresses. I was lying back on the hot rock, staring at the trees and the bright-blue sky, and the big black bugs playing tag.

"Dragonflies," he said.

"I know what a dragonfly is," I told him. "I'm talking about *those*."

"Which? The buzzards?"

I didn't want us talking past each other again, so I stopped talking.

Liam and I met back when I was working in the leasing office of Marq Uptown. Almost immediately upon arriving in Texas, I saw the job posting and felt brilliant for finding it: although they paid less than my starting salary at AUTHENTIC and without the benefits, they gave all their leasing associates a fully furnished studio in the affordable housing wing of their sister property for only seven hundred and fifty a month. This property was right on the highway, in a nonwalkable dead zone up past Anderson, ten minutes north of downtown. All the apartments had sleek modern appliances, and I didn't mind the things that other leasing associates complained about, like the carpet and constant rush of trucks through the windows. At night, the sounds of I-35 easily turned into waves or rain, and the shushing helped me fall asleep.

My first months there were slow season, and few came in. Every morning, I straightened the courtyard furniture and pool chairs, wiped down the ellipticals in the gym, helped direct the delivery of packages and food, and refilled the candy bowls. Some addicted residents came by for their daily fistful of Tootsie Rolls, but few said hi. I had a big, glorious monitor all to myself. I clicked around on Google Earth, learned the names of all the rivers in Texas, memorized the streets in a Scottish town called Aberdeen, explored the tiny Thai island of Koh Tao, and clicked and clicked and clicked around the deserts of Pakistan. I flipped through three different dating apps to see who lived around me but never messaged anyone back; everyone looked the same and liked the same things. The apps were only about playing little games; I awarded myself one Tootsie Roll if I correctly guessed the next guy's first prompt, occupation, or height.

By springtime, Marq Uptown got busier, and I had to start giving more tours. At first, I liked getting dressed up in stockings and heels—I didn't look or sound anything like myself. I even bought a light-pink lipstick, with a glossy sheen that made my eyes pop, and spun my hair into a big bun on top of my head. I thrifted a pencil skirt with a slit in the back, and several turtlenecks. The AC made the leasing office very cold, but I didn't mind being buttoned up.

The people who came in were mostly young men in tech looking for one-bedrooms. There were some couples. Near zero families. And then, in the middle of April, there was Liam. His shop was building out the kitchen of the five-bedroom penthouse on the tenth floor, which belonged to the owners. Everyone in the trades was required to use the freight entrance—property rules. My manager forbade me from letting them in through the front, which had been immaculately manicured to attract rich renters. But Liam didn't seem to register that this rule applied to him, which led to a small confrontation.

"Sir, you have to use the back."

"We already brought up the stuff. I'm just going in with my toolbox."

"Only residents can come through the front."

He stared at me, chomping down on a piece of gum with his whole jaw. He had a long face and an unwavering gaze— ice blue eyes—that made me want to look away. A large reflective pair of rainbow eyewear was perched on the rim of his black baseball hat.

He said, "You're not a resident. You go through the back after every coffee break?"

"I don't drag in dust and mud," I said. For some reason, I took this opportunity to lift my foot up over the desk to show him one of my heeled clogs that always slipped off. They were stupid shoes. Backless and impossible to wear, especially in sheer stockings.

He stared at me a second longer, chewing his gum. His Sherwin-Williams tank was wet with yellow stains and dark splotches of sweat, his arms pink and slippery, face flushed. Then he groaned, and without saying another word, turned around and headed back out the front door. I felt awful. His toolbox looked heavy—I wouldn't want to be carrying that. I said to myself, What was that? That wasn't me at all. I didn't care about dust and mud. It was only because something about being in professional dress made me want to expose this man in muddy boots as another insecure, little person.

But all that had happened was I had made myself feel bad and made him go back outside in the hundred-and-ten-degree heat with all his tools.

The following week, we matched on a dating app. I almost dropped my phone when his face popped up. He was the first real person I'd ever seen on an app. What was he doing on here? His profile said he was open to a long or short relationship, was six foot two, and his occupation was furniture. I messaged him a long apology about the backless shoe incident. We agreed to meet for drinks on a Monday at six thirty.

He was already there when I showed up. An upside-down gorilla was ironed onto the front of his baseball hat, his black cargo pants caked in sawdust. He was sitting at a small table in the corner, on the bench side.

When I pulled out the chair across from him, he looked up at me and laughed.

"This will be fun," he said, lifting his beer bottle to his lips. I wasn't sure what he meant.

He explained, "You don't look like someone who's going to be picking up what I'm putting down. That's all."

"What do I look like?" I was stricken. I still hadn't sat down.

"Too good for me." He put both arms up on the back of the bench and smiled. He had freckles on his triceps.

I didn't know what to say to this. I should have felt flattered but instead was mortified. It seemed like he was already under the impression that we were very different people. I wanted to explain that my stockings and skirt were only because I had just come from work. I wished I had changed but wasn't even sure what I was supposed to have changed into. Finally, I sat down and told him I'd drink whatever he was drinking, and he said, "That's a start."

He came back to the table with a Lone Star in a can because they were out of bottles.

"I don't like ordering beer on tap," he said, placing it in front of me. "It can get gross in there."

I didn't know what that meant either but couldn't keep giving myself away. He started asking me questions to help us discover things we had in common. "Okay, tell me the worst music artist that you genuinely like. But be honest."

But I didn't know anything about music and I told him that.

He laughed. "That's beautiful."

"What is?"

"What about movies? Are you a movie person or a TV person?"

"I don't think I've watched a movie in years," I said. I was so mad at myself for continuing to speak without thinking, but I truly couldn't think of a single movie. He was looking at me attentively. He wasn't a big blinker. His eyes were a little spooky when he fixed them on me. They were very blue. I wondered if he found my eyes as unsettling as I found his. But his were also warm and playful, so even though I was failing his questions, he didn't seem to be testing me. But I didn't like feeling at a loss for things to say. It occurred to me that I hadn't been on a date like this in a long time, maybe ever. It was suddenly essential he not realize that.

I decided to ask, "Do you have any sisters or brothers?" It felt like a good thing to ask.

He told me he had one sister and one brother.

"Where are they?"

"Cincinnati. My sister was in New York, but she just had a kid so she moved back."

I asked if his sister was older.

He nodded. "Can you tell?"

"Tell what?"

He took another sip of beer and said, "I only trust dudes who have older sisters."

"Why?"

"They're less likely to be shitheads," he said. "It's not a perfect science but you can know a guy for a long time who you think is alright and not realize he's a creep."

"Do you know a lot of creeps?"

"Some."

"Are you friends with them?"

"A few."

"Why?"

He shrugged. "Once you know what to expect out of people, you can be friends with anyone. It only sucks when your friends who aren't assholes act like assholes."

"Do you try to get your friends who are assholes to not be assholes?"

"Nah."

"Why?"

He smiled at me. "I don't know. You can't blame the scorpion for killing the frog."

"What does that mean?"

"You know. The parable. Is that what you call it? A parable?"

But I didn't know, so he told me about the scorpion crossing the river on the back of the frog, promising the frog it wouldn't sting but still stinging the frog anyway, killing them both.

"And you're a frog?"

He laughed. He crossed his arms, leaning toward me over the table on his elbows. His blue eyes moved back and forth across my face. He said, "I can't tell yet if you're more attracted to frogs or scorpions." He leaned back and sipped his beer. "Ask me again later."

"Well, you have a sister," I reasoned. "Do you think I'm a scorpion or a frog?"

"Scorpion," he said.

"But I have a sister too." I felt hurt.

"The sister thing only matters for guys." He took another sip. "I guess my brother's a bit of a shithead. But he's the oldest."

"My sister's a frog," I said. I suddenly felt tremendous urgency for him and my sister to meet. I had the feeling that meeting Patty would prove to him something about me, but I wasn't sure what. I was already worried he might think I was weird since I had deleted all my social media, except LinkedIn for work. I really needed to call Patty. It had been ages since we talked. "So, basically you're saying some people are predators and some people are prey," I clarified.

"Nah," said Liam. "Swimmers and stingers maybe."

After an hour, we had moved on from scorpions to other desert animals, like a type of lizard Liam said had evolved to suck up water through its feet, then to the desert in general, and then we were back to talking about Texas.

"Do you want to live here forever?" I asked.

He shook his head. "I don't think I want to die in Texas."

"Why not?"

"Don't know. Haven't gotten that far," he said. Then he added, "It's hot."

I told him I had moved here from Maui and that I'd been here about a year.

"You don't look like you're from Maui."

When I told him I was from Boston, he said, "Ah right,

I feel like a lot of my friends did the whole Hawaii thing at some point."

I wasn't sure what that meant, but I didn't like it, so I asked, "Do you have parents?"

"Do I have parents?" he repeated, smiling.

I blushed. "Are you close with your parents?"

He didn't answer for a few seconds, then nodded slowly and said, "I like my parents a lot and we get along but I wouldn't say we're close."

"Why not?"

"I see how some people my age still call their parents every day and I've realized I'm not like that."

He had been running his hand under the table for a while, feeling for something.

"Why are you doing that?" I finally asked.

He took his hand away and said, "I was just seeing how it's made."

"How do you do that?"

"Just feeling for different parts."

"What different parts?"

"Like if there's a substrate. Or if there's an applied edge. Or if there's fasteners. Or if there's an applied top. If it's hollow. If it's solid."

"How can you tell just by feeling?"

He shrugged. "You can usually feel how things are put together on the underside." He was suddenly antsy, no longer looking at me. The ceiling lights flashed.

I placed my hand under the table too, trying to feel what he was feeling. "Is this put together well?" I wanted to know, but the bar was closing. We had been sitting there for hours. It was almost midnight. I was a little drunk.

"Want to go sober up at the shop?" he asked out in the

parking lot. "It's just around the corner." He nodded at the only other car in the lot—mine. "Is that you? It's probably okay to leave it here a little longer. I don't think they'll mind."

"The shop?"

He was talking about his woodshop. He explained that we could walk there but it was probably easiest if he drove us over in the truck. He'd had only two beers. "The roads around here get a little sketchy at this hour. No sidewalks."

"I'm not getting in your truck," I said. We hardly knew each other.

He was quiet for a second, taken aback, then he laughed. He leaned against the truck bed and looked down at the ground. He was unclipping his keys from his belt. He had them on a carabiner. Looking down at his fingers as he fiddled with his keys, he said, "Yeah, that's fair. Not great optics. Me taking you to a dark creepy warehouse late at night."

"It's dark and creepy?"

"A bit." He looked up at me from under his baseball cap— even in the dark lot, the eye contact was striking—and smiled softly. He had a very kind face. "All I mean is I get it's weird to go to a warehouse with a guy you just met. At this hour." He unlocked the truck, and the headlights flared. "But hey. I've got a sister."

It was a real shop. One of the units in a warehouse at the very end of Cesar Chavez, just across from Guerrero Park. I hadn't been that far east in the city before. He and his friend had started the company on their own. I could tell he was genuinely proud of it because when I asked him questions, he got shy, breaking eye contact to answer. He told me they were doing jobs like the one at Marq Uptown that made people think they were bigger than they were. He showed me the table saws and the credenza with the wenge veneer and the restored canoe—a passion project—and the cabinets they were in the middle of making. "Just rectangles at this point really."

I asked him about the huge slice of tree leaning against the wall, all its marvelous whorls. "How does that turn into that?" I asked. Looking at it, I tingled in the same way I would if it were a taxidermized animal. Even a real animal. I felt the way I felt the first time I saw a male lion stand on a rock at Franklin Park Zoo and roar.

"I can't read you," said Liam eventually.

A table saw was between us.

"What do you mean?"

"I'm trying to figure you out."

"Ask me more questions about myself, then."

"Can I kiss you?"

"Sure," I said.

He came around the table saw and put one hand carefully on my hip bone, then his other hand on my other hip, taking his time. I realized he was very secure, and for a moment I felt like I was about to disappear. Gently he pulled me toward him by my hips, used one hand to swivel his cap around, then moved both hands to the sides of my face and tilted up my chin. He kissed me deeply. Then he pulled away and threaded our fingers together.

"Come on," he said and led me into the office.

"So, this is the office," I commented, my hand in his. I was still feeling weak from the kiss. "Who sits there?"

"Barry." Barry ran the beer tap company that shared the shop.

"And there?"

"Me."

"What about Frank Savilino?" This was the name of Liam's

partner. Liam was sole proprietor, but he and Frank split everything fifty-fifty. Over drinks, Liam had told me he had no plans to ever hire anyone else because he'd never want to pay someone less than he paid himself.

"Frank likes the couch or the bench out front."

Liam was on the couch now. He was looking up at me. Hat still backward.

I sat on the couch too. He turned his head to hold eye contact with me but didn't move his legs. His boots looked huge. I placed a hand on his upper leg and he looked down at it.

"Yeah, I'm pretty attracted to you," he said. "Sorry."

I pressed my hand down on his zipper. He clasped his fingers in mine again and pulled me on top. With me straddling him, his warm hands under my shirt on my lower back, we kissed. I put both my hands on his neck. The back of his neck was hot, sweaty, and a little pimply. Then his lips were on my neck, under my ear. His lips moved from my neck to my collarbone, then to my cheek, then back to my lips. His skin and shirt smelled of lacquer and must, but his deodorant was fresh and tangy, cedar or juniper berry maybe—and I felt a hole open up inside me and then I felt myself get wet. This was so astonishing, I stood up.

"I'm not having sex with you tonight," I announced.

"That's alright," he said. His face was flushed. "You okay?"

"I'm going to go."

"No worries. Can I take you back to your car?"

I shook my head. "I'll walk."

A big pink splotch on his chest was spreading. A few moments were spent just us breathing together, him staring up at me. I had my arms crossed.

"Are you good to drive?" he asked.

"Yes."

—

The next day, I had to call in sick to work. My insides were uneasy, a turbulent sea, and there was nothing I could do to calm down except curl into a ball on the carpet, squeezing my knees to my chest, muzzling the roaring animal that was my stomach. I told myself, It's okay. This will go away. Just don't text him ever again. Don't see him. But by the evening, he had already texted me that he'd like to see me on Wednesday.

So on Wednesday, I had to call in sick again. I went to the Goodwill in Windsor Park and found a pair of faded camo overalls in a bin, which I paired with my dark-green tube top and a pair of bright-white socks, brand-new from CVS, that went halfway up my calves. Even though it was ninety-five degrees out, I walked all the way to the food truck, three miles, looking in every window I passed. In some of the windows, the girl was skinny. In others, she was barely there. She gazed at me helplessly, but I couldn't help her. And besides, behind her, she had so much space. She was standing in front of a cool, black lake. Out here it was so hot the pavement could make a dog's paws bleed. There were millions of guys out there who wanted to fuck me. He was just one of many. Once he understood that, my stomach would surely settle, and I'd be back to normal.

"I want you to fuck me," I decided to say an hour into our date, interrupting him in the middle of complaining about his plastic fork. He was saying, "If I'm going to eat pasta, I want to eat a fuck-ton out of a gigantic bowl. And not with this flimsy shit."

As soon as I said this, he stood up dramatically, without missing a beat, and tossed his paper plate and the rest of his pasta into the bin next to our table. "Well, let's go."

I was surprised. "Should we finish our drinks?"

"Absolutely not." He took my hand off the table and kissed it. "My place or yours?"

When we got to mine, the first thing he did was open the fridge, which was empty except for a container of oat milk and a box of strawberries. Things with expiration dates made me anxious. He said next time, we should go grocery shopping. I was on the couch, as far away from him and the fridge as possible. He walked across the apartment and pulled me up by the hand.

"Do you not like that?" he asked. Somehow, we had ended up on my bed. My legs were dangling over the sides. I was in the middle of hoping the real me had been the skinny one, not the one whose eyeliner made her face look dirty—and I had completely lost track of what he'd been doing. Luckily, he seemed to like being in charge and hadn't noticed that I was nowhere until the moment my teeth started chattering.

Next thing I knew, he was lying on his side next to me in bed, propped up on his elbow, shirtless with his chin in his hand, observing me softly. The fact that he had stopped what he was doing—right in the middle of doing it—was terrifying.

"No, I do," I corrected. My chattering teeth made it hard to speak. One of his hands was holding one of mine.

"Only if you like it," he said. He squeezed my hand. "Talk to me. What do you like?"

"I like that," I said, horrified by his question. More forcefully, I commanded, "Keep doing that," and gestured down at myself. I felt frustrated. I didn't want to keep talking.

He let go of my hand and pushed some hair out of my face. He told me that I kept squirming away, and he didn't want to do something that I didn't like. I explained that I just didn't want him anywhere too hard to reach, where I couldn't tell what he was going to do next. I didn't want him doing anything weird. He said he didn't want to be doing anything weird either.

"What do you like?" he asked again.

I hated that question. He was ruining everything by talking so much. "Actually," I said. Time was up. "Let's not have sex tonight." It seemed like a smart way to get the power back and keep him on his toes. Make him want me, then pull away. "I barely know you."

"Want to just hang out?" he said. "And talk? Or do you want me to go?"

"Actually, no," I said, getting back on top of him. "Let's fuck."

He studied me. A staring contest. He was so good at not blinking.

"How 'bout we just hang out," he said, even though his hands were holding my hips.

I rolled onto my back again, dizzy. The ceiling kept coming close to my face, then backing up.

"Hey. Do you want me to go?" he asked, from a million miles away. "I can head out. Whatever you want."

But I didn't want him to go. That was exactly the opposite of what I wanted. I realized my teeth had started chattering again. A window rattled and I bolted up. Who was there?

"You're alright," said Liam. "I think it was just a truck."

A very pale face was looking in at us through the black window, making direct eye contact with me—but it was just mine.

"Lucy?" he said again. "You okay?"

I got back on top of him and put him inside me and didn't get off until he finished and it was over. Then, I rolled onto my back again and said, "I'm really, really dehydrated."

Soon he was clinking a tall glass of ice water down on the nightstand. It was so hot in the room, but my insides were so cold, it was hard to consider drinking ice water. I didn't know what to do—everything was all mixed up. Was I hot or cold? My body had once more been taken over by little shivers. I was trembling uncontrollably.

"Oh no," he said. "Oh no. You okay? Come here." He was back on the bed and pulling me into him. I tried to push him off, but he wouldn't let me. He pressed my cheek onto his chest, and I gave in. His chest was warm and sweaty and spotted with pink. I was saying sorry a lot. "It's okay," he said. "Shh." He locked his arms around me. I felt tiny nestled into him like that.

"You want me to go?" He was talking very quietly into the top of my head. I was worried my hair was getting in his mouth. "It's really okay. Hey." I was gripping one of his arms with both my hands. I told him no, I wanted him to stay in bed with me. But saying that made me feel so embarrassed, I started to cry immediately. Still, he wouldn't let go. He held me the whole time. He held me even as we started falling asleep. We fell asleep like that.

Liam knew the city better than anyone. He had biked to the top of every single parking deck north of Ben White and south of Koenig. I told him I wanted to do that too, but he said he wanted to show me only his top five. For that date, he had fixed up one of his bikes to fit me and had mapped out our route in advance. He wanted us to make it to the Tillery Street deck in time for sunset. He said the sky above the city gets extraordinary in Texas, light and color like I'd never seen.

He knew all the secrets. He had only ever lived in Ohio

and Texas but said he preferred re-exploring places he'd already been and discovering more about them, rather than traveling to new places he knew nothing about. He didn't like when people went places, then left them without ever knowing anything about them. On another date, he told me that he wanted to show me something. So we got into his truck and drove around for a little while until he stopped right in the middle of a quiet street—Avenue B—in the most historic part of Hyde Park. "This," he announced, "is the widest street in all of Austin." He said the narrowest street was nearby too and he'd take me there next, but first he wanted to stay parked. Avenue B was so wide, any cars driving down could just go around us. That's how wide it was on both sides. We stayed parked there in the middle of the street for a while, hoping some cars would come just so we could see.

I liked him so much. Every time I left him, I was worried I'd never see him again, so every day became about defeating a debilitating vertigo. I kept having to miss work to spend more time on the floor. The carpet stopped cutting it, so I moved to the bathroom, pressing my cheek against the cold tiles, listening to the pipes coursing through the building; the walls and floors full of water, the flush of toilets in the apartments above crashing down around me, showers turning on, pipes squeaking. The tiles rehydrated me; they became the place I felt most like myself. When I wasn't with Liam, or on the bathroom floor, I moved about the world feeling weak, on the brink of passing out. But on the floor, I felt my skin darkening. I felt like I could suck up water out of anything. I'd become restored. I had deep, important visions down there. I uncovered truths—the point of life, for example, was to suck up as much as possible while you still could. Other times, though, the point felt less about becoming the lizard, drawing up water through its feet, and more about being the droplet of water itself, on a bright-green leaf.

We had sex only at the end of the day, and only in bed. Even if we started kissing on the couch, he'd pick me up and bring me to bed. He picked me up very easily. If there wasn't a bed around, we wouldn't have sex. When we had sex, I didn't feel like myself at all, and the next morning I was always certain he'd never text again. But he always did. We saw each other every few days, sometimes two days in a row. I began spending most nights with him, speeding down I-35 to get to his tiny, cozy apartment as fast as possible, then sinking into him. The rare days he didn't text, I would drive up and down the highway, just in case there was enough time left in the night that he still might want to see me.

Before my discovery about his furniture, what stunned me about Liam's apartment was all the stuff. It was full of things that he'd accumulated—camping gear under the kitchen sink, a tackle box above the fridge. In the credenza was a chessboard and several decks of cards and an original Scrabble board. He had a bookshelf full of dusty paperbacks and a drawer of batteries and loose screws. Everything in his tiny space was stored in its rightful place. He had Band-Aids in the bathroom, and witch hazel for mosquito bites. He had a medicine cabinet with five-year-old hydrocortisone cream from that time he got poison oak, and Pepto-Bismol from when an ex-girlfriend had food poisoning. A bowl of half-empty lighters, and tons of pens, and coins from when the laundry machine took only quarters. He had drain cleaner and Clorox wipes and a Swiffer, and a cabinet of important files, like his passport (expired) and the title to his truck. He had a crate in the closet with Ping-Pong balls and tennis rackets and a wiffle ball set. He had spices and sauces. A compost bin that he kept in the freezer. A wall of pothos with long tails—he'd taken care of them for years—that hung at varying heights from rope.

After being in Liam's, my apartment became unbearable— everything mundane, silver and black and beige. It contained nothing that was mine, save the beanbag chair. I didn't want to be there anymore. I wanted to move into Liam's. Work became a torture. Presenting myself to new people every day was exhausting. I dreaded showing off the dark common rooms no one used—the billiards room, the room with the printers, the coworking space. The smell of all those rooms was so thick and perfumed, and the furniture looked luxurious only at first but was in fact cheap—the tables and lamps and chairs weighed nothing. I started warning future residents on my tours, "Don't look at anything too closely. Don't pick anything up." My tights and stockings and pencil skirt made me feel like a little kid pretending to be fancy in a building that was fake. Liam's building, on the other hand, was made of brick.

"All this shit comes from years of accumulating stuff I don't need," Liam reassured me when I complained about my apartment being barren. He reminded me, "I've lived in this apartment for six years." He'd been in Austin even longer— nearly a decade.

He and his friend Grant had moved together at twenty-two after college, picking the city on a whim. They had since built a large group of friends who all hung out at the same bars all the time. All you needed to be a successful bar in Austin, according to Liam, was a patio, picnic tables, and shade. Liam's Austin was

full of friendly faces and backyard barbecues. We ran into people on the street. People waved to us in the grocery store—his
old roommates, his friends' ex-boyfriends and ex-girlfriends,
people he knew from Frank's sandlot baseball team, guys he
fished with at Mueller, contractors he'd worked with on various job sites. I tried to make the other leasing associates seem
more like my real friends, sometimes turning down plans with
Liam, or pushing them off till later, to convey that I also had
things to do on a Friday night. I understood I needed more
of a life, but I couldn't figure out who I was supposed to be.
I asked Liam to point out his ex-girlfriends, but he wouldn't.
He didn't like to dwell on the past. I was worried there was a
different type of woman that Liam was supposed to be with.
Sometimes things I thought we had in common turned out
to be not in common—after I learned he chewed Nicorette
on site, I felt relieved and smoked a cigarette in front of him,
but he was displeased. He didn't like cigarettes. He hadn't ever
been a smoker; the Nicorette was just a weird habit he'd picked
up from his old boss who used to keep boxes of it in the office.
There was a cute barista with bangs and tattoos who worked
at the coffee shop next door to Marq Uptown, who listened to
the same music Liam did. When it was her shift, she put on
the songs I had never heard before Liam but had now started
listening to over and over. I was pretty sure I was supposed to
be more like her.

Three months in, I realized I didn't want to have sex with
anyone other than Liam ever again. Because of this, I decided
it was best to end things.

"We have fundamental incompatibilities," I let him know.
He had said so himself on our very first date—we had no

common ground. I didn't know about music. I didn't watch movies. I tried to remind him of these things.

He was in the middle of cooking us an elaborate Bolognese. He patted his hands dry on the dish towel and looked at me. I was sitting on his couch, trying to be as calm and serious and emotionless as possible. Both my arms and legs were crossed, which helped.

"You're talking as if there's some mutual understanding between us that this isn't going to work out," he said. "But I don't agree. I think we're having a great time and should see where this goes."

I had to consider this.

He dumped the pasta into a strainer and steam billowed up out of the sink. He put a piece of pasta in his mouth. "Obviously, you can break up with me if that's what you want to do, but just know that that's not what I want."

I wasn't expecting him to say any of that. I thought he was going to agree with me fully, and the fact that he didn't agree shattered me—I felt so relieved. I shook my head back and forth, staring at my feet and a tangle of hair that looked like mine on the rug.

Even though I was in the middle of breaking up with him, he came over to the couch when I started crying and pulled me onto his lap. He could never stay away from me when I was in distress. I could even say mean things and instead of being mean back, he'd hug me and ask, "Where'd that come from? What does that mean?"

"I feel like you want something else."

"Nope," he said into my neck. "I just want to keep spending time with you."

—

Marq Uptown fired me in the middle of July and said I had until August to move out of my apartment. Liam made space for some of my boxes under his bed and said I could keep my beanbag chair at the shop. But I didn't want to just move in temporarily; I wanted to move in for good. Living together would solve all our problems—I wouldn't have to spend the day stressing out anymore about whether I was going to see him later.

"That's not good," he said, about my stressing out. "We should work on fixing that first."

I took a different tactic: I accused him of being stuck and never wanting to change or grow up or move forward or take risks, but he interrupted all of this and said he just didn't think we were ready yet. We'd been seeing each other only six months and he reminded me how mere weeks ago I had tried to break up with him.

"But that wasn't real," I said. I hadn't actually wanted to break up.

He said, "I think we should move in when we're both feeling really good about it."

Liam was only thirty-one. I was only twenty-five. But on the way home from the swimming hole the day of the break-in, I remember us driving by a large ranch house and Liam pointing it out and saying that he loved that house, that it was the house he'd buy in another life.

"What does that mean?"

"You know what it means." But Liam was only thirty-one. I was only twenty-five.

"Maybe we can buy it one day."

"Maybe you want more than I do."

"But you just said you wanted that house," I reminded him. "Oh, don't listen to me."

When we got back downtown, Liam dropped me off at his first, so I could take my car to H-E-B while he went to his shop for the plywood. By the time I returned, he'd already completed the window task. Blue tape framed it on the outside. He'd done a neat, clean job.

Inside the TV was on. Liam got up from the couch to help me put away the groceries. He was drinking beer and had already made me a negroni with a big ice cube and orange peel in it.

"So," Liam said, after I collapsed on the couch, in my favorite spot under his Grandma Betty's antique lamp. He clicked on the rice cooker, then rested a forearm down on the counter. He took a sip of beer. "I did find out some things about our friends over there."

It was so thrilling that he was bringing it up all on his own, without my needing to pry, that I hopped off the couch. I gripped his forearm with both my hands and leaned back, probably looking like an eager, stretching cat. Then I stood up, calmed down, and took a sip of his beer.

Liam, his eyes crinkly and bright, continued: "After I fixed the window, Greasy Liam took me outside. He wanted to give it to me straight, man-to-man." Liam said "man-to-man" with a lot of irony. "He offered up the whole story all on his own."

I got such a kick out of Liam calling Shaggy Liam Greasy Liam. We had started to think about so many things in the exact same way.

It turned out that Anna and Greasy Liam broke up last year when she left for Mexico. Now she was back in Austin, but

Greasy Liam had a new girlfriend named Ruby. Anna didn't have any place to stay and was struggling. Floating around, she started hanging out with the neon-green guy—"So it was a love triangle," I cut in. I needed credit for being right about everything—but the neon-green guy was crazy abusive, Liam explained, and things went south fast.

"What does that mean?"

"I don't know, but when Greasy Liam said it, he did this," and my Liam put both his hands on his throat to simulate the way that Greasy Liam had acted out getting choked.

"It was a love triangle," I repeated, again for some credit. "I bet the neon-green guy keyed the car and the car is Anna's. Or Ruby did it. But that car is definitely Anna's. I've seen her get out of that car before. I've seen both Anna *and* the neon-green guy get out of that car before."

"I feel so bad for her," I added about Anna, after drinking some more of Liam's beer. "Where's the neon-green guy now? They didn't get him, right? He's still out there."

"No, he's in jail."

"Really?"

"Yeah, but just for tonight."

"That's not long enough for Anna. He's still out to get her."

"Lucy, stop. We don't want to get involved."

"I know. I just feel bad for her." I took his beer with me to the couch. "I wish we could do something to help."

"Darling," said Liam. "That over there, we don't want to be around that."

"It must be so scary for her."

"It's not our problem."

"How can I be with someone who won't talk to me about stuff?"

He stopped chopping the tomatoes then and cocked his

head at me in that way that meant he had to pause and reevaluate. "Wait," he said, a little amused. "What's this about?"

He set the knife down on the cutting board and came over to the couch. He sat next to me and took back the beer I'd taken from him, then placed a firm hand on my knee.

"What's going on?" he said.

"Tie game," said one of the announcers on the TV. "Nineteens. A lucky hand for this Vegas matchup."

"Sometimes I just feel like it's up to you all the time," I said. He didn't get it.

"That's just what I feel like," I clarified.

"Okay," he said. "I'm sorry I don't care about my neighbors as much as you do."

"But you think there's something wrong with me that I do."

"I came and got you out of the truck because I knew you'd be interested to see what was going on," he said, incredulously. "I thought, Lucy will want to see this."

I considered this. Then I added reasonably, "I guess sometimes I feel like you don't know anything about me."

"Well, let's see." Liam hated tests. "I know that you have a pattern of getting pretty existential during periods of transition." I had said these exact words to him last week. He was probably referring to the upcoming move. He squinted at me, trying to figure out what else I needed. I was curious too—I wasn't that sure myself.

"Sometimes I feel like you don't think I'm a capable person."

"I think you're very capable."

"But you think you're more capable. You don't think I can change a tire, for example."

"Can you?"

I couldn't. It was a bad example.

He thought this was funny and laughed, thinking we were

now having a good time with each other. He put his arm around me. In a squishy voice, he said, "I can teach you."

"No. I don't want you to teach me anything ever again. I hate that dynamic."

My suddenly venomous voice made him let go.

"What's going on?" He looked annoyed.

I took a deep breath and apologized. I didn't know why I had been so mean. I tried to explain how I knew all about his dream to buy a ranch house, but he didn't know about any of my dreams. He clarified again that he didn't actually want that ranch house. He wanted only the things he already had.

"All I want is you, darling," he said, to prove the point. "Okay? And I'll work on asking you more questions. I can see that's something I need to work on." I think he was being a little insincere. Liam hated talking in circles. At least he was good at pulling us out of them. He kissed my forehead, then left the couch to finish making the pasta.

Every night, before falling asleep, I tried to will myself out of making any nighttime noises. Apparently, I smacked my lips randomly, at ungodly hours, which sounded like I was aggressively eating something. Liam let me know about this by tapping me awake once at 3:00 a.m. to ask if I was chewing gum.

The next day, I called my sister to fact-check this. "Oh yeah, this noise?" Patty said, and she mimicked a loud bovine smacking sound through the phone. "Yeah, you sound like you're possessed. You've always done that."

So I had to spend a great deal of energy trying to force myself out of making these noises that woke Liam up. I was horrified, worried he might leave me over it. Men hated anything that disturbed their sleep.

Still it was strange that my nighttime noises were something Liam cared enough about to mention, which weren't in my control no matter how hard I tried, but another time, early on, when I apologized to him about the stubble on my bikini line, worried it was scratching him during sex, he got angry and said, "You're kidding, right?"

I'd had to push off my wax last-minute because money had been tight around my next paycheck. But the hair growth had really started stressing me out, and for several nights, I'd been mustering up the courage to apologize to him about it before he had to bring it up himself.

But his response completely threw me off. He had pulled down his pants. "You see all this hair? Does that scratch you?" He looked legitimately upset, but not at me.

"No," I answered.

"What made you think that you're scratching me, then? What gave you that idea?"

I held it together till he was sound asleep, but then I couldn't keep from sobbing. A full body grief had possessed me out of nowhere. Snot poured from all my orifices. It felt like I was birthing something viscous and monstrous out of my mouth. For some reason, Liam's response had released a sea creature from within me. But luckily, he was fast asleep, not witnessing it.

Every morning, around three thirty or four, I woke up to step outside and smoke several cigarettes while he was still asleep. Then I'd shower and slip back into bed with him.

Out on the patio, I liked to inspect the night—mostly the cranes extending their necks of huge red lights up to the sky. Sometimes I'd walk to get coffee at the Starbucks, which was open early, and take inventory of all the half-built buildings, wondering if they'd outlast me.

The morning after Shaggy's window got shattered, when I stepped outside to smoke, I made believe I was the apartment complex patrol, on the lookout for Neon-Green Guy, in case they'd prematurely let him out of jail. I pictured him appearing in between the dumpsters. Then what would I do? His tall, slender green figure abruptly showing up in front of me, the streetlights making him literally glow in the night. I waited for a while, smoking my cigarettes, in case he appeared, but he didn't.

The plywood in the window was haloed with light. For a while, I faced the apartments smoking my cigarettes, leaning against the gate, mesmerized by the glowing sides of the plywood, without realizing that the glowing sides indicated that Liam's next-door neighbors were also awake. They were probably on high alert like me, in case the neon-green guy returned, or maybe they were just early birds, also like me. They were in there, though, that was for sure, in their apartment that was likely shaped like a U just like my Liam's.

I decided to knock on their door and check in. We were all awake, after all.

Shaggy Liam came to the door, wide-eyed, in boxers, on patrol too, just as I'd suspected. He was relieved it was only me.

"Oh hey. What's going on?" he said.

"Just checking in," I said. "Making sure the plywood's all good."

"Oh wow. Yeah. It's so late," said Shaggy. But he opened the door and let me inside. On the couch was Anna, with bright-red eyes and those spectacular nails, still holding her vape.

The apartment was indeed the same shape as my Liam's. But there was garbage everywhere. Bags of chips, e-cigarette wrappers, clothes on the floor, unwashed dishes. Nothing built-in. There wasn't even any furniture besides a mattress and a saggy loveseat.

"Where's Rosa?" I asked. Then, realizing this probably sounded weird, and also judging by Anna's face, I added, "Sorry, my Liam told me about Rosa."

"Ruby," Shaggy corrected. He didn't seem to care that I knew all about him.

I sat down on the couch with Anna. Shaggy apologized if the cushions were wet and passed me a pink beach towel to sit on. Then he asked if I wanted a beer.

"At this hour?" I said.

"Oh yeah. I guess it's pretty late. We've been up all night."

"What have you been doing?"

"Just watching movies."

Once all of us were sitting on the loveseat, Shaggy unpaused the horror movie they were watching about witches in New Hampshire. I was so relieved to be sitting in between Shaggy and Anna, the three of us squished in as if we already knew each other well, as if we had all been through so much together. Because the loveseat was sagging in the middle, each of my knees were touching one of theirs. Pretty soon, though, I realized that none of us actually had a lot to say to each other—but maybe that was just because we were watching a movie. Then I realized I wasn't so interested in these people at all, but here I was sitting with them. I felt a lot of gratitude gust through me then for Liam and for where I was in my life. It was a dazzling, deadly feeling. It was cause for celebration. I had a job and I was in love with a kind, talented man. We were trying our best to have a life together. One day, we'd buy a house, maybe in Wimberley, maybe that ranch. Inside, I'd have my own desk, built by him, where I could read in the morning, and drink tea, and gaze out at birds. Two little girls would one day press against Liam's chest as he read picture books to them in bed. I could waste days thinking this way. I could sit on this stained a-little-bit-wet couch in Shaggy Liam's apartment forever, drinking his weird beer, planning out all the meaningful lives Liam and I were going to have, asking Anna if I could hit her kiwi vape again, just feeling grateful, my Liam breathing close by, just on the other side of the wall.

I left their apartment around six, just as the sun was coming up. Stepping outside, I was shocked to see two deer, sleeping together in front of the yellow house across the street. Does. One rested on top of the other, their bodies breathing together like lovers, the sun glossing over their tired, velvet muscles, filling in the creases. I had never seen deer sleeping together like that before, and right in the middle of Austin! Then I realized that they weren't breathing. They were dead. Then I realized that they were just two rolled-up rugs that someone had dumped out on the curb.

THE KIDS' ROOM

THE DIRT ROAD THAT CONNECTED THEIR LAKE HOUSE
to I-140 was closed that weekend because a hurricane had
somehow made its way into Tennessee. So, the cab dropped
us off at the marina and Liam's father picked us up in their
Boston Whaler. Tom Davies Sr. was old, with bright-white
hair and boat shoes and orange wraparound sunglasses. He
was also the tallest old man I'd ever seen, though when I
described him as "tall" to Liam later, Liam looked confused,
claiming his dad was only five eleven.

On the whaler, Tom Sr. got us up to speed on the setup.
Liam and his dad seemed most at ease together when talking
about logistics. Tom Sr. told us that we were going to be in
"the Kids' Room," Claire and her family would be in the
treehouse—they weren't arriving until the afternoon—and
Tommy's family was in "the Babysitter's Room."

"What babysitter?" I asked over the motor.

"We had a billion," said Liam.

"Liam, get down," said his dad as we pulled into the boat-house. "You're in my view." Liam squatted down; he had a line in his hand and was trying to help tie up the boat.

"Jesus, son. You stand up right as I'm pulling in."

Liam didn't say anything, just finished looping the line around the cleat.

At 2:00 p.m., Liam's father took the pontoon boat to pick up Claire and her husband and their four-year-old son from the marina. A half hour later, they arrived at the dock. Liam was floating out on a bundle of pool noodles, distracted by his six-year-old nephew, who'd been hanging on to his arm and chatting nonstop, both of them in goggles. I was sitting on the dock with Liam's mom, both of us drinking Aperol spritzes.

Taking my cue from Liam's mom, who had stood from the Adirondack chair as soon as they pulled up to the dock, I took my spritz over to where they were getting out of the boat. Claire looked up from where she was looping the line around the cleat to greet me. She was as skinny as Patty and just as perfectly pale, except that Claire had striking long blond hair. Red toenails, gold flip-flops. Her husband lifted the boy by the armpits out of the bow and placed him on the dock. The boy was holding the shoulder straps of a blue life vest that was slightly too big. Liam's mom gave the boy a big hug, his life vest squishing, then she kissed him on the top of his head.

"Can you say hi to Lucy?" Claire asked her son as she took another bag from her husband, who was unloading things from the stern.

But the boy just hung his head, held his life vest, and stared at his feet.

"Hi, Wyatt," I said. Then I tried to give him a hug just as Liam's mom had. But Wyatt backed away from me right as I approached. I tried harder, hoping that Claire and Alaine hadn't seen him squirm away, but on my second attempt, as I was leaning down to also kiss his head, Wyatt shrieked "Ow, ow" and shrank away from me, running for his mother's legs.

Claire put a hand on her son's head, and then said, in front of everyone, "In our family, we like to ask before hugging." She was talking to me. Then she said to her son, "Wyatt, honey? Are you hurt?" Wyatt nodded and held out his arm.

"Can I give it a kiss?" asked Claire. Wyatt nodded again, and Claire took his little wrist in her hand, bent down, and made a kissing sound but didn't actually touch her lips to his arm. Then she sang out, "All better!" Standing up, she looked at me and said in the same singsong voice, "When did you guys get in?"

The hugging incident made it clear that there was something wrong with me. And unfortunately, everyone in Liam's family—besides Liam, who had not seen since he was out on the noodles—knew it now too. For the rest of the afternoon, I sat in the Adirondacks, next to Liam's mom, on high alert. I needed to make sure that Claire wasn't ever alone with Liam, or she might tell him about the hug. Luckily, Liam had gotten caught in an endless round of cannonballs with Griffin, who kept bouncing around, saying, "Do it again, Uncle Em, do it again!" It didn't seem like Griffin was anywhere close to stopping. Wyatt was in water wings by the ladder, with his dad (Scott), who was teaching him how to kick. Tommy Jr. and Liam's father (Tom Sr.) were hitting golf balls off the end of the dock. Claire had sat down in an Adirondack next to me and Liam's mom. She was in the middle of tallying up everything that was wrong with the house. Liam's sister-in-law (Tommy's wife), Janet, was either chiming in from where she was supervising her daughter collecting pinecones on the path, or interrupting everybody to yell, "Griffin, Griffin, Griffin, get off that part of the dock. Tommy, get Griffin off that part of the dock." That part of the dock was rotting. Several boards had big holes.

We were all down at the dock till dinnertime. I wanted to get in the water—it probably seemed weird that I hadn't yet, and I wanted to show Liam what an excellent swimmer I was. The lake was calm in a way that seemed fake, and Alaine liked telling me about how the water had once been potable, back when Liam was a baby boy. But it was only a matter of time before Claire would tell Liam about me, and I couldn't risk letting my guard down.

But then: Alaine asked me if I wanted to come up with her to the house to help make a cheese plate. I couldn't say no—this was Liam's mom, and I already loved her. Upon our arrival, she had immediately pulled a bottle of prosecco out of the fridge because Liam had told her I liked Aperol spritzes. She had also tugged both of us into the downstairs bathroom to show off her new sink and point out the brand-new razor and toothbrush that she had set out for me in case I had forgotten any essentials. When Claire had been complaining about the mildewy towels and daddy longlegs problem, Liam's mom hadn't said a word even though I could tell she thought the house could use some light improvements too, though I deduced that only because of the new sink.

So, I went up with her to assemble the cheese board, trying to do it quickly even though Liam's mom moved slowly because of bad knees. I pulled the charcuterie out of the fridge, arranged the apricots and raisins and nuts, even added the chocolate truffles that Alaine had suggested—I'd had to pull out the stepladder to reach the top shelf of the pantry. We were making fine time—and it was entirely possible that Liam was still doing cannonballs—but unfortunately Alaine's knees made it take us a while to get down the path, which was full of rocks and roots. I held the cheese plate as she gripped the railing, focusing on every step.

Back at the dock, Liam and Griffin were out of the water. At first, Claire was nowhere to be seen. Liam was wrapping a towel around Griffin, patting him dry in a way that made Griffin giggle. Liam picked up his nephew and then started swinging him back and forth, Griffin wriggling and giggling and squealing as Liam pretended to toss him into the water.

"Careful with him, Liam," said Claire, but she was smiling. She was in the lake with her hair down, treading water.

Liam's father was done hosing down the pontoon boat, which he'd moved to the other dock, and now he looked up at Liam and Griffin and said, "Hey. Time to wind down." Liam's father hadn't taken off his orange sunglasses once since Liam and I had arrived.

At dinnertime, when everyone was in the kitchen, it was chaos. Liam wasn't looking at me or speaking to me at all, but also there were a ton of other things going on: Janet was feeding Goldfish and pieces of peach to Ellie, who was in her pink bib and high chair, her fingers either in her mouth or wrapping around the bangles on Janet's left arm; Claire was pulling chicken nuggets out of the freezer, counting the nuggets under her breath, then looking at the back of the box; Scott was supervising Wyatt, who was playing with trucks on the floor; Liam was pouring vodka in his ears over the sink, his eyes still bright red from all the cannonballs; Alaine was preheating the oven for slice-and-bake cookies; Janet was repeatedly calling Tommy into the kitchen, asking him to either make Griffin a grilled cheese please or take Ellie up to give her a bath, but Tommy kept coming in for only a second and then drifting back out to the TV, where he and his dad were watching a game. Eventually Tommy took Ellie upstairs, then brought her back down so she could show off her footsie onesie that had giraffes on it.

The Kids' Room was a tiny room on the first floor with two twin beds separated by a bedside table. That night, when I entered, Liam was already in his twin bed, reading, glasses on, which was always the last thing he did before turning off the light. He hadn't pushed the beds together and the door was wide open to the living room, where his dad had fallen asleep on the couch while reading, a paperback mystery now splayed on his rising falling chest.

When I went to close the door, Liam said, "I think we should leave it open. No A/C."

I got in bed silently, waiting for him to invite me into his. But he didn't say anything else. He just closed his book, flicked off the light, and rolled over, his back to me.

I stared at the ceiling. The fan was thump-thump-thumping, and Tom's snores kept getting louder. Well that settled it: Claire had told him about the hug. Otherwise, he would've pushed the beds together, and we'd be cuddling and debriefing the day and reveling together in how good everything felt. He would be telling me about what he and Griffin had been talking about

out on the noodles. I also wanted to know if he had caught a fish down at the dock when he threw in a line with Scott after dinner. At the very least, I wanted to know what he thought of his mother's new sink. But the undulation of his back indicated he had fallen asleep.

I tallied up everything else, in case it wasn't just about the hug: For example, I had probably had one spritz too many, and I knew I asked too many questions. I was also probably hogging his mother by sitting with her all day. And then, there had been that moment when I was doing dishes. Liam's father came into the kitchen to mumble something to Alaine and then Alaine said to me, after Tom left, "Honey, just be a little gentler setting down the dishes when the babies are sleeping." I had adjusted right away, becoming so careful that it took me twice as long to finish the dishes, which was why Liam had gotten into bed first. He had probably overheard his dad complaining about me. Clearly, I lacked critical instincts about how to be helpful. I should've offered Alaine my arm when we were walking down to the dock, for example. I had noticed later that Liam had given his mom his arm to hold.

Early the next morning, a stampede of little feet thundered through the living room and then we heard Janet's pitchy whisper as she gave them bowls of cereal ("Fosted fakes," said Griffin loudly, "And Wy wants foot loops.") and ushered them outside. Soon after this, Liam was up, doing the things he always did to get ready, buckling his belt, zipping his pants, his glasses clinking down on the bedside table. I hoped that I had imagined everything from the day before and he was going to come over, kiss my cheek, and say that he was just going out to make us coffees, but he didn't. Soon, I heard the low rumbling of his voice speaking to someone in the kitchen, discussing how to get rid of me.

I decided that the best thing I could do was wait until the house was empty, then run down to the dock and dive into the water before anyone had the chance to speak to me. If I was able to go on a long swim, at least to the other side of the lake, I could get myself into a headspace where I wouldn't care about Liam sending me home. After all, I could survive on my own. I was untouchable. Once I got myself into the middle of the lake, no one would even be able to reach me— Liam wasn't a good swimmer at all. That's why he'd needed the noodles.

I changed into my bikini, then sprinted barefoot down to the dock. Liam's father was on the porch crunching on some toast, but I ran right past him, without even saying good morning. That was okay: Tom Sr. wasn't a talker. At the dock, Liam was in the boathouse with his brother. Scott was examining the sunfish. Claire was nowhere to be seen. I dove off the dock into the water, hoping that at least Liam had witnessed my beautiful form, the warm water rushing up right away to embrace me. Without looking back, I swam out, straight into the middle, feeling all their eyes on my back. Out ahead of me on the opposite shore, the sun was selecting just one house, lighting up its entire roof. I decided to swim toward that house. Swim, swim, swim. Breathe. Swim, swim, swim. Breathe. I'd swim for however long it took to find the right headspace.

I could stay out here treading water forever, I realized. It was easy. After all, I had been out in water like this before. I could swim long distances. What makes me different from people, I thought as I continued to tread, is that at my core, I have no fear. Liam had no idea about this—he thought I was more scared of the world than I really was. But remember, I said to myself. You can be anything you want. There are hundreds of other guys out there who'd want to be with you—Liam is one of many. You can have anything you want. You can get everything you've ever wanted. You don't need to be anything. It doesn't matter what they think of you, those people back there on the dock. Most people are too scared to swim out into the middle of the lake like this—but not you. You're not scared of anything. You're not even scared of drowning. You're good underwater. You know how to make tiny adjustments down there to keep still while still breathing, how to exhale slowly until your body becomes just breath descending, all the colors disappearing the deeper you go, you as in you and your body, red first, then yellow, until it is all just blue. It could be nice—breathing would be a lot easier down there. You'd become just one thing, without any interruptions. If this wasn't a lake, I thought to myself, there'd be pink anemones and white sharks beneath me.

I pulled myself onto the dock, using just my arms, no ladder, then ran back to the house, the bottoms of my feet picking up pine needles. They were probably all wondering why I was running, but who cared. When I got out of the shower, no one was in the kitchen, but clearly, some people at some point had gone to get donuts: the box was already empty on the counter, but I needed a snack. Claire's skinniness was making me self-conscious of everything I put in my mouth, so I tried to eat just three Triscuits but ended up eating twenty, then stopped counting.

Suddenly, Liam was in the kitchen. He went to the sink and started washing his hands. Where had he come from? He was in his Sherwin-Williams tank top and smelled the way he did after work. His mother came into the kitchen, too, and said something to Liam about an armoire, something like, "Thanks for your help with the armoire." He was wiping his forehead with one of the handkerchiefs I'd gotten him for Christmas.

"Well, shall we?" I realized Liam was talking to me. It felt like the first thing he'd said to me in days. He dried his hands with the dish towel, then took a ChapStick out of a drawer.

"What are you two up to?" asked Alaine, who was now straightening up a pile of junk mail. Liam's mom was one of those people who was always looking for something to do.

"We're going out on the kayaks," Liam replied, greasing his lips.

We walked down to the dock together in silence. I followed him obediently to the shed and we each dragged a kayak out onto the orange pine needles, then by their noses down the muddy bank, into the water. My kayak was yellow and red, Liam's baby blue. They were flat kayaks, so you sat on top of them, every part of you exposed. They weren't the kind my dad used to have that trapped your legs in.

Liam was kayaking slowly, just a few paddles at a time, then floating, gazing out and around. I lagged only a little. It was like he was taking me out to the middle of the lake to do away with me. It was like following my executioner.

"That one's roofy," he finally said, pointing his paddle at a sparkling mansion.

"Roofy?"

"It's got a lot of roof."

Next, Liam paddled us into an inlet that jutted off from

the main lake. The inlet had smaller boathouses and zero mansions. We kayaked to the end, where the trees met the water.

"Well," he said. "Shall we go in here?"

He wasn't really asking. He started kayaking into the woods, pushing up branches and ducking under them. It was a tiny passage through the pines and poplars that were growing up out of the water. We bumped our kayaks over fallen shrubs, using our paddles to knock back the sticks and ferns, the sunlight slipping away as the foliage thickened, the mosquitoes starting to land on my legs in multiples, until Liam stopped paddling in a small circle of sunlight coming in through the trees, light glossing over the back of his boat. There was just enough space for Liam to push against a birch to turn his kayak around, the noses of our boats touching. He didn't make eye contact with me, just gazed up at the trees. We bobbed there, listening to the gentle knock of our kayaks, the swish of water against their sides, the loud bugs overhead, the birds. Under different circumstances, it might've been romantic.

"There used to be running water coming in over there," said Liam after a lot of quiet. "Or, actually"—he paused— "maybe that was just once, after a rain."

I couldn't figure out what he wanted to do with me in here—far away from everybody and out of the way, deep in the trees, where no one would see us. What was happening? There were two options: he was either trying to fuck me or he was going to break up with me.

"It used to feel more wild because there weren't any houses back here," Liam was saying. He wasn't even looking at me. He was just looking up at the trees. What was he looking at up there? Songbirds? Tree snakes? He was quiet for a long time, the only noise just the rustling of leaves and little critters, then still looking up at the canopy, he said, "I used to think this place was so far away." I didn't say a word—I had no idea what he was after.

"Well," he said after some more silence. "Shall we?" He glanced at me before looking down at his oar, scooching his kayak past mine to head back out the way we came.

What a pointless journey, I wanted to say. Nothing had happened.

Out in the open and despairing again, I decided to kayak really slowly, just to see if he noticed. He was already kayaking slowly, so it was hard to kayak even slower.

"I'm hungry," he called back.

"You can go back," I said.

"I'm not going without you." He laughed. "Come, my darling. Come." I sped up a little, feeling like a dog that you have to constantly walk just to keep it from peeing everywhere.

As we tugged the kayaks up the shore, Claire called out from the dock, where she was reading a magazine, Wyatt on her lap. "Did he show you his secret place?" She was in her big floppy sun hat, a blue cover-up, and aviators.

I shook my head.

"Yes, I did," said Liam, laughing again. "The slough."

But I didn't know what a slough was. I hadn't heard that word before.

"The place where I used to catch tadpoles," he said. Tadpoles?

"Leave them there," commanded Liam's father from the

boathouse, as we started to drag the kayaks back to the shed. "I need to hose them down."

So, we abandoned our kayaks. Liam walked back to the dock to sit in the broken Adirondack next to Claire, and I decided to go up to the house to find Liam's mom. She was my safest bet for the rest of the weekend because she didn't like talking about anything serious. Whenever there was a lull in conversation, Alaine resorted to going over what was next on the docket—what was for lunch, for dinner, for breakfast tomorrow. After covering all the meals, she'd then move on to talking through weekend departure plans, then Thanksgiving plans, then Christmas plans, then next summer's plans, then next fall's plans. She was already talking about Christmas plans as if it were a given I was going to be at Christmas with them that year. I could tell Alaine was a little religious but only because Liam had taken off his gold cross when we arrived in case his mother found it blasphemous. When we got onto the topic of next fall's plan, Alaine told me about her sister, Emily, who lived in Albany, and how her sister didn't do much to take care of their mother in her final days. But Emily had felt guilty about it and had gifted Tom and Alaine with a cruise to anywhere in the world.

"You know the worst is when someone isn't involved and then comes in with all these opinions about this and that," said Alaine. "But with Emily, it wasn't like that. She stayed out of my way and let me make all the decisions about Mother."

"What cruise are you going to go on?" I asked.

Alaine did a big sigh. "Well, Tom will only go if he can fish. So out of the cruises Emily sent, that leaves Scotland and Alaska. And I only want to do one of the ones she suggested."

"Scotland would be beautiful."

"Well, I've already been to Scotland," said Alaine. "I'd

love to go to Greece or Italy. The Mediterranean. I'd like to see that part of the world." Alaine decided we should bring our spritzes outside and get some sun before it set. It was Janet's night to cook, and she was going to do her vodka sauce, and she wanted us to eat down at the dock.

Dinner on the dock came to an abrupt end when Ellie snatched Wyatt's blueberry Nutri-Grain bar right out of his hand and dropped it between the planks into the water. Wyatt watched it fall, then began a full-blown meltdown. Claire leapt up to try and calm him down, but Wyatt screamed, slapping her multiple times and saying, "No, Mom, no, no, no."

Then he bit her arm and held on for at least four full seconds.

That's when Scott came over. He knelt in front of his son and said gently, "Wyatt, let's not bite your mom. We don't do that in this family. Can you say you're sorry?"

"No!" screeched Wyatt.

"At least someone in your family knows the word *no*," said Liam's father softly, staring at his daughter. I watched Claire darken, then shake her head faintly. Tom got on his feet then, picking up Ellie, who had started screaming because Wyatt was screaming. Tom bounced his granddaughter around the dock, Ellie on his hip, singing sailor songs.

Scott, still crouching down in front of Wyatt, finally got his son to stop screaming.

"Mamma. Why is Wyatt sad?" asked Griffin.

"He's sad because he dropped his snack," explained Janet. "Tommy? Can you please take Griffin up to bed?"

"No," shouted Griffin.

"Yep," said Tommy, scooping up Griffin. "Bedtime. Let's go."

Griffin's little chin bounced on his dad's shoulder as they headed up the path. "Uncle Em too," he yelled. "Uncle Em!"

"Liam, you're getting summoned," sang Janet, who was still watching Tom sing to Ellie. They were at the end of the dock now and Tom was pointing out at two Jet Skis. Liam sighed and pushed himself up from the dock. "He's coming, sweetie," yelled Janet. Liam grabbed two of his brother's empty beer cans from the ground before making his way slowly after them. Soon, Tom was heading up the path too. He was going to give his granddaughter a bath.

That left just me, Janet, and Alaine. It got quiet fast, just the boats knocking against the dock. A hundred yards off, two more Jet Skis roared by—or maybe they were the same Jet Skis just coming back.

"Did we tell you about the time Tinkerbell swam all the way to the marina?" Alaine asked. Tinkerbell had been the name of their St. Bernard. "I miss that dog. She was such a good dog." I let Alaine tell me the story again.

After ten minutes, Tommy came back down with a beer for himself and an Ohio State sweatshirt for Janet, in case she was cold. "They're fine," he said to Janet, who was already scolding him for leaving the kids. "Probably shouldn't have left Dad up there with Claire though, huh? World War Three."

"Hush, dear," said Alaine. "They're figuring it out."

"I've been trying to help," said Janet. "She and Scott are way too down the rabbit hole of gentle parenting. She doesn't want any advice. Maybe because I'm younger? But I've only *just* been through it with Griffy. It's a tricky age."

"Come on. Griff didn't do that at three and a half," said Tommy.

"They're doing their best," said Alaine. There was a long pause.

Then, spectacularly, Janet asked me a question: "What about you, Lucy? Any siblings?"

"One sister," I said. "She lives in New York. She does theater. Sort of like comedy."

"So, you get the whole sister thing," said Janet, even though Claire was her sister-in-law and not her sister-sister. "I keep trying with Claire, but she just won't take my advice. She doesn't want to hear it."

"That's cool your sister's a comedian," said Tommy, taking out his phone. "Give me her info. I want to look her up." But thankfully, before I could, Tom Sr. was calling Tommy Jr. to the house and Tommy Jr. was bounding athletically up the path. I didn't like the idea of watching Tommy Jr. watch my sister. I was worried he wasn't going to find her funny.

When Alaine headed up to the house to help with bath time, I decided to get ready for bed. When I came out of the shower, I spotted Liam and Claire sitting together on the porch, just the two of them, talking quietly. Liam was leaning back in the swing, his arms outstretched behind him, gently rocking back and forth, one boot on the ground. Claire sat crisscrossed on the sofa covered in dog hair, clutching a mug. Because I left the door open, the creak of the swing and their soft mutterings kept entering the Kids' Room. They talked for a long time. I left to get a glass of water from the kitchen and on my way back saw Claire buckled over, her head on her knees, her shoulder blades trembling and sticking up out of her back like fins. I thought she was sobbing but when she picked up her head, she was laughing.

It was another hour before Liam came in to get his glasses off the bedside table and his towel off the bedpost. Then without a word to me (even though I was still awake, reading), he left. Twenty minutes later, he came back in, hung up his towel, and got into bed, his skin still pink from the shower and steaming.

At four forty-five, I woke up soaked with sweat. I was so upset at Liam I could barely breathe. All day he hadn't even been man enough to send me home. Every time, he left it up to me to confront things. I was about to shake him awake when a little voice in my head said, "No. Don't do that. Resist that." The little voice was right: Liam hated being ambushed.

But the distance between my body over here in this bed and his body over there in that bed was too prickly. I wanted to swoop down upon him and bite the back of his neck. I wanted to bite his neck and hold it in my teeth forever and shake my head back and forth, and back and forth—

"It's done, it's done," the little voice kept saying to me. "Leave it. Drop it."

I pulled the covers over me and squeezed my eyes shut so I could listen to the little voice better. I needed to keep listening to it and then I'd be able to fall asleep. I had to stay away from Liam and think of nothing else other than what the little voice was saying to me. "It's done, it's done," it kept repeating. I was almost asleep. "It's done," it said. "Just come back. Come back."

But then Liam's father coughed—three, four, five times— completely scaring away the little voice and making me jump.

I heard his big body shift around on the couch. Then, the light in the living room flicked on. His footsteps went up the stairs, and the ceiling above us creaked, creaked, creaked. For a few minutes, the house got totally silent. Then the creaks started again: Tom Sr. was coming back down the stairs. From the kitchen came several clinks.

Luckily, sneaking out of bed was my specialty. Tom was cooking up eggs and bacon and making a pot of coffee.

"Good morning." The microwave said it was five fifteen.

"Early bird, huh," he acknowledged. He poured me a coffee, then brought both his plate and mine out with us to the living room. We sat on the couch together, crunching on our toast.

"Your chessboard is set up incorrectly," I pointed out, just to make conversation. Tom grunted, his mouth full, then he put his plate on his lap and leaned over the table. He switched the rook and the queen, a pawn and another rook. The game that ensued didn't last long. He beat me in four moves.

After he checkmated me, he put his plate full of crumbs on the ground. Then he leaned back on the pillows, with a big sigh, and opened his knees. He removed his silver wristwatch, unbuckled his belt, slid the leather off the clasp, but left the fly be.

"Come," he said, tapping his thigh.

"I can't have this kind of thing happen to me again," I tried to explain, but he put his hands under my armpits, picked me up, and with another grunt, placed me on his lap so I was straddling him. I readjusted my right leg, so my heel wasn't trapped under my butt.

"Nothing's happening to you," he told me.

I had started crying a little bit. He placed his whole calloused hand on my cheek. He wiped my face for me (my tears were making my cheeks itchy, and I tasted sunscreen). The skin on his arms was loose, sun-spotted, and soft.

"My mascara's in my eyes," I said, hoping for a brief pause.

He took my right hand, knotting his fingers with mine, and lifted both our hands up to my face to wipe my cheek again.

Then he said, "Like this. Here. Feel this."

He guided my hand down and pressed. I could feel all the blood bulging up.

"Wait," I said, panic stampeding into me. "Can we hold off for just a second?"

"Feel it," he instructed, pressing my hand down harder.

"Can we talk a little bit more first?" I asked.

"Keep your hand there." He shifted around beneath me, wriggling his hand down so he could cup me between my legs. "What do you want to talk about?" he said, closing his eyes. He let out a long sigh. He put his mouth right up against the side of my face, his white beard scratching my lips. His breath smelled like eggs and the underside of an engine. I wanted to adjust myself but didn't want him to grab me any harder than he already was. He had quite a hold on me down there.

"I'll do this," I reassured him. "I'm just worried about the door." I nodded my head in the direction of the Kids' Room. The door was still wide open and even though we were speaking quietly, Liam could wake up at any moment. I had no idea if he had taken his Benadryl, since we had gotten ready for bed separately. "I don't want to have to explain this to him."

"Don't worry about that," said Tom.

"Can we at least close the door?"

"You stay," he commanded.

He pushed me off him, then walked to the door, holding up the sides of his pants.

"I really can't have something like this happen again," I tried once more, as he was coming back. He pulled me back on top of him. "Something like this has already happened to me."

"That's all fine," said Tom.

"No, but this has already happened," I explained again. The back of my head was bumping against the back of the couch, Tom's body pushing against every part of me, his bones loose under his skin.

"I'm twenty-six," I managed, my throat choked, my chin digging into my collarbone because of the angle of my neck against the wall. "Can you even be raped at twenty-six?"

"You can be whatever you want to be," Tom told me, easing off for a moment, but his voice was also tight, constrained, because of how hard he was focusing. He was huffing and puffing, his skin like a sheet. He had a fast, shallow heartbeat.

"I was the one who got out of bed," I told him. "I chose to come out here." I wanted to make sure we were on the same page about everything, about exactly how this happened.

"Of course you did," he said, his eyes closed.

Out on the porch, I sat on the swing. It was six o'clock and the sun was starting. The only sound around was from one loon. She sounded sad. Suddenly the screen door clacked behind me, and I almost gasped. But it was just Liam. Liam was coming out to the porch, all groggy, rubbing his eyes. I didn't want him to get too close, but he sat down right next to me on the swing.

"Hey." He even put his arm around me. I felt too weak to scooch away. "What are you doing out here? Are you alright?"

I didn't know what to say, so I said, "Why are you being such a dick?"

"What?" Liam removed his arm from my shoulders, surprised. My voice had come out loud. At first, he looked dumbstruck. Then, bemused. He put a hand on my knee. I stared at his big hand, feeling his eyes on my cheek.

"What's that, darling?" He sounded like he was about to laugh.

"Do you not want me here?" Asking this made me tear up.

"Are you kidding?" He squeezed my knee. That made me cry harder. "I love that you're here." He was baffled. "We're only here because I've been dying for my family to meet you."

"But now you think I don't fit in with your family."

"What?" He started stumbling over his words probably because of how hard I was crying. "You fit in perfectly. Everyone loves you."

"Well, you're being a dick," I said again, too loudly. Also, this time, it came out even meaner and he looked like he'd been shot.

"Hey," he said. He took his hand off my knee. "Don't talk to me like that. We're with my family." He glanced back at the door. "I don't like being called names."

I stared at our four feet.

"Help me understand," he was saying. "I'm not sure what I did wrong."

"You didn't talk to me at all on the kayaks."

But unfortunately, I was now having one of those moments where I had no idea what was real, and I was without access to any of the tools I needed to figure it out. It was now becoming possible that I had singlehandedly ruined our second day at the lake by being anxious when everything had been fine.

"I thought we were having a nice time," said Liam. He sounded hurt. "Did you not have a nice time? It was so nice just being out on the water with you." Then, in a lower voice, he added, "This house can get so crazy with all the kids."

"Why didn't you push the beds together?" I hiccupped.

"Oh." He was at a loss. "I haven't . . . I get hot, so . . . I don't know." He rubbed his forehead. "I'm sorry. I've really been over here thinking we've been having a nice time."

Down at the dock, a boat started—their Boston Whaler. We watched it pull out of the boathouse and roar away, its fluffy white tail disappearing behind an island.

"I don't like that," said Liam.

"What?"

"I don't like when you and I have totally different experiences of the same thing." He was still rubbing his forehead. "That makes me feel far away from you."

"Oh no," I said. "Oh no, no." I was no longer slipping off the face of the earth. Instead, I was here, just a little panicked. I didn't want to be far away. He needed to know that we weren't actually having different experiences. I told him. I'd tell him a hundred times if I had to. "It was so nice being out on the kayaks with you!"

Liam shushed me again. He pointed up above us. Unfortunately, he was right. I was speaking very loudly. But he needed to know that I understood now.

Then, the boat came back. We could smell the gasoline even from up here. A few moments passed, and then Tom Sr. was walking up the path, wearing his hat and orange sunglasses, holding a box of donuts.

"Morning," he said. This was the real Tom, I realized. He was opening up the box for us. Suddenly, I felt like I was sinking and soaring. I did a big exhale and my whole body rattled with relief. He was extending the open box to us.

"Willow Point?" asked Liam.

"The best," said his dad. Liam took a glazed donut. Tom Sr. bent down to offer one to me—he bent slowly. His knees were not so good. I took a glazed donut too. Tom closed the box. Then he headed inside, the screen door clacking behind him.

It was the best donut I had ever eaten.

"I'm really, really sorry," I finally said to Liam, feeling amazing. "I'm really sorry about calling you a dick." I whispered this last part so no one would hear. I didn't want to call Liam names. "Silence makes me feel lonely, I think," I said, but then I felt embarrassed.

Liam considered this, then said, "I feel like we haven't had any silence in this house."

I shook my head at how right he was, then started trembling because all my anxiety was now disassembling into hiccups and little laughs. I was being ridiculous. Liam pushed away from me to check that I wasn't crying. Then, he started laughing too, but a little nervously.

I pressed my mouth against Liam's shoulder, feeling my body collapse into his. He rocked us back and forth in the swing, holding me. There really was nothing wrong.

"I just want to be a part of your family," I admitted, when I was finally done crying.

He sighed but said, "I want that too." He patted my head with his big hand.

It was a gorgeous morning. Now that the sun was lighting everything up, it felt like Liam and I were the king and queen, gazing out over our flat dazzling kingdom, everything the light was touching. The light fluttering on the surface looked like millions of brilliant fish. Two loons carved a cross into the lake, turning the water to gold. Why would I ever be angry, why ever cry, when I had all of this? It was more than I could have ever imagined. I started telling Liam about the two winter breaks in college when Cole had come home with me, and my family was at its absolute happiest and how even the memory of those winter breaks couldn't compete with how I now felt with Liam's family. Liam's family was so joyful and noisy and full of magnetic energy. In this house, kids were growing up right in front of our eyes.

"Alright," he said, cutting me off. I was probably speaking too loudly again, or he thought I was exaggerating. But I wasn't exaggerating. I was already so excited for Christmas. I had been waiting to have a Christmas tree my whole life. My mother had always forbidden them because of the needles getting on the floor. But now we had all of this and so much more to look forward to if and when we had our own kids. Everything I'd ever wanted was spilling out—

But then Liam interrupted me to say, "I don't want kids," knocking the wind right out of me. For several seconds, I lost the ability to speak.

"What?" I finally said. "Why?"

He shrugged. "I never saw myself with them."

But what about bringing our kids up to the lake? What about our kids being cousins with these kids? What about the Kids' Room?

"I don't really want any part of this," he said.

I had to ask him a few times what he meant until he finally clarified about the lake house: "It's a shitshow. I want to eventually be bought out."

How could he say that when we already had it?

"But what about me?" I asked.

"What do you mean?"

"I want kids." Now I closed my eyes. Oh dear. What were we going to do?

"I don't think we need to do anything," said Liam. "It's a far in the future thing."

"But how can we move in together when we're not on the same page about this?"

Liam laughed. "I don't think we need to figure this out right now."

"When are we going to figure it out?"

"I don't know," said Liam. "Let's talk about it down the line, when it's actually an option for us." He didn't sound stressed at all, but I had no idea what that meant either. "When we're in a position where we can actually have kids," he explained. He meant financially. He said it was hard for him to imagine that we'd ever be in a position to comfortably have kids since our combined income was under six figures.

"Well, I'm going to make us a ton of money," I said. Was that all it was about? "I'll get a tech job. Is it just about money?" Of course, it'd be very hard to get a tech job. Especially considering I was too embarrassed to reach out to any connections from college for help after having not spoken to anyone in years. On LinkedIn, my old friends were always getting promoted for vice president this, senior that. They could have as many kids as they wanted.

"I only want two kids," I reassured him, in case that helped. The sun was insisting on burning a hole in my head. "I'm not even good with kids," I added, but quickly regretted it.

Liam thought we were getting ahead of ourselves. He wanted us to focus on right now since right now was so good.

Behind us, the kids started waking up. Liam said it was going to be a long day for us since we hadn't slept at all. He asked if I wanted to go water-skiing. I hadn't ever water-skied, but I was sure I could do it. He said he bet I could.

"You pick up things very quickly. You're very capable."

Of course, the problem also was: we only ever did what Liam wanted. If that stayed the case, we were going to remain in Texas forever, just the two of us, surrounded by deserts.

Suddenly, big fat tears were rolling down my face. So much for never crying again. Liam leapt into action: "Baby, no. Don't do that." He looked behind us, back at the house, then hugged me tightly again. "We don't need to figure any of this out right now. I believe in us. We'll be okay." He was wiping my face with his thumb. He was laughing a little. He thought I was being ridiculous.

"No, it's not that," I finally clarified, pulling it together. It wasn't about the kids. "I think I'm upset because your mom isn't going on her cruise."

Liam was very confused. I guess he didn't know about the cruise.

I told him. Then I said, "And I want her to go on the cruise that she wants to go on. I don't want her to change it for your dad."

He took this in. Then he said carefully, "I'll take you on as many cruises as you want."

"It's okay," I said. I didn't even like cruises.

"Good," said Liam. "Me neither."

"All I want is for your mom to go on her Mediterranean cruise."

"I'll talk to them about it," he reassured me.

Neither of us said anything for a while. When I looked up at him, his eyes were closed but he wasn't asleep: he was holding me too tightly and his foot on the floor was still rocking us back and forth. What was going on back there?

"Why are your eyes closed?" I asked.

"Hm?" He opened his eyes. "Oh. I don't have my contacts in, and I left my glasses inside." The swing creaked, creaked, creaked. It was funny thinking of Liam on a cruise when he didn't even like to leave Texas. This weekend was the first time we'd ever traveled outside of the state together. But it was nice to think of him going on a cruise for me. From the kitchen came a loud clatter, then a lot of overlapping voices: kids, Janet, Liam's father.

Against my cheek, Liam whispered, "It makes me nervous that one day, I'll still be thinking you want me when you no longer do. And I'll just be that guy who's happy but oblivious."

It was a crazy thing for him to think. I had never loved anyone more than I loved him. "That won't happen," I told him. "I've loved you since the moment I met you."

"That can't be true."

"It is." It sounded cheesy, but it was. "Since the moment I saw you at Marq Uptown."

We were quiet. "I'm very lucky, then," he said.

Maybe the little things we didn't agree on wouldn't matter in the end because of how much we loved each other. But this one mattered, didn't it? At least it was comforting to already know the reason our relationship would end if it ever had to. At least it wouldn't be because we stopped loving each other. It would just be because we wanted different things. That would be heartbreaking. I hoped it wouldn't happen with us. But if it did happen that way, at least I knew it in advance.

That's when I finally understood: I had seen this lake before! That's why everything that had happened that weekend felt like it had already happened. I could picture the lake perfectly, especially the sloughs, but just the way it looked from above—the whole lake at once, not part by part. I'd have to get Liam to show me a map of it later just to confirm. If I closed my eyes, it felt like I knew everything about it. I didn't know when I'd seen it—but I wasn't bothered by that—all I knew was that at some point in the deep past, I'd seen this exact lake. I didn't need to know anything else. And knowing this, without needing to know anything else, felt very important—it felt bigger than me. It felt like God, or something. It felt like God was telling me that the lake represented the source of something, and the sloughs were the offshoots. And I understood what God was saying: God was saying that the problem with Liam was that he was the source of everything, and yet he lived under the mistaken impression that he was a slough.

Later that same year, a month after we moved in together, Liam came with me to attend my mother's Thanksgiving. Thanksgiving that year was just me, my mother, Liam, and Patty. Patty was still back and forth from Boston to New York a lot, and she said Mom was hoping to keep things simple that year. It was Liam's first time ever in New England. Liam taught my mother how to spatchcock a turkey, which he claimed was the only way to cook it without drying out the meat. Liam got into a ball on the kitchen floor, all tucked in, then splayed out his limbs to demonstrate spatchcocking. Then Patty got on the floor, too, because she also had to have a turn demonstrating. On Friday, the day before we were flying back, my mother pulled me aside in her way, holding me captive on the porch after Liam and Patty left to bring in their dessert plates.

Gripping my forearm, she hissed, "You smoke cigarettes."

"No, I don't," I said. Oh no. The sudden change in her affect was piercing.

"Well, Liam smokes."

"He doesn't."

"He does. You can't hide that from me. I know he does."

I had put some things in the laundry that week. It was possible there'd been an old cigarette in the pocket of my pants. I wanted to tell her that the reason I no longer smoked was because Liam had caught me outside one morning, and we had gotten into a big fight about me "hiding things" from him, and that had led me to stop five weeks later, cold turkey, but saying this would of course reveal to her that I had once smoked, which would undo her.

But I took a deep breath and promised her that he didn't.

"Well, he chews Nicorette," she hissed.

"Oh." Whoops. I had asked him to hide the Nicorette thing from my mother, but he had thought that was ridiculous: "We're adults." Still, it was an inconspicuous enough habit, I didn't think she'd notice, unless she went through the trash. "Have you seen the wrappers?"

She shook her head and told me she could tell just by watching Liam chew. "I'm sixty-three years old. I can tell the difference between someone chewing Nicorette and someone chewing bubblegum."

Frankly, I was impressed. And I laughed—I couldn't help it—which actually made her laugh too. Her fingers loosened around my arm, then slid down to my wrist, and then she was holding my hand. I squeezed her fingers back. I told her how the dumb Nicorette thing was just a bad habit he'd picked up from his old boss, and she got these tiny tears in her eyes and said, "I'm just scared, sweetheart. You understand that." And that was it really.

THE HALLS

EVELYN HALL GAVE BIRTH TO HER SECOND SET OF twins the same day her husband fell from their attic window. He'd been removing the storm shutters. Only after the birth did Mrs. Hall find out her husband was dead. She was already at the hospital, accompanied by her own mother, who moved in with her daughter and grandchildren immediately after this tragedy and never left. The Halls were our next-door neighbors. The first set of twins were in my grade, Johnny Junior and Philip. At the time of this tragedy, we were all ten years old. Philip was a quiet, fastidious kid, but Johnny Junior was mean and athletic, always getting into trouble, flanked by two other boys, Jackson Cooper and Jake McCormick. They'd been the gang of *J*s. To simulate real war, Johnny Junior liked to set fire to those tiny green toy soldiers in the middle of our street. He also liked lining up kids at recess if he suspected someone of farting on the playground and he'd go down the line, one by one, smelling each of our butts, to nail down who.

For several years, this was the story: Mr. Hall had decided to remove the storm shutters while Mrs. Hall was at the hospital giving birth, and a terrible ill-fated accident had occurred. Then, at some point when I was still young, it became clear to everyone that Mr. Hall had killed himself. The investigators confirmed it, and it took no time for all the mothers in the neighborhood to embrace this new reality. Suicide made more sense than the story of the storm shutters. One of my clearest memories is of my parents debriefing this latest iteration in quiet voices, as they cleaned up the kitchen together after dinner. Patty and I were watching TV in the other room. I can see it so distinctly: my mother washing her hands at the sink, looking down at Dad as he loaded the dishwasher next to her, and saying fiercely, "It's just so inconsiderate, making someone clean you up." These words haunted me later when Liam's ninety-six-year-old grandmother took advantage of the seconds between the nurse exiting the room to refill her juice and entering again, to hoist her frail body up onto the sill, then launch herself out of the sixteenth-story hospital window. I was deeply disturbed by that, but Liam had said with pride, "No one was letting her go the way she wanted. She'd been begging my mom to pull the plug."

But then the story changed again when, upon Evelyn's request, the investigators reexamined the footprints and discovered that, in fact, their meandering path through the room suggested that John Hall had been pursued. Furthermore, the way he'd fallen onto the driveway, the way his footsteps had backed into the window, indicated that he'd been pushed. My mother and Mrs. Hall were good friends at this point—once a week, she was over for tea. For Mrs. Hall, it'd been a number of stressful years, raising four boys on her own. She had never believed that her husband had killed himself—she didn't know how that rumor had started (I'm almost sure it was my mother)—but she was terrified to think that someone else had killed him. At school, it became vastly accepted lore that the dad had been in trouble with the mob, killed off by none other than Whitey Bulger. The investigation dragged on for years, the Hall boys having to just go about their lives, their dad's killer still out there.

I had been over to the Halls' house only twice growing up, both times before the age of ten. I remember sheepskin rugs in every room, and fluffy white throws draped over the chairs, and, hung above their fireplace, a gigantic bearskin, head and all. To me, their house was a castle in the North Pole—so different from ours, which was the smallest on the block, standing out in the neighborhood, which swelled with McMansions and big shiny renovations built on the bones of historic homes. Ours was the same as it had always been, overcrowded and aging, our kitchen a time capsule. Pinned to the fridge was what seemed like every Christmas card we'd ever received, stacks held together by big magnetic clips that sometimes slid onto the floor due to the weight. Faded lilac wallpaper, spotted with tiny daisies, covered the kitchen walls, and blue masking tape held together the oven handle. In a corner of the kitchen counter, my mother kept two stacks of Day-Timers, twenty years' worth, and referenced them like encyclopedias when recalling things. A toy box in our living room still contained at least a hundred of my animal figurines and all of Patty's Polly Pockets. My mother stored things neatly but still had trouble throwing anything out. She had boxes of old T-shirts that she'd forever been wanting to stitch into blankets. Dad had always loved a project, and usually had multiple going on, like repainting the hallway or installing a new faucet or retiling the bathroom—but his projects nettled my mother, so he had to chip away at them slowly. She hated big changes.

That's why my mother's plan for the two of us that Thanksgiving was so shocking. Upon my arrival, she announced that she wanted us to focus the week around deciding how to renovate the house. Everything was already set up on the kitchen table the morning I arrived: three booklets of graph paper, a variety of highlighters, crayons, two rulers, a pack of unopened pens.

"Just get it all down on paper. No bad ideas. Whatever we want this house to be. Glen helped me get the current dimensions. He wrote them down somewhere." She moved a few papers around until she found the Post-it with Glen's handwriting. Glen was a general contractor in town and an old friend of Dad's. "We're going to gut this place," she continued. "Here. Take a pen. Take this paper. The crayons are for making it pretty." She tried to rip off a piece of graph paper for me but split it in two. She went slower on the next piece. Her hands were shaking.

"I'd like to just tear it all down and start from scratch," she continued, uncapping one of the new pens with a shockingly loud snap. But, she explained, it'd be less of an ordeal to build on top of what we already had. If there were dimensions that I needed that Glen had missed, she said, there was a measuring tape in the drawer.

She had made a list: another bedroom, turn the half bath into a full bath, tear down the wall between the kitchen and the den. Those were her biggest wishes, and all of it needed to fit in the new layouts. She wanted the home to be a comfortable place for all of us to stay, especially for the holidays. "All of us" included a few people who didn't exist yet, such as whomever Patty ended up marrying, and all of the grandkids.

"We've got to gut the walls," said my mother again. She seemed to be really loving the verb *gut*, and I didn't want to admit that I was unclear as to what it signified in this context. "There are still too many mice. I see one at least once a month." Getting rid of the mice had been one of Dad's ongoing projects. He always used humane traps instead of snap traps because, as a kid, I had begged him to. The two of us spent many weekends driving out to the Arnold Arboretum, near where my dad grew up, to release them. We had a theory that the same ones kept coming back to us.

My mother patted the other pack of graph paper. "It would've been great to get Liam's input on this. This booklet is his."

This year, Liam hadn't been able to come. Unlike last year when he and Frank only had residential pieces left come November, this year they had taken on two huge millwork jobs and were at the mercy of vying year-end timelines. Patty also couldn't come because she had just moved back to New York, after having spent several months living at home with Mom. She had agreed to work Thanksgiving in order to take off Christmas. Timing-wise it made sense for her to settle into the city now and be back with our mother at the end of the year, since Liam and I did Christmas in Cincinnati, which was unmissable for us.

"We can FaceTime him later," I said. "He'd love it."

"Will he be all alone tomorrow?"

I shook my head. "He's going over to Grant and Naomi's for Friendsgiving. He only has to work during the day."

"Friendsgiving," repeated my mother. "Well, let's not bother him until we have our final drafts."

Truth be told, I found the whole idea of my mother's project hideous. I was adamantly opposed. But I was also nervous about being alone with her all week, and I didn't want to mess up the energy between us, so I tried to hold back all negativity. That evening, however, when my mother headed out on her exercise walk, I called Patty.

"I don't want to change the house," I said. "Do you?"

Patty encouraged me to go along with it. She said our mother had been talking to her about doing this project with me for weeks. Patty talked to our mother on the phone every day.

"She thought it'd be good to do an activity together rather than spend the week in front of the TV or something," explained Patty.

After we hung up, I thought about calling Liam, but resisted. Instead, I went upstairs and found some of Patty's old nail polish—light bright blue—and painted my toes. The night before I had left, Liam and I had argued about kids again, and the conversation was still sitting in my stomach like a half-dead bird. Trying to get to the bottom of it, I had asked if it was because of climate change, but he had said it was because "when I picture our life together, I picture it just us." When I explained how I just wished he could picture having kids with me, he told me not to worry: "The only future I want is one with you." The problem was, in the future with me, he was reading our kids picture books in bed.

I had to get up at 4:30 a.m. the next morning to catch my flight. I didn't like leaving him in the wake of such a teary conversation, and I also didn't like the idea of being around my mother when such a conversation was still on my mind. It was so much on my mind, in fact, I even considered talking to her about it, but had a feeling her response would make me want to leave him, and I still loved him too much. Anticipating the way my mother would feel if she never got to be a grandmother was so excruciating, the feeling felt too big to belong to just me. Sometimes, I really wasn't sure which feelings inside me were hers and which were mine.

That night, my mother and I ordered pizza and two Caesar salads from Mikey's. Patty and my mother never had any trouble coming up with things to say to each other, and could chat for hours about anything, especially other people. They liked to gossip about my mother's friends, their kids, the parents of Patty's old friends, Patty's old friends, and whomever they were dating. Patty always had an impressive amount of intel to share, I assumed because of social media. I had nothing interesting to offer my mother, but that night, I managed to keep the conversation flowing by asking her about every single mother in town I could remember and every single one of my mother's friends. Sandy, Jordie, Georgia Klein. According to my mother, a lot of these women were choosing to "throw in the towel" now that the kids were out of the house. She believed that Georgia Klein had kicked off the trend when she left Doug, and my mother suspected Sandy would be next. Sandy had been threatening to leave Bobby for years.

During dinner, snow had started bunching up in the windows, so when my mother took the pizza box out to the recycling bin, I decided to build us a fire using the birch logs in the basket. I also filled the tea kettle and spread peanut butter on graham crackers—with some chocolate bits stuck in—to make us little sandwiches for dessert. Unfortunately, the birch logs turned out to be decorative, not burning well, and my mother got upset about the smoke when she came back inside. In silence, she cleared the table and returned to her graph paper as I tried to beat the smoke away, opening up the vent and a window.

When I went to close the window, I saw Mrs. Hall tugging her trash and recycling bins up her snow-dusted driveway. Bundled up and hunched over, her breath swirling in skinny clouds ahead of her, she—for some reason—suddenly looked like an elderly woman. But she was younger than my mother, maybe fifty-five.

"Is Mrs. Hall doing okay?" I asked my mother, breaking the silence.

My mother had her elbows on the table like a little kid, kneeling on her chair, tipping it slightly forward, pressing her forearms down to keep her hands steady as she traced her red pen against the edge of the ruler. You'd think there'd only be so many ways to renovate the house to fit in all the things she wanted, but she seemed to keep coming up with new ways.

Suddenly she lifted up her head to look me straight in the eyes. "Did I tell you the latest? I must have."

I didn't know what "latest" she was referring to, so she went on to say that they had finally figured out what had happened to John Hall. After seventeen years, they had solved the case. Since it was being classified as a murder case, there was no statute of limitations, and my mother told me that at some point in the last couple of years, the detectives had re-examined all the evidence and had determined that although the footprints implied he'd been pursued, there was zero evidence to support that anyone else had been in the attic, or the rest of the house, that day besides Mr. Hall himself. They had thereby concluded that Mr. Hall had only believed there was someone inside the house, even though there hadn't been, and it was this imagined pursuer who'd stalked him through every floor of the entire home, eventually backing him into the attic, where he felt forced to make his final escape.

"He was hallucinating," I clarified. "Was he drunk or high?"

"No, no. They checked for that early on," said my mother. Then she added, "They think schizophrenia. Evelyn found out from John's aunt that he'd had a break in his early twenties."

"Wow," I said. "You think it's one way and it turns out to be another."

"The thing is," said my mother, "John Hall never wanted kids. I'm not saying that's what caused it, but Evelyn pushed and pushed that man into having children. She said it to me herself." My mother shook her head, rolled her eyes, and let out a sharp tsk. Then she capped her marker and said abruptly, "There's something else I want to get your thoughts on." And she stood up and headed upstairs.

After a few moments, she came back down with a stack of colorful construction paper in her hands. At first, I thought, Oh no, another art project. But when she put it on the table in front of me, I saw it was spiral-bound in a booklet, and the first page—a piece of light-pink construction paper—had a kid's handwriting on it. In black were the words "Places Beyond."

"Do you remember this?" asked my mother, flipping the

page. The first page said, "Africa," and had a drawing of a lion and a big sun and a giraffe. Next was "China" and there was a panda bear. Then "India" and a Siberian tiger. "You wrote this in the first grade."

"For school?" I asked.

"No. Just here at home. And you asked me to get it bound for you. So we went to Staples. I thought you might remember. Anyway, I found it upstairs." She sat down at the table and took a deep breath. Then, sitting very rigidly and speaking very seriously, her hands clasped, she said, "I've decided that when your kids and Patty's kids turn thirteen, I'm going to take them anywhere they want to go in the whole world."

There was a long silence.

"They can pick any place," continued my mother, her voice a little trembly. "And I'll take them. What do you think?"

I had a lot of thoughts about this, but didn't want to say anything to hurt my mother's feelings. What would Patty say? It was a little confusing. Our mother had barely ever left the Northeast.

"Do Patty and I get to come?" I decided to ask.

My mother shook her head. "I was thinking of it as just a me and the grandkids thing. Jordie's mother did it with Andy and Miles. Remember that? They went to Costa Rica, and, I think, British Columbia."

"Not really," I said. Silence again. The fire was casting flickers through the whole kitchen, which made everything feel a little agitated. My mother was looking down at her clasped hands, and I realized what I thought were specks of light in her eyes were actually tiny tears.

Quickly, I said, "I think that's really nice, Mom. It's a good idea."

"Well, good," she said. She took a deep breath, opened

her eyes, and pulled a piece of graph paper toward her. "Your dad really wanted to go to South Africa." She uncapped a pen, grabbed a ruler, and started counting out the squares under her breath to draw her next line to scale. The snow was high in the windows now, packing us in. I wanted to tell her that I'd go to South Africa with her.

"Mom," I began.

"Cap that marker, honey," she interrupted sharply, before I could say anything else. "It's drying out." She started gathering up the highlighters and putting them back in their plastic case. Then she said, "Okay," and took in a long audible inhale through her nose, then let out an even longer, dramatic, exhausted sigh. "What? What is it?" She looked tense and unhappy, her jaw fixed. She thought I was preparing to tell her something she didn't want to hear.

For whatever reason, instead of saying what I'd meant to say, I said, "Oh, just that I got pregnant once," surprising myself.

She stopped putting away the markers and froze. Then her hand grabbed my wrist, quick as an insect bite, and said fervently, "Have you two been trying?"

"No," I responded, stunned. "This wasn't recent. This was years ago."

She kept her hand on my wrist, but her grip loosened. She didn't say anything.

"I didn't know I was pregnant," I explained. "It was a total surprise." I suddenly felt a little feverish. What was I doing? It was like I was talking about a life that hadn't existed in her lifetime. A life when I wasn't her daughter. "It came out of me into the toilet."

Her face was unreadable.

"This was years ago." I suddenly had no idea what I was

talking about. "I don't know why I'm saying this. This isn't even what I wanted to talk about." My voice was many distances away from me, over hills. I realized that this thing about the baby and the toilet that for years I thought mattered so much, maybe didn't. I think I had been waiting to tell someone about it, but maybe I had waited too long and it had expired in relevance. Babies in toilets was maybe something that had happened to a lot of people, and now I was giving myself away as someone who didn't know the difference between things that distinguished me and things that didn't. "I guess, it was just a weird thing that happened to me once. Sorry. It's not a big deal."

She looked either in pain or enraged—her face all wrinkly and scrunched up.

There was no good way forward now. I really wanted her to ask me a question, any question, so that I'd at least get to tell someone the story: I had been cat-sitting. The bleeding had stopped after a few days but for weeks I kept reaching a hand down my pants, multiple times in a workday, because I kept feeling this wetness that didn't exist drip down my inner thighs, a feeling that had only filled me with fury at my own body. This friend of mine named Darnie Phillips had taken care of me, so sweetly. Where was Darnie now? We used to be such good friends. My eyes were now hot and swollen from holding back tears, and I realized the tears were for Darnie, that friend of mine who'd been so good to me, such a good friend, who was now far away from my life. I didn't want to lose any more people. I couldn't bear it. I'd work hard not to. Life was getting simpler anyway. It was easier to prioritize who was important. Liam, Mom, Patty. They were the only ones.

"When was this?" asked my mother quietly, breaking the silence suddenly.

"This was when I was living in Indianapolis," I said. But I didn't want to talk about it anymore. We were on the precipice of something awful. We had to back up—beep, beep, beep.

"That city was awful," she said, still quietly. She let go of my wrist. "That was a hellscape you were living in." Silence again. She was looking out the window now, at the snow. Then, she said, at the window, "Where was I?"

"This was when I was in Indianapolis," I said again, a little confused. I added, "You weren't speaking to me."

She continued staring at the window.

"You were mad at me," I said, "about the barefoot hike."

Silence still. My voice was shaking a little. "I took you and Dad on a hike. Barefoot. And you got mad at me and stopped talking to me." I had run out of breath. She still wasn't moving her face at all. It was all so stupid. "It doesn't matter anymore, Mom. I'm sorry." For some reason, I started unzipping the pack of highlighters again, even though she had just put everything away. I ripped off another piece of graph paper. I put a ruler to the paper. I couldn't let her see that I was crying—I was crying over Darnie, but she might think I was crying just to make her feel bad about this thing that happened years ago that didn't even matter anymore.

"You were trying to punish me," she said suddenly. I looked up at her and saw that she was livid. She spoke in a whisper. "Just like you're trying to punish me now."

"I'm not," I said. I shook my head rigorously. "This isn't even what I wanted to talk about. Liam doesn't want kids and I don't know what to do—"

"Don't do that," she interrupted. "Don't do that to me."

Then, she got up from the table and headed upstairs.

—

Everyone—Mom, Dad, Patty—knew that the window seat was the place in the house I most preferred to be, and because of this the window seat always felt like it belonged to me. It was built into the wall next to the front door, and looked out west at the sunny field across the street—private land belonging to an ancient estate that was big but hidden deep in the trees so even in the winter, you could see only bits of the main house, which was built of stone. My dad used to call it Lucy's Field because of how much I loved it. I imagined it to be full of fawns. Very young, I'd go out there alone, committing the ferns and flight paths of birds to memory; it seemed to go into infinity, like I could get lost in the middle of its tall grasses, which to me contained whole worlds, and never find my way back. In the summer, the field became dense with monarchs and swallowtails, red wildflowers, milkweed and goldenrod, pollen puffing up over the grasses like shy adrift fairies. My mother didn't like me playing out there alone, on property that wasn't ours, and yet I remember her once proudly telling Mrs. Hall in the driveway about how I could entertain myself for hours outside, just exploring.

I really wasn't sure what my mother wanted for me. Did she want me to explore the world, and experience all the people and places beyond this? Or did she want me to live here with her at home for the rest of her life? And then: What did I want? The question hit me like a ton of bricks and suddenly, I felt like an infant. I had no idea what she wanted out of my life versus what I wanted. How could I possibly entertain the idea of having kids? I was still at the beginning of my existence.

Above the field now was a V of geese, all of them getting away. Going somewhere. That's how I define happiness, I decided. A big sunny field, full of fawns, beneath geese, with white butterflies and blue sky and tall grasses waving together back and forth for hours and light floating in circles across it all day, and herds of frolicking antelope and hippopotamus clouds. And life, I decided, was just about finding your field. Liam's was his ranch. Ellis's, an ocean full of golden treasures. Cole's, a brilliant company saving people every day. But what was mine? And then I thought, maybe mine is just this big sunny field.

I needed to do a better job painting the picture so that Liam could see what I was seeing—and see how close it was to what he was already picturing: him and me buying the field across the street and building a not-so-big house on its outskirts, a house that would be flooded with sunlight at all times, and decorated with furniture of white pine, all the wood running in the right direction, no exposed ingrain, only perfect trim. We'd have tall impressive bookshelves packed with paperbacks and a ladder on wheels gliding easily over our blazing bamboo floors, and a window seat, this time facing east, built right into the wall, with a light-green cushion and pale floral pillows, and a shed out back for his tools and table saws and passion-project canoes. He just needed to see it as clearly as I did: him and me sitting on our back porch, drinking sweet tea in tall glasses, with bright lemon slices and big ice cubes, watching doves build a nest in our flowerbox.

The next morning, while I was drinking my tea, I heard the door open and clack shut. My mother had returned from a walk. She came into the kitchen and poured herself a glass of water. She was sweaty. We didn't say anything to each other. She finished her water, then went upstairs to shower.

That night, we ate dinner together at the table, in silence, pushing away the art supplies to make room. I cleared both our plates when we finished. She brought a cup of tea back to the table for herself. She bobbed the tea bag in and out of the mug, staring off into the darkness, through the window that faced the bay window of the Halls' house, their huge tree already in it, professionally decorated and squinting, gold and white. Even though my mother didn't like Christmas trees inside the house, Dad did always get her to agree to letting the two of us string lights up on the crab apple tree out front. Only white lights though—every year, Dad told me rainbow would be pushing our luck.

By now, I had forgotten all the things I wanted to say to make things better. But I knew I couldn't leave things like this between us. I was done spending months living far away from her without knowing what it would take to make her speak to me again. What had broken it last time was Dad dying, and if I hadn't had Liam, that ambush was one I wouldn't have survived. But then my mother spoke first.

"Something's breathing," she said.

"What?"

"I hear something breathing." Her tone had turned my body to ice. Her gaze was still fixed on the window above the kitchen sink.

"What?" I said again. "Mom? Stop that."

"Shh," she hissed at me. Silence. And then, she said, in a shrill, terrified voice, "There. Someone's outside."

She was covering her mouth with her hand. Her face white. Slowly, but still in a whisper, she said shakily into her hand, "There's someone there."

"Who? A person?"

"Quiet," she hissed. "Somebody's walking around out there."

"Did you actually see someone?" My voice was also increasing in pitch. She was scaring me. "Or are you just hearing something? An animal, maybe."

"A person," hissed my mother. "They're trying to get inside. They were right there, right in the window. I heard them breathing."

"How could you hear them breathing when they're outside?" I said. But I felt terrified.

She got off her chair and frantically started making her way around to all the windows and doors trying to shut everything, to lock everything up. She even blew out the candle.

"Mom, stop," I said. Everything smelled like candle now.

"Get down here." She was crawling under the kitchen table.

"Blowing out the candle won't help," I pleaded. But it did feel like now there were eyes on me from every angle. And then: I heard it too. The knocking.

My mother's hand clasped around my ankle. We were both hearing it. That was clear. Someone was knocking on the back door. Suddenly my head got very cold, like I had no scalp, like wind was blowing straight across the surface of my brain.

After a few moments, the knocks stopped. And all was quiet. But my mother continued to hold my ankle. And then, it resumed—this time a gentle, single knuckle tapping on glass. One of our windows was rattling, but it was hard to tell which window since darkness surrounded us, and I was too scared to even turn my head.

We ended up sitting together, squished under the kitchen table, for a long time.

At one point, to break the silence, I said, "This is a good table," feeling the silky wood above my head. "It's put together well." I didn't know if that was true, but I wanted my mother to feel good about the table.

My mother decided to make her way on hands and knees over to the mudroom, where she grabbed two old blankets out of the wicker basket under the bench and brought them back to us—the white feathery one draped completely around her, making her look like a goose, just her head popping up out of the fluff, and the thin gray one covering my knees.

"Did you hear that? What was that?" She was trembling again.

"It might just be the branch hitting the window," I said, but my teeth were chattering.

"No. It's him. He's still tapping." My mother spoke in tight little sentences.

We both fell quiet again, trying to hear the tapping. Her nails were cutting into the back of my wrist.

"Mom, it's okay," I said, gently unlatching her hand finger by finger. "It's just the wind, I think." I was still trying hard to listen. Through the kitchen window you could see a single orange lamppost buried in snow, and the northern bit of our slushy street. The wind started picking up, making the windows rattle.

After another half hour or so, my mother whispered, "If Sadie was here, we wouldn't be so scared." My lower back was starting to hurt. I was realizing it was going to have to be up to me when we got out from under the table. My mother would stay here all night. "I can't believe they're all getting divorces. It'll be a shock to their systems when they're all alone in their big terrible houses." Her soft arm was quivering against mine.

"Should we try and go to bed?" I asked. The snow was changing to rain, and somehow the sound of it was calming me down.

"No, Lucy. Wait," she said. She looked angry again. "There's someone out there. I don't want him to see that it's just the two of us in here."

"They're not out there anymore," I let her know. "Come on. Let's go to bed." Even though it still felt like there were eyes on me from every angle, I took a few deep breaths and scooted out from under the table and stood up, the gray blanket falling off my legs. When I looked at the time on the microwave, I saw it wasn't late at all, only eight fifteen. And that made me feel much better. It felt like the middle of the night, but it wasn't.

"We can't go yet," she said. "Please." Her eyes were welling with tears. Her body was shaking so much, it made me nervous. "Oh, honey, please. I'm so scared." She was gasping. "I'm so scared."

"The doors are locked," I reminded her.

She was shaking her head slowly back and forth. She didn't want to get up. She was terrified. Big fat tears were rolling down her face. She tried to say something else but couldn't. Her upper teeth latched onto her bottom lip. I reached down my hand again and this time she took it. Still shaking, she pressed her other palm onto the floor to steady herself so I could pull her up. I led her by the hand up the stairs. But at the door to my bedroom, she wouldn't let go of me, so I told her I would come with her to her room.

We both got into her bed. It took a while for us to fall asleep.

At some point in the darkness, my mother started to speak.

"You know," she said and took a deep breath. "Once, when

I was a little girl—" I was on my side facing away. But I rolled over onto my back when she started talking so she knew I was listening. Both her hands were clutching the duvet, and she was staring at the ceiling. "Once, when I was a little girl," she started again, her voice steadying, "Isaac and I were home alone, and we thought there was a ghost in the house. We kept hearing something shuffle around. And then the piano started playing. Oh, it terrified us. I mean, imagine. Then finally, Isaac worked up the courage to look. It was just a mouse scampering over the keys."

I had never heard my mother talk about her brother like this. I had only one memory of him, and it was vague: he had come for a holiday. This was before kindergarten even. There had been some fight. I was too little to know what it had been about, but for some reason I remember it as being about him taking something. I had asked my mother about him only one time after that, and she had gotten very angry with me. She had told me to "cut it out."

"Where is Isaac?" I decided to try now. "Where does he live?"

She didn't say anything for a moment, and for a moment I worried I had once again overstepped. But then she said shortly, "He died."

"He did?" I was stunned. "When?"

"2012," she said. "I found out a few months ago."

"How?"

"It didn't say," she said. Then: "Drugs."

But I had meant how did she discover—

"Oh," she said. A pause. "I felt like reaching out. After your dad."

I fell asleep listening to her breath. Her breaths sounded shallow and a little bit wet, with long gaps in between each one. I tried comparing the gaps to mine, to see if hers were longer. Looking back, I think this was the moment I realized my mother was sick.

The following morning, Thanksgiving Day, as I was rolling up the trash bins from the curb, I found footprints in the snow. I considered not telling my mother about them—I didn't want her to get worked up again—but she'd already spotted them herself when she came out to the porch to have her morning tea. We walked around the house together, following the feet. It was just one set of tracks, not too big. My mother wanted to call the police but before we could, we were interrupted by an older woman with short white hair, cut cleanly around her ears and round glasses, and a little boy, walking up the path toward our porch, both in mittens, holding hands. It was still early in the day, not yet 9:30 a.m.

"I grew up here," explained the woman. "I love to see it's still here. Hasn't changed a bit. I came by last night, but I don't think anyone was home. I was just curious to see the house. I'm back in town for the first time in—it must be over thirty years."

My mother was not amused by this.

"This is Howard," said the woman, introducing her grandson. He looked to be Wyatt's age, though to be certain, I'd need to see them side by side.

"That's a strange name for a boy," said my mother. "This is my daughter, Lucy."

"I already introduced myself," I reminded her. I had greeted them on the walkway.

My mother didn't invite them in but gave them permission to look at the house from the outside. I wasn't sure why she wasn't being nicer. It should've been a relief that the mystery of last night had been resolved so easily and quickly for us.

"Well, I'm sure you two have a full day ahead of you packed with fun things," said my mother, when they came back around to the porch, maybe seeing if they could have another shot at getting inside the house. The woman had started sharing some memories about how she used to walk through the woods behind the house to get to school. Was the little deer path still there? But my mother interrupted, "We really don't want to be keeping you."

"Oh no, this is the big event of the day," said the woman. She wasn't picking up on any of my mother's cues.

"You two should get some donuts from Frank's," suggested my mother. "What do you say to that, Howard?" The little boy was still attached to his grandmother's hand.

"You frightened us last night," my mother let the little boy know. "You shouldn't come by somebody's house so late."

"It was just me last night," said the woman. Now, she seemed to understand my mother was displeased and she looked a little hurt. In a sweet quiet voice, she said as if only musing to herself, "It was only half past six. I guess it does get dark so early these days."

"All winter days, for my whole life in New England," said my mother. "I don't think that's changed."

"I just meant these winter days."

"Oh," said my mother.

I decided to chime in. "It is crazy how dark it gets here. I live in Texas. There are a lot of downsides to that state, but at least we don't have four p.m. sunsets."

"I could never live in Texas," said the woman, shaking her head back and forth. "How do you stand it?"

"My boyfriend's there," I explained. But I felt offended.

The thing with people from New England is that they think they know about everywhere else in the country, but they only know about New England. Liam said that once and I agreed it was true.

My mother and I stayed on the porch after the woman and her grandson left.

"I think you should stay here with me until the end of the year," she commanded. "The end of the year is not far off, and then you'll get to see Patty and we can all be together."

"I have to get back to Liam," I reminded her.

"Bring that extra pack of graph paper back to him, please."

"We have paper at home, I think."

"Just take it."

Next door, Johnny Hall was pulling into the driveway and getting out of a jeep, holding the hand of a slender woman in a long silver slip and jean jacket.

We both watched the woman gingerly step up the driveway in her heels, following Johnny to the door, where Mrs. Hall stood to greet them. Mrs. Hall caught us watching and waved enthusiastically.

"Oh, I hope she doesn't invite us over," said my mother. "I don't have that in me today." She unwrapped one of her scarves, the plush light-brown one, from around her neck and rewrapped it around her shoulders.

"Did she know I was coming home?"

"I told her. I said we'd just be spending time just the two of us, but she's been insistent that we at least come over for pie."

"I'd go over for pie."

My mother yawned. "Let's wait and see if we're up for it."

—

We ended up choosing to turn down pie and instead spend the sundown hour walking her favorite route around the town. It was strange to see all the unused retail space. So many shops had closed. A whole strip near the main square that used to have the deli, hardware store, and Radio Coffee now had nothing, just tawny awnings drooping and empty windows.

Halfway up Allendale was when my mother coughed up some blood into her hand. At first, she didn't even stop, just looked at it and then wiped it off on her leggings—she hated stopping while walking—but then she coughed again, lost her breath, and fell onto the gravel, scraping up her palms and knees. When Patty went home that year for the holidays, she stayed. She stayed with Mom for the full year and a half, going back to the city only briefly in the middle.

A few months ago, sticking out of a coffee-table book, I found three short essays that my mother had written—"Places Beyond," "Giving Thanks," and "Abe's Hands." It was a book that Liam had bought her for her sixty-fifth birthday—*Texas Interiors: How to Decorate Small Spaces.* Each essay was dated about a month apart. Patty had mentioned the writing group to me once, telling me that Jordie Williams had suggested it. I wasn't sure if Patty was the one who had printed out my mother's essays or if my mother had. I've read them each several times now—I still read them sometimes before bed—but unfortunately, they're not enough. They end too soon. She should have written ten more essays, and thirty or forty pages of each, at least. I've looked for more, flipping through every book in the house, clicking into folders on her desktop, reading through her old Day-Timers that were supposed to be a cornucopia of information but had in the margins only reminders about soccer lessons, lunches, recitals, school projects, talent shows. But the only essays I've ever found are the three from inside that coffee-table book.

She couldn't have been writing them for herself—they're not long enough to be her way of reliving life. Upon understanding that, I stopped reading them as a way of figuring out what it was like to be her, and started reading them as a way of figuring out what she was trying to say to us. My favorite sentence is *Lucy and Abe have the same heart-shaped chin.* We didn't, but I wanted to believe it. She and I were the same that way. We both wanted to see things that weren't true.

Here are the parts I've reread the most:

In "Places Beyond":

> In 1973, my father and his pilot friend John Geer hit bad air over Ferris Lake. I was thirteen. My mother never stepped aboard another plane, or train, or ship ever again. She never traveled any farther north than Allentown, and nowhere south of Saratoga Springs. I didn't want to be like that, so I moved to a new state and a new city to start a new life. My brother did the same, but he went to San Diego.
>
> Still, I didn't fly on a plane until a few years ago. The plan was to drive to Indianapolis, then fly home. Abe signed me up for a fear-of-flying course, to prepare. It met for over five months, mostly online and only a few times in person. Luckily, the flight wasn't so bad in the end. My primary care gave me something to take, and Abe held my hand the whole time.

Both my girls have lived all over the place. Patty has spent time in Chicago. Now she's in the big city. Lucy was in Indiana, now Texas. When I found out Lucy was in Texas all of a sudden, I cried to Sandy about it and Sandy's response was totally opposite mine. She said, "Wow! Lucy is so brave!" She was very impressed that Lucy had driven to Texas all by herself.

In "Abe's Hands":

When we first started going steady, he informed me, very seriously, that he didn't like holding hands. Back then, boys and girls held hands all the time.

I'll never forget the first time he reached for mine crossing Beacon Street. After that, he kept reaching for it. He started holding my hand for entire movies, even if our palms got sweaty. I always thought I'd have those hands to hold when it came time to die. It'd be so nice if that was the case. I wouldn't be so scared.

In "Giving Thanks":

Lucy and Abe have the same heart-shaped chin. They have the same big eyes and long eyelashes and wild laugh. They both like being in nature too. But everyone says Lucy looks and acts exactly like me.

The week before Patty called to say Mom was really dying now and it was time to come home, Liam took me on the most beautiful bike ride of my life. It was a route called Willow City Loop, out past Gillespie. The color and abundance of the bluebonnets was extreme. Passing black Galloway cows with bands of white fur around their bellies, Liam stopped to say, "Wow, those cows are crazy." He liked to stop a lot when we biked. He liked to moo back at cows. We continued up and down the hills of the borderless road, in astonished silence. We felt we were somewhere else, a different earth. The bluebonnets were boundless, plush, in full bloom. Around every bend, when we came upon them again, we groaned. "My heart might explode," he said. There were white flowers that looked like tulips but with more delicate petals. Fiery wildflowers, too, of oranges, yellows, and reds. Indian paintbrush. The air was dreamy and sweet with the smell of flowers and horses. Buzzards floated above. Days before, it had finally rained, which drew out all the greens in Texas in a way I'd never seen. It remained cloudy that day—rare for us. It made the sunset insane. It put a red streak in the middle of the sky, like a vein.

DUPLICITOUS EXISTENCE

IN LATE APRIL, WE HAD A WEIRD STRETCH OF FREEZ-
ing rain. Every evening that week, Liam and I took a walk
before dinner. We liked how the ice turned the city into a mu-
seum, encasing everything. The pecans became skeletal and
translucent and intricate and perfect, their branches bending
down over the sidewalks like bridges. The ice made you see
right through them. Our neighborhood looked full of sculptures and ghosts. It felt like we were at the end of everything,
branches falling down all around us.

"It must be sad for people when the trees go down outside
their home," I said.

"Oh yeah," he agreed. "It's heartbreaking."

That was the spring that Grant and Naomi split up. They
had been together eleven years, but that first week of May,

Naomi moved out. They weren't married but owned a house and a four-year-old boxer named Winston. Grant was thirty-four, and Naomi thirty-five. At first, I didn't know who had broken up with whom or why, since all Liam would tell me was "They've been having problems for a while." Eventually though, it became clear that Naomi was the one who ended things. Grant started coming over to ours four or five nights a week, to play video games with Liam, drink beer, and rehash the relationship, mostly the same inane details from that past year, just trying to understand what had happened. He was boggled and shell-shocked.

Still, I couldn't help but feel extremely concerned for Naomi. It seemed to me that all of her friends had been Grant's friends first, and I was worried she was going to lose that group of friends entirely. But Liam explained that he couldn't be there for Naomi while Grant was leaning on him so much. It was too complicated for him to receive both of their feelings at once. And despite having known Naomi for over a decade, he still felt like he had to prioritize Grant.

So, when Naomi reached out to me to get coffee, I was eager to show up for her. Out of all the girlfriends in that group, she said she'd reached out to only me, even though we'd never hung out just the two of us before. I had always been a little intimidated by her: she was not only older than me, but a beautiful, politically perfect ceramicist who sewed her own clothes, worked part-time at the apothecary, and still shaved her legs—the exact type of person Liam adored.

We met for coffee on a Sunday at noon, at a place called Hopscotch in Barton, which had a large back patio area with shade and pink picnic tables. She had gotten there first, her elbow nearly knocking over her kombucha when she stood up to greet me. She came around the table, arms crossed, seeming unsure whether we'd hug. I decided to hug her right away because she was on the brink of tears. She asked how Liam was, her faint voice giving away just how much she missed everybody. She was the one who needed me as a friend, not the other way around.

Soon, she was chronicling all their problems, the early warning signs that had reared their heads years ago, which she had chosen to ignore. Their problems sounded so much like our problems; it was spooky. She kept explaining the difference in how she and Grant shared their feelings with each other. She wanted connection on a deep emotional level that he wasn't giving her. She wanted adventure and romance, and he also failed at this. He had told her, believe it or not, that he'd been more open and vulnerable with her than he'd ever been with anyone, that she was the person who knew him the best in the world. But she had needed more.

"It's these emotionally stunted men," she said fiercely. Naomi was a strong and decisive person. I admired this about her. It made me slap my palms down on the pink table also and sit up straighter. "I need to be with someone who'll talk about anything with me for hours."

Another slap-slap on the table, from both of us. I, too, was nodding vigorously.

She continued, "I need us to always be nurturing a genuine curiosity in the other person. I need us to be constantly uncovering each other's darkness and depth of being. And I need romance. We'd never even have sex anymore. It was always just fucking."

"Totally," I agreed, shielding the sun from my eyes. It was my turn: "Sometimes I feel like I can ask Liam only so many questions before he wants to shut down the conversation."

Naomi shook her head in sympathy. "That's probably because he had severe depression in college that he never got properly treated. Grant's the same way. A suicidal kid who always had to figure it out on his own. His family didn't believe in mental health."

I hadn't known about Liam's history of severe depression, and I felt a little sick. I also wasn't sure if by "suicidal kid" she was referring to Grant or Liam or both?

"I was always dragging Grant into every decision," continued Naomi. "Moving in together, meeting parents, buying a house, getting a dog."

"We have that dynamic too," I interrupted.

"It got exhausting. Everything was just another thing I had to convince him of. And now, of course, he's suddenly all in. As soon as he sensed me actually pulling away, he panicked. He was asking for my ring size just the other week. But too bad. Too late. He's made me a ghost."

By now, our conversation had devolved into both of us absolutely shitting on Grant and Liam. I had to go to the bathroom, but it felt so good to air all our grievances and I had so much more to say that I didn't want to leave my seat, even with the sun in my eyes. My sweaty thighs were glued to the bench. If I stood up, they'd surely peel off paint chips.

"Oh no," said Naomi, interrupting me. "You want kids?" She pushed the queso out of the way, then reached for my hand with a fierceness that made me flinch. Her nails were chewed down like mine. "Lucy, you can't be with him, then. Liam definitely does not want kids."

"I think he does now," I said, feeling tipsy from the two

sangrias and all the sun. After all, the last two Christmases I had watched him very carefully, the tireless way he'd played with his niece and nephews. I took out my phone to show her the video of him playing piano with Wyatt, who was in candy-cane pajamas, wearing Liam's reading glasses, and swinging his footsied feet back and forth under the bench.

"You need to have that conversation," said Naomi, looking up from the piano video before it had played all the way through. "You can't guess."

"I'm not guessing," I reassured the both of us.

But she wouldn't give it up. She ended her speech by saying, "He doesn't want the same life as you." This felt like a violent thing to say, and it kick-started a little emergency inside me.

Luckily that was also the moment that Naomi decided to change the subject. Suddenly, she threw her head back and laughed wildly.

"Okay," she said, dropping her chin to her collar as if her head was now the heaviest thing in the world. She looked ecstatic. "Want to know a secret?"

"Yes, yes!" I said. I did. I so did.

"I met someone," she said, and she slapped her hand down on the table again. She had stacks of black and silver rings on almost every finger. Also, a silver bracelet on her right wrist beaded with turquoise stones.

She and her yoga teacher named Aron had fallen in love a year ago, and now they were planning to move in together. At first, she said that nothing had happened between them until *after* she had broken up with Grant. But when I said, "I'm so happy for you," she then launched into every single detail of the affair, starting with the moment they first kissed after class, then when they first had sex (six months ago), then all the things she did to keep it a secret from Grant.

When she was done, I said again, "I'm happy for you," and her eyes welled with tears. She was so relieved. A yellow jacket landed on the lip of her kombucha, and neither of us flinched, and I remember briefly thinking, We're both big girls.

"Does Grant know?" I asked, even though I knew he didn't. But Naomi wasn't aware that Grant was over at ours for dinner so many nights a week.

"God no," she said. "He can never know. He'll just discredit all the very real reasons I listed as to why we needed to break up. He'll just hear that I cheated on him."

For another whole hour, Naomi talked about Aron. It got a bit boring to keep hearing her reiterate how in love she was. She seemed to really want to prove it.

Then, she stopped talking about herself, grabbed my hand again, and said, "Lucy, listen. I *know* Liam. You two don't want the same things. I let that dynamic play out between me and Grant for years. I convinced myself that I didn't really need to travel. I didn't really need kids. I didn't *need* to get married. But now, with Aron, it's like, oh wait. I would like those things. Aron lets me be myself! He reactivates my old desires! I feel alive again after years of holding myself back! I feel alive after years of trying to make a relationship work that just wasn't working!"

Not telling Liam about Naomi's affair gave me bad diarrhea for weeks. I probably should've told him right away, but I had given her my confidence even though it was hard to pinpoint the exact moment I had given it to her. It was probably when she said, "Want to know a secret?" and I had said "Yes, yes!" But had she explicitly told me not to tell Liam? No. But also, I genuinely believed that Naomi's affair was information Liam would not consent to knowing. He would feel implicated by it; he would feel like he had to tell Grant. The longer I held it on my own, however, the more complicit I felt in Naomi's lies, and I already had committed myself to living a less duplicitous existence for the rest of my life, since my life was going to be spent with Liam and Liam was an honest man.

Ultimately, I decided to call Patty for advice.

"You have to tell Liam," she said. "I would've told Ben."

Ben was Patty's new boyfriend. Supposedly, they'd been dating for five months. I wanted to tell Patty that her situation with Ben was very different from mine with Liam, but I let it be.

"Whenever I tell my friends something, I just assume they're going to tell their partners. Especially people who've been together as long as you and Liam," added Patty. "Want me to ask my friends what they'd do?"

"Don't say it has anything to do with me."

I waited on the phone while she texted all her group chats. Then she said, "Okay, yep. Everyone says they would've told their partners immediately. Sydney, Anne, Eloise, and Bee."

So, in the truck, on our way to the grocery store, I finally worked up the courage to say, verbatim to the script I had typed out on my phone (and gut-checked with Patty): "Naomi told me this thing about the breakup that's complicated. I don't want to betray her confidence, but I feel uncomfortable keeping it from you. What do you think I should do?"

Liam was snacking on the pistachios that he kept in the cupholder. He was silent for a second, just chewing, then he laughed a little heartlessly. "What am I supposed to do with that?"

I tried again. "I don't want to tell you something you might not want to know."

"She told you not to tell me?" He sounded annoyed. Liam could get self-conscious that I knew more things about his friends than he did. But that's because I asked them questions when we were all hanging out at the bar, and he didn't.

"Right," I said.

He parked the truck and turned off the engine. "Honestly, it feels like you're just dangling this over my head."

"I'm trying to handle this the best I can," I said, heart broken already by his response.

"Can I guess what it is? It has to do with the breakup?"

"Don't guess."

"She got a job in New York."

"It's not that," I said, stunned by how dumb his guess was. "Please don't guess."

He was unbuckling and craning around to grab the tote bags from the back seat. "Come on," he said. "Let's go."

"Wait! What do you think I should do?"

He settled back down into the driver's seat. Took off his baseball hat. Put it back on. Finally, he sighed and said, "If you want to tell me, fine, but first you need to let Naomi know that's what you're doing. After you tell her that you're going to tell me, then you can tell me."

I didn't do this, of course. Naomi had picked me as the person to trust, and I needed to rise to the occasion. I also didn't want her to think I was prioritizing Liam over her; I had to be a good friend. So, I took a different tactic: I gently suggested to her over text that she confess to the affair herself. Didn't she want to exist freely in Austin without always having to glance over her shoulder? Her long paragraphs back let me know that she was terrified of three main things: that this would forever define their breakup, that she would be seen as the villain and Grant as the victim, and that all their mutual friends, like Liam, would hate her.

"Yes," I texted back, "but it's going to be more authentic for your relationship with Aron if you're able to start it from a liberated place, instead of building it in this illicit place." Also, I told her, "Liam won't hate you; he and everybody else will come around." This convinced her.

"Is this the thing you've been keeping from me?" Liam asked, getting off the phone with Grant a few nights later. I'd rarely seen him so angry and couldn't tell if he was angry at me.

"Yes, but I didn't know all the details," I said. "Does Grant know that I knew?"

"It's just so fucked," he said, cracking open a beer, pressing the cold can against his forehead. "Grant's last girlfriend cheated on him as well."

"His college girlfriend?"

"Yeah. Missy."

"Well, that's different from this," I said. "That was in college."

"You don't get it. He's going to be so fucked up over this."

Liam didn't seem mad at me, but he also wasn't acknowledging what a difficult position Naomi had put me in by telling me first. All he could think about was how fucked up it was that Naomi had made Grant process a breakup for months without giving him all the information.

"She's worried that you're never going to be friends with her now," I let Liam know.

"Naomi? Yeah, no way."

I wasn't expecting that. "You're not going to be friends with her just because of this?"

"Grant got the friends, and she got the boyfriend. That's how it works. The way she handled this was her choice."

"I still want to be there for her. I was the one who told her to tell him."

Liam didn't like this. "It's not your job to take care of her. Grant's really suffering."

"But she's suffering too," I said. "She's all alone feeling awful. I cheated on my college boyfriend once and it was excruciating."

Liam was quiet. Then he said, "You never told me that."

"It was in college," I went on. "It made me feel terrible. I'm just worried that Naomi is feeling all of this by herself. She needs at least me to talk to."

"Was this Cole? Weren't you guys together for years?"

"Yeah, but that whole last year I was cheating on him. I still feel bad about it."

"How did he handle finding out?"

"I never told him."

"He doesn't know you cheated on him?" Something was happening between us again. Lately, things had been a little sticky.

Louder than I was expecting, Liam said, "I hate that." His mouth was twisted up in a weird way, the expression on his face new to me. I still couldn't tell if he was angry.

"Well, I should've told him. Definitely. But it's not important anymore. It's in the past."

"It's sort of important. He's been living his life with the wrong idea about you."

This troubled me. "It's water under the bridge," I managed to say.

"It's not though," said Liam. "You guys still have a relationship with each other."

"No, we don't." We hadn't talked in years.

"Weren't he and your mom close?" asked Liam, and for a second, it was like he'd shot me in the stomach. I had forgotten that Cole had been at the funeral—he and Liam had met.

"Not really," I said.

"She used to bring him up."

I shook my head. "No, she didn't. When did she bring him up?"

"Last Thanksgiving. She mentioned seeing him."

"I think he brought over a lasagna, like once," I said, which I knew only because Patty had called that day to tell me that Cole had not only bleached his hair but was also balding.

"It's not fair that he doesn't know the truth," said Liam.

"Everyone remembers relationships differently." I was ready for the conversation to stop. "You can't control how or what people remember about things. That's not my job."

"It's your job to tell the truth," he said.

"This was in college, Liam. I really don't think it matters anymore."

He didn't say anything.

"What?" I said. "What? What are you thinking?"

He pulled a half sheet of Nicorette from his back pocket. He tore off a square, dug it out with his nail, then flicked the empty square in the direction of the kitchen. It fluttered to the floor. Lately, his gum trash had been accumulating everywhere, his habit back with a vengeance. Before I could tell him to pick it up, he bent down and picked it up himself. He put it in his pocket and headed over to the couch.

It was always up to him to decide when and how to end

a conversation. "Let's put on a movie," he said, fishing the remote out of the cushions. "Something funny."

Twelve of my sister's friends had shown up for my mother's funeral, people from New York, college, and home. The only person there for me besides Liam was Cole. He had come with his fiancée, Daphne, a blond labor and delivery nurse. He was bulkier than he'd been in college and Patty was right—his hair was not good. But he looked happy and this made me happy. He and Daphne had hovered in the back, gazing over the pews, and Cole, holding a program in one hand and Daphne's hand in the other, was looking for a spot where he wouldn't get in the way. I watched him guide the clerk from Donaldson's into one of the pews, handing her his program as if he were an usher. Liam witnessed me burst into tears at this. Cole was always so good at being polite and helpful. It was funny remembering how trapped I felt in that relationship when really, I'd had all this space. Cole had let me do whatever I wanted.

At the reception, Cole's tweed jacket looked exceptionally preppy next to Liam's skinny tie. Cole wanted to hear all about Liam's work, asking him a number of enthusiastic questions. He even told Liam about his uncle who did woodworking as a hobby. Daphne turned out to be the exact person Cole was supposed to marry. They were two of the nicest people, and I liked how funny she found Patty. She was an attentive listener and laughed a lot at Patty's stories.

But afterward, when I asked Liam what he thought of Cole, he answered, "Not my first choice of a guy to hang out with."

"What does that mean?"

"He's just not my first-choice type of person."
"He's one of my oldest friends."
"He's your ex."
"Am I your first-choice type of person?"
"Okay, what's going on? I'm sorry, alright? Okay?"

My sister had asked everyone to wear bright colors. No black. Sandy Lewis had shown up in a blue gown and big hat and was a little drunk the whole time, which was classic Sandy. She always used to tell our mother that she was at her wit's end with Bobby's drinking, even though everyone knew Sandy drank just as much as her husband if not more. Sandy had offered to host the reception at her country club, which was also Evelyn Hall's country club. She must have gusted over to us a hundred times to tell us again just how much she loved our mother. As people were leaving, I told Patty I'd stay behind, to help Sandy and Mrs. Hall pack up the good leftovers for us—they were planning to bring them over to ours later. Patty told me to see if I could find out more from Sandy about Tiff's boob job; apparently Mom was certain Sandy had paid for it, but had never been able to confirm. Liam went with Patty because there had been an issue with the window unit that morning—I think it had been on his mind all day. We had woken up to it leaking water, and Liam hated when water accumulated indoors. As soon as Patty and Liam left together, I snuck out to the back parking lot and hid behind the white vans. I had no intention of helping with the leftovers; I just wanted to smoke a cigarette, and this seemed like my only chance. I didn't want Sandy or Evelyn or any of the other stragglers to know I was still at the club; the day had been a lot of socializing. It was when I was about done with my second cigarette that Evelyn and Sandy burst out of the back door, both carrying large trays covered in plastic wrap, talking loudly. Their twin white Suburbans, I realized, were parked side by side, close to where I was smoking.

Sandy had always been a tall woman, with an abnormally long neck. She towered over Evelyn, who wore a pink skirt and white fluffy sweater. It may as well have been Easter Sunday. Sandy's dress had puff sleeves. Together they looked like an ostrich and a bunny.

Clearly, they didn't think anyone else was around or they wouldn't have been talking so loudly, the lot empty besides their cars and the vans. As they approached, I stomped out my cigarette and squatted down behind the front tire of the closest van, listening for any gossip I might be able to relay to Patty later. Patty loved gossip.

As they crossed the lot, they started talking more quietly and I couldn't hear what they were saying. But then, when they were standing maybe twenty or thirty feet away, Sandy said clearly, "I used to just *ache* thinking about Abe." She sounded less slurry than earlier.

"Awful," said Evelyn, in a hushed voice. Two beeps and a trunk opened.

"When I saw her today, I just— It's hard to see."

"I can't imagine."

"Plain as day."

"You know she never mentioned a word to me about it? And there were many years when we really did talk all the time."

"Oh, she'd *never*." Another trunk opened. "Of course, when she was pregnant with Lucy, she told us everything. Everything. She was so anxious. We were worried she might miscarry." Silence. "I don't excuse it, of course, but it was really a terrible time for her."

"Oh, I know. I didn't even meet Linda until the boys started day care. And we moved next door in '94."

"Days and days and *days* of her not getting out of bed. And she just kept saying over and over to us that she felt *nothing*. Jordie and I would go over and just find her *sobbing*. I can still picture Jordie, you know Jordie, poor Jordie, trying to swaddle up little Patty, who would also be *wailing*. It was awful. The dogs next door. I mean, we had all just had our first. Tiffany was only nine months." Another trunk opened. "Abe really had no idea the extent of it. He wanted another! He would've had more, I know that. He wanted a big, big family. He always said that." More silence. "We should've done more. But at the time, you know, I was about to be made partner, and Tiffany was only nine months . . . I know, I know, I know." Another pause. "Abe *asked* Lloyd to check in on them during the day because he just couldn't get there from downtown. That's the thing. Lloyd showed up. Lloyd was there. That's what I mean when I—"

"And remind me, Lloyd's . . . ?"

"Dead. Did you never . . . ?"

"No, I did, I did. I can remember him at Eagle Farms." Another long pause. "Awful. For her to grow up and look exactly like his good friend."

"I always told Bobby if he could be even half the dad Abe was . . ." A trunk shut. "Oh, I adored that man. He really threw himself into fathering both those girls."

A tsk, then silence. Then in a much louder voice, no longer hushed, Evelyn said, "Well, the girls seem to be doing great, all things considered. Patricia did a beautiful job today—"

"Oh, just beautiful—"

"And that man Lucy's with seems fine."

"I mean, thank *god*. And Linda really liked him. It was

always Lucy this, Lucy that. She never caught a break. Did I tell you Tiffany is starting at McKinsey in the fall?"

I had learned this technique of retreating into the most inanimate parts of my body as a way of escaping feelings of extreme discomfort. My elbows were a safe space for me and also, occasionally, the edges of my shoulders. I did this for a few days but then a week or so after the funeral, instead of reading in bed as Liam was, I rolled over and took out my phone and scrolled through old photos of the four of us— holding my breath the whole time. I looked like a giant alien dropped into this family of midgets. I was the spotted beast among them—these pale, dark-haired others. It was a crazy place to be, the inside of me; a flock of birds kept swooping in and out of this black sand pit that was my stomach, thousands of them, and then up and out into this blue-sky space of what I can only describe as weird, sunny relief. If I put too much pressure on interrogating the things stupid Sandy had said, I knew my life would just give and give. So, I had a choice, and I didn't want to go barreling into a black crater. But then Liam was asking me if I was okay. I realized I had been rolling all over the bed, kicking off the sheets, trying to get comfortable.

"Are you hot? I can turn on the AC, but I'm worried you'll get cold," he was saying.

"No, I'm good. My stomach just hurts." But after a few seconds, I said into the pillow, "I want to talk to you about how I'm feeling."

He made me pick up my head and repeat myself. Then he said, "Of course, baby. I'm listening."

I considered my options. They were all scary. What could he possibly say? Would he say it made sense? Would he say that he had suspected something like this? I could see him trying to convince me it didn't matter. Did it matter? I had no idea. Would he try and tell me it wasn't true? Or would he just reassure me that everybody loved me no matter what, and it wasn't worth dwelling on? Liam hated dwelling. I could ask him: Well, do you think my dad loved me as much as Patty? Or was there something missing? Was there something missing in my mother? I always knew there was. But what was the point of talking to Liam? I really thought about it. There wasn't anything technically different about what I was dealing with. It was all still just grief. There was also a world in which all of this became a stabilizing thing, not destabilizing. After all, I was just like her. I was also someone who broke vows.

The back of my skull throbbed. It had suddenly struck me that, from this moment forward, every new person I'd meet would never get to meet her. Nobody after Liam—and because of that, I would always be that much less known by those people. But that was okay. I didn't want those people anyway; I wanted only the people I already had.

"I want to get married," I finally said to Liam. "Why aren't we married?"

Liam took a long pause to consider this. Then he said carefully, "I thought you wanted to figure out the kids thing first."

I told him I didn't want to put off our life any longer.

"This is our life," said Liam.

"Well, I'm sick of the hypotheticals," I said. I rolled back onto my back. I had this feeling that marriage would eliminate all the hypotheticals. "I want to get started," I said, clapping my hands at the ceiling. "I want us to get a move on."

"Hypotheticals?" repeated Liam. He sat up and looked down at me. The bedside lamp was still on from when he'd been reading. "I didn't realize marriage was so important to you."

I sighed. I kept getting hot, then cold. I rolled over again. The sheets were all twisted up now. My stomach did really hurt. "I wish you had met my dad," I said into the pillow. Liam lay next to me, then pulled me up softly onto my side. He was trying to get my mouth somewhere he could hear me. He pushed some of my hair behind my ear, then hugged me into him, my back against his stomach. It wasn't his fault that he didn't get to meet my dad. It was just no longer a life we could have together. There was no more, Well, life could still be this way. It couldn't.

"I'm grateful that I got to spend so much time with your mom," Liam was saying, his chin on my shoulder. He may have been saying more things before this, but I hadn't heard them.

"It just sucks," I reiterated.

"What if you tell me more about him? Show me more pictures."

"No," I said.

"I'm sorry," he whispered.

The freight train went by, so there was a long pause of huge sounds. Then they finished. I turned around to face his sad beautiful eyes behind his gold-rimmed reading glasses. And my chest throbbed with love for him. I loved him so much.

"I think what I want is," I started, but then ran out of breath, which made my body shake violently. I inhaled and tried again: "What I want is to tell you about a feeling, and for you to just say, 'I see that you're having that feeling. I'm here for you and I love you.'"

He kissed me on the cheek, then pressed his stubbly one against it.

"What are you feeling now?" he asked my cheek.

"Pain," I said. "A lot a lot of pain."

He tightened his arms now. "I see that you're in pain," said Liam, squeezing. "And I'm here for you." He draped his leg over my stomach. "And I love you."

It was my favorite way for us to sleep, me on my back with his leg on my stomach.

That summer, Liam and I attempted to get back into the swing of things—the way we'd been the year before, when we were the happiest people on the planet. Most mornings though, I woke up feeling exhausted and dense, my insides piled high with the sweet debris that comes from the collapsing of a poorly constructed skyscraper that had probably been begging to fall for years. I felt just as ruined as I did relieved, but still was barely able to move. Liam tried to help with this by making sure that every weekend we got out of the house to walk the greenbelt, or find more swimming holes, or drive around the Hill Country, sometimes heading all the way out to Blanco or Fredericksburg, occasionally Fort Stockton and Marfa, in order to lose ourselves in the landscapes of West Texas—landscapes that made me feel like I was suppressing a long, blood-curdling scream but that consistently compelled Liam to pull the car over every hundred miles or so, even in a hundred plus degrees. He liked to walk out into the middle of the mesquite and stand by himself for a second under the humongous sky. Sometimes, he'd pee.

If we had been talking to each other on those drives, I would've felt different. If we spent that time not silently staring out at land but instead talking for hours and hours and hours . . . I wanted to tell him all about my life. There was still so much to say. I wanted to write down every detail from the past decade—I had several hundred pages worth of stories—and make him read all of them, even the terrible ones, so he could finally understand what it was like to be Lucy and why Lucy loved Liam so much. I needed him to look at me—at me! Not at the land!—and say, Wow, you've had some really big experiences. You've been through a lot. I didn't need him to tell me it was any more or any less than anybody else, but just to confirm that I was capable of bearing a lot and making it through. But Liam didn't seem to want to learn any more about my past. He was always steering us away from it.

All summer, Naomi kept inviting me to volunteer with her at the DSA office, to bop around galleries on East Sixth, to attend a protest on a campus where neither of us were students, to have wine, to go on a walk. I usually said no because Liam didn't like Naomi anymore and I didn't want him to think I was still her friend. I managed to see her once in July, in the middle of the day for forty-five minutes—and I kept this from Liam. Naomi and I didn't even talk about me at all, because she was worse than ever. Insecure, tense, she felt like her life was slipping out from under her. She had started seeing a therapist. She didn't want to be in Austin anymore but didn't know where else to go. She was trying to find friends by joining a knitting club, a book club, a run club, and a French club. I was the only friendly face still in her life that wasn't totally fresh.

At the end of our coffee, she invited me to her birthday party and nervously asked if I thought Liam might come too. She was hoping he was done being upset with her.

"Naomi invited us to her birthday party," I told him later, as casually as possible.

"Yeah, that's not happening," said Liam. "Are you guys still in touch?"

"Not really," I said. "I think she's probably just lonely. You want to go?"

"No," Liam said.

"Is it okay if I go?"

Silence. "I mean yeah, you can go. You can do whatever you want."

"But you'd be upset with me if I went."

"Look, we've talked about this. I don't care if you're friends with Naomi. Do whatever you want. I just think you should let Grant know, because he thinks you're fully on his side."

So, I didn't go to the birthday party. However, when Naomi reached out next about the dominoes night she was organizing with a couple new girlfriends, I decided to go without telling Liam. Naomi told me over text that she'd heard on a podcast that the secret to building adult friendships was to organize recurrent get-togethers over mutually enjoyed activities, as a way of taking the pressure off any one person to have to plan it each time. The others joining us were women she'd never met in person but had connected with on a new app for making platonic friends in the city. I said I would go if we did it on a Tuesday, when Liam thought I was at yoga.

I knew going into dominoes that I'd be the youngest in the group by a lot. For example, that evening I'd chosen to wear over-the-knee heeled black boots and Liam's cut-off paint-stained tank over a black lace bralette—whereas the other three women all dressed like kid-less, middle-aged women, which is what they were. Not Naomi obviously, but Katherine and Norah had a never-had-sex look about them.

During the dominoes, Naomi kept glancing at me, to either make eye contact or check that I was having fun. It was clear the group needed me. The fact that I'd chosen to show up gave these women validation because I wasn't looking for friends online. I was attending this dominoes night out of philanthropy, not necessity.

Strangely, no one was sharing anything about their lives or making any attempts to get to know each other. It seemed like all three just wanted to play dominoes. I was also the only one drinking. Even though we were at a bar, both Naomi and Norah had ordered hot tea, and Katherine was sipping club soda with lime. On the second round of dominoes and my second negroni, I resolved to take one for the team, to help Naomi forge some bonds, by asking Norah a personal question: "So, Norah," I said, "how long have you been in Austin?"

Norah looked shocked that I was asking about her life. "Oh," she said. "I'm from here."

Now I was shocked. She was from here and she was looking for friends on an app? "What about you, Katherine?" I asked.

Tight-lipped Katherine looked at the sky and then back down at her clasped hands, calculating, calculating . . . and then said, "Hmmm. Seventeen years."

Now I needed to know everything about these women to understand why they were in this situation. Having been in Austin for decades and not having any friends. How had they become so desperate for company? How had they ended up destitute?

"What brought you to Austin?" I asked Katherine. Naomi

looked nervous, and I wasn't sure why. It seemed to me my questions were tactful and not at all overstepping. I just needed to find out about these women without making it seem like I was finding out about them.

"You mean seventeen years ago?" Katherine clarified. "My partner at the time wanted to be closer to family."

Partner? Man? Woman? Nonbinary? I had no clue, so I said, "At the time? Do you have a partner now?"

"Oh yes, same partner. I just meant that at that time, he had wanted to be closer to his family." So, a man.

"Are you married?" I asked.

She shook her head in this tiny way, like a snobby elementary school principal. "God no. I don't know why anyone would do something like that." She snorted, as if I were a silly little kid asking a grown-up an idealistic question about life. I realized Katherine was a mean person. This was why she didn't have any friends. It wasn't complicated: she was unlikable.

But Naomi laughed at Katherine's marriage comment and Katherine beamed at her across the table. They were bonding. Then the conversation died, and we were back to dominoes.

After an hour, I was bored out of my mind. How many more rounds? I decided to ask everyone what they were watching.

Katherine went, "Oh, I don't watch a lot of TV."

"What about movies?"

"Not really. I like to read."

"Okay," I said. "What are you reading?"

"I just read that novel about the Manson family girls," said Norah.

"I didn't love that one," said Katherine, in her terse, snippy voice. "Writing about white girls getting lured into cults and sexually assaulted . . . it's only ever so interesting."

"So true," said Norah. "It's tired. It's like the only bad thing that happens to girls in books is rape." They were both getting worked up together over this.

Katherine again: "Women are really challenged in only the one way. Female characters should be more than just bodies waiting to be violated. It's bad for the culture."

"Every time, it's like: Here's a pretty white woman," said Norah. "And now here comes the big tragic rape. And now here are all the graphic details."

"It'd be better to have more of a variety of narratives," added Naomi. "More representation. I do agree that most women in books are marked as victims."

"It's just so typical," Katherine sniffed.

I hadn't spoken in several minutes because I was seeing red everywhere. I was desperate to leave, but I didn't want to be the first to go in case they thought I was upset. Luckily, at last Norah said, "This has been so fun, but I need to get to bed early tonight. Let's do this again. Where's everyone located? I realize I don't even know." She chuckled.

It turned out Katherine and I lived in the same bizarre zone south of campus. She was on Nueces, in the stretch by the jail and all the bail offices.

"We could try somewhere near you two next time," said Naomi.

I was on the brink of something terrible. I was cresting a black rogue wave. My heart a beluga whale. But, so no one would know, I chimed in, "There's that bar that opened up on West Sixth. Gemini's?"

"Oh god, I hate that place," said Katherine.

"Oh. Why?" I asked. "I haven't been."

"I hate all the new places," she said, doing her minuscule headshake again. She had a small mouth, and a pointy chin, and tight, thin lips. She probably gave terrible blowjobs. She'd probably never even given a blowjob before. Her poor partner, who'd never gotten to feel a woman's lips around his penis, who never would for the rest of his life. I silently added that to the reasons Katherine didn't have any friends: she was unlikable and closed-off, and she shot down ideas.

The highway was blurry. Venomous me, barreling down 183. I was capable of causing a massive car wreck. I didn't even want to go home anymore. I wanted to go anywhere else. Far, far away. Somewhere on the other side of the world, or Manitoba, or the moon. In the night, surrounding me, were thousands of pulsing alarms. The headlights passing seemed to be screaming. Out in the dark the stadium lights cast down their funnels of fuzz. My car rattled manically every time another car passed. We were going fast but some of them were going even faster. I was whipping down the road, trapped inside this long-nosed narrow bullet, this baby-blue Crown Vic, red-hot energy reverberating off me. In the far-left lane, my foot pressed down to ninety, then off to eighty, then back to ninety, ninety-five, a hundred, then off again to eighty. Wee-woo, wee-woo. It was too dangerous for me to be out here like this. If I kept at it, I wouldn't make it home. Was it the three negronis? Or was it that cunt called Katherine and the things she'd said? I couldn't even feel my elbows or shoulders anymore. I tried summoning into my car the little voice that was good at telling me what I needed to hear: "I can see you're suffering," the little voice tried. I replied, "But it's so stupid I'm suffering over this." The little voice said, "It doesn't matter why you're suffering. It only matters that you're in pain." "I'm in so much pain," I agreed. I continued,

"I have to calm down or I'm going to fuck things up at home. I'm going to accidentally ruin my life. I have to get into a better mood before I see Liam. Sometimes I have all this pain inside, and I don't know why." I tried explaining for the little voice, but the little voice was long gone. The little voice didn't want to be in this crazy car with me either.

Oh wait, no. The little voice was back. "Don't merge yet," it said. "Blinker on."

It said, "Be kind to yourself. You're just in an extra sensitive space right now, so even a small comment from someone can get you really worked up, but that's not what this is about."

"What's it's about?" I wanted to know.

"It doesn't matter," said the little voice.

"I don't think I can keep going," I said. It was too dangerous.

"Just two more exits, sweets," said the voice. "I'll tell you when to get over to the right. Stay in this lane for another mile. Just follow that red Kia there. Okay, get over now."

I made it home. The car beeped. Locked. Click, click. I had it parallel parked beautifully on the side of the street. Now that I was home, I could better evaluate. My bad mood was the result of what Katherine had said about rape being the only bad thing that happens to white girls in books. She was talking about literature, but still. It made me think, There's nothing original about me. My life is typical, dull. But also, Katherine was white! Katherine was a girl!

I needed to unpack all of this with someone. Who could I call? I obviously couldn't talk about any of it with Liam, since he thought I'd been at yoga. Besides his Grandma Betty, Liam didn't know anyone who'd died. Both his dad's parents were still alive, living it up in Chicago in their late nineties. It was to Liam that nothing bad had ever happened!

I didn't know so much anger could be in me all at once. What a stupid, boring emotion. It made me unable to feel anything else. I wanted to fling dishes around. I wanted to shatter my life! I couldn't risk having this anger inside me when Liam got home, or who knew what would happen. But getting rid of it anytime soon also felt impossible. Liam knew nothing about grief.

I decided to take out my phone and call Patty, but instead I responded to Ellis's LinkedIn message from three years ago.

"Hi sorry," I messaged, referring to the fact that I'd never replied.

Less than a minute passed, and he'd written back, "wow that you??" It was so fast it sucked my heart right out of me. But that was okay—my heart was doing me zero favors at that moment. Its excessive beating had only been making me sick.

"How do you have LinkedIn?" I typed.

Suddenly he was video chatting me. Buzz, buzz, buzzzzzzz went my phone. Alive again. A hummingbird in my hand.

His face split into that big old grin. He looked the same. My heart was floundering all over the place. I couldn't believe this tiny screen had this person inside it who'd been so right about everyone. He'd seen it all. He'd seen right through me.

"Wow," he said, dropping open his jaw in that exaggerated, goofy way. "Look at you!" He seemed genuinely thrilled to be looking at me. "Feels like a dream. Hold the camera closer. Let me see you." He fell backward onto something, maybe a bed. "Wow. You look amazing."

"You look the same," I said. I felt shy, but knew he wouldn't mind. He'd know that I just needed some time to warm up. "Where are you?"

"Thailand. Me and the missus are scuba instructors."

"Really? That's wild."

"Yeah, I got me a girlfriend."

"No," I said. "That you're teaching scuba."

"Oh right," and he rolled his eyes. He was just joking around. "It's unbelievable over here. You'd love it. Come visit!"

"Maybe," I said. "Where in Thailand are you?"

"Koh Tao. You know it? We got here a year ago." He paused to smile more, with all his long teeth, then he brought the camera closer to his face. He tilted it left, right. Was he looking at himself or at me? He was sucking in his cheeks. "Look at you. Wow. Can't believe I'm chatting with you. It feels like a dream."

"Guess what? I'm married," I lied.

"Fuck off!" He stuck out his tongue. "Who's the lucky lad?"

"This guy I met in Texas."

"Texas? Wow." He was grinning. We could be quiet with each other, and it was always fine. We knew we were both always dying to say something else to each other, so not speaking was just teasing. "Wow," he eventually said. "You live in Texas. And you're *married*. I wasn't invited!"

"Didn't know your address in Thailand."

"You's a little married lady. A real penguin now, aren't you? You staying faithful and all that? Or you still fucking other guys on the side?"

"Fuck off," I said. Whoops. I realized I actually hated him. "You don't know anything."

"Come on, baby. I'm just taking the piss. Keep talking to me! Tell me, what's he like?"

But Liam walked in then with the groceries.

Immediately, I ended the call and shoved my phone under my ass. It kept buzzing against me. Buzz, buzz, buzz. I knew

Liam knew I had just hung up on someone, but he didn't ask who was on the phone. He didn't care. He never asked about me. He was humming, tapping a beat on the counter as he unpacked the bags, opened and closed the fridge, put things in the cupboard. In my eyes, headlights were going by. I was so far away. What missus? Who was his missus? Was she like me? How old? Also: Was she like me?

"We need to talk," he said, holding up the empty box of Honey Nut Cheerios, "about the rate at which you consume cereal."

Where was my voice? Anywhere. What missus though? What did she look like? I realized I didn't care. I hoped I'd never meet her or ever get any idea of her. I hoped she was older, forty-six, forty-seven, somewhere around there, older than Ellis. But was she like me? There were many girls out in the world, just out and about, exactly like me. Women. Young women? Girls. Or, whoever. Anyone! But was she like me? Hopefully not. I hoped she was okay, with whatever she was doing. Did they do what we had done together? Maybe so. Hopefully, she liked her life.

Liam was still holding the Cheerios. Now he could tell my energy was off.

"My love," he said, to check I was alive. "You okay? How was your day?"

He tossed the box in the recycling bin, unloaded the eggs and beer into the fridge, then came over to the couch to stand in front of me. He reached down a hand to pull me up.

"You alright?" he said. He kissed my forehead, then held me by the shoulders out in front of him, studying me quizzically. Liam liked to tell people that my moods kept him on his toes. He still hadn't taken off his boots, which made him a giant in comparison to me, barefoot. He squinted at me playfully, then pressed my head to his chest. I breathed in his armpit; the day still on him, stain, lacquer, sweat. "What can I do for you? What do you need?"

I just had to breathe through this; his heart thumped steadily against my temple. This was one of those choice moments. It wasn't worth a big reaction. He held me a little longer, then gave me a final squeeze. He headed back to the kitchen to start dinner. He thought we were done. He thought all I needed was for him to ask what I needed. He was so bad at finding out about me!

"I'm worried that nothing bad has ever happened to me," I said.

Liam turned around, cocking his head. "Well, that's obviously not true," he said slowly, carefully, trying to figure me out.

"I'm worried I'm a boring person," I clarified.

"Darling." Now he laughed, but I was being dead serious. Clearly, he'd had a lovely day and I was about to ruin it. "You're the least boring person I've ever met. You're the most captivating woman in the world." He came back to give me a quick squeeze, his eyes sparkly. "And anyway," he said. "Boring isn't bad. It's okay for life to be a little boring. That doesn't mean you're boring."

I pulled away from him. "I want a scintillating existence, actually."

"Scintillating?" he repeated. My sharp tone had sent a tiny dagger into his good mood. He rubbed his forehead. He sighed. "What do you mean?"

What I meant was: It had once been an unimaginable future, the one without him, but the world had just started letting on that it might not have to be. There could still be more . . .

But what I said was: "We don't talk about anything with each other. That's why we don't know each other that well."

"Well, that hurts my feelings," said Liam. "That devastates me, actually."

I sucked the snot back into my nose and backed away from him. My long arms winged out on either side of me, I tried to take up all the space I could. He had no idea how big I could be. "If our life together was more exciting, I wouldn't want as much."

"If our life together was more exciting, I wouldn't want as much," Liam repeated slowly. "I don't know what that means."

I could be in Thailand! Living! Living! I felt so confused. He had no idea—I had a sky in my stomach. I had an endless cavern. I contained birds! Great migrations took place inside me.

"I could have such a bigger life than this one. Is this it?" I wanted to know. I asked again, "Is this all?" I gestured around the room, my arms still flying out at my sides. I picked up one of my coasters from the coffee table even though he said we didn't need coasters because his furniture was all properly varnished. I put it back down.

"This is us," he said. "Yes."

"Sometimes I want to start my life over and make every single different choice."

A pause. Then: "See, I hear you say things like that, and it just sounds like you don't love me."

"I do love you." I had to backtrack now. "I love you in *this* life." Then, I added reasonably, "I just want to have another life too. I just want more lives. This life I have with you—I could do it with anyone."

"You're hurting my feelings," he tried to tell me.

"This isn't about you at all." I felt frustrated.

"Do you understand how I can feel that it is?"

His arms were crossed, his hairline sweaty under his hat; my hands were on the back of my head, armpits facing him.

We were quiet. "Okay," said Liam, taking a deep breath. "Can we start over? I don't think we're saying things that we mean."

I took a few deep breaths too. Suddenly I felt very heavy. I started to cry a little.

"We can't now," I sniffed, feeling awful. "I've already ruined your mood with all the mean things I've said."

"It's okay," said Liam, still rubbing his forehead. "Let's just shake it off. Alright? Let's try and have a nice evening. I'll put on a show."

So, I excused myself to the bathroom, to splash water on my face and calm down. It was time to calm down. He was right—it wasn't even true what I'd been saying. I had no interest in having multiple existences. I really didn't. I just wanted one existence. A consistent, stable one. Or I wanted many different single existences. But one after the other. Not all at once.

When I came out of the bathroom, Liam said, "Ellis messaged you."

My phone, stupidly, was lit up on the couch cushion. How'd it get there?

"Oh," I said, picking it up. "That's just a coworker." Then I clicked it off and placed it on the coffee table, face down.

But Liam darkened. Something was up.

Finally, I inquired, "Okay, what's wrong?"

"Nothing."

"Your energy's weird."

"My energy?" That bite in his voice. It didn't suit him. I was bringing it out. He continued, "Yours was off the moment I walked in."

"Why won't you tell me what's wrong? I hate it when you don't talk to me."

"Alright," he shot back. He sounded angry. "I guess I don't trust you."

I was stunned. "What? Why?"

"That." He pointed at my phone. "That's your ex. You've told me his name and now you just lied. I know that Ellis is your ex."

Shit. So dumb. "It's nothing. I just didn't want to make it a thing because it's truly nothing. You want to see? It's nothing." I picked up the phone. "He reached out to me to see how I was. But he has a girlfriend and they live in Thailand. I didn't even text back. It's nothing. You want to see? I'll show you."

"No," said Liam fiercely. "I don't care. It just sucks that you lied."

Of course, Liam wouldn't want to see. But I opened my phone anyway to see for myself what Ellis had messaged in case Liam had wanted to see and I would've had to show him. Ellis's messages since our video chat read, "Are you still there??? I lost ya," "haha ok fuck you," "lucyyyyyyy," "fuck you!!!" "I still love ya btw. You was something special."

And then the next one read, "ok take care baby xx," and then he wrote again, "I'll never forget us and the stuff we did together. That was special," and then "also!!!!! Fuck you for leaving me hahahha!!!!"

"This is so dumb," I said, but I didn't want to show him any of the messages now. Luckily, he still didn't want to see them. "He reached out to me," I tried to tell him again.

"It's not about that," said Liam, waving away the phone I was once again thrusting in his face. "It's that you lied."

"I said coworker because I thought it was easier. I didn't want to make it a big thing."

"You lie in these little ways sometimes and I really don't like it," he said. Then he snapped, "Get that away from me."

I had been thrusting my phone once more in his face. He had never snapped at me like that before. He sounded mean and threatened, like an animal backed into a corner. He didn't want me or my phone anywhere near him.

So, I backed away quickly, into the bookshelf. A couple paperbacks fell onto the floor.

"You know what?" he said, his voice was trembling. "This is why I don't know with you. I'm worried I can't trust you."

"Fuck fuck fuck fuck," I said, mostly to myself. I accidentally dropped my phone on the floor. My head was in my hands. "Fuck." Sometimes I really couldn't stand who I was. "It's not my fault that Ellis reached out to me," I tried. Then, I added, "You once called me Becky."

Now Liam looked like he was about to explode. I'd never seen him so out of control. He half groaned, half roared, his hands holding his head as if it was about to pop off.

"Seriously?" He paced around in a furious circle. "That's crazy, Lucy. I mean, that's crazy. That was years ago." So, he *had* called me Becky! Ha!

"Do you wish I was Becky?" I suggested. I couldn't stop.

I realized he'd gotten completely frozen. Ice. His eyes were closed, and his jaw was clenched. Not just his jaw. Every single muscle in his body. Why were his eyes closed?

"Why are your eyes closed? Liam?" I was now panicked. The fact that he hadn't taken off his shoes was also starting to shoot anxiety through me. "Why are your eyes closed?"

My panicky voice was so pitchy it didn't even sound like it belonged to me. But his eyes being closed was petrifying.

"Where are you?" I commanded. I had no idea what was going on inside his head, but he definitely wasn't here in the kitchen with me. "I don't know where you are." My voice cracked. "Talk to me. Say something."

"Hey," he said. He opened his eyes and locked his gaze on me. He didn't like it when I raised my voice. But before I could apologize, he said, "I can't be with someone who lies. It makes me feel unsafe."

Suddenly, I felt very high up. My head got very cold. From a bird's-eye view, I was looking down at us and seeing that we were on the edge of a cliff. Liam inhaled loudly through his nose, his shoulders and chest lifting. Even from up here, I could hear his hot breath getting sucked up, and then he exhaled like a dragon—I could see the smoke. The cliff we were on, we'd never survive the fall; the ground was way too far away, and it was up to me to back us up from the edge and get us off of there. That was the most important thing right now: I had to stay focused on that. I needed to back us up—but oh, I felt so heavy still, so full of ruins, I could barely move. With all the breath I had, I tried to explain, in a much calmer, softer, quieter voice: "I shouldn't have lied. I'm sorry. That was a mistake." Every word was making the next word easier. And he was giving me the time and space I needed to get us off the death-edge, back from dire to good. "I just didn't want to make it a big thing," I said again. Liam chuckled a little bit at this, so I chuckled too. He lifted up his hat and rubbed his sweaty forehead and took a deep breath and his shoulders fell away from his ears. Things were going to be fine. He was relaxing; the farther we got away from the edge, we were both calming down. "And I can also see how it's not just about that," I said—this was the most important part; I had to bring us back to the present, and to what was next, and how things were going to be better now—"it's about how I need to work on being more honest with you about the little things." Solid ground, here we come. Good, good, good. "I should've been honest tonight. That was really dumb. I promise to be completely honest with you moving forward." We were already moving forward. "This really doesn't need to be a big thing. I won't do something like that again. I'm sorry."

"I don't know," he said, and zoom, zoom, zoomie zoom zoom. We were back at the edge. "I think there's some trust missing between us."

How could he say that? I was baffled. "But you don't have any reason not to trust me," I said. "I'm honest with you about everything." I pointed at the phone again. "That was a one-time mistake."

He shook his head.

"Is this because I cheated on Cole? I've never cheated on you."

"No," said Liam fiercely. He was mad again.

"I've only ever been honest in the context of us."

"What about the smoking?"

My voice got very high then. "I have to do it secretly because you don't like it. If you let me—"

"Stop. We're talking in circles." He took a deep breath. He squeezed his eyes shut. He took another deep breath. "I guess I'm also having this reaction, having a hard time with this, because I hate thinking about that stuff. All that stuff you told me about."

"What stuff?"

"You know. Your weird sex shit."

I was shocked. "What do you mean?"

He continued, "It's not like I care. I know it has nothing to do with me. I just don't like being reminded of it."

"What weird sex shit?"

"You know."

But I truly felt as though I didn't know.

He dropped his head back and groaned again and told the ceiling, "All that stuff you told me about on our first or second date. Like, way back."

"Was I drunk?"

"Come on." He put his head back on top of his neck but wouldn't look at me. "Don't make me talk about this stuff. I hate this kind of stuff."

But I still had no idea what he was talking about.

"Did I tell you about Australia?" I asked.

He immediately put up both his hands to stop me. "Don't tell me any more. Don't tell me about anything else." There was a lot of panic in his voice. "Please."

He only took his hands down when he was sure I was staying quiet. But what had I told him about? I needed to know.

"But what did I tell you?" I tried to speak as softly as possible so as not to spook him.

He seemed to be in a tremendous amount of pain. He held his face and stared at his boots. I didn't know what to do with myself. I didn't want to torture him. I just needed to know what he knew.

At last, he snapped, stopping me mid-question. "Alright. You asked me all these questions to find out if I choked girls." He wasn't shouting, but he also wasn't totally in control of his volume. "And then you told me about the whole Tinder thing." He could barely get it out.

"But that was years ago." I was dumbfounded. "That was in the past."

"You were just talking to him," he said into the fist that was pressing into his face.

"He reached out to me. I can show you—"

But Liam looked terrified again and held up his hands. "Don't," he said, his voice shaking. He looked genuinely frightened. "Don't."

"That was all in the past," I said again. "None of that's important anymore." I couldn't feel my feet. "You have a past too," I reminded him. "Becky—"

"Stop it. No." He shook his head rigorously. "I've never done anything like that. The type of thing you were doing makes me really uncomfortable." That made me feel like I wanted to die. "You and I are just different," continued Liam. "I could never . . . with random people. I'm just not like that. You're interested in something that's not me. We're different."

"No, no, no," I said. That was the worst thing he could possibly say. "No, we're not. We are the same. You and me are not different." I really needed to make sure he understood. "That was the whole problem," I tried to explain. "You and me are not different." Stupidly, I pointed at his chest, then at mine. But he needed to understand this. "We are the ones who are the same."

But Liam shook his head again. "I could never do that kind of thing with my partner. And I really hate thinking about you doing that with him. I don't want to talk about it anymore." He took a big breath. "I guess sometimes it feels like you don't want to be in a relationship like this. Or you just don't want to be with me." A pause. "Or, you don't know what you want yet."

"No, no, no," I said again. He was misunderstanding everything, and it was critical that he understand. He was the only thing I wanted in the whole world. "I fell in love with you the moment I saw you," I told him. And he smiled weakly at this, which made me think we were going to be okay. He just needed reassurance. That was all. He just needed to know how much I loved him. I took a deep breath to continue—

"Lucy. I think we're just different."

"No," I said. How did he still not get it? "That wasn't me." I pointed at the phone again. "This is me." And I pointed at my chest. "This." I knocked on my chest with my fist. My voice was losing volume again. But I had to get us off the cliff. "This is me." It was life or death. "I want to be with you more than anyone else. I've never wanted to be with anyone as much as I want to be with you." He needed to know how special he was. "I could be with hundreds of guys, but I choose to be with you."

"Seriously? Come on. Why would you say something like that?"

I was confused.

"I really hate that," he said. "I hate that so much. You're trying to make me feel small."

I didn't understand . . .

"When you say things like that," he said. "When you remind me how you've been with hundreds of guys—" He waved his arms around. "Do you not get how that makes me feel insecure?"

"Not hundreds," I said. That was an exaggeration—surely it wasn't hundreds. All I was trying to tell him was that I wanted to be with him the most—

"Stop," he said. He held up his hands again. "I don't want to talk about this anymore. I really can't keep talking about this. I won't be able to fall asleep."

It was excruciating to be inside my body now. "This makes me want to die," I let him know.

We were quiet for a long time then. Liam worked through things with a lot of big sighs and a lot of holding his breath. Finally, when he was finished breathing, he said, "Okay. I can see that this might be a me problem. It's just . . ." he trailed off. "It's not that I'm jealous or anything." Why did he say *jealous*? That was such a weird word. What was he even talking about? "I'm embarrassed that I get so uncomfortable talking about this with you."

"Talking about what?"

"I don't know. Your past."

I sat down on the couch, feeling dizzy.

"I want to be able to talk to you about it," he said. "But it just makes me really uncomfortable."

"Why?" I was so confused. The room was spinning.

"It's just that you told me about all that weird shit early on. And I've tried really hard to forget about it. It's not—I don't judge you for it. It's fine. I just don't like thinking about it."

"I just wanted you to know all about me at the front end," I explained. I still couldn't remember what conversation he was referencing, but if I had told him about Ellis, my reasoning must've been that I had wanted him to know all about me right away so he couldn't leave me later for things he already knew.

"Like that old guy in Hawaii? Fuck. Yeah, see? I hate thinking about that stuff."

"That stuff is my life," I said, surprising myself.

And then it dawned on me: "You think I'm gross," and I started to sob.

"Oh fuck." He lifted his head and looked me in the eyes. "Lucy. Please," he said. He sat down on the couch too. But when he tried to get closer to me, I scooted away immediately. He reached out to try and grab my socked foot but I pulled that away too. I didn't want him touching me when he thought I was gross. Also, it was obvious that he didn't really want to be touching me either because when I pulled my foot away, he didn't try to grab it again. He always tried again. "Lucy. Come on. Please."

I curled my knees into my chest so I was a tiny ball. I knew it, I knew it.

"Please. Lucy. Let's— Can we—" he put his face in his hands too.

"Is this just about my past?" I needed to know. "Because"— I was sobbing still—"because you have stuff too. Like with your dad."

"My dad?"

"You have problems with your dad."

"I love my dad."

"You wanted to commit suicide."

"Lucy." A little blizzard whipped across his face, and then it got calm again. "What are you trying to do here?"

I was trying to remind him about how we all have stuff. "We all have stuff," I said, the breath in my throat still sounding like a rattle. "Someone else will just have something else."

"It's not just about your past. It's—" His voice cracked the tiniest bit. "It's that I feel like you're not always fully honest with me."

"That's fixable though," I said. "Let's just stay focused on that. How do we fix that?"

He shook his head. We were quiet for a long time. Sitting far away from each other, on opposite sides of the couch, just breathing. Neither one of us knew what to do. I think we were both praying for the smallest chance we could get loose from this, the smallest chance . . .

But then at some point, that night or another night soon after, he said, "Lucy? Hey. I don't think this is working anymore." And we began our slow tumble down, down, down . . .

He said, "I feel like the more we talk about our relationship, the less we're in it."

"Yes," I said, "I see."

He said, "I think we're both in a lot of pain. I wish we didn't need to have hard conversations like this. Sometimes I feel like if we understood each other better, or if we were more similar people, we wouldn't need to."

"I agree," I agreed.

He said, "And you say these things sometimes that make me feel so bad about myself. Like I'm not giving you what you want. Like I'm not enough."

"I'm sorry."

He said, "I love you. But we're not on the same page about what we want out of life."

"We should both want the same things," I agreed.

—

He said, "I don't want us to keep talking in circles." He hated circles.

And yet, I would keep talking with him forever, even like this . . .

He said, "I think we need to talk about how we're going to end this."

I put my head in my hands for what felt like hours but when I rose the clock told me only twenty-three minutes. He was still there, but all the way on the other side of the couch, staring my way, waiting for me all this time, all twenty-three minutes. But now that we were looking at each other, he wasn't moving closer to hold me, to tell me, I choose you, Lucy. I'm always going to choose you. The only future I want is one with you. He wasn't saying that this time.

Finally, I said, "Okay. I understand."

"But, so, it was me?" I asked. We had continued to be frozen with each other. Sitting in our separate spots on the couch, both of us still in shock. "About the kids thing. You haven't been sure about kids with *me*."

"Oh, no, baby, no. Don't think of it that way," he said. "There's just some trust missing between us. Both ways."

"But I trust you," I explained. I could barely get the words out.

"I don't think you always do. I think you worry I'm going to abandon you."

"But you are. You are abandoning me."

"Baby, please," he said. "Come here."

"I can't. I can't come here anymore."

"This is breaking my heart," he said.

He was crying just like me. We were both gasping at each other like shipwrecked fish.

THE ORPHANAGE

I<small>T STARTED AS A CONVERSATION ABOUT A NEIGHBOR</small> my sister and I both knew who'd asked a friend of a friend of a friend, whom this neighbor had met only once at a holiday party, to be her sperm donor. They were attracted to each other and decided to go about it the natural way, but before it happened, he backed out. We'd heard about this from our mother's friend Meg. It got us talking about whether, if we were in his position, we would donate our eggs to someone else. This got us talking about whether we would ever be surrogate mothers. It was my sister and I talking. Mom was there too, making dinner, moving around behind the kitchen island, and Patty and I were sitting on our respective swivel stools. We were both home from college for the holidays. I said that if Patty asked me to be her surrogate mother, I would do it, but I wouldn't do it for anyone else, and the only person I would ever want to carry my own baby would be Patty.

"Absolutely not," she said.

"Absolutely not what?"

"You'd be the last person I'd want carrying my kid."

"What?"

"And I probably wouldn't carry your baby for you."

"*What?*"

"Yeah. You'd be the last person."

"Are you serious?"

"It'd be like you were my baby's real mother. It'd always feel like that."

"Are you hearing this?" I asked our mother, but she didn't say anything. She was humming and washing her hands, patting them dry with a dish towel, those sorts of things.

"It'd still be your egg and your husband's sperm," I informed Patty. "It would just be inside me because in the case we're talking about, your body wouldn't be able to have a baby and so you'd be asking me to have your baby for you because you'd really want a baby and this would be a way for me to give that to you."

"But the baby would know that you were the one who had it, and it would have a special connection to you," Patty said. "I wouldn't be able to hand my baby over to you to feed and babysit and stuff when deep down, you'd be thinking the whole time that you were the baby's real mother."

"You would rather have a stranger birth your baby than me."

"Absolutely."

Dad was there too. He looked up at us from whatever he was doing.

"Well, this is fascinating," he said. "Fascinating stuff."

He was sitting on the stool to my right, probably eating raw vegetables and doing the crossword. Whenever we were home from college, our parents liked to spend as much time with us as possible and it was always around this kitchen island.

My sister looked tense and cold. She could be such a cold person. And whenever she got tense, she wouldn't look at me. She'd gaze forward and down and pull all her limbs in as if preparing to take a punch. It made her look small. She was a very small person.

Patty leaned forward on the island. "What I'm saying is: if you carried my baby, my baby would have this special connection to you and you would have this special connection to it. I wouldn't be able to handle that."

"That's the whole point," I said. "I'd want that for my baby and you. I'd trust you the most out of anybody having my kid. I would want my baby to be carried by only you." I felt suddenly desperate, expressing this, and my voice got thin. I couldn't let it go. "You're saying that you would not carry my baby for me if I asked you to?"

Our dad craned past me to look at Patty and asked curiously, "What if you already had two kids and Lucy couldn't have any? You've already had kids. You'd carry her baby then."

"I already have kids? I already have two three-year-olds or whatever running around the house and then you come up to me and ask if I can carry your baby when I already have a house full of kids? You'd want me to be pregnant for you for another nine months? I'd think about it, I guess, but I probably wouldn't."

I started to cry a little now. It was ridiculous, but I was tearing up. "Are you serious, Patty? I can't have any kids. I'm *unable* to have kids. And you already have two little kids. And I come up to you asking if you can help me by carrying my baby so that I can also have kids and you would say no?"

"If it were me, I'd adopt."

"It's not you."

"I think you would probably do that for your sister," said our dad. "You would see how awesome it was to have kids and you'd be like, 'Oh, Lucy, you've got to have a kid, too, I'm telling you, everything changes once you have kids.' And you'd want to help Lucy have that."

My mom could tell things were getting tense. "Well, you have to consider the complications," she said. "It makes a relationship really complex. There can be death in childbirth, even still. You'd be asking your sister to do a huge thing—what if she died and you had that on your plate? Or if the baby didn't make it, or came out with health complications?"

"Well, yeah," I said, "if Patty was listing those as her reasons for not doing it, if she was saying that she was scared for her own life, or for having the responsibility of messing up my kid. But that's not what she's saying. She's saying she wouldn't do it because she wouldn't want to be pregnant for me for nine months of her life, because it'd be too much of an inconvenience."

I put my feet on the metal bar under Patty's stool and forced her to swivel around and look at me. She was all stony and sucked in. "If you said it was because of any of Mom's reasons, I'd understand, and then I'd have responded that I wouldn't want to put you in that position either, if I really thought it through, but those are things we would think through together after the initial, instinctual fact of it. And my initial, instinctual fact is that if you, my *sister*, wanted me to be a surrogate for you, I would absolutely say yes and then we'd discuss the rest of it and make sure we were both willing to take on the risks. You weren't saying that."

"Would you give Lucy your kidney?" our dad jumped in.

"A kidney? Probably," said Patty.

"I don't care about a kidney," I said, and I swiveled back around to look at him. I still had tears in my eyes. "We're not talking about kidneys. Patty doesn't want me carrying her baby because she'd be too jealous of me." It was a nasty reason. I told her. "That's nasty, Patty."

A decade later, our parents were both dead, and Patty joined me back at our childhood home to finally decide what we were going to do with the house. Patty had brought her new boyfriend with her so that I could meet him. They were going to stay in our old bedroom, and I was on an air mattress in the pink room on the first floor that used to have an antique dollhouse inside it but in recent years must've become our mother's office.

It was the first time Patty had ever brought a boy to this house, whereas I'd been bringing boys home since the seventh grade. At thirty-one, she was in her first real relationship, with this man named Ben whom she met on the train to Long Island, where she sometimes still staffed children's birthday parties as a clown or Disney princess.

Ben had it more together. He was a couple of inches shorter than Patty, from Connecticut, with a goatee and a handsome, clean face. He was the sales director at a fully remote software company and an ex–college hockey player, and his family was rich. His dad was an executive at a big bank. He also seemed to adore Patty, which was exhilarating, but in a way that put me on high alert, like I was sitting in a lifeguard's chair. When I came out to greet them on Friday evening as they exited the cab, we all stood in the driveway chitchatting, and he reached up to place a hand on the back of Patty's neck, even though Patty had always declared herself to be someone who didn't like being touched.

Up to that point, Patty had handled most things related to the estate—funeral arrangements, public notice, probate, insurance. She was generally better at organizing small details and managing paperwork. I said I'd take care of going through all of Mom's things, and had been home already for three weeks. I was resolved to stay for however long it took to get everything sorted. Being back in the house had also made me reconsider all the plans our mother had for improving the place, and I was excited to share her ideas with Patty. Maybe now we could finally renovate it in the way she had described to me. We could redo the kitchen cabinets and turn the half bath into a full bath and knock down the wall between the kitchen and the den. We could add built-in bookshelves and a nook for reading and watching the sun rise. We could get the garden going again. Patty could move back here too, and we could work on getting the house back into the shape it was in when we were kids—tidy up the lawn, repaint the porch, that sort of thing.

But on the first night of that weekend, when Patty, Ben, and I were sitting on the front stoop having wine—I was enjoying Ben; he was warm, enthusiastic, a good laugher, and I kept feeling happier and happier for my sister—Patty implied that she wanted us to consider selling. I didn't say anything. I was working on being less reactive and had repeated to myself during the days when I cleaned and prepped for their visit that I would be calm and strong for Patty throughout the whole weekend, especially since I was meeting her boyfriend. I even told myself I wouldn't smoke. But I didn't feel good. I kept feeling tortured by this memory of me and my mother sitting on the porch together, and my mother saying something to me. We're having a conversation, and she says something, and it's a good memory. But I can't see it totally.

I think we're watching the rabbits together, and at one point my dad's headlights burst around the corner and we both stand up, happy. But I can't remember any more than that and the harder I try, the more my mother's face disappears, and I end up feeling enraged. I wish I could remember it better, any of it; I wish I had written down more things as they were happening to me, when the people were right there in front of me—I'd be sure of so many more things—instead of waiting till now.

That first night of the weekend, after the three of us had finished dinner and they went to bed, I got up at two in the morning to smoke a cigarette. I was tying my shoelaces when I heard someone coming down the stairs. I stuffed the cigarettes into the pocket of my purple puffer jacket but when I turned around it was Ben, not Patty.

"Oh my god. You scared me," I said.

Ben stood at the bottom of the stairs, barefoot, in his boxers, and wearing glasses.

"What are you doing up?" he asked, his voice raspy.

"Oh," I said. "I can't have Patty knowing I smoke." I pulled the cigarettes out of my pocket to show him. He took a glass out of a cabinet and started filling it from the tap.

He took a sip. "Let me throw on some pants," he said. "I'll keep you company."

I didn't want to smoke too close to the house, so Ben and I walked toward the edge of the new development, where our old tire swing still hung from an ancient maple. Our dad used to pile mulch under the tree to give us a hill to swing off of, but the mulch was long gone. It was early April and still cold out, but the trees had only some leaves on them, so you could still see the streetlights. I used the flashlight on my phone as we walked, but at one point heard Ben trip over something and grunt. I asked if he was okay. He was fine. When we got to the swing, I offered him a cigarette, but he declined. Back at the house, just that kitchen light was on.

"I don't want to sell," I finally said. "Is Patty really set on that?"

"I don't think so," he said. "It's a great house. I don't think you should sell it."

"Why does she want to?"

"Have you two not talked about it?"

"Not before this evening."

"Well, I'm sure you'll talk about it and come to a good decision."

"But she's talked to you about it?"

"A bit."

"And you don't think we should sell?"

"I think it's a great house."

I pushed the tire swing lightly with my foot. He started to put his foot through the hole but I told him not to because I didn't know how strong the rope was, or whether the branch that held it was still alive.

"We used to play on this all the time," I told him. "We had this weird game where we pretended the swing was a swan. God, we spent hours playing out here."

"You were happy kids," Ben said.

"We were," I agreed.

I wanted to talk more about the game my sister and I used to play but I couldn't remember all of the details. It seemed incredible that we had created an entire universe together and I needed to know how it had worked. I finished a second cigarette, then Ben and I walked back to the house and I thanked him for his company.

The next day, after breakfast, I went back out to the tire swing to get a better look at the rope, and soon Ben and Patty joined me.

"Do you remember that game we used to play?" I finally asked Patty, tugging on the rope to test it. I had been thinking about the game all morning. The mechanics of it fascinated me. Did we speak out loud to each other? Did we speak at all? Was she under the impression that she'd visualized whatever world we'd created the same way I had? How had we known we were playing the same thing in the same way?

"Don't get on it," Patty said.

"I'm not." I backed away from the swing and looked up at the branch. It didn't look too dead. Then I asked again, "You remember that game with the swan?"

"Obviously."

"How did we play it?"

"Like any kid game. We were on some sort of adventure and we had all these special ways of riding the swing and depending on the way we jumped on the swing, the swan would take us somewhere different. There used to be that mound here, and you'd swing out and I'd hold on to the rope and it'd yank me up and we called that flying."

"Oh right. That was something."

"We were doing secret missions for the queen. And there were also big storms that would happen and we would pretend the swing was bucking us off."

"How do you remember that?"

"We played that game for years."

"That's so weird about kids," I said. "How do kids do that?"

"What do you mean?"

"How were we both seeing the swan at the same time when the swan wasn't even there?"

"Well, I don't think we were seeing the same swan."

"My brother and I did this thing," Ben cut in, "where we pretended the floor was lava."

"Everybody does that."

"Did we have any other games," I asked Patty, "where we made up stuff?"

"Did we, or did I?"

"What do you mean?"

"I mean I did."

"You did what?"

"I had other games. I had this one game that I played for years."

"What was it?"

"It was weird."

"What was it?"

She hesitated. Then she said, "It was called Orphanage."

"Orphanage?"

"I think I started making it up after Dad read *Matilda* to us, because the Trunchbull was in it. And there was the Chokey, too, for the bad orphans."

"What orphans?"

"Well, the whole world was this orphanage, so everyone was an orphan. The poor kids were on the bottom floor, in steerage—that was where Hillary and I were—"

"Hillary?"

"She was my best friend, in the orphanage. I can remember

all the names of the other orphans too, and what floor of the orphanage they were assigned. And then at one point, Hillary and I had these pet mice that we kept in our pockets. And the mice could talk. That was a whole storyline. It was pretty complex."

"Where was I?"

"What do you mean?"

"When you were playing this."

"I don't know. You were around."

"But I didn't know you were playing."

"Well, I was playing by myself. It was my game."

"But I was in the game?"

"No, it was just me and everyone in the orphanage."

"I never saw you playing it."

"It was in my head."

"Okay."

"What? I feel like every kid has something like this."

"Well, sure. I know I did. I just can't remember the details of mine."

"Ben, don't climb on that."

"I'm not. I just want to see something." Ben was sticking his foot through the tire again and looking up at the branch.

"I don't want it falling."

"I bet we could replace the rope," he said. "We just need to make sure that the branch will hold. Does it look dead?"

"Wait. So, you were playing in another world this whole time?" I said.

"Well, no. Not always."

"When were you playing it?"

"I don't know. A lot of the time. On errands with Mom and stuff. I remember playing at Aunt Rebecca's wedding reception at that house with the outdoor shower, and that girl Nancy was there. Remember that?"

"Sort of."

"I mostly played at school, or walking to school in the morning. There was that restroom at school, the single-stall one by the cafeteria, that was important to the orphanage."

"But we'd be talking when we walked to school."

"We weren't always talking."

"How old were you when you were doing this?"

"I think I played that game for like fifteen years. I played it through high school."

"That's so interesting," said Ben. I thought he was referring to an interesting part of the swing, but he was looking at Patty.

Patty said, "I was really shy growing up."

Ben let go of the rope and shook his head. "That always blows my mind." He was beaming at her. "You love being onstage. You love an audience."

"Well, I used to be invisible."

"What changed?" His eyes were sparkling. "How'd you become such a force?" He opened up his arms at the sky. Patty shrugged. Ben seemed keen to keep on asking things, but Patty's mouth was twisted up. She was fiddling with her dead ends. I was glad Ben held himself back. I knew Patty, and I didn't want to watch him make her cry. So we all walked back to the house in silence. It sort of felt like too much had been said.

Then, pushing open the door, Patty said to no one in particular, "Leaving home, I think."

Later that night, Ben came downstairs again, around the same time as the night before. I hadn't fallen asleep yet, and when I heard someone in the kitchen turning on the tap, I came out of the pink room, and there he was.

"You want some company out there?" he asked.

We put on our jackets and set out. We ended up back at the tire swing and somehow, I started telling him about a short story I had read years ago.

"It was about this clown murderer. It was told from the clown's perspective. And this clown went around murdering couples, and you know what I thought as I was reading it? I thought: *You get it*. You, Clown, get something, and that's why you're able to do these things where you murder people who don't get it. And I felt like I was actually understanding what the writer was trying to say, and it felt insane that everybody wasn't a clown murderer."

"Hm," said Ben.

I continued, "Or maybe the writer was saying we are all clown murderers. Or he was asking about what keeps us from being clown murderers. I could be a clown murderer. I used to think that only some of us were capable of being clown murderers. But I've been realizing lately that actually, we're all murderers. Isn't it funny how writers make you think things like that?"

"I think I see what you're saying," said Ben. "I guess I never considered the possibility of being a clown murderer before."

"It's okay if you haven't," I said. "Just something to think about."

"A little food for thought," he said.

I asked, "How much do you think this house is worth?"

He answered more quickly than I expected: "I think you could get a million for it."

"And she wants the million."

"Well, half a million each. When you split it," said Ben.

"What would I do with half a million dollars?" I actually wanted to know his thoughts.

He seemed ready to rise to the occasion. "Do you have student debt? You should pay that off first," he said. I didn't have any student debt. It was one of the luckiest things about me. "Then you could put it in the stock market," he continued. "An ETF or index fund. Right now, a high-yield savings account is also a solid option. With a good bank, you could just live off that interest for a while, depending on your cost of living. You can get four-point-three percent right now. And that's all liquid. Or you could buy property, which is what Pat and I want to do."

Property? "But this is property," I said, waving my left hand around.

"Well, yes, if this is the property you want," said Ben. "We've been thinking about an apartment in Brooklyn."

"You said this is a great house."

"It is," he said. "I don't think you need to sell it. I think we could fix it up." He opened his mouth, then closed it. Then after another moment, he opened his mouth again to say very slowly, "I think whatever you're sensing isn't because she doesn't like your ideas. She just likes being in the city." A pause. Then he added, "We both really love that big city life."

But there was a big life to be had right here. Hadn't I been talking about making the house bigger? There was a big field just across the street. Here we could have whole fields.

Ben had started talking about Patty's latest show. "I have a really good feeling about this one," he was saying. "I knew it the first time I saw it. This is the one that's going to make her a star."

"Well," I asked after another silence. "What else?" I wanted to keep talking.

Ben kicked the swing with his boot. "I've been meaning to tell you," he began now. "I'm sorry about your relationship. Breakups are so hard. I'm sure it's been devastating."

What had Patty told him? But I said, "Thanks." Then I added, for context: "We weren't on the same page about kids."

"That's really tough," said Ben, shaking his head. "I'm divorced. I remember how scary it can feel to start all over."

"You're divorced?"

"Yeah."

"Huh," I said. I accidentally exhaled in his face and waved my hands around to get the smoke away. I didn't know what to think of this, except that this whole time, I guess I had assumed that Ben was coming into this relationship with Patty from a similar point in his life as she was. But of course he was divorced. He was almost forty.

"What's so interesting about that?" Ben asked.

It wasn't my place to say anything, but I said, "Oh, just that Patty hasn't been in any sort of relationship before you. I guess it strikes me as a little uneven."

Ben didn't say anything and it was too dark for me to tell what he was thinking. I wished he would look at me so I could tell. Then I felt panicked that I had made a mistake, that I had given away something about my sister, and I said, "Don't think badly of her."

Now Ben looked at me. "Why would I think badly of her?"

I didn't know what to say to that. I also felt confused about what I had said.

"I don't know. Sorry. I don't know what I'm saying."

"That was a weird thing to say."

"Sorry. There's something wrong with me," I said. "I don't know what it is." I was still hoping someone might tell me. Maybe Ben would.

I was also now worried that Ben might not like me anymore, and I didn't want that. I needed Ben and me to be on a team about saving the house. Why had I talked about clowns murdering people, and why had I said that I felt like a clown murderer? I offered him a cigarette again, but he wouldn't take it. I felt queasy. It was probably time to go back inside.

But neither of us moved. All I knew was, I really needed him to touch me now. It would make everything better. I felt compelled to ask him outright to touch me. To put a hand on my neck or my arm. Something. I didn't ask, but I could also see a situation in which he and I started kissing. I could see it happening. Would I let it if it did? Was it all supposed to lead up to this moment where Ben and I kissed and the two of us got together instead, and would Patty ever accept that as the case? She'd have to. She and I were all each other had now. I bet his hands were warm and strong, and I realized, to my astonishment that, in fact, I wanted him inside me. My teeth were clenched. I tried to relax my face. If he did kiss me, I wanted to have a soft face.

He was in the middle of saying something.

I heard him say, "You've got to just keep moving forward, you know."

"I know," I responded, without missing a beat, because at that exact moment, I was somewhere in the future, imagining my past, which included that exact moment, plus at least five prior worlds that existed long before the version of the world that was this one, and all I could do to keep from falling off the face of all five earths was respond to the words he was saying.

"You're still a young beautiful woman," Ben continued, and I came back to where we were again—the now. I felt the rubber of the tire swing under my right palm—I was pushing it lightly back and forth as we talked. Ben was leaning against the tree's trunk with his hands behind his head. The cigarette butt was still between my fingers. "And you can have whatever you want from your life. Don't give up on things yet."

"I know," I said. I felt dizzy. I said, "Should we go back inside?"

"Sure."

Patty was in the kitchen when Ben and I walked in. She was sitting on one of the stools, and didn't move a muscle, even when I said, "Patty, you're up!"

"Are you alright?" Ben's voice came out much softer than mine and I suddenly felt like an intruder. Patty didn't say anything. Her back was to us, her hair pulled into a bun. Still in his boots and jacket, Ben went right over to the island and pulled a stool toward her and hopped up onto it so he was sitting very close to her.

"You okay, Pat?" He put a hand on her knee. "What's wrong?"

"Yeah," I said, heat in my throat. "What's wrong? You have something to say? Speak."

But I was shouting. I think we were all astonished by this. Especially Ben, who jumped up off the stool to face me.

"Whoa, Lucy. Hold it—"

But I shouted again. "What? What? Why are you so upset?"

Patty wasn't moving. Her back was to me still. She was in a white spaghetti strap tank top and I could see her ribcage through it, down her back like a braid. "You think I've gone and done something right behind your back?"

Ben held his hands out in front of him, his mouth ajar. He looked like a jockey under a rearing horse. I knew I had to stop shouting.

"What? What's wrong with you? Speak," I commanded. I was huge. My neck was stiff as a trunk. I towered over them.

Patty swiveled around then and faced me too. The skin

under her eyes was so pale it was blue. She always got the same look on her face whenever I raised my voice at her. "I'm fine," she said. "No one was in bed. I didn't know where you had gone or what you were doing."

"Okay, but when you don't say anything," I tried to explain, "nobody knows what's going on with you. You're just sitting there, looking upset, and we have to guess what's going on. You should just speak up if there's something wrong. Tell us what you're feeling."

The problem was that I realized in my hand was our long kitchen knife. I was waving it around as I reasoned with Ben and Patty. Noticing this, I tightened my grip around the handle to keep it from flying free. But Ben looked spooked and helpless, another little man who didn't know a thing about himself. And there I was, gargantuan, freakish.

It was hard to gauge what more to say and there was also all this dust in my eyes. I felt myself withdraw back into my body. I returned the knife to the cutting board. I waited for someone to say something else, but nobody did, so I said, "I'm going to bed. Maybe we can do something or talk more tomorrow. I'm sorry about yelling. I'll see you both in the morning."

I woke up early and put together a picnic for me and Patty. I used the basket that our mother kept by the front door. I pushed our largest dish towel into it to make it look pretty, then dropped in a banana, a jar of fig jam, olives, a sleeve of cranberry-rosemary crackers, and a block of Gruyère I had bought the day before they arrived, having already had this plan loosely in mind. I hoped that the picnic could be just me and Patty. The two of us hadn't had any alone time all weekend. We could go to Bridle Pond and lay out on the grass there, wherever it wasn't muddy. The day already looked like it was going to be sunny. There was no wine in the house, no Aperol, no soda water, but it was probably too early for a spritz anyway. I stuck an unopened bottle of cranberry juice in the freezer to chill it quickly. I wished I had baked cookies.

But when they came down the stairs, they were all packed up. Ben was carrying both of their suitcases.

"Were you planning on leaving today, or is this because of me?" I asked. But before they could answer, I knew.

Patty didn't say anything, but she stopped halfway down the steps, her hand on the railing. Ben kept going with their suitcases. She looked down at the basket in my hand. I put it on the floor and crossed my arms.

"It is," I said.

I kept my eyes on Patty but felt Ben stop next to me in front of the door. He left the bags, then walked back to her, kissed her cheek, and quietly said that he'd go load up the car.

"No rush," he said. The door opened, and air swept across my shoulders. We heard the suitcases bump down the front steps.

"Nothing happened," I said to the two of us. My voice cracked.

"I know that."

"Then why are you leaving?" She didn't say anything but started down the stairs. She was trying to get by me out the door. "Why are you leaving if nothing happened?"

"Stop it." She had raised her voice. This made me let go of her pointy shoulders. I backed up too quickly and bumped the back of my head against the wall. Just a tiny tap.

"No," I said when Patty took a step toward me. Her eyes had softened. But I held up my hands, feeling panicked.

"Stop acting like I'm supposed to be scared of you," said Patty. But she stopped approaching.

"So why are you leaving?"

"I'm just ready to be back in New York." Then she said firmly, "I'm allowed to prefer my own space."

"Do you let Ben into your own space?"

We stared at each other. There was a long pause. Then she said, "Come on. You get it."

"Get what?"

"It just brought up some old stuff for me." Her voice was tight, pained. "But everything's fine. I just need some space."

I dropped my head. I closed my eyes. I could hear only my own breath. I hated that I had grabbed her shoulders. Why had I done that?

"What old stuff?" I asked the floor.

"Just drop it," she said. "Okay? Lucy, look at me." But I couldn't look. She said, "It really doesn't matter. I promise. Let's just move on."

"Are you sure?"

"Yes. It's not important."

"Why not?"

Another long pause. Then she said, "I know how to be good with myself now."

We were quiet for a long enough time that I heard the door open halfway, then close. It was just Ben checking in. I looked up at Patty after that—she hadn't moved at all, her gaze fixed on me. I really didn't want her to go. "Will you come back?" I asked.

"Obviously," she said. "This is our house. You're my sister."

Soon I was on my knees on the floor, my face in my hands, weeping. After a few moments, I felt her crouch down next to me. She patted my back twice. Then, in a very unlike-Patty way, she just left her hand there. I held my breath to keep from moving a single muscle. I didn't want her to take her hand away. Luckily, she left her hand on my back for so long that when I finally opened my eyes, I thought her hand was still there, but the warmth on my back was just the sun coming in through the window, landing on the floor in a bright dazzling square.

It's strange still being in this house when all the wild animals move into our town.

I first noticed it six weeks ago when I went out to roll in the trash bins, and suddenly, from behind the woodshed, a wild boar strutted out. His ears were hairy and black, his skinny tail switching as he shuffled around the soft bed where the delphiniums used to be, pushing his snout into the mulch. I watched him, shocked. There had never been any wild boars here before. At least not in my lifetime. I'd never seen anything like it. At last, he turned and looked at me, the sun making his ears glow red. The light showed off each of his back hairs, the raised ones particularly thin and distinct. His eyes were too small and dark for me to see, and his forelocks drooped over them. Staring right at me, he flared his huge wet nostrils, then turned to the side and jogged down the driveway into the street, his little ballerina hooves clopping.

I was about to go inside when more things started jostling at the edge of the woods. Other low round shapes. Within moments, a whole herd had appeared—massive boars, medium-sized boars, baby boars with light-brown jiggly bellies and spots, little ones small enough to totter under their mothers' huge swinging stomachs, some squealing, others yipping and grunting and puffing up dirt around their feet. There were twenty of them at least. Blond, white-striped, light brown, solid black, all with coarse hair and petite feet and little wiry tails switching. Some had these round ears like bears. Others had stringy beards hanging from their thick, fuzzy faces. All of them had tiny eyes. They crossed the yard, then the whole herd went trotting off down the pavement. When they reached the street, they turned to the left and vanished.

I think about what it'd be like if Patty and Ben were still here, and I could tell them about seeing the boars. I would come inside and say, "Hey! There are all these boars out there."

"Really? Wow!"

"I also saw them," Patty would say, opening and closing cabinets in the kitchen, looking for coffee filters. Then she'd add, "I saw them yesterday."

"We've never had any boars around here before."

"You know they'll charge you if you mess with them," Ben would say.

"Anything wild will."

The local radio station says it's because of all the land that's getting built on. Also, the fires happening west and north of us. Jennifer Pellman keeps bringing on a couple experts before *Morning Edition* to talk about it. One of her favorites is a young environmental specialist for the city, what my dad used to do. The specialist says it's pretty simple: as we're building and taking over land, these animals have fewer places to go. "Undaunted by crowded urban landscapes, many species are relocating to cities and adjusting their behaviors to survive." At first the experts, and Jennifer Pellman, are talking about all the animals excitedly, especially the black bear that keeps showing up in the parking lot behind the old deli. People have named her Bella. But then it turns into fear and alarm. In the middle of the day, Mrs. Hall storms from her porch into her front yard, banging two aluminum pots together at a mother skunk and her three skinny kits, bellowing, "This is my yard! My yard!"

Fisher cats start screaming at night, and people are calling in to complain about their sleep and all their lost pets. There are lots of signs on the street posts for missing dogs and cats. I find a small skull in our lawn, skin flapping off the forehead. I clean it in the sink, then keep it on the kitchen island. It's about the size of a softball, but flatter.

Another woman calls in, all worked up. At eight thirty that morning, she looked out her bedroom window and saw on her small circular stone patio a deer carcass being torn apart by crows. All over her yard were chunks of flesh and fur and entrails. By the time the wildlife removal department arrived, the prey had been dragged by something somewhere else. A representative from the removal team comes on the program to confirm that they've identified signs of a brutal chase. "This was not your typical chase," says the representative.

If an animal encounter gets aggressive, that's when you should report it, says the county agricultural commissioner. He says your first step should be to contact animal services. There's an online form where you can report unwanted or aggressive encounters. "That's when there's definitely a concern. That's when our department will take action." His name is Kenny Something. He adds that the department will euthanize if necessary. "We'd rather not have to do that, but when it comes down to it, we're gonna protect human life." Fewer and fewer people are outside, walking around.

Weeks pass, and I keep getting older. I take a bath one night with some old soaps from under the sink, lavender and citrus ones, and scrub the bottom of my feet to get rid of the callouses. My body's tired, so I rest. I'm dirty, so I clean myself. Patty calls. The thing is, I could talk to Patty on the phone forever. I could walk miles and miles, just talking with Patty. At some point, in some conversation, she voices again her desire to sell. But this is home, I say. Also, where else would I go? I'd rather be here. But Patty is steadfast. Well then, where should I go? I actually want to know. I'm open to her suggestions. I consider going somewhere like Kansas or Iowa. I've been craving the sight of flat land. I've never seen cornfields before. I get on Google Earth to look up other places I could go. "Yes, I know, I know," I tell her. We both know that in order to sell we still need to fix up the place. The house isn't sellable in its current state but, I tell her, it's livable for me.

Patty calls again. Yes, it's all fine, I tell her, when the sign goes up in the yard. I promise I'm good. Because here's the thing, in ten years, here's what I know I'll have: I'll have a conservatory and two little kids. I'll have a partner who loves me, and I'll have friends, and I'll have a little house somewhere in a small-town community. It's just the simple things that I want, and I'll find a way. I know I am still young and I will have these things. It doesn't need to be a real conservatory. Just a room with lots of sunlight and some plants. A few bright throw pillows and at least one glass wall. And a bench built into the window where I can read and have a cup of tea in the morning. I don't think I'm asking for much. "Just the simple pleasures," says Patty. Yes, I agree, just the simple things! That's all. All I want are a few friends, two kids, and a conservatory. I know that already I am lucky, luckier than most. I am lucky to be here and have what I already have. "You are lucky," says Patty. "And you'll find a way. It's all going to be okay."

Then it happens: Jennifer Pellman tells us that an unidentified male has been found by the Rockdale trolley stop, mauled to death. So far, no witnesses, but sources say the body has been sent to St. Jude's Trauma Center for evaluation. The body was found around 5:00 or 5:15 a.m. Five trap cages have been set around the area to catch the suspected animal. Then, Jennifer moves on to warn again about the uptick in rabid raccoons.

I'm the one who spots her first. One morning, when I'm out walking, I spot her body resting under the twisted branches of a willow tree, the big one by the high school pond. I stop to study her; she's in shadow. Then, as the sun starts breaching the hill, she stands up, shudders, stretches, then starts walking slowly out from under the dappled light, one paw in front of the other, her long silken body rippling. She doesn't move toward me, but walks diagonally across the dewy soccer field, making her way toward the swing set, behind the tetherball pole, eventually disappearing into the woods where the red house used to be.

Sources from the forest department are saying that another trap has been set in the area and more cameras have been installed. And then the radio confirms it: a lion has indeed been seen wandering around. This time, no one is naming her like they did with Bella. People are trying to spot her from inside their houses or inside their cars. She's seen crossing a busy state highway. She likes to use the same spot to cross each time. She's seen crossing the tracks. The researcher with the book is saying that knowing the big cat's highway-crossing habits can help policymakers make more informed decisions about where to build animal underpasses.

Snow comes in the middle of October. The leafy trees hold up platters of ice. The spruce hang on to their orange needles like ornaments. I'd forgotten how the snow makes the light on the trolley look like a plow. I decide to put up our white lights early, unpacking the bins in the basement that are still by that old fridge.

When I head out to the crab apple tree, I see, surrounding the house, big, beautiful tracks. Solitary. Just one set. No claw marks. I follow them down Allendale and into the cemetery. It is so quiet out, the snow gently falling on my lashes and my hair and all the pine needles, the tiniest quietest critters stirring in the branches above that are still so full of leaves. A plane rumbles overhead. Snowflakes on my eyelashes, hair wet to my cheeks. Power lines sag with the gathering snow. I follow the tracks to the little bridge behind the mill that takes the sidewalk over the stream. If anyone else comes out to walk around, they'll see my tracks right next to hers. But no one else is out. Just us. Above the naked maples, whole clouds are disassembling, and two hawks are swooping down, then rising back up, their wings tilting. It must feel so good to have wind lift you up like that. The air is pilling with snow.

But I'll follow these tracks forever if I must! I'll follow them for as long as it takes to find her. Everyone thinks she's a lion, but I know what she really is. Ultimately, it's just about being good with yourself. Once you can stand being out in the dark cold alone, you're good anywhere. I didn't understand that before, but I understand it now. I understand that after a few more nights of walking, I will get to see all that flat land again, all those large endless ranches. I will get to hear the slow long creak of trees by the rivers, the tremble of birds lifting off their leaves all at once. I'll never get tired of following her. I'll follow her tracks straight into the den! Suddenly, it's spring again. I stop to watch baby wood ducks fall out of a tree. A whole series of them: one, two, three, four. Then they waddle in a line over the mud and duff and soft pine needles to where their mother is floating in the reeds. She has been calling. One more day on this rock, and one of the ducklings will hop its fluffy body into my lap. Someone will witness it.

ACKNOWLEDGMENTS

Thank you, Marya Spence and Mackenzie Williams, for your incredible conviction, insights, and belief. Thank you, Michener Center, all my teachers and classmates: in particular Elizabeth McCracken and Bret Anthony Johnston, for over a decade of wisdom and support. Thank you, Catapult team, for believing in this book and giving it everything you've got. You are magical people.

Thank you, Kendall Storey, the best editor in the world. You have spoiled me, stunned me, changed me. Obviously, this book would not exist without you, and now, I wonder, how any book does?

Thank you, Zack Schlosberg, Molly Williams, Sophia Emmons-Bell, brilliant friends, brilliant writers. With you three, there's no such thing as wasted time. I would extend an afternoon by an infinite number of hours if it meant continuing to hang out together, "write," and talk about everything under the sun.

Thank you, Allie Freiwald, my best friend. Writing a book can be a lonely thing—so how lucky am I that, because of you, loneliness in this life is only ever fleeting? How did I survive for eighteen years without you? I really don't know. I love you with all my heart. I will follow you anywhere.

Thank you to my family for being readers and dreamers. Uncle Dan and Uncle Mitch and Thom, I can trace all my dreams back to you; thank you for reading this book. Thank you, Jake and Livvie, my brother and sister, the sparkliest people in the world; I miss you so much when we're not together. Thank you, Mom and Dad, for loving us so fiercely, for giving us everything, for always being home, and for reading this book so many times. There are no words. I love you so much.

And thank you, Chris, for making everything so beautiful, for making me never want the days to end. I want to live every single one with you over and over and over again.

EMELINE ATWOOD graduated from the Michener Center for Writers in 2023. She writes fiction and poetry and is a recipient of the Thomas T. Hoopes Prize, the Louis Begley Prize, the Roger Conant Hatch Prize for Lyric Poetry, and the Le Baron Russell Briggs Fiction Prize. She lives in Austin, Texas.